Merryhearth Manor & Me

Abigail Darby

Dægbrecan  Publishing

Winchester, Virginia

Merryhearth Manor & Me
A Dægbrecan Publishing Book / March 2022

Published by Dægbrecan Publishing

Book design by Nicholas Edward

Cover design by Will Garrett

First Edition ᛚ

Library of Congress Control Number: 2022933519

Darby, Abigail.

ISBN 978-1-955810-16-6 (Paperback)

Dedicated to all those who love and save old houses.

Merryhearth Manor & Me

Part One

Finding

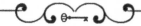

"I've got the key to my castle in the air, but whether I can unlock the door remains to be seen."

— Louisa May Alcott, *Little Women*

Chapter 1

From the other end of my cell phone came Bob Norseman's deep voice, with a hint of an old Virginia drawl, "Hmm, so you wanna see the old house. Well, I can tell you the ole girl's seen better days, but she has potential for the right buyer. I can be there in about twenny minutes if that'll work for you?"

"That's perfect! I'll be here . . . in the driveway."

I stood, mesmerized by the structure looming in front of me. I let my cell phone drop onto the driver's seat of my little two-door coupe and carefully picked my path through the waist-high weeds toward the front of the house. Discovering the bottom step of the crumbling brick stairs, I stood motionless, looking up at the tall, burgundy brick structure with its once grand, two-story pedimented portico, and multiple sets of Tuscan columns. It was a big house and I liked the symmetry of it—the left side was a perfect reflection of the right side. There were at least two full stories, a half story attic, and what appeared to be a full basement.

But what a state she was in, white paint was peeling from the decaying wood trimwork, vines had snaked through the windows, breaking the windowpanes in many of the old sashes, and the portico was sagging at a dangerous angle. I knew upon approaching the house that it was a mid-nine-teenth-century Greek Revival, the only one of the historic houses that day that was this architectural style. I liked it immediately and was glad it was last on my list. My house-hunting treasure trip had started with high hopes, but little expectation that I'd actually find anything suitable. This house appealed to me, but whether or not it was suitable remained to be seen.

☙——✳

I'd started my day early that morning, leaving my Leesburg apartment with a travel mug of coffee, and a handful of real-estate listings that I'd grabbed from my printer. I was exploring houses over a span of about 150 miles, and the first house I'd mapped out was in Berryville, so I'd headed west on Route 7. My plan was a simple one, I was doing drive-bys of five houses that I found for sale on the internet, and if I liked any of them I would call the listing agent and ask to see the inside. I was doing this each weekend until *the house* presented itself, I'd know it when I saw it.

Deciding where to live had been a question consuming my thoughts since the day of the explosion—more on that later. This, however, was the first house-hunting treasure trip I was taking in the opposite direction of my horrific daily commute. Like any of us know, who live and work in crowded metropolitan areas, distance is measured in time, not miles, and Washington, D.C., is a prime example of this. So, as I headed in a direction that would make my commute to work worse—much worse—I looked at the budding spring land-scape and threw logic to the wind.

Out on the open road, I opened my sunroof to enjoy the unusually warm weather for mid-March in Northern Vir-ginia. I inhaled the fresh scent of springtime and took in the scenery unfolding around me. The blooming bright-yellow daffodils that filled the space between the east- and west-bound lanes gave a visual performance that could only be out-done by the lush early green rolling fields. Rows of suburban townhouses were replaced with pastures dotted with grazing, jet-black cows. Miles of painted, black farm fencing led to long tree-lined driveways. Stone-foundation barns popped up, mostly in classic oxblood red, but there were also beautifully painted white ones with green trim, set back into the fields.

As I topped the Blue Ridge Mountains at Snickers Gap and headed down the other side toward the Shenandoah River, I felt like I was soaring above the ground. It was such a strong feeling that nonsensically I looked up through my open sunroof to see if a tether was pulling me upward, off the road. When I got to the bridge crossing the Shenandoah at the bottom of the mountain, I nearly floated, midair, over the gentle springtime whitecaps as they gurgled northward to meet the Potomac River at Harpers Ferry. It struck me as both ironic and sad that I hadn't felt this happy and hopeful in a long time.

Upon reaching Berryville, I navigated my way through the little historic downtown and onto a side country lane that led to the first house on my trek. As I approached the house, I slowed to get a closer look and realized at once that it wasn't for me. The house was a plain white farmhouse with little architectural detail. My best friend Danielle's questions from the night before flooded my thoughts as I looked at it from the road.

"I thought you were going to buy a historic row house in D.C., so that you could be closer to work. Didn't you like any of the ones you've been looking at?"

"I loved them, and yes, that was my original plan. But they're too expensive. I can't afford any of the nice ones, and the ones that need total restoration would cost even more in the end."

"So now you're looking at houses in the opposite direction, but still historic?"

"Yes, houses that are one hundred years or older, away from the high-priced neighborhoods, not to mention the congestion and traffic."

"Why would you want an old house in the middle of nowhere?"

"Not any old house. I'm looking for an elegant historic house with a lot of character. Something refined, peaceful, away from the chaos, with pretty vistas and lots of space."

"So you're not going for a rustic house look?"

"No, I want a house that's genteel . . . even feminine looking . . . if that makes any sense."

"And you think you can find this by heading west?"

"I don't know. For my first day, I've picked five houses to drive past. This will give me an idea of the possibilities."

"I get it, after the explosion you need to . . . well, I get it, and I'm all in favor of whatever makes you happy. But maybe a new-construction house would be more practical?"

I smiled at this suggestion. Danielle could not have understood my desire—my actual need—to buy a historic house. She didn't know about the car rides I used to take with my grandmother when I was five years old. My grandmother loved to drive past her favorite old houses and tell me who lived in them and their stories. My favorite house, by far, was the princess's house, a beautiful Queen Anne Victorian with turrets, stained-glass windows, and an elegant wraparound porch filled with big wicker chairs loaded with plump pink pillows. It was quintessential fairy-tale, and so feminine. My grandmother didn't know why the princess lived there, in her house in Uniontown, Pennsylvania, instead of with the Prince of Thurn and Taxis in his castle in Bavaria. But I was pretty sure it was because she had such a beautiful house of her own.

As I left Berryville I set my GPS directions for the next house and headed north on Route 340 for Charles Town. The route provided more stunning vistas and horse farms that matched the cattle farms in charm and oil-on-canvas landscape scene potential. The drive was proving to be delightful, even if the house search came up empty. The nightmare of the past eighteen months was the furthest thing from my mind as I focused on my mission and the possibilities for the future.

Entering Charles Town, I was delighted to see an abundance of beautifully restored, mostly Victorian-era homes. I easily found the second house, which was absolutely lovely and fit my criteria. As I sat in my parked car looking at the house and the pretty street it sat on, I tried to imagine living in the house, but I couldn't. It was flawless and in perfect order, without the need for so much as a polishing cloth taken to the brass knob on the front door, and this disappointed me.

There was also the unfortunate circumstance of a historical event that had taken place near the house. The event and its location were immortalized with a big historic civil-war marker. I don't believe much in ghosts, but I could well imagine feeling creepy at nighttime, knowing such an event had taken place near where my house was now standing. Another deterrent was the possibility of tourist traffic, and that might be a lot worse than the potential ghosts. So, I mapped my route to the third house and left the tranquility of charming downtown Charles Town.

As I entered the outskirts of Shepherdstown from the south on Route 230, the third house came up on my left. I knew immediately it wasn't a fit. The house had dark-brown wood siding and dark-red trim that made it appear, well, dark and unfriendly. Of course, it could be painted bright colors and the overgrown bushes cut back—but I couldn't see myself there.

At this point, I was hungry and ready for a break, so I headed into downtown Shepherdstown. This little historic college town, known for its charming mix of shops and restaurants, well-preserved and restored historic architecture, and a congenial mix of interesting people, was the perfect spot for reenergizing. I lost no time finding a parking spot on German Street and headed to the bakery café for a sandwich, coffee, and a little people watching. I settled into a window table after ordering the daily special from the counter, and opened my cell phone to check for email and text messages. I had a text from Danielle and another from Alex, they both wanted to know how my day was going. Danielle asked about the house hunting and Alex wondered if I was working. I responded to Danielle first: I'm having a marvelous day! Haven't found "my" house yet—three down and two to go.

Danielle: Where are you now? Have you found any good locations for us to do a day trip and some shopping?

Me: I have! We'll plan a day soon. I'll surprise you!

Danielle: Emoji heart bubble.

I thought to myself how including Danielle in my plans for the future was only natural. She had been my sanity savior during the last eighteen months—listening when I needed to vent, asking the right questions at the right times, being a distraction when I needed one, and even providing court testimony when I asked. She didn't always agree with me, but her loyalty was unwavering.

Next, a text response to Alex: No, I'm not working. I'm out having fun today!

Alex: About time you actually enjoyed your Saturday. What are you doing?

Me: Check this out. It's the chalkboard where I'm having lunch today.

<u>*Coffeeology*</u>
Stay Grounded
Espresso Yourself
Better Latte than Never
Take Life One Cup at a Time
Take Time to Smell the Coffee

Alex: Where are you? I love that coffee quote!

Me: I thought of you as soon as I saw it. I'll fill you in on Monday about my adventures today. Should be a good story.

Alex: I can't wait to hear it!

Me: See you at the departure gate at Dulles on Monday morning.

Alex: Don't freak if I'm late.

Alex is Alex Jenkins, a member of my work team. I thought of him as soon as I saw the coffee quote chalkboard on the café wall. He and I have this thing where, no matter where we are or what's going on, we have to have morning coffee—and that includes making a coffee stop, if need be, on the way to a meeting or training workshop. This has led to some embarrassing moments, like arriving late, or finding no seats were left in the meeting room. On Monday, my little team of three—Alex, Jill, and me—was traveling to attend a weeklong training bootcamp. I fully expected Alex to arrive at the boarding gate at the last minute, he was notorious for stepping onto the plane just as the flight attendants were closing the hatch door. Somehow, this added to his charm.

I finished my sandwich and checked my printouts for directions to the last two houses. One was on the way out of town and the other was about thirty miles away in Winchester. I packed up my papers and walked to the car. As I headed southwest on Route 480, I found the fourth house easily—and it did not disappoint. It was a white-clapboard Georgian with deep-green shutters and front door. The house was large and

9

well-balanced, with two additions added sequentially to the left side that gave the vague impression of the house being a telescoping spyglass. The polished-brass pineapple knocker on the front door made a welcoming first impression, and the thick, antique glass in the windowpanes reflected wavy, mid-day sunlight. *Note to self, must have wavy glass and a pineapple door knocker!* The house was beautifully situated, with a curving driveway that looped into a half circle in front. The landscaping was gorgeous, complete with mature trees, boxwoods and hollies, and several flower beds that promised to be exquisite once the weather warmed and summer was in full swing. I had no trouble imagining myself living in this house. I did, however, have a lot of trouble imagining being able to make the mortgage payment!

I had added this one to the list because I was going to pass it anyway on my way to house number five, and I thought, *why not?* And now I was reminded that on my federal government salary, even my manager's salary, this one was way out of my price range. This was probably the weekend getaway for one of those government contractor executives who make the big money. I could imagine him sending an email to his Capitol Hill friends saying, "I'm opening the country house this weekend. Come on out. I'm picking up a couple of cases of Virginia wine, a great Viognier, and an excellent Cab Franc. Kat is getting steaks from Washington Farm, all organic and grass-fed, you know. We'll get some townies to be waitstaff, so we can relax. See you Saturday!" *Umm . . . definitely not my house.*

The drive to the fifth and last house took me over to Interstate 81 and south to Winchester. When I exited the interstate onto a country lane, my first sight was an extremely well-kept apple orchard. Hundreds of apple trees were standing in straight rows at exactly the same height and stage of maturity. They looked a little like line dancers on Broadway. I expected at any moment their hazy pink-hued apple blossom headdresses would bob as they began high kicking in unison—it was quite impressive, actually.

I no sooner drove past the apple tree Rockettes when a pasture of the prettiest Jersey dairy cows came into full view. Now, I'm not a cow expert, but Jerseys are very distinctive, and they're the cow image of choice for most of the children's books of my youth. There were clusters of these lovely creamy-beige, doe-eyed ladies standing with their heads together as if catching up on the latest dairy-farm gossip while soaking up the warm midday sun. I imagined their conversation . . . , "Have you heard? The farm is going to start piping classical music into the barn at milking time."

"No, really?"

"Yes, they say it's what all the best dairies are doing, and we want to remain world-class don't we?"

"We certainly do!"

"We'll have to brush up on our knowledge of the great classical composers. We don't want to appear ignorant when the music starts!"

I didn't know what the fifth house would have to offer, but the drive into Winchester was proving to be pleasantly unexpected. Just as I was refocusing on the road, I came upon a historic stone building with a sign announcing, "Hopewell Centre Meeting, Religious Society of Friends (Quakers), Established 1734, Built 1759." I swerved the car into the crushed-stone driveway and skidded to a stop. It was quite a setting with the old stone building set back off the road, an ancient cemetery to one side, and venerable, timeworn trees hovering above it all as quiet observers. As I got out of the car and slowly walked toward the nearly three-hundred-year-old structure, I took in the details of its simple architecture.

With each step toward the meetinghouse, I felt closer to the past. My little coupe disappeared, and I was surrounded by humble buggies pulled by handsomely groomed horses.

There were ladies in long skirts and modest bonnets, and men in black coats with white cravats and black, broad-brimmed hats. They were chatting amiably as they prepared to enter for their Sunday meeting of the Friends. The setting was welcoming, and the images felt familiar and friendly. As they entered through separate, sturdy wood doors to start the meeting, I slipped through the white gate in the stone wall surrounding the cemetery. The ground was soft and lumpy under my feet. Bright white-petaled snowdrops pushed their way up through the soft ground in random patterns between the tombstones. I stopped to read the names and dates on some of them, many of which were very old and reflected the same surnames. One tombstone effigy in particular caught my attention, and struck me as very touching.

Mary Rebecca Wife and Mother
She was the Sunshine of our House

To be remembered by your family as "the sunshine of our house," seemed a monumental honor.

I reluctantly stepped back into the present and headed the car in the direction of the last house. After turning down a series of country roads, I knew the house from a distance as soon as I saw it. Something akin to a small billboard was positioned in front announcing, "Historic Property For Sale." I eased into the lower portion of the driveway and turned off the engine. "You've seen better days, old girl," I said aloud. *Come to think of it, the house could have said to me, "You've seen better days too, old girl!"*

Bob Norseman pulled up in a polished white pickup and parked behind me in the driveway. He stepped into the tall, weedy grass and crossed the distance between us in a couple of long strides. Before I could say hello, he was shaking my hand with genuine warmth. He appeared to be about sixty, tall and slender, with thick white hair and a well-groomed mustache. He was dressed in a salmon-colored, button-down shirt with the sleeves rolled up, a pair of tan-colored jeans, and brown-suede boots. He reminded me so much of the actor, Sam Elliot, that I almost called him Sam.

"Hi Bob. I'm Amanda Grayson."

"Nice to meet you, Ms. Grayson."

"Oh, please, call me Amanda."

"Is it just you today, Amanda?"

"It's always just me," I said.

Bob ever-so-slightly raised an eyebrow but didn't ask any questions. Later I realized that he was probably referring to whether or not I had a buyer's real estate agent with me, but he didn't embarrass me by making that clarification.

I followed him as he carefully made his way up the crumbling brick steps. "Well, let's see if I can get this cranky, old door open and show you 'round the house. Ask me any questions you like as we go through. Watch out for rotten boards here, don't want you slippin' through the porch floor."

I looked through a bowling-ball-sized hole, down to the ground a half story below. "Yeah, it might be hard to fish me out."

"Oh, we'd get you out with no trouble. Don't you worry 'bout that."

I waited as Bob extracted the front-door key from the lockbox and slipped it into the ornate, antique-iron door lock. The big formal front door glided open effortlessly.

"Huh! That's unusual, I usually have to wrestle with it quite a bit to get it open."

We stepped across the threshold and I found myself standing in a large center hall surrounded by dust-diffused beams of sunlight. The light came from various doorways from my right and left. A considerable staircase lead upward from the right side of the hall. I could see the dark walnut banister and white painted stair pickets looping continuously up, and up again, three stories. *I love this!*

Chapter 2

After going through security at Dulles, I made my way to the boarding gate. Barring any complications, we'd touch down in Orlando around noon, giving us plenty of time to get settled before the training bootcamp check-in and icebreaker. Jill was already settled at the gate and was saving seats for Alex and me. I doubted Alex would need the seat, he'd probably breeze in at the last minute, but I was grateful to be able to leave my carry-on with Jill and go in search of coffee. While we waited for the plane to board, I asked Jill about her weekend. She was looking a little down, and I could guess the reason. She and her husband were trying to have a baby, going on about seven months, and Jill was beginning to worry that there was a problem. We talked about the options that a lot of couples we know consider when they find they aren't succeeding in getting pregnant. Jill wasn't there yet, but I could tell she was anxious, and she admitted the stress was beginning to negatively affect her relationship with Tom.

I was keenly aware that my team's recent travel schedule was not helping Jill's stress levels. The three of us were on the road a lot, and we had a brand new nationwide project we were leading for the agency across all the regional offices.

"Do you really think we need this training course?" asked Jill.

"It will be helpful for the new project, and we'll be certified PMPs once we take and pass the exam."

"Project Management Professional certified, I guess that does sound good, and I've seen people putting 'PMP' after their names like it's some kind of higher education degree."

"Rory certainly likes us having certifications to add to our professional portfolios," I added.

"Yeah, I've noticed. Why do you think that is?"

"When the agency hired him last October, he promised to focus on training and staff development. You know, the federal government hasn't always been big on that. When budget cuts hit, the first thing to go is always training."

"Can you believe he's our fifth department manager in seven years?"

"I know, the job has been a revolving door of executives. Let's hope he survives and sticks around for a while. We need stability," I said.

Jill, Alex, and I traveled well together and generally enjoyed each other's company. We were the agency's strategic planning team and our work was challenging, but also rewarding. When we were on the road, I tried to make it as enjoyable as possible, spending hours searching for the best locations and hotels that positioned us near good restaurants and local attractions, while keeping us within ridiculously low government spending restrictions. We always ended up supplementing our trips with our own money, but being able to enjoy some of our after-work time together made it worth the personal expense.

Jill, however, now needed more balance in her life and time to make sure she and Tom could achieve their long-term life goals, one of which was to start a family. I wasn't about to put pressure on her to choose between her career and what would make her happy for the rest of her life. If Jill wasn't on the road traveling so often, and if she could minimize the long days and commute when we were in D.C., she and Tom might have better success. I decided that when we were back from Orlando, I'd figure something out and convince Rory that it was the right path forward.

The plane was nearly finished boarding. Jill was three rows in front of me. I was in an aisle seat and was wrestling my laptop case and purse under the seat in front when I heard a familiar voice, "Hi there! I believe the window seat is mine."

I smiled and stood up so that Alex could slide into the seat next to me. "You're early, as usual."

"Had to grab coffee," and he held up his favorite iced brew.

"I didn't think we had seats together. How did you end up next to me?"

"Ha, perks of arriving late. I asked if there were any no-shows to see if I could get a better seat than mine in the back next to the toilets, and your window seat was a no-show."

"You were born under a lucky star! I've never seen anyone with your good luck."

"Hey, I don't want to miss the story about where you were and what you were doing on Saturday. You have the most interesting adventures!"

"And this was a good one!"

We settled into our seats and the plane lifted off. At reaching cruising altitude, Alex prompted for details, "I was trying to figure out where you were on Saturday, but it didn't look familiar."

"You would have loved it. I was in Shepherdstown."

"Shepherdstown, West Virginia? What were you doing way out there?"

"I was looking at houses."

"Shepherdstown, that's like at least two hours outside the city, right?"

"Well, it won't be Shepherdstown exactly, but it might be Winchester."

"What did you find? This sounds interesting."

"It is, and after driving all day to look at five houses, my last stop was very intriguing!"

"Give me the details."

☞━━

As I began describing the house to Alex, I was transported back to Saturday afternoon when Bob Norseman swung open the big front door with more ease than usual, and I stepped across the threshold.

Bob was quiet, he intuitively knew to let me experience the scene unfolding in front of me. I stood silently for a minute or two, observing everything I could. As I began to meander through the rooms, the layout and flow of the house fascinated me. It was so unlike today's modern open floor plans with no boundaries between spaces. Yet, there was incredible flow and connectedness as the rooms were joined to one another and to the expansive hall. Each adjoining room had a broad opening with a hinged, three-part folding door that could be closed to create inner walls between the rooms, with an individual small door in the center of the three-part bifold door. I had never seen anything like these doors, pocket doors yes, but not doors like these. Every room had a large fireplace with distinctive mantels, no two were exactly alike. The high ceilings and liberal number of expansive windows gave the rooms a light and airy feeling. *And there it was, my wavy glass!* Through the dust, I could see the imperfections in the glass in the six-over-six window sashes. Unfortunately, a number of the glass panes were cracked and the vines I saw from the outside of the house had made their way inside through several pieces of broken glass. The inner doors between the rooms and the hall still showcased their original locks, little brass doorknobs, and ball bearing hinges. The oversized trimwork was painted white and displayed carved detailing that you only see in historic homes.

I drank it all in as deeply as if I'd been given a glass of fresh mountain spring water after walking through the desert. The floors were glorious, wood planks of different sizes, many of them wider than my shoe from heel to toe. Covered as they were in a layer of thick, earthy-smelling dust, I could see they were original to the house and nothing like hardwood floors today. Bob, watching me study the floors, finally spoke, "All the floors throughout the house are heart pine. Original-growth heart pine is as rare as sunken treasure nowadays. There are fewer than ten thousand protected acres of original-growth longleaf pine forests remainin' in the U.S. The slow-growth heart pine from longleafs was so valuable that the settlers timbered the trees in record numbers and left nothin' in their place. By the late eighteen hundreds, virtually the entire range of original growth was wiped out. The only place now to find this antique wood is reclamation from old buildings. This here old girl took her fair share of that fine wood."

I liked how he referred to the house as feminine. I felt that too.

"The floors, trim, doors, mantels, all of it's heart pine."

I reached out and ran my hand over one of the deep-set windowsills, then wiped the dust on my jeans. "Are you a historic house expert?"

Bob laughed. "Me? Oh, no. But I like old houses. My real estate company specializes in historic properties. My wife, Marie, and I run the business. She's the real expert."

"Do you and your wife live in a historic house?"

"Yes ma'am, we have an early eighteen hundreds Colonial. It's not a big house but Marie's a historic-house

19

snob. She'd never live in a new house. She says, 'Just give me a house with character and a soul, and for goodness' sake a kitchen with a door that I can shut. I don't wanna smell Sunday's pot roast in the family room sofa next week.' She hates these new house open floor plans."

I smiled and thought to myself that I'd like to meet Marie.

We headed up the stairs to see the bedrooms. The floor plan was the same as below. Two of the five bedrooms had huge pocket doors that separated them when closed. *This may have been the nursery at one time*, I thought to myself. There were two very outdated bathrooms, probably added in the 1940s and the 1980s. Old wallpaper was in a half state of being ripped down, and the dirt and grime from below had not ended at the top of the stairs. I asked Bob how long the house had been sitting vacant.

"Well, the heirs of the last owner sold the house and the three hundred acres that came with it to a developer 'bout five years ago. He parceled out the land and started to build a couple of spec homes. These are houses that are mostly finished, but new buyers can still pick some of their own options like carpet color. He didn't make a success of it and the bank ended up takin' ownership. As far as I know, the house has been sittin' empty, basically abandoned, for goin' on five years now."

"Hmm, that explains a lot of the damage. Does the bank own it now?"

"Yep, been on their books for several years, and they keep lowerin' the price. They're ready to unload it. There've been a couple of different contracts written, but they fell through. Buyers couldn't get funding or got cold feet after assessin' all the work the house needs."

"Oh, interesting," I said. I was getting more excited by the minute about the possibilities, but I played it cool and asked if we could head to the next level.

Bob warned me as we approached the top of the stairs, "Now things look pretty bad up here. This is where most people say they've seen enough. It's mostly cosmetic in my opinion, but I just wantcha to be prepared."

I stepped into the hall of the third level of the house. I was both thrilled at the layout and appalled by the conditions. To the left of the center hall were two more bedrooms, the same size as those on the floor below. To the right was one large room, the size of two bedrooms combined. I could easily imagine a number of great uses for this room. Unfortunately, the plaster ceiling on this level was collapsing in most places. There were broad cracks in the plaster walls. Old, defunct, window-unit air conditioners were in three windows, and they had caused leakage around the windows leading to further plaster damage. One of the historic windows was missing altogether, and the plastic sheeting covering the opening was torn and flapping in the wind. A multitude of mud dauber wasp nests were visible on the walls and ceiling. I began to get a sinking feeling. I could see why this was the end of the line for most buyers. I didn't want it to be the end of the line for me.

"So, are you going to buy it?" asked Alex. "It sounds amazing! I mean, you just don't get features like that in new houses."

"Not to mention it sits on four acres, surrounded by farmland, rolling pastures, and apple groves," I added.

"And the winding staircase, the twelve fireplaces, and the English basement—that would make the perfect wine cellar—how can you pass it up?"

"I did love it and I can picture it totally restored, fully furnished, beautiful from top to bottom. I can see myself living there and making memories with friends and family. I feel connected to this house, like it's meant to be."

21

"So, what are you waiting for? What's the downside?"

"More like what isn't the downside? But the fun I could have with this house!"

"You'd never get bored, you'd always have a project."

"True, because the projects are never-ending! The house has so much potential, but it's so impractical. And I can't even imagine how much it would cost to restore it."

"I think a project of this magnitude would be great for you!"

I thought about what Alex said. *Is this what I need at this point in my life?* I was just beginning to move beyond the turmoil and stress of the last eighteen months, brought on by the explosion. I felt tired and hardly recognized the person looking back at me in the mirror. My once thick, blond wavy curls were thin and drab, my bright, sea-green eyes were masked by dark circles, and unlike Elizabeth Gilbert, who wrote in her memoir, *Eat, Pray, Love*, that at the low point of her depression she was so thin her body hurt, my eighteen months of anguish had led to a weight gain of fifteen pounds. I also had a demanding job with a new project just getting off the ground, not to mention the fact that I knew nothing of old houses and how to restore them.

"Enough about me. How was *your* weekend?" I asked.

"It was good. We started kickball practice this weekend."

"Oh, I wondered when that would start up again. Kickball. It must be a D.C. thing."

"It is, and a gay thing. The D.C. gay community is huge, and they sponsor activities for just about anything you want to do."

I thought to myself, *Kickball would not be anything I wanted to do.* But then, I was ten years older than Alex, and lately I felt a lot older than that!

We spent the remainder of the two-hour flight talking about the Winchester house. He was fascinated and asked questions about the condition of the house and the grounds, who I would hire to help me, and how long it would take to finish the work. He never questioned the wisdom of me taking on a project of this magnitude. Even later, when I thought about that conversation, I don't think Alex ever doubted for a minute that I could do it.

As soon as we landed and got the green light to turn on our cell phones, I texted a message to Danielle: I'm setting up a time for us to look at the Winchester House this weekend.

Danielle: Great!

Me: I've asked Bob, he's the listing agent, to meet us out there.

Danielle: I can't wait to see it.

Me: I want you to tell me why buying it is a terrible idea!

Danielle: The only terrible idea is doing nothing.

She was right, doing nothing was dangerous, and I'd been in a state of limbo for too long. But to fully understand why I was considering a house that was completely unrealistic for my life—we have to go back in time to a very bleak, snowy December day.

Chapter 3

I sat in the driveway that miserable, dreary December day, looking for the last time at a very different kind of house. I thought to myself then, *I will never be able to replace this house. How do you replace THIS?*

I was tired, so unbelievably tired. It had been more than a year of ongoing, ugly legal battles brought on by the person who I'd spent years building a life with, my life, *our* life. Today was the appointment to sign the final paperwork completing the sale of our house and transfer of the title to the new owners. This was the last milestone in our miserable divorce proceedings. Our real estate agent, Ron, had arranged it so that Richard and I would not have to see one another during the settlement, and I knew he understood more than he let on. The morning of the settlement, he called me to say that the new owners were being real jerks about the large four-tiered fountain in the middle of the circular drive. They said it had not been covered for the winter as promised. He had called Richard first about covering it, but got nowhere, so he asked me if I would find the cover, so he could do it himself.

The predicted snowstorm was in full force and there were

a couple of inches on the ground by the time we met at the house. The wind was gusting from the west, and it was bitter cold as the two of us struggled to get the cover up and over the top of the fountain without causing any damage or knocking the top bowl off. Blowing, icy snow was blinding us both and in the process, Ron lost his balance—one foot went down into the fountain pool base. His expensive leather shoe, and the leg of his suit pants to the knee, were immersed in icy, cold water. We eventually managed to get the cover over the fountain and secured it with bungee cords. Shivering and wet, Ron snapped a photo of the covered fountain and texted it to the new owners. I heard him mumble under his breath, "*There*, asshole." Despite the miserable circumstances, he mustered a smile for me and said, "All done! Thank you for coming out here. I'll see you in a little while at the settlement office."

As Ron drove away, I sat in my car looking at the house. It was as though the exhaustion and the sadness I'd been keeping pushed down for months finally broke through the floodgates. I began to sob—uncontrollable, gut-wrenching, loud sobs. I dug around in the glove box for fast-food napkins to soak up the mess on my face. The tears kept coming. Before long, the passenger seat was covered in half-disintegrated napkins of various colors, depending upon their restaurant of origin. We had worked so hard—I had worked so hard—to finally be able to buy and improve this house. It started out a no-frills, plain tract-house McMansion when we bought it for a bargain price. The developer was closing out the last of the lots in what had once been a beautiful, rolling-hill farm of thousands of acres. It was a nicely laid out housing development with a mix of estate lots, those that were three to five acres, and village lots, those that were one acre. We'd been looking for a while to upgrade from our initial starter house.

After leaving the gorgeous model home, we took a map of the development and walked the remaining available lots. We fell in love with one that was at the end of a long drive and sat high above the other lots in that section. It had just become available because the contract that was written against it fell through. We jumped at the chance to have it. We walked the lot, visualizing the orientation of the house and the views from each side, then signed the purchase contract. We picked from the available tract-house models and went about choosing our options like so many happy suburbanites before us. We labored over every decision as though it was of monumental importance, three sides of pink brick, a side-load three-car garage, oak hardwood floors, kitchen cabinet upgrade, granite countertops, stainless steel appliances, and so on. We opted for an unfinished basement because we had big plans for the space, much more than the developer would do. We visited the house every weekend as it was going up, took pictures for the scrapbook, and imagined what it would be like living in it when it was finished.

Over the course of seven years there together, it had become one of the prettiest estate-lot houses in our tract-house McMansion neighborhood. With the banks willing to throw money at homeowners with good credit, we were able to add the circular drive and fountain, the pool and pool house, landscaping, trees, bushes, you name it, and we did it. Inside we added ridiculous luxuries like a 650-bottle capacity wine room, a nine-seat sloped-floor movie theater, and a steam room and dry sauna. To save money, I did all the design work and Richard did much of the physical labor himself. We'd walk around the house and property for hours, talking and planning and imagining what we wanted to do next. We didn't take vacations because we were on vacation in our own house, enjoying every square inch, every free minute we had. We both had demanding jobs and typical D.C. commutes, meaning Monday through Friday were easily fourteen-hour days, but in the evenings and on the weekends, we treated ourselves to the luxuries of home.

☒•——x

Looking at the time on my cell phone, I realized I had to get cleaned up and be ready to sign the settlement papers. I pulled myself together and stopped crying so that I could see well enough to drive. The house had been a lot of work and a lot of expense, but I loved it, and I thought Richard loved it too. We jokingly referred to it as "the cruise ship." Keeping the cruise ship afloat and on course was not an easy task, but the rewards were worth the effort, or so I thought. Richard, as it turned out, must not have thought so. The day he told me that he wanted a divorce, sitting on our pretty back deck that was the same height as the tree branches in the patch of woods behind the house, I felt my world explode. A bomb went off, and it was sending the cruise ship, our years together, and all that we had built into a giant dust cloud. I refer to this episode in my life as "the explosion." The ensuing divorce would result in nothing being left. It was just as if everything had been blown to bits and was gone forever.

Richard had done this once before, early in our marriage. That time it was an extramarital affair, but he regretted it. After time apart and counseling, I forgave the indiscretion, and we put the marriage back together, seemingly stronger than it had been before.

This was different, there'd be no reconciliation. I asked him point-blank, "Who is she this time?"

He screamed at me, "I knew you'd say that! I told my family you'd blame it on me. I told your mother you'd blame it on me!"

He had been paving the way for the explosion since he first met her, months earlier. He'd talked to our families before talking to me, he'd consulted an attorney, and he'd moved assets around. I had been blissfully ignorant, coming home

27

from work to join him for dinner that we would prepare to-gether on the outdoor grill, and spending the weekends to-gether at the pool. I never had an inkling it was coming. I had no idea he was positioning the dynamite in the shaft and was preparing to push the plunger. Nothing more was said. I knew it was over.

With an air of calmness that surprised me as much as it surprised him, I said, "Don't let the door hit you in the ass on the way out."

I don't know if it was this last statement, or just his resolve to never look back, but he made the next year of my life as miserable as any human could. I tried to carry on with work and managing the cruise ship as the legal battle launched by his vicious attorney advanced. He moved out, leaving me to cover the full amount of the mortgage and all expenses, even though our separation agreement required us to pay expenses fifty/fifty until the house was sold. This quickly dissolved all cash assets that I had. He filed frivolous motion after motion with the court, running up my legal fees as my attorney had to respond to them, baseless as they were. When Ron sheepishly brought us an offer on the house that was for $36,000 less than what we owed, he threatened to sue me to pay the short-fall. With all of my assets completely exhausted and living paycheck to paycheck, I realized the cruise ship was going to sink. I told him we'd have to let the house go back to the bank. I couldn't pay anymore. I was flat broke. It was at this point that he produced the shortfall $36K in cash for the sale, and the buyers with the lowball offer got quite a bargain.

I made it to the settlement office and, true to his word, Ron had scheduled Richard and gotten him out of the door before I arrived. I signed all the paperwork. I could see Richard's name and signature on all the documents; each one was like a grain of salt sprinkled in the open wound. I could picture him scanning each document and confidently scribbling his signature with his Montblanc pen, while checking his Rolex as if he had a million better places to be. I wondered if she was with him, watching over his shoulder, as he expunged one more aspect of his life with me. I got through it without crying. I don't think I had any tears left. I just felt so, so tired and so sad.

As I was leaving, Ron held out his hand and said, "I wish you all the luck in the world."

Shaking his hand, I said, "Thank you. And Ron, thank you for being so good through all of this. I really appreciate all that you've done."

"What will you do now? What are your plans?"

I don't know exactly why I said it or where it came from. I think I wanted to say something that would make him feel better and less sorry for me, "My next adventure is to buy and restore a big old historic house and make it my forever home."

And this became my standard response when the "What now, Amanda?" question inevitably came from my friends and family. It made them feel better, and that made me feel a little better too.

Chapter 4

I checked my email as the three of us watched for our black suitcases to circle around on the baggage conveyor carousel, mangled between all the other black suitcases. I was pleased to see that I had a message from Bob, "Good Morning, I'd be happy to show you around the house again. I can meet you and your friend out there Sunday morning about ten o'clock. Let me know if that's a good time for you. Best, Bob P.S. I'm glad you're coming back for another look, and I've attached some history on the house. I think you'll find it interesting."

I confirmed the time with Bob and let Danielle know to block her Sunday. I took a quick look at the information he attached and saw that the house had been featured in a couple of different books published about the homes and architecture of the region. The mere fact that I might own a house that was featured in two books was thrilling. The land had been purchased in 1840, and construction on the house was complete by 1845. The owner was a farmer, and his family was recorded in early Quaker records in Frederick County. *Wait—Quakers!* I wondered if they were connected to the Quakers who established the Hopewell Society of Friends. That would be an amazing coincidence considering my recent discovery of the Hopewell Friends Meetinghouse. I shared this intel with Alex, and he suggested I keep digging. He offered to do research with me at the local libraries if I bought the house.

We loaded our luggage into the rental, an SUV with enough room for us to share, and Alex did the driving. The team always gave me a pass on driving when we were traveling. I had the worst sense of direction in unfamiliar locations. On our first trip together, I drove us around lost for an hour before Alex spoke up and asked if I wanted him to drive. From that point on he always drove, I rode shotgun, and Jill preferred the safety of the back seat where she could ignore how fast Alex was driving and weaving in and out of traffic. I would frequently "help" Alex by giving him directions, and then I would say, "But you know to ignore everything I'm telling you, right?" He would smile the way he does and say, "Yes, I know." After stopping for lunch, we checked into the hotel and headed to our rooms. We agreed to meet in the lobby at five o'clock for the training-class registration and icebreaker.

It turned out to be a pretty big group, about fifty people from all over the country and a few from outside the United States. Alex and Jill did most of the small talking, not my forte, as we meandered through the reception with our mini plates of hotel, fancy finger-food fare. Business cards were doled out by the dozens as the training participants networked in hope of making contacts that would benefit their businesses. We were the only government agency participants. We stayed a respectable amount of time and met some interesting people, then we headed to the outdoor lagoon bar and restaurant, where we each ordered a glass of wine.

"Orlando has some of the prettiest *man-made* scenery I have seen anywhere," said Jill.

I agreed that the lagoon was impressive. There was no end to the lush plantings, palm trees, tropical flowers, and right there in the middle—sticking up out of the water—was an impressive half-sunken fiberglass pirate ship. Gliding around the lagoon were swan boats, propelled by tourists paddling their legs off, and wiping sweat from their faces.

Jill had an idea, "Let's have a team-building exercise. We'll rent one of those swan boats and paddle around the lagoon before we leave."

I'm not sure if it was the wine or the allure of being in kid-central U.S.A., but Alex and I agreed to Jill's plan and said we'd do it before we left. After finishing her glass of wine, Jill headed back to her room to call Tom. Alex and I hung out for a while longer and compared notes on whom we had met and the surprising mix of industries that were represented. A continental breakfast was provided by the training sponsor, so we said goodnight with plans to meet in the training room in the morning. We each promised to save seats if we got there first.

As the week progressed, the training went well, and we talked about when to schedule our certification exam, preferably soon before we forgot the material, but with enough time to study. The evenings were enjoyable as the three of us did some shopping, ate great food, and shared what was happening in our lives. I thought a lot about the old house in Winchester. We would talk about it over wine in the lagoon bar, enjoying the subtle, warm night air. Alex said if I bought the house, he'd introduce me to two of his friends, Ken and Mitch, who recently bought a circa 1880 house in the quaint, historic town of Middleburg. He said they gave up the D.C. lifestyle and were thoroughly enjoying country living. Alex had been out to visit them a number of times and said they really liked the whole experience and planned to be there for a long time. He cringed when he quoted Mitch as saying, "The only way I'm leaving here is in a wooden box." *Spoken like a loyal resident of a nineteenth-century house,* I thought. I got it, though—I was beginning to imagine myself enjoying country living. The daydreaming was top quality as I pictured the Winchester house fully restored and with me living in it.

We were finished with training by eleven thirty on Friday morning. We were glad to have the intense days behind us, much like that feeling you used to get on the last day of school or after finishing final exams. Most of the people from the class were eager to catch flights home that afternoon, but Jill, Alex, and I had time to kill since our flights were scheduled for Saturday—or in Alex's case Sunday. He was hosting family who lived on the Florida Gulf Coast to a day at Disney and was meeting them later that afternoon. We headed to the lagoon bar for sandwiches, where Jill reminded us we had a swan paddleboat team-building session scheduled. After we ordered our sandwiches, the waitress asked if we were interested in the lagoon bar drink of the day.

"What's your drink of the day?" asked Alex.

The waitress, a cute twentysomething with long honey-colored hair, who was clearly flirting with Alex (this happened a lot, much to the amusement of Jill and me), said, "It's this really yummy blueberry margarita. The bartender uses fresh blueberries, and he doesn't skimp on the tequila. I can't wait until I'm off work today, so I can start drinking."

Good grief, I thought, it was the perfect lead. Even I wanted to say, "And what time do you get off work today?"

But Alex's response was a little different . . . . "They sound great, bring one for each of us," and then he glanced my way and smiled mischievously.

After the waitress headed for the bar to put the order in, Jill and I both protested.

"You know I'm good for one glass of wine. After that, you don't want to see me!" said Jill.

Alex laughed. "If I have to get in one of those swan boats, it's going to be after something stronger than wine."

"Okay, fair enough!" I said.

I don't remember for sure, but I think one delicious blueberry margarita turned into three for me, for Alex it was more, and Jill was at two . . . I think. By the time we boarded the really big swan, which could hold four people, we were laughing so hard we couldn't fasten our enormous orange life vests. Fortunately, it was a quiet day on the lagoon and the staff seemed completely impervious to our drunken silliness.

Jill nearly fell in the lagoon as we were boarding the swan, "Mounting a swan is harder than it looks," she announced.

This resulted in roars of laughter. Alex handed his cell to the swan operator to take a picture of us. I could imagine how that would look when it hit his social media. I tried to hide myself in the vast depths of my florescent orange life vest. To tag the photo on social media, we thought we should name our swan. This idea generated more rounds of laughter.

Alex started, "How about Brawny Swany, because this mother clucker's enormous!"

Peals of laughter ensued.

Jill asked, "Do swans cluck?"

More uncontrollable laughter, *Only Jill*, I thought to myself.

"I mean, is that the sound they make?" she said.

We all knew where Jill's mind was these days. As we paddled around like the other tourists, I tried to help with the naming.

"Is this a boy or a girl swan?"

"Does it matter?" asked Alex.

"How do you tell? Should I lift up its tail and check?" said Jill, standing up in the swan boat.

We heard the swan operator yell across the lagoon from the dock, "No standing in the swan! Stay seated in the swan at all times!"

Fits of laughter followed. I was crying so hard I couldn't

see. I defended my question, "If it's a girl, the name shouldn't be *Brawny* Swany."

"Okay," said Alex, "How about GargantuSwan?"

New rounds of laughter.

"Enough," said Jill. "I can't take any more."

Alex agreed, "Let's dock this duck before we sink it. I need another blueberry margarita."

Still laughing, we sat at the bar and ordered one more round. Jill finally reached her limit and said she was going to shower and take a nap before meeting me for dinner at six thirty.

I stayed with Alex, keeping him company while he waited for his family to arrive. They had been texting their progress from the time they left Tampa. As the two of us sat in side-by-side barstools, heads together chatting softly so as not to be overheard in the quiet of the now nearly empty lagoon bar, a warm breeze and the scent of creamy white gardenias added to the effects of fresh blueberries mixed with tequila. For northerners, that first taste of warm weather after the end of winter, and the joy of shedding heavy sweaters and boots for shorts, T-shirts, and sandals, is a magical moment—like being set free. That's exactly how I think we were both feeling. The week was over, it was warm and sunny, even our clothing was saying—be free! It was at this point that Alex said something, something that maybe any other time would not have meant much. But this day, in this setting, at this moment in my life, it had an effect—quite an effect. He leaned toward me . . . and touching his forefinger to his lower lip, said, "I'm considered a really good kisser."

WHAT!!? I remember space and time slowing to a standstill as I looked at his lips where his forefinger was resting— then at his eyes—and then at his lips again. I had the strongest urge to move his hand away from his mouth and lean into those beautiful lips with my own in a slow, deliberate, sensual

35

kiss. I wanted to pull his head toward me and just keep kissing him. *Oh no! Oh no-no-no!* This cannot be happening. This must not be happening. Alex is much, much younger than I am. He is my employee. And—Alex is gay. I cannot be feeling this way about him. I thought to myself, *Damn tequila! Damn, damn blueberry margaritas!* I pulled myself together. He seemed to be looking at me expectantly. I wondered how much of what I was thinking was written all over my face. I could only hope he had too many margaritas to remember the details of the afternoon when tomorrow came.

I didn't have a chance to respond, not that I know what I would have said, because from behind us, I heard a woman yell excitedly, "ALEX!" We both turned to see Alex's sister, brother-in-law, niece, and mother walking toward us. Alex stepped down from the barstool and, picking his sister up off the ground, twirled her in a circle. Hugs were happening, and I could see that Alex and his family were close. I wondered if they knew him well enough to have wondered about the scene at the bar, as it must have looked just as they were arriving. It may have been my imagination, but I thought his sister looked at me with more than a hint of curiosity. Introductions were made, and the family gave me the "you're his boss" deference that I hate. I found myself complimenting Mrs. Jenkins on her excellent son. I felt ridiculous, like this was parent-teacher night, and we were finishing the first semester of kindergarten. Alex seemed amused by my discomfort. I couldn't help but wonder what his mother would think if she knew just minutes ago I was imagining being locked in a seductive kiss with her son. I extricated myself from the scene as quickly as I could, wished them fun at Disney, and told Alex I'd see him at work on Monday.

On the flight home, I kept thinking about Alex. It was like I was seeing him for the first time. I was always fond of him and I liked the dynamics of our team. We were friends. Jill and I knew he was good-looking, but it wasn't any different than acknowledging the waitress at the lagoon bar was cute. But after yesterday . . . after the "I'm a great kisser" proclamation, I was seeing him differently. Alex was a gorgeous man—tall, slender, and athletic. He had dark hair with a short, boxed-cut beard, and gray eyes. He was a runner, up to six miles a day, and he did weight training. Often when we were traveling, I would run into him in the hotel gyms. He had those arms and chest that had definition through his clothes—you couldn't see the muscles, but you knew they were there. A former partner of his had been a sports trainer, and Alex never gave up working out and staying fit. Women were always checking him out, and people generally said he looked like Channing Tatum—but I never thought of him in that way. Now I couldn't *stop* thinking of him in that way.

I'd be spending the day with Danielle tomorrow, I needed to keep my forbidden thoughts under wraps, and she had an uncanny knack for picking up on my feelings. *Amanda, get yourself under control. You're his boss, and he's not into women, and you're ten years older than he is.* The irony of not being able to decide the order of precedence for which of these facts was the most compelling argument for stopping my current trend of thinking, was not lost upon me. *It's ALL a big NO!* But was it? And, what was Alex thinking?

Chapter 5

Sunday morning was proving to be another pretty spring day. As I pulled up to Danielle's new, three-story townhouse in Leesburg, I thought to myself that I was glad she would be seeing the house on a nice day. Old houses in a state of abandon look depressing and sometimes creepy, especially when it's dark and overcast outside. Already, I was personalizing what others would think of the house, I wanted it to make a good first impression. I wanted Danielle to be as awestruck as I was when first seeing it.

Danielle popped out of her front door and waved. "Can we make a coffee run before we head to Winchester?" she asked. "How was your trip last week to Orlando? Poor you. Orlando in March."

I laughed. "It was good. The training was intense, like all these bootcamps, but the certification will be good to have."

"Did you do anything fun? You mentioned in one of your texts that the hotel had a really nice outdoor bar and a lake with ducks or something."

"A lagoon, with swans . . . umm yeah, we did some fun things. Jill and Alex are fun to travel with. We have great chemistry. I mean . . . we have camaraderie . . . that is, we get along."

With my stuttering around, I thought I detected a funny sideways look from Danielle, probably just my imagination. I changed the subject, and with it eliminated the risk of blurting out my newly discovered awareness of Alex.

"I can't wait for you to see the house. But I have to warn you, it's in awful shape. And I want your honest opinion. If it's a terrible idea to buy it, just tell me."

"I will," said Danielle.

The drive was as beautiful this week as it had been last weekend when I drove out by myself. The fields were a slightly deeper shade of green and pops of pink were now visible everywhere as the wild red buds and the neatly planted cherries were in full bloom.

Danielle commented on how lush the scenery was when driving west toward the Blue Ridge mountains, "I forget what it looks like when the suburban housing developments end and the land returns to farms, and mountains, and woodland."

We skirted downtown Winchester by taking Route 81 and exited at the same location I had last week, when I found the house. I pointed out the tidy apple grove and the dairy-farm girls. As we went by the Quaker meetinghouse, I said, "Isn't that awesome?" I could tell she wanted more time to see it, but we were on a mission—no time for dallying. As we approached the house, I didn't say anything. I wanted to give her the same opportunity to process the scene in front of her that I had had when I drove up to the house the weekend before. I slowed the car as we approached and pulled into the lower drive to provide her with the view from a distance. I was glad to see my timing was on target, and we made it to the house before Bob Norseman arrived.

"This is quite a house!" she said.

I explained the history of how it had been sitting vacant for nearly five years after the developer that bought the three-hundred-acre farm had gone belly up.

"Why do you think the bank didn't take better care of it?" asked Danielle.

I wondered that too. I had seen the history of the bank's listing prices on the internet site I used for house hunting. They had started ridiculously high at nearly a million dollars, and steadily dropped the price to just under half of where they had started. Apparently, it didn't occur to them that the longer the house sat vacant, the more its value depreciated.

"This could be a really beautiful house. But it's going to take a lot of work and probably a lot of money," said Danielle.

Those were my thoughts too. *Was it too much work and too much money? Was the house too far gone to save?* These were the questions that I needed to answer.

As we waited for Bob to arrive, we walked around the property. With Danielle, I had more courage to enter the overgrown jungle surrounding the house, *safety in numbers or something like that*, I thought. As she questioned the wisdom of wading through waist-high weeds, I put on a brave front, "Don't worry, anything that is hiding in this mess will hear us coming and get out of our way." I wasn't so sure, actually, but it sounded logical. As we rounded the back of the house and stepped out of the tall brambles onto an old concrete patio, we came toe to toe with an enormous black snake. It was at least six feet long and with a diameter the size of a baseball! Taken by total surprise, we both let out with high-pitched screams. The snake didn't seem at all perturbed by our presence. Considering our options for exiting, jumping forward toward the driveway seemed the best course of action, rather than heading back into the bedlam from which we had emerged. Still screaming, we ran for it, going as far around the giant snake as possible.

Of course, as luck would have it, there was Bob Norseman. He was standing in the driveway right where we emerged from behind the house. We practically bowled him over. He half smiled and in that deep Virginia drawl said, "You ladies encounter a snake?"

I was so embarrassed. Here I was, trying to seem like a serious buyer of a complicated house, and I was running and screaming with my friend like a couple of middle-school girls watching a scary movie. I tried to justify it by saying, "I've never seen such a large snake. It had to be eight feet long (I embellished), and as round as a kickball." *Kickball—where did that come from?*

Bob patiently explained, like a parent would do with a hysterical child, "That would be a black rat snake. They're completely harmless. I've seen 'em out here quite a bit. They keep the venomous snakes away, and they eat rodents. If you're gonna have a snake around, this is the one you want."

Okaaaay, I thought to myself.

Bob continued with a serious tone, "Do you know the difference between a venomous snake and a poisonous snake?"

Could my mortification get any worse? "Umm, no," I said. I was trying to remember high school biology class. *Was it a genus thing? What exactly are genera and species? Which comes first, species or genus?* I generally zoned in high school when biology started to sound like a foreign language.

"Well . . . a venomous snake is deadly if it bites you. And a poisonous snake is deadly if *you* bite it."

Danielle let out with her famous laugh, the one she's known for when something is really funny, "HA! That's great! I like you!"

This elicited a broad smile from under Bob's perfectly manicured gray mustache, and he said, "Well, come on then, let's see what this grand old girl has to show us today."

41

This being my second time through the house, I looked at details with a more practical eye and less of an emotional re-action. Danielle I could tell was still at emotional, and I thought that was fine, let her enjoy being at that stage. I focused on what I could see would mean dollar signs if I bought the house. For anything that was going to need more than a good cleaning, I wanted to assess the cost. As Bob put it, there was all the cosmetic stuff—including the failing plaster, the windows that would need to be fully restored (how many? sixty-seven individual sashes comprising fifty-four windows as it turned out), twelve fireplaces (four needing to be opened and all of them probably requiring their chimneys be restored), repairs to the floors in many areas (with extinct heart pine no less), the rotting boards and handrails on the two-story portico and the long veranda running down the east side of the house, and probably much more.

Then there was the make modern stuff—new bathrooms, a new kitchen, laundry, heating and air-conditioning (the house had no central air-conditioning), and plumbing and electric to code. *What else was there that I wasn't even aware of?* Oh, there was the demolition of numerous unoriginal, falling-down outbuildings along with the twentieth-century lean-to addition on the back of the house, not to mention restoring the grounds. As we headed down the steps from the kitchen into the English basement (a basement that is partially underground with windows and a separate entrance of its own), I heard water running. "What's that noise?"

"After it rains, the groundwater sometimes comes in through the walls and up through the floor," said Bob.

"That doesn't sound good at all. How much water is it?"

"Well, you'll see," and Bob turned on the hideous, single-tube fluorescent ceiling light that supplied the only source of electric light in the basement.

Danielle burst out, "Oh, you have a Roman bath in your

basement!"

I could see water trickling down the brick walls in at least three places. Last weekend, the basement was dry, and the floor appeared to be a dirt floor. Someone had set up a sump pump by digging out some of the dirt floor and placing the sump pump in the dug out area. It was pumping away as fast as it could, but that wasn't fast enough for all the water that was coming in.

"Where did that come from?" I said, pointing at the sump pump.

"I set it up a while back when I saw water was a problem down here. It doesn't do much, but every little bit helps."

"Said the frog when he spit in the ocean!" exclaimed Danielle.

I was not feeling so jovial, "I thought water inside the house was a really bad thing."

"Oh, these old houses aren't like new houses. You've got all-natural materials down here. There's no drywall, or carpet, or electric wires in the walls. Some old houses were actually designed to have springs run freely through the basement, an old-fashioned solution for running water. But yes, you would need to get this water infiltration dealt with. You don't want water standin' in the basement. That's why I set up that little sump pump."

Bob had this way of making something that seemed just awful sound like no big deal. *This doesn't look good though*, I thought to myself. I couldn't imagine that groundwater leaking through the brick walls and up from under the floor was doing the house much good. I started a third list in my cell phone's notepad, "Structural Stuff" and I added "Deal with water in the basement," to that list.

"Bob, the walls throughout the house are solid brick, right? The plaster is applied directly to the brick and there are no hollow areas?"

"That's right. The inside walls are two bricks thick, and the outside walls are three bricks thick, except the inside wall that separates the kitchen from the house. That one's three bricks thick, like an outside wall. You can see it when you look at the door and window casings."

Danielle and I both instinctively started counting bricks in the openings.

"So, is it a problem that some of these solid, interior basement walls are crumbling?" I pointed to a section of wall between two basement rooms, "And this wall here is actually missing a huge section."

"Well, I'm not a structural engineer, but this place is built like a fortress. I don't think one wall is going to bring the whole thing down, if that's what you mean."

I knew there would be masonry work to be done, but I hoped it wasn't urgent. I added "Fix brick walls in basement" to my "Structural Stuff" list.

Bob pointed out that the exposed solid oak beams and floor joists were all in good shape, no rotted wood. I knew that was a good sign. There was no doubt about it, a lot of work needed to be done to make the house first livable, then comfortable, and finally beautiful again, but the potential was real.

We thanked Bob for showing us the house and before parting I asked him, "Do you think the price is negotiable? Will the bank accept less than what they are asking for the house?"

"Well, you've hit on a bit of a delicate subject. You see, I'm the selling agent, representin' the bank who owns the house. It's not really proper for me to advise you about what the seller will do. Are you gonna have your own agent? Usually the buyer has their own agent."

I had not even considered this. Of course, I knew there were usually two agents involved. I'd bought and sold houses and just got done dealing with the cruise ship sale. In the excitement of finding the house and wrapping my head around the rehabilitation potential, I more or less forgot that Bob wasn't my agent. I didn't have an agent. I thought briefly about calling Ron, but he once told me that Leesburg was as far west as he would go from D.C. I also needed to put that chapter of my life behind me, and Ron was a painful reminder of the explosion. *What should I do?* I knew it wasn't exactly a shrewd move, but there was something about Bob that made me feel like I could trust him. It might have been the whole Sam Elliot vibe, and the fact that he and his wife loved historic houses.

"Bob, could you represent me to the seller if I decide to make an offer on the house?"

"Yes, I can do that. You'll have to sign a disclosure statement sayin' you understand that I'm a dual agent."

"Okay, I'd like you to be my buyer's agent. So . . . will the bank accept a lower price?"

"Ah, you got me now! Well . . . my guess is after havin' it sit for years without a buyer, they're ready to unload it. You make them any offer you want. The worst that can happen is they say no, it's too low, and you offer a little more until they see a number they can live with. They won't get hurt feelings. They just need a number that works for them."

"Sounds good. I need to try to get a sense for the costs involved in rehabilitating the house and see where I stand with money. I'll aim for no later than the end of the week to let you know if I'm going to make an offer."

As I backed out of the driveway, Danielle searched on her cell for a place to have lunch in Winchester. My mind was reeling, and I couldn't wait to break it down with Danielle and get her thoughts.

We found a restaurant in town that had been converted from a railroad depot warehouse into an industrial chic bar and grill. It was quite impressive, and I found myself studying the engineering of the exposed ceilings, beams, support posts, and the obviously original hardwood floors. I was becoming one of those people! Our cheeseburgers and battered French fries were excellent. The waitress was great about refilling our iced tea as we sat for what seemed like hours talking about the house. Danielle was not the voice of reason that I thought she would be. I began to wonder if she had seen any of the numerous disaster zones in the house. She talked about it as though it was already restored, and I was living in it. I found myself in the role of being the practical one. Last weekend was all about dreaming and imagining. This weekend was all about reality!

"Danielle, I can't buy it if I can't afford to restore it. From what I can readily see, I've made a long list of the things that need to be done. What if there is something I can't see, and it's really expensive? I don't know anything about historic houses or how to rehabilitate them. Do you know there are universities that offer four-year degrees and even master's degrees in historic restoration? It's a big deal, despite what Bob says."

"Are you done with your rant? How much money *do* you have?"

"I don't have *any* money. The explosion wiped me out. I have a good job, steady and decent income, but no money. I'll have to take a loan against my 401K for the down payment and hopefully some of the preliminary work."

"So, what was your plan to pay for the restoration work?"

"I'll have to get a loan to cover the cost of the work. That can be a little tricky, as banks want to use the equity in the house as a measure of how much money they will loan."

"Then the problem is solved!"

"What do you mean *the problem is solved*?"

"Banks lend money, right? You're buying the house from a bank. A bank that *knows* the house intimately. Make it part of the sales contract that when you buy the house, they mortgage it *and* lend you the money to restore it. Problem solved!"

46

I thought about what she was saying, *This was a stroke of sheer genius,* and I laughed out loud. "You're right! That's a great idea. I wonder if they would go for it?"

Sometimes it takes someone with a fresh perspective to come up with a new idea, and Danielle was definitely the fresh perspective that I needed. Going through the lists on my phone's notepad, we began guesstimating the cost of the items that needed to be addressed. Danielle asked how I could guess the costs.

"All those years of improvements to the cruise ship gave me a good deal of experience talking with contractors and reviewing estimates. I have a pretty good idea of what things cost. Problem is . . . my experience has been with new construction."

"And you think the costs are different with a historic house?"

"I don't know much about historic houses, but I know repairing and restoring them has to be handled carefully and with respect for historic building materials and design. I don't have any experience at all in this type of work."

"So you'll have to ballpark it based on modern homes."

I was able to come up with general costs for everything that I could identify, and it was a sobering amount. Just as I began to doubt that I could or should take on the house, Danielle prodded me. "What are you waiting for? Call Bob! Let him know what you can pay for the house and the amount of the loan you think you'll need. The worst that can happen is he'll say you're crazy!"

She had a point—nothing ventured, nothing gained. I hit the number for Bob in my cell phone, and he answered on the first ring. "Hi, Bob. Can I run an idea past you? I've done a rough estimate of the work that will need to be done and the cost."

"Well, okay then, what are you thinkin' of?"

47

I told him my price and about my restoration loan terms.

"Whoa, that's a good $155,000 below their askin' price. You don't mess around. I don't see a problem with the restoration loan. They need good-credit borrowers on their books. I'll write up the offer and send it over to you tomorrow to look at. We can review it together over the phone."

"That sounds great, thanks, Bob."

"Well, alright then. I'll talk to you tomorrow."

I looked at Danielle. "I feel like a just took a leap off the side of a cliff."

"I haven't seen you like this in a long time."

"What do you mean?"

"Back to yourself! Planning, strategizing, excited about the future!"

She was right. This leap of faith was the start of living again. I didn't know what I would do if the bank didn't accept my offer. My excitement and desire to restore a once beautiful, one-hundred-and-seventy-five-year-old house, prevented me from asking myself too seriously if I could actually do it.

Chapter 6

When my alarm sounded at 5:00 a.m. on Monday morning, I was wide awake. I was wide awake because I never went to sleep. A million thoughts of what could go wrong in the purchase of the house, or worse, if I couldn't purchase the house at all, nagged and badgered me. All night a round of *What if this happens*, and *What if that happens*, and *What will I do if this occurs* kept playing over and again. I created a worst-case scenario and then ran through the options and costs for dealing with it. It was like a game-show marathon was running in my head.

For $50,000—Cause for the house partially collapsing: What is a deteriorating foundation wall?

For $40,000—Solution for keeping water out of the basement: What are foundation drains and sump pumps?

I was glad when the alarm went off because I was forced to end the cycle and get on with my day. Shower, hair, makeup, clothes, shoes, jewelry—the usual routine was done with a little more care. Actually, it was done with a lot more care. I wanted to look cute, and sexy, and yes, appealing. It occurred to me that I was on the edge of running so late, due to wardrobe changes, that I might miss getting a parking space at the commuter bus lot—catastrophe! I hadn't cared this much about looking good in quite a long time. I wanted to make a good impression. Was it because I had a big day ahead and the start of what could be a major shift in my life if the bank accepted my offer on the house? Maybe that was part of it, but mostly, it was knowing I would see Alex.

Bob was true to his word, and my offer to the bank with all conditions arrived attached to an email at nine o'clock. I read through it, had no questions, and signed it. I responded to Bob's email, "Thanks, Bob, for having this done so quickly. I don't have any questions. Let me know what the bank has to say." I attached the signed copy and hit the send button. I checked the time and noted it was nine thirty. How long would it take for the bank to respond?

Alex and Jill slid into the chairs around the little table in my office just as I was finishing my email to Bob. We had a routine team sync-up meeting at nine thirty. I filled them in on what was happening, and both seemed genuinely pleased that I had decided to buy the house. Alex said if the deal went through, he wanted to come out and see it before the work got started. I thought this was a great idea, and it generated a very real flutter of excitement in the pit of my stomach.

The morning was dragging: 10:00, 10:30, 11:00. My cell rang, and I saw it was Bob!

"Hi, Bob. What did they say?"

"In a word . . . no. I spoke directly with the bank president, and he said, I quote, 'This number is disappointing.' But don't take that too hard, we just need to go back in with a better number."

"Did they counter?"

"No, but they didn't slam the door. I think they liked the idea of doin' the restoration loan. They wanna run your credit and learn more about your ability to take on a historic rehabilitation project of this size and complexity. I think they were a little surprised you were a woman, takin' on such a big project by yourself. Gilbert, or Gil as he likes to be called, is kinda old school. He isn't used to women being so self-assured about a project like this."

Was I self-assured? Naïve was more like it!

Bob continued, "I think we just need to go back with a more realistic offer, a better number, not a big deal."

"Okay. I knew that was a possibility. I just wanted to start low because I thought there would be a back-and-forth with counter offers and I wanted room to go up, but not too far up. I'll just jump to what would have been my final offer. Raise my first offer by $40,000. I know that's still $115,000 less than their listed price, but their listed price isn't realistic considering all the work the house needs. My ballpark estimate is that the house will need close to $300,000 to restore it and make it comfortable, and that doesn't include anything like major structural work, should that be discovered down the line."

"Speakin' of restoration costs . . . Gil told me that about a year ago, when the bank was considerin' fixin' the house up to sell it, he had a local guy by the name of Josh Edden give him an estimate to do everything the house needs. This guy Josh told him $215,000. Now, I don't know all the particulars or what that included, but it's not a bad price."

"Interesting. It sounds a little low, but good to know. Is Josh a historic house contractor or someone who specializes in historic rehabilitation?"

"Oh, I seriously doubt that. Gil and his buddies at the bank don't give a damn about the historic aspects of the house. They were just tryin' to see if they could make more money off of it by fixin' it up. I'll see what I can find out about this Josh Edden. In the meantime, I'll update the offer and get it over to them."

The afternoon dragged: 1:00, 1:30, 2:00, 2:30. An email

from Bob!

"The bank accepted your offer with a few caveats. Call me when you have a break in the action."

I grabbed my cell and shut the door to my office. "Hi, Bob. They accepted the offer?! What were the caveats?"

"Well, the final price you gave 'em was fine. I think they were relieved after seein' the first number. And . . . they will agree to loan you the money as a condition of the sale. Here's the big caveat . . . they're cappin' the restoration loan amount at $215,000. They say they know the house can be made livable for that number. And, before they'll release the money, they want a project plan that shows how you'll tackle the restoration work and the costs involved. They recommended you meet with Josh Edden and hinted that his written estimate of the work and costs would be acceptable to them as your project plan."

"I think $215,000 is low for all the work that needs done. This isn't one of those TV fixer-upper shows where they seem to be able to get work done for unbelievably low prices."

"No, but look at it this way, if you prioritize what needs to be done, $215,000 can get you into the house and functionin' while you do the pretty stuff over time. Hell, you'll like havin' projects, and you'll enjoy seein' the progress evolve slowly. It's what Marie and I have done with our house."

He had a point. I was used to new house construction and the turnkey perfection of every aspect of the cruise ship. This was a different situation all together.

"But back to Josh Edden, I'll meet with him but is the bank requiring me to use him for the work?"

"No, they aren't. They know they can't do that, and I'd shut 'em down if they tried. I'll still plan to do a little research on him and let you know what I find out before you meet with him."

"Thank you. I appreciate that."

"Amanda, one more thing . . . in the updated offer I sent them I added a clause that you have thirty days to have engineers, historic restoration experts, Santa Claus, and anyone else you like to come through the house and assess the work it needs, and the cost. If you see anythin' that looks like more than you wanna bite off, you can call it quits. They pushed back a little on that, but then accepted it when I didn't budge."

"Yes, I saw that in the updated version of the offer. Thank you."

"I want you to take this seriously. Just between you and me, I'm givin' you a key to the house so that you can go in there whenever you need to. I don't think there's anythin' that's too big a deal, but I don't want you left holdin' the bag if you buy the house and then find somethin' seriously wrong with it. Do you understand what I'm sayin'?"

"I do, and thank you. I'll start today to line up some of the right experts to look at the house. Santa Claus might be a little hard to get on such short notice, but I'm on it!"

"Alright then, let's meet—where and when? I wanna give you this key and make sure you can get in without any problems."

That evening, after meeting Bob halfway between Leesburg and Winchester to pick up the key to the house, I started researching contractors who specialized in historic house rehabilitation. There were surprisingly few of them. Almost all the contractors did work like what I had done with the cruise ship. This was going to be more challenging than I had imagined. I was able to put together a small list of contractors within fifty miles of Winchester and would start calling them in the morning. I had mostly general contractors on the list, but there was one who specialized in structural engineering. Those basement walls had me worried, and I thought to myself that it goes to reason that the walls that hold up three stories and a massive hip roof needed to be solid and not missing sections.

In the course of doing internet research to find historic restoration contractors, I also stumbled across a plethora of educational information, including the U.S. National Park Service Historic Preservation website. It was a treasure trove, including a series of how-to preservation briefs. The website stated, "Preservation Briefs provide information on preserving, rehabilitating, and restoring historic buildings. These NPS Publications help historic building owners recognize and resolve common problems prior to work." The first preservation brief on the list of fifty briefs was *Cleaning and Water-Repellent Treatments for Historic Masonry Buildings.* It was like the site had been created for me! Other topics included things like the repair of historic wooden windows, pointing mortar joints on historic masonry, repairing flat plaster walls. I hadn't been this excited since I didn't know when. *Well, maybe that's a stretch,* I thought, *perhaps not this excited since Alex announced he was a really good kisser.* It was midnight by the time I closed my laptop.

As I began setting up appointments to meet historic restoration contractors at the house, I realized I would need to take some days off work. I couldn't be in Winchester and D.C. on the same days. I tried to line up more than one contractor per day. This resulted in me spending a lot of time at the house between appointments and gave me the opportunity to study the house and learn more about its rehabilitation priorities. As the appointments progressed, I was finding not one of the contractors would give me a price for all the needed work. They seemed overwhelmed with the enormity of the house and the variety and number of restoration projects. Even the engineer needed to undertake an expensive study of the house to give me an answer about the integrity of the foundation walls. I decided to change my approach and started breaking the work down into specific jobs, starting with the ones that I judged to be the most urgent: water in the basement, masonry work to close up foundation wall holes, broken windows, falling plaster ceilings. I was beginning to have to rely on myself and my limited knowledge just to communicate with the contractors and get what I needed.

There was one contractor who seemed like a good fit from my conversation with him over the phone. He was an older gentleman who had done a lot of work with historic homes around the nearby towns of Purcellville and Hamilton. We met at the house and after introductions and going over the type of work he had done, and some of his bigger projects, I had a sense that he was a careful man and an honest one. We started in the basement, with me asking if he thought the house was stable. He waded through the basement floor mud with me, looking at the beams and floor joists, examining the brick walls, and pointing out things like the original wooden pegs that held joints together. He generally seemed very pensive. He, like all the contractors I had spoken with, was quick to share his knowledge of certain things. Each of them, in sharing little nuggets about historic house construction, was giving me valuable information that I could piece together. I absorbed this information like a sponge and added it to the information I read in the NPS historic preservation briefs. However, when I probed for specifics he was evasive, saying things like, "That depends," and "It might be alright," and "It's hard to tell." I was getting frustrated. I needed specific information about what had to be done, the order of precedence, and the cost!

I tried one last time, "Mr. McCullough, I know, as you've said, you can't have a solid understanding of the cost until after you begin work and can see exactly what you are dealing with, but ballpark—what are we looking at?"

He replied, "It's really hard to say. I'd need to have an engineer come out and take a look and then once we get into the work there are things that can start to add up quickly."

We parted on friendly terms, with him promising to send a rough estimate of the items he would work on and the cost. The estimate never came, and this is how it went with each of the contractors.

As I finished meeting with everyone on my list, I was no closer to a solid understanding of the needed work and the overall cost. I decided to try one more internet search. An article that had been published in the the local paper, the year before, came up on my list of hits. I clicked on the article and read with fascination. Near Winchester was a company owned and operated by two young men who had college degrees in historic restoration and a long list of very impressive projects in their portfolio. They had restored buildings that were on the National Register of Historical Places and had expertise in all areas from woodworking to historic masonry. I wondered if they were still in business and searched the internet for the name of their company. I found them almost immediately, and I was ecstatic! *This could be the answer to my dilemma*, I thought. I set up an appointment to meet them at the house.

I kept Danielle and Jill and Alex up to date on the progress of finding a contractor. I found myself sounding like a construction industry representative. Jill was definitely not into it and besides, she had other pressing matters on her mind. She and Tom had decided to see a fertility specialist. I needed to talk soon with our department manager to see what would be allowed to ease the stress that work was causing her. Danielle was eager to have the work done and the house looking beautiful. I could see that the construction and contracting details of how that would happen were more than she wanted to wrap her head around.

More and more, Alex was the person I could talk to about anything and everything. We would meet for happy hour after work, and I would fill him in on the latest. He would ask questions and give me great suggestions that I really appreciated. He was genuinely interested, and it had been a very, very long time since anyone (especially a smart, engaging, and gorgeous man) wanted to know the details of what was going on in my world. I found myself looking forward to our conversations and social time together. Neither of us mentioned what was said in Orlando. For all I knew, he didn't remember it. I remembered it very well and felt a warm flush to my face every time I thought about it. We had a trip to Denver coming up in May to kick off our new, yearlong, nationwide project. I found myself looking forward to the amount of time we would have together while traveling. Alex must have also been thinking about it. He asked me if I had found a nice hotel near good restaurants and bars, and wanted to know what kind of rental car I wanted him to reserve. We talked about driving up into the mountains outside of Denver and doing some sightseeing. Alex had never been to Colorado.

⚷━━

It was mid-April and true to the rhyme, April showers were giving it their best to ensure May flowers were on schedule. I hoped the basement wasn't a muddy Roman bath as I was meeting the latest contractors from Restore It, LLC, at the house. I liked them immediately. I felt for the first time in weeks that I had found true restoration experts who fully understood my needs for the house. They walked the house, checked things out, and shared information about what they were seeing and how to tackle the projects. They were knowledgeable, direct, and self-confident. A few times I thought they went a little far afield, like when they started describing the custom-made cabinets they would make for the kitchen, and at one point they went into great detail about how they pack a construction dumpster better than anyone—not leaving a gap of unused space to be found. But all in all they seemed perfect for the job. We parted with the promise of them having an estimate to me within a week. That would leave me one week before the end of my thirty-day assessment window and my commitment to the bank to either move forward with the purchase or cancel the sales contract.

Now that I had found Restore It, LLC, I stopped searching for contractors. Bob Norseman and I kept in touch. When I excitedly told him about the company, he was not as enthusiastic as I expected. I sensed he knew something he wasn't saying.

He asked me if I'd spoken with Josh Edden and I said, "Honestly, no. I know you said after checking into him, he has a good reputation, but he is a small-time, new construction, tract house builder. I know he's not a good fit for my work, and I haven't had time to spare for a nonproductive call."

"Yeah, I get it. You want the best for the house, and to be able to turn it over to the pros and know it's gettin' done the way you want."

"Thanks, Bob. I'll let you know as soon as I receive Restore It's proposal and the breakdown of the work."

This conversation with Bob prompted me to call Derek at Restore It, LLC. The week had come and gone, and I hadn't heard from him. The call did not go well. He had not even started on the proposal. I was livid but kept my cool. I explained again how important the proposal was and the time sensitivity. He said he was slammed with work and didn't know when he'd be able to get to it. I said I would provide him with a list of each of the restoration projects on a spreadsheet, and all he needed to do was fill in the amount next to the projects. He agreed that would speed things up. I had already created this list for myself, so it wasn't difficult to just clean it up a bit. I sent it via email to him within the hour.

I met Alex for an early dinner in D.C. that evening and vented my frustration, but I was still certain they were right for the job and that we could work well together. Alex listened and looked worried for me. As the calendar ticked off the final days—April 25 . . . 26 . . . 27 . . . 28—I still had nothing from Restore It, LLC, and I had no other contractors I could call.

I got Derek on the phone and said, "I have to have a number. What is the cost, even if it's an estimate, you've got to give me a number!"

Derek nonchalantly apologized for being too busy to work on the proposal and said, "Based on what's on your spreadsheet and what we saw at the house, it's going to be about $500,000."

I felt like I'd just been hit by a freight train. There was an intense ringing in my ears, and I saw little flashes of light from my peripheral vision. I couldn't speak. I was in shock, complete shock. After asking time and again for the proposal, and receiving nothing, he threw out a figure of half a million dollars! That was way more than I paid for the entire house. Was this a realistic amount? If so, I couldn't buy the house—financially, it was impossible. The house would sit abandoned and continue to deteriorate until sections of it caved in, and it was gone. I was sick, actually sick. Should I tell Bob the deal was off? I called Alex. In a panic-stricken voice, I told him the figure I'd received from Restore It, LLC, and how I thought it was game over.

Alex, in his levelheaded, logical way, said, "Now wait a minute. None of this makes sense. On the low end you have an estimate of $215,000 and on the high end $500,000. You don't know what either of those estimates really involves. Your own estimate is closer to the low end at $300,000 and that involves everything under the sun, except some unforeseen issue. The real question is, can you either come up with the difference between $300K and $215K—that's $85,000—on your own, or knock $85,000 in costs off of your list?"

Still panicked, I said, "But what if the house isn't structurally sound?"

Alex had an answer for that too. "Look, the bank wouldn't be tying up their money on a mortgage and a rehabilitation loan to you if the house was going to fall down. I think you should stop worrying about that. Bob Norseman said as much as well."

He had great points. "You're right, of course. I'm feeling a little better about this. Yes, I can definitely find $85,000 worth of projects that can be done later . . . over time. The big stuff that has to be done now fits within the $215K range—I think. I guess I'd better talk with Josh Edden. I only have two days left."

I called Bob Norseman, "Bob, I need Josh Edden's number. I seem to have misplaced it."

Bob didn't sound surprised, "No problem. Did you get your estimate from the Fix It guys?"

"Umm yeah . . . I got it. It was unbelievable. After waiting for weeks to get their proposal, Derek threw out a figure of half-a-million dollars, with nothing in writing to even break down the costs. I thought I was going to have a heart attack or pass out. I'm stunned, not to mention pissed!"

Bob chuckled heartily, "I thought somethin' like that might be the case. A fool and his money are soon parted, and they must have taken you for a fool. They were wrong. Let me know how your call with Josh Edden goes." Still chuckling, he said goodbye and hung up.

As I started to dial Josh Edden's number, I thought to myself how much I had learned in the last twenty-eight days. From nonstop reading of historic preservation briefs, to picking contractors' brains, to spending hours and hours in the house, learning its construction secrets.

Chapter 7

I met Josh Edden at the house to go over the $215,000 pro-
posal he had presented to the bank the previous year. We
wiped layers of grime and dead bees off of the circa 1985
kitchen island. I sensed a bit of tension in the air and figured
that he knew I only called him because no one else had
worked out. To lighten the mood a bit, I said, "What's with all
of these dead bees? Do you think there's a problem here?"
From my first walk through the house I noticed piles of dead
bees in the deep-set kitchen windowsills, all over the floor,
and trapped in the ugly fluorescent ceiling light's plastic cover.
There were a number of live bees doing their best to get out
through the window, and they no doubt would end up in the
pile with the rest. It was terrible to see so many dead honeybees.

Josh looked around and studied the ceiling, then fixed his
gaze on one side of the big kitchen fireplace chimney and said,
"Looks to me like there's an active beehive. We'll want to deal
with that. Don't want bees dying in the house when they need
to be outside making honey."

I looked across the counter at Josh, studying his features.

He sounded exactly like Eeyore from the *Winnie the Pooh,* cartoons. His voice was a dead ringer for Eeyore, and he kind of looked like Eeyore too. *How fabulous,* I thought; Eeyore was one of my favorite childhood characters. Josh appeared to be in his early forties, with thinning black hair that he combed straight down on his forehead. He had a traditional dad bod with extra weight in the middle and was wearing jeans and a dark, gray-colored, polo-style shirt with his company logo over the left front pocket. I already knew from Bob Norseman's poking around that he had a reputation for being decent to work with and very honest.

"How do we deal with it? I know honeybees need to be protected. I wouldn't want to exterminate them."

"No, we'll just move them out of the house."

"Move them?"

"You can call Blandy Farm at the State Arboretum of Virginia. They'll have experts who can take the queen bee and relocate the hive."

"Oh, I see. That's great. Thanks."

I was impressed. He could have said to just buy a spray can of insect killer, but no, he cared about saving the bees. Given that in the Old-World way bees are symbolic and represent activity, work, diligence, and good order, I took this as a good omen.

Josh opened his project proposal folder and a flurry of papers fell out across the center island countertop. The proposal was partially typed and partially handwritten on plain white paper with numbers written, crossed out, and rewritten in the margins. This was definitely not the level of professionalism I was accustomed to, but I had already learned my lesson about the professional looking contractors. Josh handed me a bundle of the crumpled papers and the two of us began to go through the line items together. The first item on the list took my breath away.

- *Tear off hip roof, replace with prefabricated front-gable trusses, add ceiling insulation.*
- *Tear off two-story front entrance portico and columns, tear off long side porch on east side, replace both with a one-story, wraparound porch.*
- *Remove all original windows and replace with new, vinyl, energy efficient windows.*
- *Remove original exterior doors and replace with new insulated energy efficient doors and keypad entrance locks.*
- *Remodel kitchen and two bathrooms.*
- *Tear down damaged plaster throughout and replace with wallboard.*
- *Paint walls and ceilings.*

That was it, the whole list, totaling $215,000. I felt an intense wave of nausea. Who knew restoring a historic house could frequently produce physical symptoms that mimicked heart attacks, intense stomach flu, and the urge to faint? I could see the house after this work was done being in *Old House Journal* as the featured "Remuddle of the Month." I had enjoyed looking at the monthly remuddles in the back of the magazines Bob Norseman loaned to me. It was astonishing what people did to beautiful old houses. I wondered, when looking at the photos, how on earth such atrocities occurred. Now I could see it, the photo caption would read:

We'll call this remuddle a Greek Anne. Amanda Grayson, remuddled this circa 1840 Greek Revival by adding a traditional neocolonial gable roof and Queen Anne Victorian wraparound porch. For added flare, she installed mid-century modern exterior doors and windows. This Greek Anne gets the best example remuddle-ribbon of the year!

Okay, I needed to save this situation quickly. Josh was going to be my contractor if I bought the house—the events of the past month meant that was now certain—but I'd rather not buy the house at all, than buy it and do this to it. I was back at square one! I would need to correct Josh's plan of action, without wounding his ego. Considering my lack of credibility in historic house rehabilitation, and his mistaken sense of expertise and competence, this was going to be a very delicate dance. The same dance women had been choreographing for millennia when it came to partnering and working with men. I was no stranger to the dance.

"Umm, Josh, I like how you've hit on all the big-ticket items here, however, some of the things on your list I don't want to do right now—maybe later."

"Oh? But most of these items are badly needed now."

"And Josh, there are some things that I need, er, want, to do . . . that aren't on the list."

"Okay, what do you want to cross off?"

"Umm, well, I think you can cross off the first four items for sure. Let's plan to just repair what's already there. That should save money, right?"

"That's not a good idea. You won't save money in the long run. You'll have a really high heating bill if we cross those items off. To make the house comfortable and affordable, you better modernize and keep those items on the list."

Oh no. We're on totally different wavelengths with completely divergent ideals for restoring a historic home. Think fast, how do I get us on the same page? He thinks I'm ignorant about what makes a house comfortable, and I think—no, I know—he's out of touch with restoration principles for historic houses. Clearly, he had not been reading the NPS historic preservation briefs! I had to find a way to get us working together toward the same goals. If my time as a federal manager had taught me anything, it was that your team has to have the same end goal in mind and be in agreement that it's the right end goal! I'd spent half my career developing strategic plans for federal agencies to achieve their goals. Most of the time they ended up collecting dust on a shelf because no one understood or agreed on the end goal, even when it was mapped out in a twenty-page, step-by-step operations plan. *How do I get Josh's buy-in?* I had an idea!

"Here's the thing. I plan to apply to have the house added to the Virginia Landmarks Register when it's finished. To do that, it has to be as original as possible. Every single original element needs to be left intact to the degree possible. I know it means sacrificing a lot of modern comfort, but I really want the house to be accepted for placement on the register."

"Is it old enough for that. When was it built?"

Silent groan. Amanda, keep your face neutral, don't react. Hold it together!

"The original family bought the land in 1840 and the house was finished by 1845." *And for added effect,* "It dates to before the Civil War."

My research, limited as it was at this point, was paying off. The two books that featured the house were clear about its origins and the dates.

Josh nodded, "Winchester does have a lot of houses on the historical register, especially in the downtown area. But I hear the historical register people are really picky about everything. They expect the houses to practically be museums—not places that people can live in comfortably. Is that what you want?"

"Yes! It's always been a dream of mine to have a house that was on the historical register. Will you help me with making sure I don't make any bad decisions that would destroy or eliminate an original element? One wrong move on my part could be the end of my dream."

I saw the flash of understanding cross his face, and he looked up from the papers scattered across the center island.

"Okay, well then what I have here isn't much help. Where do you want to start?"

Josh is on board! Thank goodness! I thought to myself. We had a common end goal—keep the house original. Now we had to keep it within a very tight budget. I'd tackle that goal next.

"This might help. I put together a list of projects for the house that I came up with on my own. Do you want to see it?"

"Sure. Let me take a look."

I opened my laptop. I had two versions of the list, one with estimated costs and one with the cost column blank. I opened the version with the blank cost column. I reviewed each must-have item with Josh, providing explanations of what I intended.

- *Dig down basement floor 12" to increase ceiling height and allow for floor drainage and the installation of a sump pump, replace mud floor with poured concrete.*
- *Repair holes in basement masonry walls and repoint mortar throughout the basement.*
- *Rebuild and restore original basement cooking fireplace.*
- *Tear old lean-to addition off the back of the house and remove other outbuildings, except the smokehouse.*
- *Demo existing kitchen, remove plaster to expose brick walls, install new kitchen (Amanda will design).*
- *Remove two existing bathrooms and all old plumbing— add three full bathrooms and one half bathroom (Amanda will design).*
- *Remove failing plaster from ceilings on the gallery level, add ceiling insulation, replace with wallboard.*
- *Add lighting and electric outlets throughout the house (Amanda will specify locations).*
- *Add new heating and air-conditioning system. Type to be determined.*

66

• *Remove existing storm windows and add new minimally visible storm windows.*

I decided to avoid the voluminous "Nice to Haves" list for the moment. I imagined Josh might feel a bit overwhelmed by all the items on that list, things like plaster repairs, interior painting, restoring historic window sashes, flooring repairs, painting the metal roof, etc.

"You've given this a lot of thought. There's a lot on this list."

"Umm, one more thing you should keep in mind . . . the bank is loaning me exactly $215,000. This is all the money I will have to get the work done. I absolutely must stay within that budget."

I braced myself for his reaction, which could be anything from laughing outright to scooping up his papers and walking out the door. However, to my surprise, Josh seemed to take the list and the budget in stride.

He replied, "Hmm, okay, good to know. I'll work the estimates for each line item with that number in mind. There's a lot here for the limited budget you have, but some of the big-ticket items that I had on my list, like a new roof and windows, aren't going to eat up the money, so it can go to other items. Some of the cost will come down to things like how many electric outlets and recessed lights you want. Also, the kitchen and bathroom details will drive the price. How about if I give you a base price with an allowance for upgrades for the kitchen, bathrooms, outlets, and lighting. Will that work for you?"

I was incredibly relieved, *This was much like Eeyore would do*, I thought. I could hear Eeyore now, *"Well, if that's all we have to work with, and all these things need to get done, we'll have to make it work . . . somehow."*

"Yes, that sounds like a really good way to tackle this. I

hate to rush you, but when do you think you'll have the esti-mate done? I need to let my real estate agent know by the end of the month if I am going to go through with buying the house." *And the end of the month was only a day away!*

"Because I know the house pretty well, I think I can give you the estimate within that timeframe."

We parted with Josh promising to email me the estimate by Friday. My being able to buy the house depended now en-tirely on Josh Edden. I hoped I would have better luck with Josh than I had had with all of the other contractors so far. If not, I was dead in the water.

☷━━✗

On my way back to Leesburg, I called Alex. I filled him in on my impressions of Josh, how the meeting went, and my fast-thinking idea to get the two of us on the same page about the restoration work.

"Just be careful you don't start calling him Eeyore. You know how you do that mental association thing and call peo-ple by the wrong name," laughed Alex.

"Great, now you've done it! The idea of mixing up the names is in my head, and I'll have to fight it every time I look at him."

"I hope you are more successful with him than you are at work with Deborah. She knows you call her Delores because she looks and acts like Delores Umbridge from *Harry Potter*."

He was right. Deborah Callahan was the special advisor to our agency's director. At work, she was my nemesis, always finding reasons for why the projects my team was proposing wouldn't work. That wouldn't be so bad, but she was sneaky about it and backstabbing. Alex, Jill, and I had decided she was the real-life Delores Umbridge, evil to the core. Once I made the association, I kept calling her by the wrong name. I didn't do it on purpose, it would just come out. It was terrible,

68

and to make matters worse, Alex and Jill fought to keep a straight face when I did it. We didn't dare look at each other, or it would have been game over. We were all one uncontrollable outburst of laughter away from formal reprimands, or worse.

"Well, Delores . . . damn it . . . *Deborah,* should work on changing her appearance, not to mention her personality! All of those Pepto Bismol-colored pink suits with the matching pink shoes and purse, and the candy football helmet hair—and all the while she's killing our projects and our credibility with them."

"Fortunately, Josh and Eeyore are two very different names, so hopefully you don't insult this poor guy."

"No, I hope not. I like Josh and for better or worse, if I buy this house, he's my guy for the long haul."

"I thought I was your guy for the long haul."

My stomach did a somersault worthy of Sunisa Lee. Could Alex hear my smile through the phone?

"Of course you are. How else would we pull off the multitude of projects we have going on?"

I purposefully pretended like he was talking about his important role on the work team, but I really hoped he was speaking on a personal level. The idea that he was my guy for the long haul had many implications, and I liked all of them!

"So, you think you will be able to buy the house? His numbers will be what you need?" asked Alex.

"There are a lot of incentives for him to work out as my contractor, none the least of which is the bank. Mind you, this is the same bank that is selling me the house and lending me the money to restore it. It's also Josh's bank for funding his business and his new house construction projects. Bob Norseman discovered that little fact when he was asking around about Josh. It makes more sense now when you think about how hard they pushed for me to use Josh for the work."

"So, let me see if I have this straight," said Alex. "The bank loans you the money to buy the house, then they loan you the money to restore it, they push for Josh to do the work and loan him the money to finance the work until you pay him. Wow, what a complicated web, and you are right in the middle of it."

"For sure—and it's this crazy, complicated web that's making it possible to buy and restore the house—maybe."

"If we were doing a project risk analysis like we do at work, I'd say there are some serious risks. But I think it will work out—I hope it works out. It would be great to have a friend with a country manor home estate where I could get away from the city when I need a break."

"Oh, I see how it is. You'll have the best of both worlds—city excitement and country relaxation! But, if it all works out, you're absolutely welcome."

"By the way, this is all happening around the same time we have our Denver trip to launch the new project. Are you going to be able to manage all this house stuff from halfway across the country?"

"Good point. I'll need to talk with Bob Norseman about the timing if it looks like I'm going to be able to buy the house."

"When will you know for sure?"

"There's one day left in April. That's the deadline. I should know by tomorrow."

I ended the call with Alex just as I was getting back to my apartment. It would be a tense twenty-four hours while I waited to hear from Josh.

Chapter 8

As the week progressed, I didn't have much time at work to worry about how Josh was doing with the restoration list and my limited budget. Fortunately, the team and I were crazy busy getting ready for the launch of our big yearlong project to reengineer the human resources operations at our agency, including automation of many manual processes. The trip to Denver was the kickoff and things had to go well. I decided to meet with my department manager to ask him about allowing our team to be a 100 percent virtual team. We'd be on the road a lot anyway, and when we weren't traveling, we could work as well from home as in the office. Actually, we could work better as a virtual team because we wouldn't have exhausting long commutes and the continuous disruptions that are typical at the office.

The idea came to me when I was thinking about how to lighten up the stress on Jill. I knew I had to come up with a plan that didn't involve telling the boss she needed more time with her husband because they were trying to have a baby and things weren't going well. That could be the kiss of death for Jill's career. An executive, who didn't know her and didn't know her work ethic or how much she contributed, would hear me say that I have an employee who wants to slack off at work so that she can have more romantic, candlelit dinners with her husband. And this could result in a scenario that would ultimately lead to maternity leave and then "mother priorities" for an infant. *Yeah—better that I make my case for a virtual team based on how it benefits our work and travel schedule.*

I met with Jill and Alex to get their buy-in and suggestions for how to approach the virtual team idea with the boss. Jill was very excited and said if we could work from home full-time, only going into the office when we had important meetings, she would gain three full hours a day. My situation was the same and if I bought the house in Winchester, my commute would be a round trip of 180 miles every day, and easily two-and-a-half hours each way due to traffic. Alex was less excited about the idea. He lived in the city and was only a few Metro stops up town from the office. On the worst day, his commute was twenty minutes, but he sympathized with us and said he could be the one to run into the office for small things and to make an appearance when needed.

Our new department manager, who liked the staff to call him by his first name, Rory, prided himself on being innovative and creative. He held frequent town hall meetings with the staff and boasted that his "open door policy" had helped him build successful teams. He wanted to set up a corner in our office space with Lego blocks and beanbag chairs to encourage "imaginative collaboration," but the agency human resources department shut him down on that idea. He settled instead for a huge jar full of Chex Mix that he personally refilled once a week in hope that, as we filled plastic cups with the stuff, we would talk with each other and magically great ideas and improved work performance would spontaneously bloom. All in all, he was a well-meaning and decent guy. I was pretty sure the environment that prevailed at our federal agency would chew him up and spit him out pretty quickly. That's how we'd had five department managers in seven years. For the managers like me who reported to Rory's position, it was exhausting. Every time we got a new executive, we had to prove ourselves all over again. I was doing pretty well with Rory, and he saw that my team produced. He had told me after being in the job a few months that the strategies and solutions we came up with were making a positive difference for the agency. Now I needed to negotiate with Rory as successfully as I'd done with Josh Edden.

I knocked lightly on Rory's open office door.

"Oh, Amanda. Hi! Come on in. Sit down. Oh, good, you brought your coffee. Mind if I warm mine up?"

"Good Morning! No, go right ahead."

I settled into a chair at the conference table in Rory's corner office and tried to position the sun at my back, so I wasn't blinded by the light. Rory had his mini blinds pulled all the way up to enjoy unimpeded views of the D.C. Southwest Business District. It was quite a view, and I'd probably do the same if I had his office. Rory was back with a full cup of coffee in less than a minute.

"So, Amanda, how are things going?"

"Great! We're finishing the last details of the project launch."

"How was your weekend?" asked Rory.

Oh, right, yes, we have to do that whole start the discussion with connecting personally thing. I had a very bad habit of jumping right into work and skipping the touchy-feely, chitchat step.

"Thank you for asking. I had a really nice weekend. I'm looking at maybe buying a house. How about you? How was your weekend?"

"I had a great weekend. My wife and I drove with our son to Williamsburg to check out the campus at the College of William and Mary."

"That's a beautiful campus! Is your son starting there in the fall?"

"Yes, we are so proud of him. It's been his dream to be accepted and eventually graduate from William and Mary for as long as I can remember, and he worked really hard to have the grades and the academic record needed."

"Wow, that's terrific. William and Mary is a really tough school to get into, as you'd expect for a public Ivy League. I think Mom and Dad need to give themselves a pat on the back too. I'm sure he didn't do it alone."

"Thank you." Rory beamed with pride.

I couldn't blame him. I knew he and his wife had just the one son, and he was the center of their world.

I proceeded to pitch my idea for allowing our team to work virtually. Rory was quick to buy into the latest workplace theory and adopt trends that were cutting edge. I leveraged that angle as I told him retaining the team was critical, and this arrangement would go a long way to keep them with the agency and avoid them being picked off by the big D.C. contract firms that paid higher salaries. He agreed but asked that we say it was provisional for one year while the project we were kicking off was under development. That way, he could get around the arcane rules that only permitted working from home one day a week.

The next morning, when Jill and Alex popped into my office for our daily sync-up meeting, I shared the good news with them. "Team, we are going virtual! We have permission to work from home full-time!"

Alex pointed out that many companies allow their employees to do this. "You'd think this idea was revolutionary, but a lot of the Fortune 500s and smaller companies have been doing this for a long time."

"I know, but for the federal government it *is* revolutionary! We're lucky that Rory thinks of himself as a modern manager who wants to change the way the government bureaucracy works."

"I can't wait to tell Tom! He'll be thrilled that I don't have to be on the road three hours a day and worn out from the commuting. Thank goodness, I'll be able to sleep one full extra hour each morning. That's huge!"

I was glad Jill was already seeing the benefits and hoped that this change in lifestyle could be the difference that helped her succeed in having a baby. Alex looked just a little bit dejected, I thought. Was he thinking that this would limit the time we were together? Did that mean he would miss me? *Don't get carried away, Amanda, he's just very social.*

"How will we sync up every day like we do now?" he asked.

"Everything we do now we'll keep doing. We'll use video conferencing instead of being face-to-face."

There it was again, that dejected look. I felt elated. He was going to miss our daily interactions!

"And remember, we're going to be on the road a lot this year, about one week each month."

Jill looked worried, "That much?"

"But I think it would make sense if one of us was always here. You know the problems we've run into in the past when all three of us were away. Our projects have nearly been derailed a couple of times because we were all three gone and the powers that be . . ."

Alex chimed in, "You mean Delores Umbridge."

"No wonder I call her Delores! But yes, *Deborah* has a way of waiting until we are out of reach to sabotage our work."

Jill got where I was going with this, "Oh, that's a good idea. I can stay here to man the fort, unless one of you wants to be here?"

"That's what I was thinking, you man the fort here. Alex and I have fewer commitments at home, and we can do most of the traveling, unless it's something you need to be present for."

Jill looked relieved and Alex looked very pleased. It occurred to me that I had just positioned myself to spend a lot of time, traveling, eating, shopping, and sightseeing, one-on-one with Alex. A little bolt of anticipatory electricity ran up my spine.

At that moment, my cell pinged that I had a text. I glanced down, "Oh, it's Josh Edden. He's letting me know he just emailed the restoration proposal."

I texted him back: Thanks! I'll open it now.

"We're dying as much as you are to know what it looks like. Open it!" said Alex.

I opened the proposal. It was a simple list of all the work, with a column to the right indicating a price for each item—no frills. I ran my finger down the list of items. He had basically taken my list and added subcategories for things like new electric subpanel, well water treatment system, type of insulation. It was thorough and clearly done by someone who understood the construction business.

"Well?" said Alex. "Did he stay within the budget and include all the necessities?"

"I'm afraid to look at the total. It's on the next page. Okay, here goes . . ."

I scrolled to the next page and zoned in on the number in the "Total" column.

"Oh, wow, he came in with a total of $235,000! That's not bad, just a little over my max, and this list is incredibly comprehensive!"

Jill asked the key question, "So does this mean you are going to buy the house?"

"Yes, I think so!"

"You should call Bob. Let him know to proceed based on Josh's proposal." Alex was as excited as I was.

76

"Okay, okay, I'm dialing."

"Hi Bob, I just got Josh Edden's proposal for the work on the house."

"Hi, Amanda. How's it look?"

"It's good. It's better than anything I got out of all those other guys I spoke with."

"And the total price works for you?"

"It's a little over the loan's max, but I think I can make that up with my own money. It's a good price for what's on the list, and what's on the list will get me into the house. A lot of the 'pretty stuff' as you put it will have to come later, but I can live with that."

"That-a-girl, now you're talkin' like an old-house enthusiast. I'll go ahead and work with the settlement company to set things up for the closing. It'll take 'em a couple a weeks at best. Any dates this month that won't work for you?"

I looked across the table at Alex as I responded to Bob, "I'll be gone for the entire third week in May. I have a work trip to Denver and will be out of pocket days and evenings for the most part." It wasn't my imagination, Alex smiled.

"No problem. Let's look at the last week in May. I'll let you know the exact date and time when it's all set up."

"Okay, sounds good."

Bob cleared his throat, "Amanda, I don't mean to sound condescendin' or anythin', but you handled this like a pro. I know a lot of people who would've thrown in the towel after the month you just had. Congratulations!"

"Thanks, Bob, see you in a few weeks!"

I turned to Jill and Alex, "This is pretty scary, actually. I hope I'm not making a big mistake. It seems like I'm positioned now to be able to buy and rehabilitate the house. And we are positioned as a virtual team, to be able to meet the demands of this new project without killing ourselves. Not a bad week as it turns out!"

Chapter 9

I was incredibly excited and nervous too. Having work as a distraction would be a great way to get through the next few weeks until I closed on the house. Jill, Alex, and I worked virtually via video conference on our presentation for the project launch meeting, scheduled for mid-May. Alex would do the main presentation and I would ad-lib and supplement what he was presenting based on the feedback we were getting from the audience. Sometimes we would lighten up the briefing a bit if the audience seemed disengaged. The two of us had been presenting this way for a while, and we had the routine down pat. People always complimented us after our presentations. As I thought about it, I realized there was real professional chemistry between us . . . but was it more than just professional . . . I wondered.

As we discussed the kickoff meeting, Jill asked me, "Should I cancel my flight to Denver?"

"Yes, there will be portions of the Denver meeting that we'll have you join via video conference, but you don't need to be there in person for the whole thing."

"Tom will be relieved. I can't wait to tell him I won't be

gone for a week!"

"Don't forget," said Alex, "I'm flying out nonstop from Reagan National, not Dulles."

"Right. Our flights get in about the same time, and we'll meet at the rental car desk. Which rental car company did you use?"

"The same one I always use, and I was able to reserve a roomy SUV. What hotel did you scope out for us?"

"It's the big chain hotel nearest the office out there. The coordinator reserved a block of rooms for all the meeting participants."

"Uh-oh, so you weren't able to apply your picky standards?"

"No, but hopefully it's okay."

Jill rolled her eyes, "If she has one of her decoraphobia fits, you'll have to deal with it on your own, Alex."

Alex smiled. "I can handle it. And besides, her hotel decoraphobia has meant we landed in some pretty nice four-star resorts, within government per diem rates."

"Hey, you two," I said. "I'm sitting right here. You know I can hear you AND see you, right?"

By the time Alex and I left for Denver, we had things well organized for the project kickoff. On the day of the trip, I met Alex as scheduled at the Denver International Airport. I had been to the airport many times, but I never got blasé about how pretty and unique the architecture was. I looked up into the underside of the fabric roof that formed white peaks emulating the tips of the snow-covered Rocky Mountains.

As I was thinking, it seemed almost mystical. I heard Alex call my name. "Amanda, over here!"

I watched Alex approaching from the other side of the big expanse of the central zone. He was wearing jeans, a black

Calvin Klein V-neck T-shirt, and a silver chain around his neck. His well-defined muscles were on full display in the T-shirt. The silver chain subtly drew my attention to his chest and the sculpted pecs right beneath the cotton fabric. His arms were perfection, smooth skin, not too hairy, with biceps and triceps that rippled as he maneuvered his luggage while walking toward me. His T-shirt was loose, not tucked in, and it was obvious his flat stomach would be as well-defined as the rest of him. *Amanda, stop it, get a grip! You're too old, you're his boss, and you're a woman! Cut it out!*

"We can head out to the rental lot and get the SUV. I've got the key. Do you want to head straight to the hotel and get settled in?" offered Alex.

"Yes, let's do that and then figure out where we want to go. Since we gained two hours by flying west, we have more time than usual."

As we pulled out of the rental parking lot, I let Alex know that, as I'd been here many times before, he could trust my navigation. From Peña Boulevard, leaving the airport, I instructed him to head east.

"Amanda, Lakewood is west of the airport."

"I meant west. I don't know why I said east. I think it's because at home, the mountains are always in the east."

"At home, the mountains are always in the west."

"Just ignore me. I may give you directions, but you should just totally ignore them."

"I know."

As Alex navigated Denver traffic like a pro, I thought about where to take him. It was his first trip to Colorado and there was so much to see. He needed to see the mountains and ski resorts, even though they were closed for skiing. Boulder was also a fun place to visit. Downtown historic Denver was full of great restaurants. We had a week, with our evenings free, I'd figure it out.

We pulled into the hotel and parked. As we entered the lobby, I looked around and noticed it looked pretty shabby and there was an odd smell permeating the lobby space. Our rooms were opposite one another on the main floor down a hallway off the lobby. The smell followed us—a cross between old mop water and yesterday's fish dinner.

Alex commented first, "We must be near the kitchen, this place smells terrible."

I just nodded and opened my room door with the key card. I heard Alex enter his room behind me. I flipped on the lights. It was really bad, like a room from *Hotel Impossible*. At any moment, Anthony Melchiorri and his team would arrive to do a total makeover and save the miserable place. Only this wasn't reality TV—this was reality. The carpet was worn nearly to holes in places and was dirty. The bed linens looked like something Granny took to the Salvation Army thrift shop . . . twenty years ago. The one upholstered chair in the room didn't match anything, and it had a large grease stain on the back cushion. I was afraid to look in the bathroom, but I did. It was reasonably clean looking . . . for the bathroom in the prison cell at the county jail. It had a plain white plastic shower curtain and two threadbare towels. I felt the melt-down coming.

I've always had this need for an aesthetically pleasing environment. When traveling, my requirement for "pretty down-time space" increases exponentially. It goes beyond cleanliness: I need designer sheets, a soothing color palette where the wallpaper coordinates with the drapes, which coordinate with the carpet, which coordinates with the upholstery on the big comfy reading chair, next to the stylistically appropriate floor lamp. I've been known to enter a hotel room and do things like straighten the lampshades, adjust the dust ruffle on the bed frame, and hide the electric cords behind the bedside tables. On a few occasions I have even moved chairs and side tables around to make the room more appealing. Ritualistically, I always completely unpack my luggage and store it away and set up the desk with my work things.

I heard a knock on my door. It was Alex, "How are you doing? This isn't going to work for you, is it?"

"No, I can't deal with this. There is no way I can sleep in this room, much less operate out of this room for an entire week. I can't do it. I should never have trusted the meeting co-ordinator out here to make the hotel arrangements. This is a nightmare."

"I'm on it. I'll find us a place you will like. How about you walk down to the front desk and check us out. I'll meet you at the car. By the time you come out, I should have some options for us."

"Okay, I'm sorry. I hate to be such a pain in the ass, but I just can't take this hotel."

"Forget about it. I'll take care of it."

The same guy that checked us in was still at the front desk. He didn't seem surprised that we were checking out and said he would ensure our credit cards weren't charged. When I got to the SUV, Alex had already loaded up our luggage and said we were headed to another hotel about fifteen minutes away. That fast, he had used his cell to locate several places and found one that had vacancies.

Alex was true to his word. As we walked into the brand-new Kentin chain boutique hotel, I knew my room would be all I could want and more. Decoraphobia is a real thing, and Alex understood. No one had ever been as thoughtful and considerate. My heart warmed quite a bit as I thought about how he understood me and went the extra mile to make my life a little easier. When your life has been really tough going, as mine had been over the last eighteen months, the small touches make a big difference and are appreciated that much more.

"This hotel is lovely! Thank you for finding it. I hate to ask, but is it even close to our allotted government rate for hotels?"

"Actually it is. When I called, they told me that Denver is a big hub for government travelers, and they offer rooms at the per diem rate."

"Oh, that's perfect. I was willing to kick in my own money, as we sometimes do, but I'm glad this is within the budget."

"Meet you back here in the lobby in half an hour?" asked Alex.

"That sounds great, and we'll figure out where to go for dinner."

The hotel concierge recommended a restaurant within walking distance of the Kentin. It specialized in unique local dishes that couldn't be found anywhere else. It was also in the historic downtown area, so we could do some shopping and look around. As we walked to the restaurant, we talked about how nice our rooms were and that we'd want to make it back to the hotel in the evenings for the complimentary wine hour.

The restaurant was a well-done repurposed warehouse with three levels. The menu was full of locally sourced, farm-to-table options that changed based on availability. I ordered braised pork chops in creamy white wine sauce and Alex ordered herb-marinated, grilled buffalo steak. We each sipped a glass of wine and talked about our upcoming presentation. There was a comfortable ease between us that I hadn't noticed before. The food looked delicious when it arrived and tasted as good as it looked. Alex was more of a foodie than I was, and it was fun to travel with him because he never settled for the mundane.

Looking at my plate, he said, "That looks delicious."

"It is, do you want to taste it?"

I wasn't sure exactly how to share it with him, but I didn't

83

have to wonder for long. With complete ease, he used his fork to pierce a piece of the meat that I had cut up on my plate and popped it into his mouth.

"Oh, wow, that's excellent. Do you want to try my grilled buffalo steak?"

"Sure," I replied.

He cut a piece of his steak for me, and I reached over with my fork and picked it up. That day started a trend. Wherever we went, if it was just the two of us, we ate from each other's plates. We stopped asking, and it just became the norm to reach over and sample the other one's selection. Sometimes, with things like French fries or onion rings, the sampling evolved into sharing. We did the same with drinks. Alex would say, "You'd love this wine, try it." Or when we ordered specialty drinks, he'd say, "Let me try yours, and you can try mine." Neither of us turned the glass around to sip from the opposite side. I loved this subtle intimacy that we shared.

Leaving the restaurant, we walked around the downtown area and strolled in and out of the little shops. In an estate jewelry store, I bought an antique gold teapot charm with a tiny lid that opened on even tinier hinges. Tea pots were my thing, and I collected them when I found especially rare or distinctive ones. Alex mentioned he wanted to pick up something for his niece, and we entered an indie bookstore. I introduced him to the *Growing Up with Polly* series, a darling set of stories about a little girl and her best friend, a pet poodle named Polly. Alex selected *Tea with Polly*, perhaps a nod to my gold teapot charm?

It was getting late by the time we got back to the Kentin. We decided on a time to meet in the morning and to get an early start. Since we were kicking off the meeting, we needed adequate time to get set up, and it would be a disaster to be late. Alex pointed out that the hotel had a round-the-clock setup for coffee, and that would save us from having to make a coffee stop on our way to the meeting. We said good night and headed to our rooms on different floors of the hotel. As I slid between Italian crafted Frette sheets, in my impeccably designed and beautifully decorated city-view room, I thought about how much I enjoyed Alex's company. He was just so easy to be with, and I felt happy when we were together. Feeling happy was a state of being I did not take for granted, especially lately.

I awakened a few minutes before my alarm to the sound of a text ping on my cell. It was Alex: "Coffee awaits you outside your room door." I opened my door and discovered a cup of coffee with two creamers—just the way I like it. Alex had dropped it off on his way back to his room after an early morning workout in the hotel gym. I texted him back with a heart emoji.

Chapter 10

As the week progressed, our meetings went well, and the project was getting started on a firm footing. Jill joined many of the meetings via video conference, and we kept her up to date on the sidebar conversations and the internal politics that always drive big projects like this one. During the day, we lunched and networked with others attending the meetings, but in the evenings, it was just Alex and me. We drove to Boulder one evening and found a historic former row house that specialized in Italian cuisine and designer cocktails—very expensive but delicious designer cocktails. I learned that Alex liked to experiment with creating his own designer cocktails using uncommon types of alcohol, bitters, and fruit nectar. The way he described it, it was a science unto itself. We found another bookstore in Boulder and killed an hour in the blink of an eye. This was something else we had in common, a love of getting lost in bookshops—the old-fashioned kind and finding the perfect book. We agreed it was like the ultimate treasure hunt. Next, we spent a fair amount of time perusing a unique organic tea shop that offered tea leaves of hundreds of varieties and combinations.

On Thursday, the last day of our meetings, we ended at midday and wrapped things up on a positive note. As everyone was saying their goodbyes, a couple of the women I had known for years, Jan and Sheryl, cornered me.

Jan said, "You and Alex are a good team. We've enjoyed watching your dynamic together all week."

Sheryl, the more outspoken of the two, said, "We've enjoyed watching Alex all week!"

"Sheryl! What are you saying?" I said with mock astonishment and smiled.

Jan responded for her, "Just saying it's nice to have some young blood and not the same stodgy, boring, old farts we usually deal with on these big government initiatives."

At that point, Alex walked over to us and stood at my side and smiled. "So, do you think this new process and the automation are going to be an improvement over the current way of doing things?" he asked.

Sheryl reached out and patted Alex on his arm, "As long as you and Amanda are involved in leading it, it's going to be great."

What was this? I didn't even touch Alex's arms! Here was this woman being so brazen as to touch the arms that I only dared to admire from a distance!

Alex took it in stride, and they launched a new discussion about the next round of meetings we would have to keep the momentum going. Jan and Sheryl were all compliments and full of excitement about the project. When it was time to head out, I watched astounded as each of them—casual as could be, reached up and gave Alex a hug goodbye. Then, as if to make it seem perfectly normal, they gave me a hug goodbye. For as long as I had known them, they had never hugged me!

When we got into the SUV, I said to Alex, "All that hugging. I wasn't expecting that."

"We're in the West. People out here are a lot more

friendly. You're used to the uptight D.C. crowd."

"I've heard people from the Midwest are friendly, but not necessarily people from the West. You're from the Midwest, aren't you?"

"Born and raised in Kansas. But I was glad to move to D.C. when I got accepted to George Washington University for my B.A. Being gay in Kansas is not ideal, or at least it wasn't then."

Why didn't I want to think about Alex being gay? I changed the subject, "Okay, since we have the rest of the afternoon, and don't fly home until tomorrow, I want you to see the mountains and one of the ski resorts. Even though it's not ski season, the village shops and restaurants are open, and we can eat there. I'll show you the slopes, ski lifts, and all that."

"Do you want to go back to the hotel to change clothes before we head out?"

"Absolutely, and I'm dying for a vanilla latte. I've had all of this meeting coffee I can stand."

Dressed in jeans and T-shirts—I took a navy blue, summer wool blazer in case it got chilly after dark—and equipped with our favorite coffee brews, Alex headed our SUV west on Interstate 70.

"How far up into the mountains are we going?"

"Not that far, just to the exit for Dillon, but we'll be climbing pretty quickly."

"Really? The mountains don't look that high."

"Oh, those aren't the mountains. What you see in front of us now are the foothills. You haven't seen the mountains yet! Just keep driving. You'll know them when you see them. It's nothing like what we have at home."

As we headed farther away from Denver and started climbing into the higher elevations, I could see us both relaxing. The week was over and it had gone well. I sank into my roomy leather seat and crossed my legs so that I was leaning toward Alex. We sipped our coffee and listened to hits from the 2010s radio station Alex had turned on.

Alex, with a beautiful singing voice, sang along to Charlie Puth's "One Call Away." He sang through the entire song to the last stanza, "Just run into my arms, I'm only one call away."

Good gracious! Did he hear the words to this song? I looked at his profile, right arm on the top of the leather clad steering wheel, triceps rippling as his thumb tapped the beat of the music, left hand resting on his upper thigh, T-shirt tight against his flat stomach, legs apart, relaxed. My insides were molten lava. I took a big gulp of my vanilla latte and closed my eyes. *Get yourself under control, Amanda. Don't look at him that way. Cool off!*

"Are you sleepy?"

"N-no not really. Just resting my eyes for a minute. Umm . . . it's nice to have someone else driving, I can actually close my eyes for a minute."

"So, you trust my driving?"

"I do. I think you're a great driver. It's a luxury for me to just sit back and let someone else deal with traffic, directions, all of it."

"I'm glad," said Alex, and then he smiled at me.

Another song started on the radio. I hadn't recovered from the last one when One Republic's "Counting Stars" started. Oh no, not this song—I'd already been making the association between this song and what I felt for Alex since getting home from the Orlando trip. I heard the familiar lyrics . . . "Lately, I've been, I've been losing sleep . . ." When the chorus started, I sang along to my favorite part of the song—the part where Ryan Tedder sings about feeling so right doing the wrong thing and feeling so wrong doing the right thing. It fit my struggle to keep Alex in the friend zone when I was feeling like maybe I'd rather have him in a very different zone!

I heard Alex chuckle, "Don't quit your day job to become a professional singer."

"That bad? I have never been able to sing on key. When I was in college, my sorority used to make me lip-synch the songs we sang during fall rush."

Then, just as we entered a pass between two foothills, I heard Alex say, "Oh, wow. You weren't kidding. This is amazing—now those are mountains! It's like someone just pulled back the curtain and there they are!"

"They're beautiful, aren't they?"

In front of us were a series of snowcapped craggy peaks jutting straight up to the heavens. They were framed by baby blue sky giving them a deep purple hue, topped with snowy white tips, even in May.

"They look massive! How high are they?"

"They average between ten thousand and fourteen thousand feet."

"And our mountains back East are, what, like three thousand feet?"

"At the most. The Blue Ridge and Allegheny mountains are much older than these. They are weathered down with age. That's why they rarely peak three thousand feet and look rounded instead of craggy. Also notice the difference in vegetation. Our mountains are like little chia pet mountains, covered in soft green woods. These mountains are true to their name, the Rockies."

We took the exit at Dillon and headed toward the ski resort.

Alex commented on Dillon Lake, "Whoa! I didn't expect to see a huge lake with sailboats in the middle of the mountains."

"I know, kind of unexpected, isn't it, and very scenic. It's actually a man-made reservoir that helps keep Denver hydrated."

"This is beautiful country. If I worked in Denver, I think I'd want to live out here, surrounded by nature."

"I've always thought that too. I think it makes getting to work in Denver difficult, but I suppose there are people who do it."

We found the ski resort and a number of nearby restaurants and shops. I explained this was one of many ski resorts as you continue west through the Rockies. I pointed out the mountain slopes that would be covered in snow during the winter and the gondola and multitude of chairlifts. I explained the difference between the green (easiest), blue (intermediate), and black diamond (most challenging) ski runs. Alex was fascinated and had never seen anything like it. "So, do you ski?"

"I ski some, mostly blue and green slopes. Richard and I used to try to get out here at least every other year to ski. Usually I could do it in conjunction with a work trip, and he would meet me out here at the end of the week. We tried a number of different resorts along the way to Vail."

"Did the two of you enjoy skiing together?"

"He was a much better skier than I am, and so we were apart much of the day, with me on blue and green slopes while he skied black-diamond slopes. Sometimes I would take lessons and then practice what I learned. Everyone else was in groups, and I felt kind of embarrassed being by myself a lot of the time. The last time we came out here, I got really sick. I thought it was food poisoning, but it turned out to be altitude sickness. We're between ten thousand and thirteen thousand feet here at the resort. I spent the entire time in the hotel room vomiting. I made it out on the slopes our last day before we had to go home. I haven't felt like skiing again since that trip."

"Oh, that's terrible. What causes altitude sickness? I've never heard of it."

"I think I was dehydrated. They say being dehydrated can cause it."

"Would you consider coming out here again? With me this time? I mean in conjunction with one of our work trips?"

"Yeah, I think that would be a blast. I'd love to come here skiing with you! We could take a lesson on the first day so that you get the hang of it. I know the easiest green runs, and they're actually a lot of fun and really long. It can take up to an hour to complete some of them if you're a beginner. And there are really cool lodges at the tops of the mountains. My favorite is one that you can get to via a second gondola."

"Let's plan on coming back to ski in December. We have a Denver project meeting that month."

"We do. We should stay at a ski-in/ski-out condo if we can. I'll work on setting up the reservations. I'll need to start now because the good lodging options book sometimes a year in advance."

"What's that?"

"It's those condos you can see from where we're standing. The ones that open right onto the ski slopes. You just put your skis on at the door, ski over to the lift, and head to the top of the mountain. There's no parking the car, dragging your stuff all over the place, getting a locker. All of that is a big hassle and eats up time. Once you've stayed in a ski-in/ski-out place, you never want to go back to staying off-site."

"Sounds good. Let's do it!"

"Okay, we'll do it! And I'll make sure the condo has a hot tub. You haven't lived until you are sitting in the hot tub at night, with big white snowflakes falling like Ping-Pong balls all around you, watching the night skiers gliding in and out of the shadows, as they descend the slopes. It's magical!"

We ordered appetizers and steak dinners from a restaurant in the village and had views of the mountain, now covered in white, purple, and yellow wildflowers and soft spring grass. It was so peaceful that it was hard to imagine it being covered in thick layers of packed snow and teeming with hundreds of skiers of all ages, zipping in and out and jockeying for a place in the fastest chairlift line. As we enjoyed our appetizers, we shared a flight of local microbrewery beers and Alex had me taste his nitro beer, a first for me—yummy!

It was late when we got back to the hotel. Before heading to our rooms, we confirmed our airline reservations and made plans to meet early in the lobby.

"Alex, thanks for a great week. It went really well, and we're off to a great start with this project."

Maybe it was Jan and Sheryl starting a trend, or maybe it was Alex's Midwest background coming out, but much to my surprise, I felt Alex's arms encircle me and effortlessly pull me into him for a hug. I reached up, more instinctively than with any thought, and encircled his neck with both of my arms. There, for the briefest moment, the length of our entire bodies was touching. The sensation was electrifying. I pulled away, afraid Alex would sense my desire to stay entwined.

He bid me good night, "Sleep well. Since we are getting such an early start, I won't leave coffee at your door. We'll get coffee along the way."

As my plane lifted off, and I contemplated the events of the week, I thought to myself that it had been a good week, no—a great week! Work was going well, everything was on track for closing on the house at the end of the month, and my time with Alex had been enjoyable, to say the least!

Chapter 11

The remaining days of May slid by slowly as I counted down to the day Bob Norseman scheduled the closing on the house. I will always remember how I felt when I stepped out of the settlement attorney's office onto the mossy brick walkway, illuminated by filtered streams of warm morning sunlight. It was the last Friday of May and many of the buildings along Cameron Street were still wearing their green, pink, and white Apple Blossom Festival buntings. The mature silver bark maple trees standing in front of many of the old houses, now converted to lawyers' offices and other businesses, cast thousands of whirligig seedpods spinning all around me as the breeze caught them in midflight. Bright pink and white azaleas were in bloom up and down Cameron Street as far as I could see.

On my left arm was an enormous gift basket from Bob Norseman. He and Marie had carefully selected every thoughtful and delicious item it contained: local farm cheese, Winchester-made apple butter, stone-ground wheat crackers, chocolates, and a bottle of Seyval Blanc from one of the lovely wineries in Winchester. Also tucked into the basket were two delicate wineglasses and a corkscrew. In my right hand were my copies of the multitude of signed settlement papers, at least an inch thick, that meant I owned the house. The closing had gone smoothly with no unpleasant surprises. It seemed surreal that I was now the proud owner of a historic, circa 1840, Greek Revival manor home (that some would call a mansion, but I thought that sounded too pretentious), and the four acres that surrounded it.

I headed out of town to traverse the ten miles that would take me to the house, to my house. I had arranged to have the grass mowed so that I could easily walk around the house without running into snakes. As I pulled into the driveway, I was filled with joy and awe . . . and trepidation. I got out of the car and stood looking at the front of the house. I was feeling very *Frances Mayes–esque*. Frances Mayes, in her beautiful memoir, *Under the Tuscan Sun*, wrote, "I am about to buy a house in a foreign country. A house with the beautiful name of Bramasole. It is tall, square and apricot-colored with faded green shutters, ancient tile roof, and an iron balcony . . ." My house didn't look quite as pleasant as Bramasole. It could be—I was sure of that—but at the moment it was a bit over-whelming. This was a house with four levels, twenty-one rooms (or twenty-three depending on how you counted them), twelve fireplaces, fifty-four windows, and numerous outbuildings—that were completely unsuitable for human habitation. It was, in fact, in a state of extreme neglect, and most likely would fall down if left unattended for much longer. Thank goodness it wasn't in a foreign country!

It occurred to me that my house needed its own name. That was a good place to start. Having a name would make it more, well, poetic if nothing else. It would also allow me to refer to it as something other than "the house" or "the Win-chester house." I unlocked the front door, *Note to self, get new locks because who knows how many keys are floating around,* and left it pushed wide open. I next walked the length of the expansive center hall and did the same to the door at the opposite end. Immediately, a whoosh of freshly scented spring air wafted through the hall and up the wind-around staircase. It was as if the house took its first deep breath with its new owner, and I also took my first deep breath as the sole caretaker responsible for bringing her back to life. I think at that moment the house acknowledged me and accepted me, *"Thank goodness this unlikely woman found me!"* she was thinking.

I began my state of ownership by meandering through the rooms, touching the wood trimwork, the brass doorknobs, the beautifully smooth plaster walls, looking at everything now from a less forensic perspective, and more from a profoundly intimate perspective. How would I use each room, what would I call them, how would I decorate, who would share these spaces with me, what occasions would be celebrated here? Now that ownership was a reality, not just hopeful dreaming, I felt my connection to the house intensifying. Fate, or maybe my guardian angel directing the car's path last March, had brought me here. Each seemingly insurmountable roadblock threatening ownership was overcome by a viable solution. The raw truth of the matter was that I needed this house as much as it needed me. That need was born from the remnants of an explosion so powerful, nothing remained but ashes. Would focusing on transforming this bygone relic of a beautiful home be enough to rebuild and restore me?

Danielle was meeting me at the house at one o'clock. I knew that she would bring a celebratory bottle of champagne, so I decided to break into my gift basket and pour myself a glass of wine. The house and I would be the first to toast our new venture, it seemed fitting that we do this alone. The cheese and crackers were wonderful, and the wine was excellent. As I contemplated each room, its purpose revealed itself.

I let the house speak to me, taking in the orientation of the rooms—north, south, east, west, their proximity to other rooms, the dimensions, and the energy from nearly two-hundred years of living that each room had experienced. It was decided. On the first floor, east of the center hall was the "morning room" in the front, and behind it the "dining room." From the dining room was the "original kitchen" and adjoining the kitchen at the end of the center hall was the "tea room." To the west of the center hall was the "drawing room" in front and behind it was the "library." I'd have to collect more books to fill the floor-to-ceiling shelves! The big trifold doors separated (or joined) the morning room with the dining room on the east side of the house and the drawing room with the library on the west side of the house. Were these doors designed to allow large rooms that could accommodate parties and family gatherings? Did the first family, who were in the house for seventy years, dance the Virginia reel in these rooms? I had so much research to do. I wanted to know the house's families, their joys and sorrows, what made them who they were and the marks they left on their community.

The bedrooms were on the next level, and there were two to the west of the upper hall and three to the east. One of these had its own staircase access to the kitchen. I knew the two rooms to the west side of the upper hall would be my bedroom and bathroom. They were connected by a large two-piece pocket door. I would use one room as my bedroom and convert the other room to a large luxury master bath, complete with a claw-foot soaking tub and glass shower. The bedroom on the east side, that adjoined the bedroom over the kitchen, would make a great guest suite. One room could serve as the bedroom and the other as a sitting room and private bathroom—there was plenty of square footage to add a full bath within the sitting room. I thought guests would love having direct access to the kitchen for midnight snacks or to descend downstairs early in the morning without disturbing the rest of the household. The front bedroom on the east side would be a study or another guest room. The hall that adjoined these bedrooms was like a room of its own, with glass French doors that opened onto the second story of the front portico.

I started the climb to the very top level of the house, which I had already started calling "the gallery." I loved looking down through the curving staircase from the gallery level. On this level were three rooms, including two bedrooms on the east side of the gallery hall and one large room on the west side. At the end of the gallery hall was a good-sized walk-in closet with a window of its own. I intended to convert this to a nice-sized, full bathroom. The large room that ran from the front to the back of the house on the west side of the gallery hall would be the "family room." I planned to add a wet bar with under-counter refrigerator and a hidden microwave, large screen TV, multiple sitting areas, and table seating.

Finally, the English basement—I refilled my wineglass on the way down. The basement, in its current state, creeped me out considerably. I wasn't having it. I refused to have any part of this grand old girl be creepy—she deserved better! And, besides, I didn't want to be hesitant to enter any part of my own house. Every area and every room needed to be welcoming and a joy to visit. I was pleased to find that, for the moment, the mud was dried up as I descended the stairs. The first room, directly under the kitchen—from where the stairs descended—would be the "wine cellar." It had a second huge cooking fireplace, as large as the one in the kitchen above it, and its own external door and two windows. The brick walls and—if I could do it—a brick floor, would make this room the perfect Old-World-style wine cellar. The next room, under the dining room, would be a large, well-equipped "laundry." The room under the newly designated morning room also had its own fireplace, and it would be the "keeping room" outfitted with cozy leather furniture, Cuban cigars (although no one I knew smoked), and locally brewed apple brandy from crystal decanters. The English basement hall would make the perfect exercise room, not exactly romantic sounding, but big enough and necessary.

I headed upstairs thinking it was time to top off my wine and have a few more crackers, with the delicious cheese—and a chocolate. I surmised that Marie picked all the basket items, and I made a mental note to let the Norsemans know how much I had enjoyed their basket! The house and I were having a delightful time getting to know one another. I could tell she loved my ideas for each room. *But now, what to name her?* The locals called the house by the last name of the family that built it. That was not good enough, how boring! Bramasole, after all, wasn't named Romano House. Not that that was the name of the family that built it—I had no idea what their name was.

"What should I name you?" I said out loud.

In response to my question, I felt another whoosh of fresh air through the open doors. This time scented with the pleasant aroma of a camp wood fire. As the pleasing scent filtered through the rooms, I wondered, *Is someone burning their winter stick pile?* I imagined I'd have to do the same in the future, considering the number of mature trees on the property. I stopped in front of the fireplace in the morning room and looked beyond, through the dining room, to the kitchen. How fun it would be during the holidays to bring the Thanksgiving turkey out from the kitchen, fireplaces blazing, candles refracting light against crystal goblets set out on the table— which could be expanded through to the morning room if needed. Then it hit me, the house had twelve fireplaces and had been built to graciously accommodate happy gatherings of friends and family. Her name would be *Merryhearth Manor*.

"What do you think of that? Do you like Merryhearth Manor?" The house did not audibly respond, but I sensed she liked the name.

I heard a *beep-beep* from the driveway and stepped onto the front portico, being careful to avoid the rotted boards and holes. Danielle was getting out of her little blue pickup truck in the driveway. She was carrying Chinese takeout and a bottle of champagne. I could see a pop-up table and lawn chairs in the bed of her truck.

"Come on in!" Danielle had not been to the house since the day that she and I toured it with Bob Norseman, and she talked me into submitting an offer to buy it.

"You know, I pride myself on being partially responsible for you standing in that doorway today."

"And you should! I probably would have talked myself out of buying it if not for you prodding me to call Bob Norseman that day."

"So, how do you feel? Are you excited? I see you found a bottle of wine!"

"The house and I have been getting to know one another, toasting our newfound partnership. And, welcome to . . . Merryhearth Manor!"

"Merryhearth Manor, I love that! This house needed a name."

"She led me to it. I think it fits well."

Merryhearth Manor hosted her first party that afternoon. We set up the table and chairs and spread out the Chinese takeout containers. We started the party with a champagne toast. Danielle popped the cork and poured the fizzy liquid into the wineglasses. "To you . . . to Merryhearth Manor . . . and to the start of a beautiful life together!"

Part Two

Restoring

"However many years she lived, Mary always felt that she should never forget that first morning when her garden began to grow."

— Frances Hodgson Burnett, *The Secret Garden*

Chapter 12

The rehabilitation work on Merryhearth Manor began almost immediately. At the same time, I began training—yes training—for the upcoming ski trip, just six months away. If I had any hope of not looking like a complete fool on the ski slopes, I needed to build muscle, lose the fifteen pounds I'd gained as a result of the explosion, and build my cardio endurance. It would take working out nearly every day for the full six months leading to the trip. I took a week off from work to focus on collaborating with Josh Edden on our plan of attack for Merryhearth and on getting things moving. This was also my opportunity to start my plan of attack for getting in shape and starting my fitness program.

For the house, we started at ground level with the most serious issues, water infiltration and missing or deteriorating brick support walls. The bank, based on Josh's proposal, had designated roughly one-fourth of the total budget for the English basement. Josh and I discussed the work in great detail and while it seemed like a big to-do list, Josh was confident that it could be done within the allocated amount of money. He would have his dedicated crew start by digging out the basement, taking the floor down one foot.

I arrived at Merryhearth midmorning on the first day of work. As I pulled up to the house, it looked a little like the circus had come to town and was setting up, minus the elephants, thank goodness. A hum of activity surrounded the house along with a multitude of work trucks, equipment, a generator, and piles of gravel, mud, and rocks. As I headed for the lawn on the east side of the house, following the sound of Latin pop music, I found the crew—and the source of the upbeat music, an industrial-looking boom box with roll bars no less. The crew was hand digging the basement floor and literally shoving wheelbarrows of mud up hill on an improvised steep ramp that covered the basement stairs leading to the side yard. I could see it was backbreaking work. I noticed the men had been separating the contents of the wheelbarrows into two piles: mud and bricks. I asked one of them if they were finding the bricks buried in the mud. He gave me an apologetic smile and said, "No hablo English." Then he called, "Victorrrr!" Victor emerged from the basement and walked over to us.

"Hi, I'm Amanda Grayson. This is my house."

"Hello, Josh isn't here right now. He just left," said Victor.

"That's okay. I just wanted to see how things were going. Is this the crew for the basement work?"

"This is the crew for all the work. I'm Victor. I'm the boss when Josh isn't here." By now, the other men had gathered around and were watching Victor and me intently.

"Oh, then it's great to meet you and the crew. What are everyone's names?" This seemed to both surprise and please Victor.

"I am Victor. This is Ricardo, he speaks pretty good English. This is Carlos, no English. And this here is Felix, he speaks a little bit of English."

"I'm glad to meet you. Let me see if I remember the

names, Victor, Ricardo, Carlos, and Feliz."

"No señora, Felix, not Feliz," said Victor. "*Feliz* means happy in Spanish." All of the men laughed at this.

"Oh, but are you Feliz?" I said to the man who I had first asked about the bricks.

The men laughed harder, and Felix said, "Sí, sí soy muy feliz!" (*Yes, yes, I'm very happy!*)

"I'm glad to hear it!"

"Señora, you speak Spanish?" All the men waited intently for the response.

"I speak a little bit of Spanish, it's rusty, and I need practice. And please, call me Amanda."

"This is good!" said Victor, and then he translated for the men. "Esta es Amanda, la dueña de la casa. Ella habla Español!"

Oh no, he made it sound like I was fluent. "Un poco. Yo hablo un poquito de Español." And from that moment forward I found myself navigating complex rehabilitation conversations mostly in Spanish, unless I was speaking with Josh, of course, who spoke no Spanish at all.

"Victor, you and the men will be handling all the work . . . everything?"

"Most things. I am a master carpenter and Ricardo works with me on carpentry. Carlos is a brick and stone mason. And Felix, he does whatever we tell him. Josh is also the plumber, and he brings guys in for the electric and HVAC."

"How long have you all worked with Josh?"

"We have been building his houses for three years."

"Is this your first old house?"

"Yes, yes we have always worked on new houses."

"It's my first old house too. We can learn together. It's different than a new house."

"Yes, you want to see what we do in the basement?"

"Yes, I do, very much." We headed into the basement and

I managed a balance beam walk down the improvised ramp without taking a dive into the mud. I could see the foundation walls that had been under the mud line. Carlos, the mason, was concerned that the brick walls ended at granite block footers in some places before we got to the one-foot-down point. He suggested not digging near those areas and building a concrete curb around them when the new floor was poured. *Here we go*, I thought, *on day one, a critical question that if not handled properly could seriously compromise the foundation.*

"I'll check with Josh, but that sounds like a good approach. Are you finding bricks in the mud? I see a lot of bricks where you are digging."

"Sí Señora, muchos y muchos ladrillos!" said Felix.

"We are saving them. We think you will want a brick floor over the concrete floor, no?" said Victor.

"Are there enough for the whole basement floor?"

"Probably no, but we can put them in the first room. Josh said you want a wine cellar, and you can have a brick floor in the wine cellar."

"Oh, that's fantastic! Save every brick you can find. Don't throw any away."

This was an unforeseen windfall, and one that didn't cost extra! In the end, there were just enough bricks to rebuild the former summer kitchen's big cooking fireplace, fireplace hearth, and the brick floor, making the wine cellar incredibly beautiful when it was done. I never fully understood what happened to the rest of the original, handmade clay bricks that had covered the entirety of the basement floor when the house was first constructed. I guess some were used for repairs to the walls, some maybe stayed buried under the new concrete floor, and some were undoubtedly hauled away to wherever the mud was taken.

This was how the days went during the first phase of the work. I would visit Merryhearth nearly every day and now that I was working from home, I could drive out in the late afternoon hours, and I never missed a Saturday. Josh and the crew worked six days a week and started early, usually no later than 8:00 a.m. At precisely noon, they would pull a couple of old mini microwave ovens out of their trucks and plug them into the portable generator. Sitting under the big shady black elm tree, with no one to disturb them other than the nearby cows noisily munching meadow grass, they would change the music to mariachi or ranchera folk tunes and heat up homemade Mexican delicacies. To this day, I've yet to visit a Mexican or Latin American restaurant that had food that smelled as tasty as what they heated each day for lunch. This was their special time, and they took exactly one hour, never a minute more or a minute less. Even Josh respected that at noon, the work stopped for an hour. At the end of the day, the men would start to clean up the work area and by 5:30 they were gone. I never noticed any of them missing a day of work, or taking off early, or showing up late.

They always seemed pleased to see me on Saturdays, or when I arrived before they left during the week. I would look at what they had worked on and ask questions and remind them to take care with anything that was original to the house. When they were gone, I'd call Alex on my cell, text him pictures of the work, and generally keep him up to date. Alex seemed to expect and enjoy my calls. That helped to keep me going. The routine was demanding, and frequently I'd find issues that needed immediate addressing with Josh. Despite the amount of preplanning, details would be overlooked, requirements missed, and often I found a lack of respect for the old and historic original features of the house. That drove me crazy because you simply couldn't replace an original wavy glass windowpane, or a piece of trimwork that someone decided to cut off the wall because they needed a temporary crossbar.

I arrived at the house one evening just as the crew was starting to clean up. I noticed right away the music was off, and they seemed more subdued than usual. Josh stopped by to check on the job as they were pulling out of the driveway. I asked him if everything was all right. He shrugged and said, "I started a local subcontractor today to rebuild those three basement walls and repoint all the mortar in the basement and on the north exterior side of the house. It's too big of a job for Carlos. They're a local company, and I don't think the two crews hit it off."

"Should we do something, or say something to the new crew?"

"No, Victor will know how to handle it and if it gets too bad, he'll tell me."

"I don't want our guys being pushed around." I could hardly believe I was saying it—*our guys*. Josh never batted an eye at my phraseology.

"I can pull Victor and the crew onto another one of my jobs for a few days while this brick work is being done."

"Speaking of the mortar . . . the subcontractor does know that the mortar can't be portland cement based, right?"

"I told him you did a bunch of research on the mortar for these old, soft clay bricks, and he said he knew all about it."

That night I couldn't sleep. I worried and worried that the subcontractor didn't really know how to mix the mortar. It had to be done very precisely using lime and sand, and had to have just the right moisture level and consistency. How did I know this? I read all about it in one of my trusty NPS historic preservation briefs. The next morning, in the daily sync-up video call with Jill and Alex, I told them about my concerns.

"You better take a few hours off and get out there to talk to the subcontractor," implored Alex.

"What if they just blow me off and are rude about it?"

"It's your house, right?" said Jill

"This isn't any different than running a multimillion-dollar project like you do every day at work. Be nice, but be firm. As Jill said, it's your house!"

Alex was right. At work, in my capacity as a government manager, I would never have been hesitant to ask questions about how a project was being handled. It was late morning when I arrived at Merryhearth. The subcontractor was still in the phase of removing old mortar and hadn't started mixing the new mortar. Josh, Victor, and the crew were nowhere to be seen. I approached one of the men and asked who was in charge. He pointed toward a black pickup. A good-looking guy in his early thirties, wearing jeans, navy blue T-shirt, Timberland boots, and Oakley sunglasses, stepped out from the side of the black pickup.

"That would be me. And you are . . .?"

"Oh, Hi. I'm Amanda Grayson. I'm the umm, owner of this money pit." He was not at all what I was expecting when Josh indicated *locals who didn't get along with our guys.*

"Nice to meet you!" he said, shaking my hand firmly. What can I do for you?"

"I wanted to talk with you about the mortar you'll be using for the masonry work on the house. You see, it's critical that it be mixed with . . ." and before I could finish, he ended my sentence for me.

"Lime. I was just going over my notes on that when you pulled up. I've been researching the right mixture and fortunately the National Park Service—would you believe it—has a whole historic preservation brief on it, and the guys down at the Block, Brick and Stone also have a lot of knowledge and sell the right ingredients. I should even be able to match the color to the original mortar almost exactly."

"So you know what to do and how to get the mixture just right?"

"Yep. I plan to add this house to my website and portfolio

of projects. I want to be known as a historic brick mason, and getting your house right has big rewards for me."

"Okay then, well, I won't worry. I'll let you get back to work. Nice to meet you!"

Josh had done well to find these guys. They were looking to break into historic masonry and weren't as expensive as the pros, but clearly cared about getting it right. My guess was that Victor and his guys just felt a little undervalued at the moment. That could be handled easily once the subcontractor was done.

I called Alex on my way back to Leesburg. "Thanks for your suggestion! It's all under control. I feel so much better!"

"What are you doing this weekend?"

"Why, what are you thinking?"

"I haven't seen the house yet, and I haven't seen you, other than through a computer screen, since we were in Denver. I was thinking of spending the day in Virginia, starting with a tour of Merryhearth Manor. The General Store in Millwood is having a wine tasting on Saturday, and then I thought we could head over toward Delaplane. There are several wineries off Route 17 and a couple of them have great food options. What do you think? Are you ready for a break from running the construction site?"

I was so ready! Our big project at work and the Merryhearth rehab were very demanding. I felt like one of those performers who has fifty plates spinning up in the air on the end of long poles. As one starts to slow down and threatens to crash to the floor, he rushes to it and gives it a spin to keep it in the air. I worried constantly that one of my many high-stake plates would hit the ground and shatter before I could get to it and give it another spin. A day with Alex would be heavenly!

"I can't think of anything I'd like more!"

"Great. How about if I pick you up at your place in Leesburg about ten thirty? We can head to Merryhearth first, then to the wineries."

"That's perfect. I'll plan to see you Saturday morning!"

I felt the familiar butterflies in the pit of my stomach that were now the telltale sign of being delighted at the prospect of having fun time with Alex. As soon as I was back in my apartment, I headed to my closet to pick out the right outfit for Saturday. I'd recently spent a fair amount of money shopping for outfits and shoes that I hoped made me look cute. After getting home from the Denver trip, I was keenly aware that my wardrobe was not up to par for spending my days with a gorgeous man, ten years my junior. In fact, other than dress suits for work, I hadn't focused on buying clothes in a long, long time, and certainly not fun, sexy, young clothes! Being with Alex made me want to focus on myself. I smiled as I thought about how Merryhearth and I were on a parallel journey.

Chapter 13

The morning was beautiful, and I was looking forward to spending the day with Alex—the whole day, just the two of us. At the sound of his knock, I swung the apartment door wide and tried to keep my enthusiasm in check.

"Hey there! I can't believe I made it out here from D.C. in forty-five minutes," Alex announced.

"That's what having no traffic will do for you," I said.

"Yeah, and I might have been speeding a little too."

Alex leaned in to hug me in greeting. *Okay, I guess this was going to be a regular thing with us when we were together socially. Fine by me!* I hugged him back.

"Are you ready to go? Do you need to stop for coffee on the way to Winchester?"

"No, I'm good. I'm anxious to get out to see the house today. I didn't get to drive out yesterday and on Thursday it looked awful, all torn up and dirty beyond belief from all that mortar and brick dust, but that's typical, I guess. It worries me though that all that dust has infiltrated the very molecules of the house. I wonder if it will cause permanent damage. Will I be able to get it out of the floorboards, the wood trim crevasses, and . . ."

"Hey, today . . . no worrying. Today is about having fun! You look great by-the-way! Is that a new outfit?"

"Yes, I thought it was about time I did a little spring shopping and I picked up a few new things."

I thought to myself, *like a whole new wardrobe of carefully chosen clothes that showed off my attributes and hid my fattributes!*

As Alex neared the house and maneuvered slowly into the driveway, I took the opportunity to study his reaction. Turning off the engine, he sat back in his seat, motionless, and assessed the scene in front of him. He was studying the house, and I detected a hint of excitement, like some people get when faced with a puzzle or challenge.

"Is it what you expected?"

"Yes, well, no, it's bigger than I imagined, and it's much nicer than I imagined. I mean, I knew from what you said that it had been a farm, and I was thinking it would look more like an old farmhouse, but this is . . . elegant."

"So you like it?"

"Yeah, I can't wait to see the inside!"

Everything at the house was quiet, no workers in sight, as we entered through the front door. "Let me take you on the grand tour—the good, the bad, and the ugly. Just try to picture it after the restoration work is done."

I took Alex through all the rooms, rattling off their names: the morning room, the drawing room, the library . . . . He liked my plans for how I would use the rooms and mentioned more than once that it was a great house for weekend parties and get-togethers. This of course delighted me. Alex was fascinated with the original details of the house and asked a lot of questions about the construction and the design elements.

"I've always been fascinated by these old door locks," he said, studying the lock on the door to the dining room.

"I wish I had the keys that went to all of these old locks,

there are least twenty-five of them throughout the house. Do you think I could get one skeleton key that would work on all of them?"

"Probably not. They are actually rather intricate, and the keys have unique cuts that are specific to the lock."

He proceeded to explain to me the engineering behind the old locks. It was so much fun to be sharing Merryhearth with Alex; it connected us. I felt he was a historic house kindred spirit.

"*You* should buy and restore a historic house. You could get a place near Ken and Mitch and have it for weekend getaways. I could help you with the restoration and reconfiguring the floor plan if needed. It would be such a fun project! I think you'd really enjoy it."

"I've thought about it and like the idea, but the Virginia countryside might as well be Siberia for the D.C. crowd that I hang around with. I'd have to live in the weekend house *during the week* and go to D.C. on the *weekends*."

"Have you seen enough?" I said. "Shall we head toward Millwood?"

"I really like this house. I can't wait until you have it done, and I definitely want to come out here to see it and spend time."

This statement was aptly rewarded with a broad smile from me (and probably eyelash batting and dilated pupils), as I responded, "I would love that."

We arrived in Millwood and parked across the street from the General Store near the old Burwell-Morgan Mill. That's Morgan as in General Daniel Morgan, the Shenandoah's famous Revolutionary War general. I knew the mill was a National Register Historical Landmark and one of the oldest operational grist mills in the country. I assumed Alex was aware of the history surrounding this little crossroad in Clarke County. I knew he had discovered it through his friends Ken and Mitch. I wondered if, now that I owned Merryhearth Manor and was a member of the "Virginia country living crowd," Alex would introduce me to them.

As I stepped into the historic general store, I was aware that it was as authentic as you get. Even the ancient drop latch on the heavy wood plank door was the real McCoy and the rough hardwood plank floors proudly displayed their nearly two-hundred years of wear and tear. The current owners understood their twenty-first-century clientele very well and offered tempting choices that catered to foodies, wine lovers, and locavores. We were there for the wine tasting, which always resulted in me taking home at least a couple of bottles of wine. Their selections from Virginia and around the world were some of the best I'd experienced. When Merryhearth's wine cellar was ready for stocking, I planned to fill it with wines that I had personally tasted and could recount the wineries or shops where I had purchased them. I planned to only have capacity for forty bottles, in handmade wood display racks. Unlike the cruise ship, this wine cellar was going to be about quality and experience, not quantity. I wanted to be able to tell the story of each bottle I displayed and offered to friends and family, and know I was serving wine that would be enjoyed.

Alex and I stepped up to the tasting table near the back of the store. This was the only place I knew of that still offered complementary wine tastings. I doubted they could do it for much longer as the crowds grew.

"Did you know all the wine tastings—at the wineries— used to be complimentary? The idea was you tasted for free so that you'd know what to buy, and the profit was in the sale of the wine. But now, the tastings have become so popular that the wineries would lose money if they did it for free."

"Huh, I didn't know it used to be free. That's hard to imagine."

Oh, hell, I just made one of those eye-rolling pronouncements that marked my age—back when I was a youngster, we didn't have school buses, we walked the five miles to school, and I remember the time when a Northwestern timber wolf chased us all the way home. Geez, Amanda, see if you can save that one.

But as it turned out I didn't have to, the wine server saved me, "May I see some ID please?" Alex began to pull out his wallet. I stepped back, feeling even older than my comment. "You too, please, I need both of your IDs."

WHAT! Elation, ecstasy, joy! "Oh, sure, let me get it out."

The twentysomething-year-old-girl with big hoop earrings and deep green eyes looked at our driver's licenses and, without shock, horror, or surprise, simply said, "Okay, thanks. We're starting with the white wines. Our first is a . . ."

The wines were excellent and there were parings of tiny samples of cheese, charcuterie, and chocolate to enhance their flavor and to tempt wine tasters to also buy the products being sampled. I didn't dare mention that the wineries also used to have small, bite-sized pairings for free with the tastings. Now you were lucky to get a dry old cracker in between your whites and your reds.

"I think I'm going to get a few bottles to take back to D.C. with me," said Alex.

"Same, I really enjoyed the Cantine Valpane Barbera. I don't think I've had wine made from the Barbera grape before."

"Where to next? Did you want to check out any of the antique stores around here while we're in this area?" asked Alex.

"You know I wouldn't mind. There are two nearby that I really like. Red Barn Antiques is just around the corner. It's literally an old-fashioned, little red barn, and it's adorable. The owner lives in Scotland and imports most of the antiques from Europe. They have some pieces that are stunning and quite old."

"Okay, and what's the other place you like?"

"The Bee and Butterfly, it's a little way down the road in Boyce. I love the shop. They have mostly new items, with a few antique and vintage pieces. Their accessories and artwork are just the kind of look I want for Merryhearth. I can't wait until Merryhearth is at the stage where I can start decorating. That will be so much fun!"

I scored in both shops, buying a small antique wooden box that had come to the Red Barn in the latest shipment from Scotland. I also bought a large, framed, replica historic map of the Shenandoah Valley at the Bee and Butterfly. The owner was in the shop and offered to bring the map to me in Winchester since it wouldn't fit in the car.

Alex noted as we were leaving the Bee and Butterfly, "People out here are so friendly. It really does have that small-town warmth that you don't see anymore. Want to head to Delaplane Winery next? It has amazing views of the valley."

"I know the one, and their wines aren't too shabby either. Let's go."

After enjoying a tasting of the winery's white and red offerings, we chose a bottle of red, made from a blend of Virginia-grown grapes. We also ordered a loaf of warm baked bread and a cheese and charcuterie board. We settled into a bistro table for two in front of the expanse of glass windows looking out onto the rows of well-tended vines below, and the rolling Blue Ridge Mountains to the west. Alex was every bit the gentleman I had come to love being with, never allowing my wine glass to be empty, and filling my water tumbler as soon as it was dry. He reminded me frequently to drink water when drinking wine, so I didn't get dehydrated. We talked and talked about everything from his family to what I envisioned for Merryhearth and our upcoming ski trip to Colorado.

One thing neither of us brought up was relationships. I rarely mentioned my past with Richard. I didn't want to be perceived as weak, stupid, or a victim—all of which were possibilities when learning the marriage ended the way it did. There certainly was no one new that I was seeing or even had on my radar scope as a possibility. Alex never mentioned his love life to me. Once I asked about his ex, Tad, who was his first long-term relationship as near as I could tell. He brushed off the question pretty lightly by saying after a while they wanted different things. I did notice he kept his cell phone close and when a text popped in, he didn't miss glancing at the phone. I assumed a few times he was texting back from the men's room because he would take his phone with him. As much time as we had spent together, one thing was clear, neither of us wanted to talk about our relationships—and so we didn't.

When we left Delaplane we had time for one more winery and decided to head across Mount Weather on Route 601. The location of Two Pines, near the peak of Raven Rocks, offered beautiful vistas, from multiple levels of outdoor decking that hung seemingly in midair, over rows of mature vines. The winery's orientation, facing west down the mountain to the Shenandoah River and beyond, made it an ideal spot for sipping wine while watching the sun slowly sink at the end of a thoroughly enjoyable day, with just the right person at your side.

This is where Alex and I found ourselves when a very intriguing idea began to sprout. We were sitting side by side on the arc of a small round table, shoulders occasionally touching depending on which way we leaned. The late afternoon sun was sinking over the valley, and the last of our rosé had ceased to be chilled and was now the same temperature as the warm June air.

"You know," I said in a happy state of contemplative

reverie thinking about the wonderful day we'd had, "Of the wines we tried today, the ones that stand out in my mind were the couple of Italian wines from the General Store."

"I agree, there's something about Italian wine that's remarkably different. You notice the quality immediately. It's smooth without being boring."

"And there's so much flavor, it evolves and changes from the tip of your tongue all the way to the back of your tongue."

"I like that it's consistently good, regardless of the grape or the winery that produced it. I'd like to take a tour of Italy's wine regions. Just spend days learning about and trying their wines . . . not to mention cheese, meats, pasta, bread—it all goes together."

"If I went to Italy, I'd want to combine wine tasting with shopping."

"What do you want to shop for?"

"I've been thinking about how beautiful an authentic Murano glass chandelier would be in the dining room at Merryhearth. Not a huge garish one, but one that's appropriate for the house . . . but it's something I'd have to see in person before I'd want to spend that kind of money."

"So, why don't we go?" said Alex.

"Go where?"

"Go to Italy!"

"Sure, and we can swing by the French Riviera after that!" I couldn't believe he said this, just as casually as if he was suggesting we head to another winery.

"I'm totally serious. It would be fun!"

"Really? . . . I'd love to take a trip to Italy, I've never been . . . and to see it with the purpose of touring a wine region *and* shopping for a chandelier, that would be so much fun!"

"Let's go. Let's just do it."

"I haven't taken a vacation, a real vacation, in years," I said, "but wouldn't it be expensive?"

"If you're like me, you probably have enough points on your credit card to cover the airfare, and if we split the expenses it will keep the costs to a minimum."

"Huh, I see your point. Okay, let's explore going to Italy! But, oh . . . we shouldn't mention this to anyone at work," I said.

"No, we'll keep this to ourselves. No one at work needs to know what we do in our personal time."

"Yeah, the optics of it could be a little tricky to explain. And is there anyone, umm special, in your life who would wonder about us taking a vacation to Italy together? I mean, this is different than a ski trip tacked onto the end of a business trip."

"No . . . no one serious anyway," said Alex.

"Let's talk more about it while we're in Louisiana for our next project coordination meeting."

We had a weeklong trip coming up the first week in July to meet again with our project's regional leaders, this time in Mississippi, at NASA's Stennis Space Center. We had decided to stay across the state border in Louisiana, north of Lake Pontchartrain. There were a number of small historic towns that promised to have great local cuisine, and scenic main streets for strolling and shopping.

"Sounds like a plan! I think the winery is closing down. Shall we head out?" asked Alex.

Alex dropped me off at my apartment in Leesburg. As we said goodbye, a hug was now completely natural, no hesitation on my part and nothing awkward about it. I gave Alex an extra tight squeeze, and placed a tiny little kiss on his cheek.

Chapter 14

Phase one of Merryhearth's rehabilitation was going well. It looked like Josh would have the critical work needed for the foundation and English basement done by the end of July as scheduled. I could see the area that had been a mud pit was now a neat twelve-inch-deep zone. It was filled partially with gravel, on top of which lay perforated drainage pipe wrapped in sediment cloth, which led to a thirty-inch-deep well that would house a sump pump to carry water out from under the house. Finally, no more creepy Roman bath in the basement! Concrete would be poured over this, but not to the full depth of twelve inches. I would be gaining about six to seven inches of height from floor to ceiling, which was badly needed in this, the only low-ceilinged area in the house. True to his word, Carlos had been careful to avoid disturbing where there were exposed footers in the newly dug out floor—approximately one-third of the length of the basement from the north to the south end of the house. These areas would have a neat concrete curb, and the curb in the wine cellar would be wrapped in bricks.

The masonry subcontractor had finished removing the

damaging cement mortar that someone had added during a past restoration effort. It was this cement mortar that caused the structural failure of three foundation walls. I was horrified to see that not only did the past effort involve using cement as mortar, but someone actually smeared it all over the face of the bricks like crude plaster. The soft, natural clay bricks couldn't expand and contract as natural moisture levels increased and decreased, because they were wearing cement casts. As pressure built, with no release mechanism, the bricks popped under the pressure and turned into red dust.

The rebuilt walls, the newly pointed brick surfaces throughout the basement and the exterior north wall of the house, looked fantastic. The wine cellar's fireplace was beautiful. It had been a big cooking fireplace, sometimes called a summer kitchen because the cooking could be done during the warm summer months in the cooler basement and away from the living quarters. It was probably also where the laundry was done in big cauldrons of boiling water and then taken out directly to the yard to be hung for drying. I noted where in the basement I would need lighting and electrical outlets. I planned to have built-in focal lights for each of the wine racks, and the electric wiring would need to be run to the right locations.

Despite the progress, I could see that there was a tremendous amount of work still required before the house would be livable. I was still doubtful that everything that needed to be done could be accomplished with the money allocated by the bank's loan. Although, I had to admit that Josh had made the amount allotted for phase one go further than I would have thought it could. Before I could move in, I needed a kitchen, bathrooms, heating and air-conditioning, and windows that weren't broken. As if on cue, my cell rang, and I saw it was Josh's number.

"Hi, Josh, what's up? I'm at the house now. Looks like the

work is going well, and we're on schedule."

"Uh huh, about that, are you going to be there for a little while? I have some things I want to go over with you."

"Uh, yeah, I'll be here. Nothing bad, I hope?"

"Let me just go over it with you when I get out there. I should be there in about twenty minutes."

This didn't sound good. We were a little over a month into the work and a problem apparently had come up. I wondered how big, and how expensive of a problem it would be. I was standing in the drawing room when I saw Josh's truck pull into the driveway. I opened the front door to step out to greet him and got a little surprise. Sunning herself on the front portico, in between rotten boards, was yet another large black snake. This one was not as large as the black rat snake I'd seen on the old patio in the back, but it was still quite large. Josh must have noticed me stopping dead in my tracks because he yelled from the driveway, "Got a friend up there do you?"

"Yes, quite a large black snake as a matter of fact, and it doesn't appear to be concerned about me in the least."

"Let me see what you've got there. Oh, that's what they call a black racer. They're harmless. They like to eat bugs and mice and frogs. All of which are plentiful around here."

"There seem to be a lot of snakes, fortunately so far, all black snakes."

"Yeah, we've been seeing at least one just about every day. I'm sure they've been living in the house, and the old barn is full of them. Have you been out there?"

"Yes, but I didn't notice any."

"That's because you have to know where to look. They like to sit up in the rafters."

I gave an involuntary shudder. I was beginning to think it was like the little house of horrors out here. Since coming out to the house I'd found a huge dead rat floating face down in a galvanized round trash can behind the smokehouse, had dozens of bats swoop over my head at dusk, found a five-foot-long snakeskin lying in the gravel in the basement, and had tripped over the remains of a half-eaten deer carcass in the woods behind the house while searching for property markers. Now I was learning that snakes probably were living in the house!

Josh must have been reading my mind because he laughed and said, "Look, right now nature has been ruling the roost out here. When you move in, all that will change. For one thing, critters go where the food is."

I hoped none of the "critters" would see *me* as food!

Josh continued, "When you eliminate the food, they'll go away. First thing you need to do is get the mouse and bug situation under control. Those big fat black crickets that are everywhere are the dessert table at the all-you-can-eat buffet for small snakes. The mice are the favorite food for the bigger snakes."

"What about bats? There seem to be a lot of those out here too."

"Bats keep the mosquito population down. They're good to have around, as long as they don't get in your attic or take up residence in your buildings. Once you start keeping the grass around the buildings cut and the bushes trimmed back, there won't be as much for the bats to eat and some of them will move on to where the food is more plentiful."

As Josh nudged the black racer with his foot, she slipped down between two rotten boards and was out of sight.

"Come on up to the top of the hill behind the house with me. That's the best place to see what I want to show you."

Now I was really curious. We headed up the hill behind the house and stopped at the wood line. My four acres continued into the woods, and this ensured I'd always have privacy along the back of the property. The view from the top of the hill was spectacular. You could see straight down the valley, thirty-five miles to Marshall Mountain in the distance. There were farmhouses and barns sparsely scattered across rolling green pastures in front and to the sides of Merryhearth. There were half a dozen historic properties that predated 1840, when my house was started. They were all beautifully restored and half of them were still working farms. From where we were standing, we could clearly see the back side of Merryhearth and its shallow-pitched, green-metal hip roof.

Josh interrupted my reverie, "Do you see how the roof has four beams that run from the center to the four corners of the main house? There's like a square section right in the middle of the roof, and then the beams jut out from each corner of the square to each corner of the house. See what I mean?"

"Yes, I can see that clearly."

"Notice how the beam that is nearest to us is not straight? It's sagging in the middle."

"Uh-oh, yes, I see how it looks like it's bent in the middle. Is it broken?"

"Yep, we have a broken beam, one of only four beams I might add. It should be supporting the weight of one-fourth of the roof."

"What does this mean? I mean, I know it's not good, but how bad is it and how did we all miss seeing it?" I could imagine now having to factor in the cost of a whole new roof. To fix the beam, the metal roof would probably have to come off, to access it. Damn it—one of the projects that was not on the list, and therefore saving tons of money, was a massive new roof.

"You can't really see it when you're walking on the roof like we did to inspect it. You notice it when you're standing up here and can compare it to the other beams."

I had stood on this same spot to look out over the property, but I hadn't focused on the roof at that time. I wondered what prompted Josh or one of his crew to come up here and examine the roof.

"Oh, wow, so how do we fix it? Do we have to open up the roof?"

"Well . . . maybe not. As you know, we have to tear down all of that cracked plaster in the gallery because it's half down on its own. We were going to add insulation to the ceiling up there before putting up wallboard. I'm not sure what we'll find, but we may be able to access the beam from inside the house when we open up the ceiling."

"So you don't think the metal roof is attached to the beam?"

"Don't know. And we won't know for sure until we take down all that plaster and lath and can see up in there."

"How soon do we need to do this work?"

"The gallery was going to be phase two, and I think we keep it at phase two. It's not leaking when it rains, and we aren't expecting any heavy wet snow in July, as far as I know anyway."

"If you can fix the beam from inside the house, will it be very expensive?"

"That depends too. If we can repair it by adding a sister joist to strengthen it, it won't be too bad for the budget. But if we have to purchase an engineered beam and replace it entirely, it could get pretty expensive."

"Fingers crossed that this is the only surprise we encounter, and hopefully it won't be the worst-case scenario—a new engineered beam AND a new roof. If that happens, I'm dead in the water. I don't have anywhere near enough money to cover that scenario."

Josh nodded his understanding. As we headed down the hill, back toward the house, he asked me about the outbuildings. "You still want to remove these rotted, falling down buildings, including the barn, the garage, and the lean-to on the back of the house?"

"Yes, everything except the smokehouse. The smokehouse is original, and it's made of the same bricks as the house. That, I definitely want to keep!"

"So that brings up another question. While we are here to demo the buildings, it makes sense to demo the kitchen and those two old bathrooms."

"But you just got the water running in the kitchen, and that one bathroom working for me. It's nice to have some minimal functionality when I'm here."

"It's going to save money if we can do all the demo at the same time, including the gallery ceiling plaster and lath."

"Okay, but do me a favor, rig up—somehow—a working toilet and one sink?"

"Yeah, I can put some temporary fixtures in one of the new bathrooms. You can change them out when you're ready to finish the bathrooms."

"Thank you! It's the small things that sometimes make life bearable!"

Josh laughed. "Yeah, I'm not a big fan of porta potties either, but then I have a few more options than you do."

It occurred to me that I just figured out what Josh was probably doing at the wood line, on the back of the property, when he noticed the broken roof beam. Providence had seen fit to give him a reason to examine the roof from that vantage point!

"So, how are we doing with the budget? Phase one is almost done, and you're ready to get started on the demoing."

"Yeah, I've got a crew and the equipment ready to go now for demoing. How about if I take advantage of the crew's availability and get started in the next week on that?"

"Okay, I'm fine with that. I'll let the bank know to release loan money for the demo work."

"Don't worry about it too much. You can pay me for the demoing with the final payment for the basement and brickwork."

"Has the bank been on time with the payments for phase one work? I've been signing off on the invoices and sending them over as soon as you give them to me."

"Yeah, I know you have. Thanks for that. They've been dragging their feet on the last two invoices. I've made some phone calls to my buddy Danny, who handles most of my accounts, but he's avoiding me. I'm not too sure what's going on over there, but I'm not concerned. They're a bank—what are they going to do—not pay their bills?"

I didn't give the situation much more thought, I was sorry that Josh may have been getting the runaround, but the bank would get to it. Still, it was odd that they would delay in making the payments to Josh, but it was probably just something administrative.

As things were going, about one-fourth of the work would be done by the end of July. If Alex and I were really going to take a trip together to Italy, it looked like August was the best timing. The work on the house would be between phases one and two, we would just be back from our trip to Louisiana, and the work project would be at a good break point. Now I had to figure out if I could afford to go on a trip to Italy! It didn't occur to me to ask myself if I *should* go on a trip to Italy, that thought never crossed my mind.

Chapter 15

When I got back to my apartment in Leesburg, I started researching the internet for hotels in Italy. That would be the big expense, since I had my airfare covered from points earned on my credit card. To add to the complexity of this exercise was my decoraphobia syndrome. If we went to Rome (and there was no way I was going to Italy without seeing Rome), and then Tuscany for the wineries, and Venice for the Murano chandelier shopping, we'd need hotels in three different locales. I started with Rome and soon found that most of the hotels near the sights were run-down-looking and overcrowded. I could see it was going to be challenging to find a place to stay in Rome that met my very exacting requirements. There was no point in telling myself to deal with it and find the cheapest options. I knew myself too well, and for anyone who understands decoraphobia, having to stay in hotel hell—or even hotel purgatory—ruins the vacation. I didn't want to ruin my first time visiting Italy, and I wanted my time with Alex to be special. Where we stayed was key! I'd rather not go at all if I couldn't find places to stay that met my standards.

As I continued to search for hotels, a text from Danielle popped up on my phone. She was pulling into my apartment and wanted to make sure I was home. I texted her back with the thumbs-up symbol.

Danielle dropped her purse and car keys on the table next to my open laptop. "I was on your side of town and thought I'd take a chance and see if you were home."

"I'm glad you did! Have you eaten? Want to order pizza or Thai food?"

"Yeah, I could go for pizza. What's on your laptop? It looks like a map of Rome."

"It is. Alex and I are thinking about going to Italy."

"You and . . . Alex-from-work?"

"Yes, that Alex."

"I'm confused, is this a work trip?"

"No, I'm sorry, I haven't really kept you up to date on Alex. Let me order the pizza, and then I'll bring you up to speed."

I hadn't kept Danielle at all up to date on Alex. With everything that was happening at Merryhearth, it was easy to avoid the subject when she and I talked. As I ordered the pizza, I wondered how much to tell her. I didn't know how to qualify what Alex and I had. I knew it was more than average work friends, but we certainly were not a couple. *What exactly were we?*

Danielle popped the tops on a couple of cans of cold soda from the refrigerator and said, "Okay, talk!"

"You know I travel a lot with my job, right?"

Danielle nodded, "Uh huh."

"Alex and I have gotten to know each other really well from traveling together so often." *Not a lie*, I thought to myself. "And we've found that we have a lot in common, and we travel well together."

"So you've decided to take a trip . . . the two of you . . . to Italy?"

"We're talking about it. We haven't decided for certain. It depends on the cost and if we can get away from work right now."

"It seems so random. Italy? Why?"

"Alex has always wanted to do a wine tasting tour, and I want to shop for a Murano glass chandelier for Merryhearth."

"You do know how this sounds, don't you? It sounds very extravagant, and it's more than a little borderline inappropriate."

"It's none of those things, really. The cost of the trip is actually minimal because I have free airfare, and we're sharing the cost of hotels and food."

"And what about the fact that you're his boss?"

"People are allowed to be friends outside of work, and our friendship doesn't interfere with work. But that said, we also aren't making it known around the office."

"Do you think people would get the wrong idea and think you're in a relationship?"

"No, not at all. Alex is openly gay, and he's also ten years younger than I am. So no, no one would think anything like that."

What I wasn't saying is that people who didn't know us, strangers, did think we were a couple when we were out together. I was seasoned enough to recognize the appreciative looks men gave Alex when he and I were in restaurants and wineries together. The women too gave us that "what a cute couple look" because usually we were heads together talking a mile a minute, oblivious to time and space. I was beyond caring that people might think we were a cougar and cougar-fling couple—if they thought that—which I doubted because we just didn't give off that vibe. Maybe I looked a few years older than Alex, but not a decade older. If I looked my age, I wouldn't be getting carded every time we ordered alcohol together. In fact, it was my own dirty little secret that I loved that strangers thought we were a couple. It was fun, and it made me feel young, and attractive, and desirable again. *Lord knows, I hadn't felt that way in forever.*

Danielle gave me a skeptical look, "So you aren't smitten with one another?"

"Now that's a word I haven't heard in a long time!" *Hmm, smitten, meaning deeply affected with or struck by strong feelings of attraction.*

Danielle may have hit the target. I had not been able to define what Alex and I had but *mutual smitten-ness* seemed to characterize it very well.

I artfully deflected the question. "How could Alex be smitten with me, he's not into women."

"Okay, I hear you. Just be careful. Stranger things, much stranger things, have happened than a gay guy and a straight woman ending up being attracted to one another."

"Of course! And that's what makes being with Alex so safe. Nothing is going to happen that ends up with me being hurt—or him either for that matter."

I did have to wonder, *Was some of my smitten-ness due to the fact that I was in a completely safe zone with Alex?* I could test the water after the explosion without the fear of getting in too deeply or getting hurt. Intuitively, I knew there was a built-in anti-lock braking system. Danielle had unwittingly provided a bit of insight that had not to this point occurred to me.

The pizza was miraculously still hot when it arrived and as we wolfed down several slices each, I brought Danielle up to date on the Merryhearth rehabilitation work, including the broken roof support beam that could also break the budget under the worst-case scenario. She filled me in on the developments with Doug, her long-time crush from the Leesburg Harley-Davidson Riding Club. I had only seen Danielle with her beautiful sky blue and white Harley one time, and it made me smile to remember it. She was transformed to a leather clad, bandana wearing, boot stomping biker chick—and she wore it well! But that was Danielle. Whatever she was doing, she did it 100 percent. We planned a day to see the progress on the house and parted with promises of not letting so much time go by before we synced up again.

⊖⸻⚡

After Danielle left, I got back to researching where to stay if Alex and I were able to go to Italy. I was very excited when I stumbled across a boutique hotel in the Aventine Hill neighborhood of Rome. The website described a historic nineteenth-century villa, facing a square named for it, with views of a famous Benedictine convent. The photographs of the rooms and the common areas were gorgeous. I was intrigued when I read, "Guests wake to fresh flowers, songbirds, and vistas of the quaint garden filled with the scent of night jasmine and orange blossoms." That, and the pictures and description of the complimentary breakfast served in the villa's gardens each morning, totally sold me on this location.

One problem—a big problem. To save money, Alex and I talked about splitting the costs. Two rooms in places like this, the kind of room you'd want to wake up in while visiting Rome, were really, really, expensive. Would Alex be open to sharing a room? That was the only way I was going to be able to afford to go to Italy and stay in the kind of places that didn't set off a decoraphobia attack. I started searching the website for rooms at the villa that had two beds. Uh-oh ... problem ... big problem. This was not an American chain hotel. There were no rooms with two beds. There was one room, converted from a broom closet I was pretty sure, with a twin bed. The other rooms all had mostly queen-size beds, and a few had king-size beds. I started looking at other options in Rome, it was the same scenario with the beds. The idea that rooms had two double beds like in the United States was just not the way

133

it was done in the hotels I was finding. Sharing a room was one thing, sharing a bed was another.

Would I want to tour Italy, stay in historic villas, share a room, *and* sleep with Alex for the better part of ten days? *Let me think, hmm . . . Is the mitochondria the powerhouse of the cell? Is the pope Catholic? Do bears poop in the woods?* I couldn't think of anything that sounded more delightful! To be perfectly fair and honest, I wasn't thinking *sex* with Alex, I was thinking being so near him that I could feel his body heat, hear his rhythmic breathing while he slept, and maybe bump into him under the covers—strictly accidentally. Danielle, if she could hear my thoughts, would say, *What's the difference between sex and what you are thinking? Because what you are thinking leads to sex.* But there was a difference: I didn't want to have sex with Alex, I really didn't. I was just smitten-normous with him!

So the question was, would Alex be okay with this plan to share rooms across Italy, even when the rooms had just one bed? Only one way to find out. I picked up my cell and began to text him: Hi, Alex. I've been doing a lot of internet research for the Italy trip.

My cell pinged almost immediately with Alex's response: Great. What are you finding?

Me: Nice hotels are hard to come by. At least the ones I can stay in.

Alex: What, Italy can't meet your decoraphobia standards?

Me: Oh, Italy can meet them, but it will cost $$$$.

Alex: How bad?

Me: There's only one way I can afford these hotels. [link to the Aventine Hill villa inserted]

Alex: Oh, wow, that place is awesome. And the complimentary breakfast would be a really convenient amenity.

Me: If we say here, you will be waking each morning to

fresh flowers, songbirds, and vistas of the quaint garden filled with the scent of night jasmine and orange blossoms.

Alex: LOL. Sounds good to me!

Me: You'd have to wake up to something else, too.

Alex: Oh . . . what's that?

Me: The only way I can afford this trip, and this standard of luxury, is if we split a room.

Alex: Yeah, that's what people usually do when they go on vacation together and split the costs. I expected that.

Me: It's a little more than that.

To my surprise, Alex texted back: You mean splitting the bed too, right?

Me: Yeah—how'd you know?

Alex: You haven't traveled much in Europe, have you?

Me: No.

Alex: Hotels in Europe are different. And the older the city, the less likely you have big hotel rooms with two double beds like we have in the U.S.

Me: So you're okay if we have rooms with just one bed?

Alex: Yes. That's not a big deal.

Me: Okay. I'll pick some places, and we can look at them on the internet next week while we're in Louisiana.

Alex: Sounds good.

Problem solved. Not only was Alex okay with sharing a room with one bed, but he knew that was the norm when traveling in Europe. This meant I could up the hotel budget allowance and go for the best! Rome was done, Tuscany was next.

It didn't take long to find a plethora of historic, Tuscan farmhouses and villas that were doubling as boutique hotels for vacationers. It was hard to believe how many there were. Most looked almost identical—very historic, brown stacked stone, wood doors and shutters, big pots of beautiful, colorful flowers. Many offered amenities like guided tours, wine tastings, cooking classes, all the things that you'd want to do while visiting Tuscany. I came across a website for a restored farmhouse in the Chianti Region. It was surrounded by vineyards and sat high with views of rolling green hills and other quaint stone farmhouses. It was secluded but also near famous towns and wineries where we could taste the best that Italy had to offer in both wine and olive oil. One of them stood out to me because a woman owned it and had restored it from rubble. *A kindred spirit*, I thought. I'd love to talk with her, maybe over a glass of wine, about her journey to bring her beloved farmhouse back to life and how she now spends her days opening its doors to visitors from all over the world, sharing her love of Italy and all that her home has to offer. Another plus for this farmhouse was the cooking lesson that came with an overnight stay. I thought that could be fun and a nice remembrance of our time in Tuscany. I bookmarked the website for the farmhouse for the three nights we would be in Tuscany.

On to Venice, where I wanted to shop for a Murano chandelier for the dining room at Merryhearth. It took a good bit of searching because Venice was a lot like Rome in that many of the hotels were run-down-looking and overcrowded. I found one boutique hotel in the District Dorsoduro that looked promising. The website boasted, "Enjoy being out of the high traffic hubbub while still near the best that the Venice art district has to offer..." Like Rome and Tuscany, this hotel also offered a splendid-looking complimentary breakfast after a night's sleep in beautifully appointed, large rooms, many of which sported French doors and Juliet balconies that opened onto a canal. I checked Venice off my list! I would share what I had found with Alex next week. I was looking forward to our trip to Louisiana. We'd be working each day but would have some free time the day we arrived, and our evenings would be our own!

Chapter 16

I had an appointment to meet the Blandy Farm bee removal team at Merryhearth. The effort promised to be a rather significant undertaking and one that was overdue. I took Danielle with me, and Josh was meeting us there. I had been anxious to have the bees safely removed from the time I first discovered them. Since finding the house, I had cleaned up buckets and buckets of dead bees from the kitchen and other windows throughout. Every time I visited the house, there were more dead bees in the same places where I had cleaned them up the last time. It broke my heart to see these little heroes of Mother Nature fighting so hard to leave the house and eventually succumbing to the dead bee pile. When I called the University of Virginia's Blandy Experimental Farm to see if they could help me with the bee removal, they were eager to get me to the right person and pleased that I wanted to do the right thing and relocate them. I spoke to Dr. Apiar, a professor of biology and apparently a renowned expert on bees and beekeeping. He was eager to check out the hive and see if there was a way to save it by relocating the queen and as many worker bees as possible. The charge for this was, miraculously, nothing. I just had to supply the manpower, tools, and ladders necessary to remove the ceiling and give him access to the bees.

I was pleased to see, when I pulled into the driveway, that Josh brought the whole crew. Victor, Ricardo, Carlos, and Felix were dressed a little upscale I thought for what could be a dirty job, but then again it was Sunday, and they usually didn't work on Sundays. I explained that we needed to wait until Dr. Apiar arrived, so he could instruct us where to cut into the plaster ceiling and how to remove it without harming the bees. The kitchen plaster would be demoed eventually on both the ceiling and walls, so cutting into it to save the bees was no loss. I had design ideas for the kitchen that included exposed brick walls, removing the layers of ugly white paint from the bricks surrounding the big cooking fireplace—which still retained its original iron swivel rod for hanging cooking pots—adding a high-velocity exhaust fan encased in a custom-made wood chimney over a forty-eight-inch gas range that would sit in a center island, not to mention modern recessed lighting and adequate electric throughout. The current fluorescent light, covered with a bee-carcass-stained plastic cover, couldn't be gone soon enough.

Everywhere else in the house, I was trying to save the original plaster if it was in fairly good shape, which fortunately it was. I was astonished at how beautifully smooth most of the walls were, much better than many modern houses I'd seen with ugly nail pops and wallboard seam tape showing. The plaster ranged in thickness from three-fourths of an inch to an inch and a quarter and was applied directly onto the solid brick walls throughout the house. Only on the ceilings was the plaster applied to thin, hand cut pieces of pine that made up the lath.

We all moved into the kitchen, already starting to come to life with the buzz of bee activity as the mid-July morning was starting to warm up to what would eventually be a steamy Shenandoah day in the upper eighties, with enough humidity to make it feel like the upper nineties. The guys put up the big stepladders and got their tools out. I opened all the external doors around the house and climbed the wind-around staircase to the gallery level to open the frieze windows—unique single sash windows with six glass panes that folded in and up toward the ceiling. Each window had its own original iron hook that fastened it securely in place against the ceiling. By some miracle of fate, only one of the original hooks was missing.

Merryhearth's design, as is true of many homes built in earlier times, was a marvel of natural solutions; the wisdom that modern-day architects and builders seem to have lost entirely. It faced true south like the needle of a compass, was devoid of windows on the windy, cold-in-winter and hot-in-summer, west side of the house, and enjoyed five chimneys shared by twelve fireplaces. Via the unique three-part doors, it could be shut down into cozy heat-containing rooms in the winter or opened for air-circulating coolness in the hot summers. Opening the frieze windows on the gallery level was the equivalent today of turning on the air conditioner. Heat rushed up from the lower levels and exited through these windows at the top level of the house. All it took was having the right windows open on the lower levels—or in this case the right doors, because the windows were all horribly painted shut. This allowed the air to circulate through the house with a gentle breeze, scented with fresh field grass and wildflowers. It was my discoveries of features and attributes like these that steadily fed my increasing admiration for Merryhearth.

It was quite the scene by the time Dr. Apiar arrived. He pulled up in a pickup truck with half a dozen big wooden boxes in the bed. He looked a little like a professor might look who went off the grid—disheveled curly gray hair, gray beard, thick-rimmed square glasses, cutoff jean shorts (like really jeans that had the legs cut off), a T-shirt with more than one hole in it, and, to top off the look, a pair of well-worn Birkenstocks with white socks. Much to my amusement, I caught Josh giving him a once-over look and forming a slight frown. I figured the Birkenstocks with calf-high white socks were probably too much for him. With Dr. Apiar was a graduate student who looked interesting in her own right. He introduced her simply as, "Allison, a graduate student interning with me this summer." She was wearing blue jean short overalls (not cut off), with a long-sleeved yellow and black T-shirt, perfectly round, plastic, red-framed glasses, and had long auburn hair that stuck up a little at her scalp before falling in two braids onto her shoulders. Unlike Dr. Apiar, she was wearing black Chuck Taylor high tops. There was something about her that looked familiar. I asked Danielle if she reminded her of anyone we knew, but Danielle couldn't think of anyone in particular.

After the introductions were made, Dr. Apiar launched into a scientific explanation of what he intended to do to retrieve the hive and queen bee. His explanation was fascinating, and he delivered it with the zeal of a professor addressing a class of freshmen biology majors. Allison nodded her head profusely during the lecture. I could see from the corner of my eye that Josh was getting impatient as he shifted his weight from one foot to the other, looking very much like Eeyore when Winnie the Pooh got long-winded. He probably just wanted to know where to start cutting into the ceiling. I had to laugh to myself, Merryhearth brought some of the most unlikely people together. It was too bad Bob Norseman wasn't here, he'd have gotten a kick out of the whole scene.

Allison was interested to know more about the house and its history and what I was going to do with the place. I was glad to have someone who took an interest, and we chatted until Dr. Apiar called her over to look at the corner of the kitchen where the bee activity was most prolific. After giving it a good bit of thought, he said to Josh, "I think we can remove the ceiling here and be able to access the hive. It's been established between the floor joists, which are running east to west, and is probably isolated to this section that's about four feet wide between the east exterior wall and the side of the fireplace."

"Is that good?" I asked. "I mean that it's in a somewhat compact area?"

"Yes, it will allow us to better isolate the hive and increase the odds that we get the queen."

Josh motioned to Victor and Ricardo where to cut, and Carlos and Felix stood by with trash bags and shovels to scoop up the mess. The rest of us stood back, watching curiously to see what would happen next. I noticed Dr. Apiar and Allison left for this portion of the operation. I could see them out at their pickup, gathering what I assumed were beekeeper suits, and getting the big wooden boxes. As chunks of plaster and lath fell to the floor where the reciprocating saw was cutting, bees began to appear in greater numbers, flying around the kitchen. They weren't aggressive, they just seemed confused.

A few times Victor ducked, and Ricardo swatted when they flew in his face. It was definitely a good thing the bees weren't aggressive, I thought, because Victor and Ricardo had no protection, and they were up on ladders with sharp electrical tools, not an ideal situation. Finally, as the last chunks of plaster came down, we could see the extensive beehive with thousands of bees at work, neatly tucked between two sections of floor joists in the ceiling of my kitchen. I marveled at what a great bee habitat it made. Dr. Apiar and Allison, all suited up in their white beekeeper suits, took positions on ladders and began to remove sections of the hive and place them

141

in the wooden boxes that were now sitting on the old center island. "These bees are so tame we don't even need to use the smokers," said Dr. Apiar.

The rest of us kept our distance and I watched from the dining room door, where I could make a fast getaway if needed. I was relieved to be getting the bees out of the house and felt good about possibly saving them to live their next happy life at Blandy Farm. When all the bees were removed, Dr. Apiar and Allison carried the wooden boxes to the pickup and loosely covered the bed with a canvas tarp. They removed their beekeeping suits and packed them into the truck. As we stood talking about the gentle nature of the docile little honeybees, and how valuable they would be to their new home, Allison made a move that surprised us all quite a bit. She reached into the back of the truck and pulled out a piece of honeycomb the size of a large submarine sandwich. Danielle, Josh, and I all stepped back a little and were focused on what she was holding. Then, she did the last thing I could have imagined. She lifted the honeycomb to her mouth and took a huge, crunching bite out of the middle of it!

As we looked on, aghast, she continued to chomp down on it with the glee a child demonstrates when eating buttered sweet corn. She continued chomping until it was completely gone! This didn't seem to faze Dr. Apiar in the least, although I noticed he didn't join her in the act of devouring the gentle-natured, docile little honeybees' habitat. As Allison used her yellow and black T-shirt sleeve as a napkin to wipe the remains of sticky honey from her chin, I saw the uncanny resemblance . . . *Allison looked exactly like a bee.* The bees, that is, of cartoon and movie fame. She had a perfectly round face, her braids looked a little like antennae, and those round-rimmed glasses gave the exact impression of big bee eyes.

After we said our goodbyes and thank-yous, and keep-us-posted-on-the-success-of-the-relocation, I turned to Danielle,

"Do you think Allison was a bee in a past life?"

"I think she's a bee in this life! One of those bees that eats other bees!" said Danielle.

I looked toward Josh, "I hope the bees make it, and I really hope they didn't leave the queen behind in my kitchen!"

"Me too . . . we need to be done with these bees," said Josh.

Danielle chimed in, "Leave the queen in your kitchen, hell, I just hope Allison didn't eat it! The way she chomped down on that honeycomb, there could have been anything in there!"

I gave a little involuntary shudder as I thought about it.

Josh and his crew headed out. They would be back on Monday with several other guys and equipment to start the extensive demo work, including the assortment of falling down buildings. I wanted to get a last look at things as they were because I would be in Louisiana next week when they got started. Danielle and I meandered through the house and I showed her the work that had been completed so far and rattled off the names of the rooms for her as we walked through them.

"You'll have to put signs up. How will anyone ever remember which room is which?"

"It will be easier to remember when all the furniture is in and the rooms are decorated."

"How will you furnish all these rooms? It will cost a fortune."

"Actually, furniture is not something I'm lacking."

"Oh, I'm sorry. I forgot you have the remnants of the cruise ship. I didn't mean to hit a nerve."

"Don't be sorry. It's a good thing, really."

"Won't that furniture bring up sad memories of the other house?"

"No, Merryhearth has such a personality of her own that the other house is already becoming a distant memory. I can't wait to have the rehabilitation work done and to start making Merryhearth beautiful again!"

After a delicious lunch, followed by French press coffees—from one of Loudoun Street's specialty boutique restaurants, this one converted from a nineteenth century building into a cozy setting featuring wood plank floors, exposed brick walls, and multiple fireplaces—we headed back to Leesburg. I needed to pack for the trip to Louisiana and be ready to head out to the airport the next morning. I wanted to pick each outfit carefully, one for the day while Alex and I were working and a separate outfit for evenings when we were going out to eat and sightseeing. I had purchased quite a few new things to wear and wanted to make sure I packed them all. My nearly daily workouts to get in shape for skiing had definitely paid off. I felt stronger and healthier than I had in years, and I was looking shapelier in my new clothes than I had in a long time. I wondered if anyone else noticed. I wondered if *Alex* noticed. I sent him a text: All set for your flight to NOLA in the morning?

He responded right away: Yep. I even finished packing already.

Me: I'll have a funny Merryhearth story to share with you tomorrow.

Alex: Can't wait to hear it! Is this about the bee removal?

Me: Yes. The removal team was . . . interesting.

Alex: Are we meeting at the rental car counter?

Me: The airport is so small that we can just meet at the baggage claim and then go get the car.

Alex: Okay, I'll see you tomorrow around ten thirty.

Me: See you then.

I was looking forward to another week with Alex and had picked out a number of great places to see while we were there. I was also excited to talk about the Italy trip and plan our itinerary. It was going to be a good week!

Chapter 17

I glanced at my watch as I settled into a seat at the boarding gate at Dulles—juggling my coffee, laptop bag, and carry-on suitcase; I had my hands full. I missed seeing Jill at the boarding gate like I used to when she traveled with us. I was pretty sure, however, that she didn't miss the frequent work trips. The flight to Louis Armstrong Airport in New Orleans was fortunately only a couple of hours. As I waited for the boarding call, I thought about all the work that would be starting this week at Merryhearth. Dilapidated outbuildings would be torn down, the lean-to on the back of the house removed, failing plaster and lath on the gallery level taken down, and the outdated bathrooms and kitchen completely gutted. It would look very different the next time I saw it. I wished I'd taken more before photos to be able to compare them someday with the after photos, but I hated taking uncomplimentary photos of the house. Just like I didn't want any ugly pictures of myself floating around for eternity, I didn't want Merryhearth to have pictures of her ugly phase either.

After boarding the plane, I reviewed the project materials for the upcoming week of meetings and put together some speaking notes. We were fortunate to have NASA at the Stennis Space Center in Mississippi offer to host our project planning session, which allowed the government employees located in the southern part of the country to have easier access and ability to attend the meeting. Mercifully, Alex and I were not the headliners for this weeklong session, so we could relax a little and not be quite as in charge as the Denver trip had necessitated. The project was going well, in no small part due to our successful launch during the Denver meeting. Now we just had to sustain the momentum, and I had to keep my plates spinning, so everything stayed on track. Jill would be our eyes and ears in D.C. while we were away this week. I'd heard through the grapevine that Delores Umbridge (Deborah Callahan) was starting to ask a lot of questions about the project, mostly about cost and project management details. The last thing we needed was her taking an interest, which inevitably lead to her trying to derail it. We had been down that rabbit hole with her before.

In no time it seemed, the plane touched down and the passengers were disembarking. As I rolled my carry-on out of the secure zone and into the lobby at Louis Armstrong, I was pleasantly surprised to see Alex leaning casually against a column waiting for me. He looked relaxed in a cream-colored T-shirt and jeans, his Maui Jim sunglasses hanging from the V-neck of his T-shirt and his signature iced-coffee-black, in his left hand.

"Hi! I thought your flight was half an hour behind mine."

"It was. But I got to Reagan National early, imagine that, and there were openings on an earlier flight, so I took it."

"Great! Where's your luggage?"

"Already loaded in the rental. As soon as you pick up your other suitcase from the carousel, we can go."

"Cool—because I have a surprise for you this afternoon, so it's good to be getting a jump start."

My suitcase was one of the first on the baggage carousel, and I wrestled if off and onto its wheely feet. Alex led the way to the rental, parked not far from the baggage claim. As usual, it was a black SUV with tinted windows and luxury interior. Alex tossed my enormously heavy suitcase, complete with two outfits per day with matching shoes, extra clothes just in case, pj's and toiletries for the week, into the back and arranged it snugly next to his suitcase.

I enjoyed one of the many perks of our trips together, watching him load the luggage. Muscles at work, more visible in his lightweight T-shirt than usual, the biceps, triceps, pectorals, abdominal six-pack, all came into play. It was like watching a fine-tuned, synchronized orchestra playing Mozart's Serenade no. 13 in G Major. I wanted to pull up a chair and watch the act of loading the suitcase over and again. Maybe when he wasn't looking, I could drag it back out, so it would have to be lifted in again. However, I suppressed the urge, set my thinking straight, and calmed the butterflies that were dancing around in my stomach. As I settled into my roomy leather seat, Alex handed me my favorite hot weather coffee, an iced vanilla latte. The butterflies started dancing again.

"Oh, thank you so much for the coffee. And great choice of vehicle . . . as always!"

"Hey, it pays to be a Gold Club member."

Yes it does, I thought to myself. I loved being his passenger! This was the way to travel!

As we exited the airport, Alex asked, "Where to? Are we going to the hotel first, or somewhere else?"

"Somewhere else! Take Interstate 10 west to the Lake Pontchartrain Causeway and head across the lake."

"Umm . . . coming from the airport, I think we take I-10 *east*."

"You know to go in the opposite direction of whatever I

say, right?"

"I do, yes. Then what—once we cross the lake?"

"Straight ahead to Covington to find someplace for a nice lunch, someplace that serves traditional Cajun cuisine, since it's our first day here."

"Sounds good. I'm starved!"

"Covington is the first historic town in our weeklong exploration of the historic towns along the Northshore."

"Oh, wow, that sounds like fun. I didn't know there were historic towns along the northern part of Lake Pontchartrain."

"I didn't know either until I started researching where to stay and eat while we are here. There are a bunch of these cute little historic towns that date back to the early 1800s. Several of them were established as resort destinations. They look like they will have nice shopping, great restaurants, galleries, historic architecture—all the stuff we like."

"Huh, most people that I've spoken with just seem to know New Orleans for the French Quarter. I've never heard anyone mention any other historic areas."

"Same, and as many times as I've been to New Orleans on work trips, no one has ever mentioned going across the lake. I've been to the French Quarter at least half a dozen times, but never anywhere else. Today we'll explore Covington and the surprise location after lunch."

"And the rest of the week? I would like to see the French Quarter at some point because I've never been."

"Tuesday will be Madisonville, Wednesday Mandeville, and Thursday the French Quarter—we'll go down to Bourbon Street and do the traditional tourist stuff. As I'm sure you've heard, it's ... quite the interesting party scene."

"And our meetings are across the state border in Mississippi at NASA Stennis Space Center, right?"

"Yes, it sounds like a long way, but it's really not, only about a thirty-minute drive from Pearl River where our hotel is located."

"And the hotel will be okay? I mean, no decoraphobia attacks this time?"

"I think so, it's brand-new. It's not high-end, but being a new chain hotel means it will meet certain standards that I can live with."

"It's great how you figure all of this out, it makes these work trips a lot more enjoyable."

As we turned onto the causeway and headed to the Northshore, the lake opened up with blue water as far as we could see.

"This doesn't look like any lake I've seen before," said Alex.

"I agree. It reminds me of driving between the Florida Keys with open ocean in every direction."

"Yeah, exactly. This is much more like the blue waters of the Gulf than a lake. Do you know if it's fresh or salt water?"

"I read online that technically it's an estuary because it connects to the Gulf of Mexico, so it receives salt water from the ocean, and it's also fed fresh water by rivers and streams. I think that makes it brackish."

"The shoreline's nowhere in sight. Do you know how long it will take us to cross?"

"I think about thirty minutes. At twenty-four miles, the causeway is the longest bridge in the U.S."

"A twenty-four-mile-long bridge. Wow!"

We were both quiet as we drove and took in the massive size of Lake Pontchartrain and how with each mile it seemed we were leaving New Orleans behind us. Not being able to see the approaching shoreline gave the sensation of traveling toward the unknown. As we approached the end of the causeway, the character of our surroundings looked and felt very different than those from the start of the crossing. There was much less traffic and overall a more laid-back feeling on the

Northshore side of the lake. The air was fresher and as we drove we caught glimpses of docks, boats, white sand, charming little houses, and colorful plants and flowers everywhere. It felt very different on this side of the lake. I couldn't explain it, but it was as if, when we completed the twenty-four-mile trek across Lake Pontchartrain, we crossed through a portal and entered a unique realm.

I wondered if Lake Pontchartrain had its own Lady of the Lake, like the one of King Arthur fame. It would make sense, considering the lake began forming some five thousand years ago and encompassed 630 square miles. That's plenty of time and plenty of space for a mystical water goddess to take up residence and become a force of nature. Perhaps she established a portal and showed favor to those crossing the lake's boundaries, provided they were worthy. Her sister goddess, the Lady of the Lake from Brittany, after all provided Arthur with the sword Excalibur, raised Sir Lancelot after the death of his father, and eliminated Merlin when he became tiresome. Had the Lady of Lake Pontchartrain opened a portal for us, through which we had just passed? I decided to keep this fantastical thought to myself and not encumber Alex with it, although, to his credit, he probably would have loved the idea.

As we pulled into the historic district of Covington, the town did not disappoint. It didn't take long to find a restaurant that specialized in Cajun cuisine. The interior was no-frills, but the aroma emanating from the kitchen promised good things. We had the restaurant to ourselves except for one other table that was occupied by an older gentleman sitting alone. The waitress, a woman in her midfifties, wearing a pink dress and red crawfish pattern apron, seated us at a table next to the window. It seemed Monday at lunchtime was quiet in Covington. After studying the menu, Alex asked the waitress for her recommendations.

"Everything looks great. Is there anything you highly recommend? We're from out of town and want to try local cuisine."

She responded in a very friendly tone, "Honey, if you want the good stuff, you can't do better than our homemade shrimp étouffée, and jambalaya. We make 'em fresh every day."

"Ooh, those both sound really good," I said.

"Where you two from?"

Alex replied for us, "We're from Washington, D.C."

Technically, I wasn't from Washington, D.C., but I let it go. There was no need to confuse the discussion. I could tell the waitress thought we were a couple. We were sitting in chairs next to one another, versus across the table, and our heads were close as we studied the menus and pointed items out to each other.

"Well, I think you two are in for a real treat this week. You're gonna enjoy your stay in St. Tammany Parish. It's a special place."

I thought her choice of words was interesting, "It's a special place." *What did that mean?*

"Okay, so, what will it be today for you two?"

I decided on the shrimp étouffée, and Alex ordered the jambalaya. The waitress was giving us that "aren't you a cute couple" look that I had grown to recognize so well.

After she left the table, I said to Alex, "Interesting that she assumed—correctly—that we are spending the week in Northshore, or St. Tammany Parish as the locals may call it."

"It was probably just her way of making small talk," replied Alex.

Maybe it was, and maybe it wasn't, although Alex was probably right, but again, I felt that sensation that there was almost a mystical aura about the place.

The food was delicious and this time we didn't just taste from each other's plates, we out-and-out shared the entrées. It

151

was too good to stop at one taste bite. The waitress checked in on us, filling up our iced tea glasses as soon as they were half empty. At one point, she looked at us and smiled, "Just like a man. Eat the food right off your plate."

I guess she hadn't noticed I ate the food "right off his plate" too. I thought Alex might be embarrassed by what she said, but he didn't seem phased. I was a little embarrassed. When the check came, Alex said, "I'll get this one, and you can get the next one."

"That works for me."

"So where are we off to now? Is the next place the surprise you mentioned?"

"It is. Get this . . . would you believe that right down the road from here is a vineyard and winery?"

"You're kidding? I had no idea they grew grapes and made wine in Louisiana."

"I know, right? I did an internet search just for the heck of it and never expected there to be a vineyard this far south. I figured it was too humid and hot for grapes."

"Goes to show what we know."

"Or what we don't know, as the case may be."

"Alright, give me the directions, and I'll map it in my phone."

We headed north on Route 1082, and in no time we were pulling into the winery's driveway. As we parked and walked toward the door, we looked around. Well-tended, healthy-looking vines were clearly visible, proving grapes can do quite well in St. Tammany Parish, Louisiana. Our sporty SUV was the only car in the parking area, so we weren't surprised when we entered the tasting room and were the only people in sight. It was dark and cool inside. Rock music played softly from speakers we couldn't see. After we stood for a few minutes at the tasting counter, taking in the pleasant atmosphere, a cute girl in her late twenties appeared. I saw her evaluating Alex and me inquisitively. I could tell she was trying to determine how we were connected and if she should turn on her flirtatious charm, aimed at Alex, or not. Alex may have consciously, or subconsciously, picked up on the same because he stepped sideways toward me, causing our arms to touch. I saw the slight disappointment in her bright expression and in a friendly tone she asked if we wanted to do a wine tasting. We indicated that we'd love to do a tasting of their whites and reds.

Sparkling wine glasses etched with the winery's logo were set out in front of us. We made introductions and Monique started us through the wines, many made from grapes grown on the property. It reminded me of the way wine tastings used to be in Virginia, before the concept caught on and became a favorite weekend pastime of thousands from the Washington, D.C., metro area. The three of us chatted amiably as Monique explained the grapes and wine-making process behind each of the wines. Her taste pours were generous, and I was more than a little buzzed before we reached the last wine, what Monique described as their specialty. Into our glasses went a dark, tawny liquid that when held to my nose smelled pleasantly of homemade date cookies. The liquid clung to the sides of the wine glasses as it was swirled. One sip was pure heaven. Monique explained it was their own brew of port wine. It wasn't like any port I had ever tried. Alex and I both marveled at the flavor.

"This is excellent," said Alex.

"It really is. What are you tasting? I can't quite put words to it."

"There's a likeness to raisins."

"Yes! That's it! It's delicious."

"I always think of port as being a wine for wintertime, wood fires, and snowstorms," said Alex, "I think because it warms you up inside when you drink it."

I tend to get a little animated when I'm buzzed, and so the next statement came out a bit more enthusiastically than I intended. I could see Monique was hanging on every word and looked a little like she wished she was doing the wine tasting too.

"Oh, wow, you know what this would be great for?"

"No, what?" asked Alex, visibly showing anticipatory excitement of what the response might be, which egged on my animation.

"This would be wonderful to have with us in Colorado when we go skiing in December. It's tradition to drink port at the end of a long day of downhill skiing when relaxing in the hot tub!"

Okay, I totally, on the spur of the moment, made that up. I'm not aware of any such tradition, but it sounded good, and perhaps it should be a tradition!

"That's a great tradition. I think I'm going to really like skiing!" said Alex, also with a good bit of animation in his tone.

I kept going, "Picture it . . . snow falling, night skiers gliding silently down the shadowy slopes, we're in our private condo hot tub, sipping port, hot water jets soothing sore muscles. And this port is perfect!"

I could tell everyone was picturing it. The steamy, hot Louisiana day was replaced by Colorado snow squalls. Monique indicated she wanted to go skiing with us too and we, in unison, enthusiastically invited her with, "Sure, meet us in Denver in December!"

We decided to purchase and have shipped home three bottles of the port and several bottles of wine. Alex ordered a chilled bottle of white for us to enjoy on the winery's shady patio, and Monique gave us fresh wine glasses. We headed out to the patio with our wine and glasses and again, had the entire area to ourselves, just the two of us. We slid into deep cushioned wicker chairs and Alex poured the wine. We settled back, sipping our cool, slightly sweet, and very flavorful white wine. It was so relaxing, all alone on the cool patio. It was then that we noticed something very unusual . . . floating in midair, drifting slowly all around us, like the snow in a snow globe. Cute little black insects, joined together and flying in pairs, were everywhere, hundreds of them. We hadn't seen them until we settled onto the patio.

"Look at these bugs. I wonder what they are?" asked Alex.

I looked thoughtfully at the little black bugs with orange stripes, "I actually know what they are, but I haven't seen any since I was a kid living in Florida."

"You've seen them before?"

"Yes, a long, long time ago."

"What are they?"

"You won't believe this, but they're *lovebugs*. That's what they're called."

"Let me guess, they're making love?"

I felt my face flush pink at hearing Alex say *making love*."

"Umm yes. It's kind of sweet, actually. They stay together, flying as one, for several days, even after the . . . umm you know, lovemaking, is done."

"I've never seen or heard of anything like them," said Alex.

"It's strange though. If I remember correctly, this isn't the time of year you usually see them in abundance. I think their, umm . . . mating season, is in the spring and in the fall. This is the middle of summer."

"Maybe in Louisiana they mate in the summertime," surmised Alex.

"Maybe, but how come we didn't see them anywhere else today?"

"Probably because they like being in the vineyard, surrounded by the vines and sipping the grapes," said Alex, smiling.

"Yes, must be. There's more nature here than anywhere else we've been today."

Motioning for me to lean toward him, Alex said, "Come here."

As I leaned in, he brushed a piece of my hair away from my face and held up a tiny pair of lovebugs, "They were in your hair."

"Oh, thank you. I think they're attracted to light surfaces. I remember that from when we lived in Florida. Blond hair attracts them."

Alex smiled at what seemed a personal thought, and I didn't press for more.

Our hotel, when we finally checked in, was pleasant enough. It was so new that I wondered if I was the first to stay in my room; fine by me if I was. Alex and I arranged to meet in the lobby in the morning and allow enough time to get coffee before getting on the road to Stennis. I had to admit, for two people who were not a couple, we had all the fun of being a couple without the pitfalls, risks, or potential hurt when it all fell apart, or worse, exploded!

Chapter 18

When the alarm went off at 5:30 a.m. I felt well rested and was looking forward to the day ahead. Alex was waiting for me in the hotel lobby and had located the nearest coffee shop on our route to the Stennis Space Center. We arrived early enough to find two chairs together at a side table in the big conference room where the planning session meetings would be taking place throughout the week. We waved at familiar faces, and I saw Jan and Sheryl opposite us at a table on the other side of the room. When they saw us, they started waving wildly and yelled in unison across the room, "Hi, Amanda! Hi, Alex!" This caused everyone to look in our direction as we were setting our stuff down, still wearing our sunglasses, coffee in hand.

"The celebrities have arrived!" announced Sheryl, much to my mortification.

Alex smiled and I heard him chuckle softly as he sat down. I could feel my face turning bright red.

Apart from our unintentional grand entrance, the meeting went well, and we were able to network over lunch and catch up with much of the group. Jill joined for most of the meeting topics via conference call from her home office and Alex and I were able to fill her in on the sidebar conversations in a private call during the afternoon break. The meeting finished up for the day at five o'clock. Some of the group asked if we wanted to join them for dinner, but since our hotel was relatively far from the meeting location, in Pearl River, we had the perfect excuse to politely decline. As we dumped our laptop bags in the back seat and Alex started the SUV, he asked, "Where to now?"

"Let's head back to the hotel. I want to freshen up and change clothes, and then we'll head to our next historic town destination, Madisonville!"

Back in my hotel room I slipped into one of the new outfits I bought specifically for the Northshore evenings and freshened my makeup and hair. I felt good in my white-denim jeans with a mauve linen button-down blouse tied at the waist, and matching moderately high-heeled slip-on sandals, sporting a leather ruffle around the ankle. My stomach gave a little leap as I stepped off the elevator and saw Alex waiting for me in the lobby. He had taken a quick shower and changed into jeans and a black V-neck T-shirt. He looked cool and relaxed.

"You look nice!" he said as I walked toward him.

"Thanks. You look ready for dinner on the water!"

"Yeah, I wanted to get out of those work clothes. I've already mapped the route to Madisonville on my phone."

"Great, let's head out."

Madisonville sits along the shore of the Tchefuncte (pronounced chew-funk-te) River and when we entered the town it was plain to see that it retained its historic charm and river town character. One of the most distinguishing landmarks, the Tchefuncte River Lighthouse, marks the spot where the river meets Lake Pontchartrain. Everywhere we looked we saw marinas, recreational boats, many of them sailboats, and maritime activities of all kinds. There was no shortage of specialty shops and riverfront restaurants. Mixed in with the commercial entities were nicely restored historic homes. The little town and its many buildings were eye-catching, and we drove slowly, taking it in, trying not to miss anything as we pointed out to each other noteworthy houses and pretty scenery.

"This is a great little town," remarked Alex.

"I'm glad it's as cute as it looked online when I researched the Northshore."

"Do you have a place picked out for dinner?"

"Let's try one of the restaurants that has waterfront tables. I wouldn't mind some good seafood tonight."

Slowing the car in front of one of the restaurants, Alex pointed out, "This one has tables out on the deck overlooking the river and says they have live music starting at eight o'clock. Want to check it out?"

"Let's do it."

The hostess who greeted us as we walked in said we were just barely beating the evening crowd who come in for the music, "Take your pick of the riverside tables while you can!"

We chose one that was a little out of the mainstream but still close enough to hear the music when it started.

"Can I get you something from the bar while you look over the menu?"

"Do you have a drink special tonight?" asked Alex.

"We certainly do. It's one of our house favorites, everybody loves them—the sand scooper. It's a mix of vodka, orange juice, and peach schnapps. It's very refreshing, and it's served in a souvenir sand-scooper bucket."

Alex and I both laughed at this.

"We'll each have one of those to start out while we decide what to order," said Alex.

"Good choice! I'll get your order when I come back with

the drinks."

Heads together, we scanned the menu and looked up when the waitress arrived with our drinks.

"Oh, my goodness, these are actually little buckets, well not so little!" I said as the waitress set our drinks down in front of us.

Alex was chuckling, almost as if it was a private joke of his own and shook his head.

"Thank you," he said and took a sip out of his bucket. "It's good, really good," then he laughed again and shook his head.

I took a sip to see what the fuss was and stated, "Umm—yes—it's good. I'd say heavy on the alcohol and light on the sand!"

"That's why they're one of our favorites," said the waitress. "We serve them every Tuesday night with the live music. This place will be so packed with people—you won't be able to move. So, now, what can I get you for dinner?"

We indicated we were thinking of seafood and the waitress stated they had the best oysters, shellfish, and seasonal catches anywhere in the Northshore. We opted this time for the same thing and both got fried local shrimp. It was still relatively quiet on the deck where we were sitting, and Alex wanted to get some pics of the water and the restaurant. He snapped a shot of his sand scooper drink and laughed again. I decided to also take a few pictures, not something I usually did because I avoided social media and posting pictures as much as possible. I ended up with a great picture of Alex, smiling brilliantly in front of the first bucket of sand. I made this photo my "Alex contact photo" in my phone, and it was a fun reminder of that second night in the Northshore.

When the shrimp arrived, it was a huge basketful, with more shrimp than we could really eat. The sand scooper drink buckets were refilled just as the music started. The band was excellent, playing mostly folk and indie rock, and the place was packed, just as the waitress said it would be. Not long after the music started the crowd got very lively. People were friendly and chatted with total strangers. I hadn't really experienced a party scene like this since my college days. There was even a mile-long line for the ladies' room and women ducking into the men's room out of sheer necessity. *I didn't miss that from my college days.* The patrons knew the lyrics to the songs the band was playing and belted them out, singing in unison, mostly off-key. Many were dancing, with sand scooper buckets in hand for quick sips without having to leave the dance floor. When the mosquitoes got too abundant and too aggressive for us sitting out near the water, we moved inside. It was a fun evening, and I wasn't looking forward to my 5:30 a.m. alarm going off.

The next morning, I texted Alex a few minutes before our scheduled departure time: GM! I'm running a little late. Will be down in about ten minutes.

Alex: Take your time. I'll meet you at the car.

I rushed as fast as I could but having slept beyond my alarm, I was way behind schedule. When I got off the elevator I could see the SUV pulled up to the hotel lobby front door and I ran out and jumped in. We headed for the nearest coffee stop.

"I really need coffee! Do you think we'll be very late?" I asked.

"I'll make up the time once we get out on the main road."

Much to my surprise we were walking into the meeting room right at the start time for the meeting. It had been Mr. Toad's wild ride getting there, but at least we weren't late!

"I hope no one took our seats from yesterday," I said in a low voice.

Alex looked around. "They did. But here are a couple in

161

the back at the far table."

"Whew. That's better anyway, we can just slip in and sit down, unnoticed hopefully."

The daylong planning session went well, and, despite the slow start, I was on top of my game and kept the project focus discussions on target and moving in the right direction. We caught up again with Jill during the afternoon break. She reported things were a little dicey back in the office. She attended a meeting for me that morning in the D.C. office and was surprised to see Deborah Callahan sitting in a chair along the wall. She said she invited her to come sit at the conference room table, but Deborah, looking sour, shook her head and said she was fine where she was.

"This is not a good sign, she's out of sorts about something. I'll need to figure it out and smooth things over when I get back."

"Is there anything you want me to do?" asked Jill.

"Yes, schedule a meeting for me with Rory one day next week, in his office rather than video conference."

"Will do. Do you want to get his help if Delores—Oh, damn, now you have me doing it—*Deborah* is looking to start trouble?"

"Exactly, and to see if he knows what may have set her off."

Alex, always the optimist, chimed in, "Do you think you are overreading the incident in the conference room? Maybe she's just interested in the project and wants to support it."

"Not a chance!" said Jill and I in unison.

I couldn't get Deborah Callahan off my mind as we headed to Mandeville for dinner and sightseeing. I hoped I wasn't going to experience one of my spinning plates falling off its stick and crashing to the floor. I needed to deal with this as soon as I got back.

Mandeville, as it turned out, was delightful and we got

there early enough to stroll through a couple of the little specialty shops. Lakeshore Drive was beautiful, and the care given to establishing beautiful parks and protecting the natural assets, like huge oak trees that were over one hundred years old, was impressive. We looked for a restaurant with a view of Lake Pontchartrain and a little more quiet atmosphere than our choice of restaurant the night before. We found the perfect place and settled into a table overlooking the water from a second-story covered porch. The restaurant had a casual atmosphere and was not crowded or, thankfully, noisy.

We decided on the cheese board as an appetizer and tonight, no drink specials. We chatted about work and when the cheese board arrived we were pleasantly surprised at the size and quality of the selection, including slivers of strawberries, pears, and apples to pair with the thin slices of gourmet cheese. It was delicious and the setting was perfect. We found ourselves alone on the covered porch after the only other table that was occupied became vacated, and we decided to make the delicious cheese platter our dinner, and nibbled slowly so it would last. Alex reminded me that we wanted to talk about our plans for the Italy vacation. The trip was right around the corner and if it was anything like our time in the Northshore, it would be wonderful.

"Are you excited about the Italy trip?" Alex asked as we looked out at the still waters on Lake Pontchartrain.

"Very, and I'm glad my first visit to Italy will include Rome, Tuscany, and Venice."

"If I know you, you've got the itinerary all planned out. Am I right?" he said smiling.

"Here's what I was thinking, but of course it's completely open to your suggestions and preferences . . ."

I pulled my laptop out of my bag and proceeded to go over what I had planned and the hotels I found—flying into Rome and spending four nights, then north to Tuscany for three more nights, followed by a train trip to Venice for an additional three nights.

What I didn't mention to Alex is that I'd spent hours and hours, over many days, looking for and booking the right places to stay. I wanted each place where we stayed to reflect the history and ambience of the region we were visiting. Rome needed to be an elegant historic villa that made us feel like time travelers to another era and lifestyle. Tuscany had to be a sprawling historic farm villa nested among the grape vines with magnificent views of the rolling Tuscan countryside. Venice, without a doubt, had to be an elegant boutique hotel converted from a historic palazzo, one that afforded a balcony overlooking one of the canals, and away from the most crowded tourist zones. Having never visited Italy before, I had to learn about the neighborhoods and towns in each region, understand the areas that were most likely to be overcrowded, and identify where we would be close enough to the things we wanted to see that the trip didn't end up being an exercise in coming and going with no time for the sites and experiences. In addition, I spent hours researching reviews for each hotel to ensure the pictures on their websites were authentic and taken recently.

I literally developed a day-by-day itinerary for how we would spend our time maximizing all that Rome, Tuscany, and Venice had to offer. I showed Alex the daily breakdown and what I thought would be a good way to spend each day, taking in the sights that were most interesting for us. "What do you think of this?"

Looking carefully over what I presented, Alex said, "That looks like a great itinerary and will give us ample time in each place to do the things we want to do."

"That's what I thought too. I've picked out what look like really nice places for us to stay in all three locations. A bit pricey, but I think worth the extra money. And besides, we save by being able to share a room."

"Did you go ahead and reserve the hotels?"

"Yes, I was afraid they'd sell out and with our trip coming up in about a month, I didn't want to lose them after I found them."

"Okay, just let me know what my half is for the hotels."

"I was thinking it may be easier to just leave them on my credit card, and I'll pay for the rooms when we check in. You can pay for our meals, entertainment, and transportation costs throughout Italy. That could really save us a lot of aggravation while we're traveling."

"Are you sure the rooms won't be more than the food and transportation?"

"I doubt it and we can keep an informal tab so that if either of us is too far out of bounds we can even it up at the end of the trip."

"Yeah, that works for me."

"Of course we'll each pay for our own airline tickets. Have you found any good deals on flights?"

"I think our best bet will be to fly out of Dulles into Frankfurt and then Rome. On the way back it's going to be Venice to Munich and then Dulles. The rates are pretty good and hopefully your free miles will work on those flights to cover the cost of your ticket."

"Sounds good. I think we're all set. I'll just need to do a little shopping for some new clothes. We'll be there in August so that means mostly shorts and lightweight clothing, I guess."

"Yeah, I'm not sure what it's like in August. When I was there a few years back, it was November and that meant dressing for cooler weather."

"What are you thinking in terms of transportation?"

"We won't need much in Rome. We can get around using public transportation, even from the gorgeous nineteenth-century villa you booked for us. I saw on their website that they offer complimentary pickup and ride from the airport, so we'll take advantage of that."

"Oh, that's great. And I guess there will be a lot of walking in Rome and I'm fine with that."

"Yes, then we'll take a train to Tuscany and pick up a rental car. We'll want to have a car to drive around Tuscany and visit the wineries and historic towns."

"You don't mind doing the driving? I'd rather not try to navigate in Italy."

Alex laughed. "I'd rather that too, and no, I don't mind doing all the driving. On our last day we'll drive to Florence, have a few hours to look around, and then catch a train to Venice. In Venice, we don't need transportation, it's walking only."

"This sounds perfect! I'm not sure which area I'm most excited to see, they're all so different."

We headed back to the hotel and parted ways at the elevator with plans to meet a little earlier in the morning, so we could get coffee without being rushed.

⊖•—×

That night I had an unusual dream that left me wondering about its meaning long after the trip to Northshore was over.

Alex was driving very fast in a sporty black SUV. He was cutting on and off the highway, sometimes taking us off-road, with the SUV in four-wheel drive. It was exhilarating and fun as we went over hills, into valleys, cut back onto the highway, and then sped off-road again. I was holding on tight to the grip bar and laughing when he cut through some woods and pulled up hard and fast in front of a hidden little bungalow with a front porch and pretty green front door.

We got out of the SUV and I asked, "Where are we? What is this place?"

Alex just smiled and said, "Come on," as he headed up the steps to the porch. I followed him as he opened the front door for me and said, "Go in."

I stepped into the house and was surprised to be surrounded by a dozen or more darling, little furry kittens of all colors. There was a nice lady there, and she was caring for the kittens and some adult cats too. I looked around in wonder, "What is this place? Why are these kittens here?"

Alex responded, "They are up for adoption."

"All of them? Ooh, this one is so cute, can I pick it up?" A gray kitten with a furry white face and neck and an extremely unusual orange-tipped tail was walking through my ankles and purring while nuzzling its face in my pant legs.

"Sure," said the lady in the house, "Just watch out, they have sharp little claws."

Alex was standing back with his arms crossed, watching me with an amused look on his face. He was enjoying my reaction to the kittens and the surprise destination.

I picked up the kitten and cuddled it in the crook of my neck. It was squirmy and gripped my blouse with its front-paw claws, "Ouch, that hurts," I said, and tried to put the kitten down, but it was now holding on with its claws.

Alex reached over and gently pulled the kitten off and sat it down. I continued to look around and despite the need to have one pried loose from my neck, I was enthralled with them.

"I want to adopt one!" I said.

Alex smiled and said, "Okay, but you need to remember it's not all fluff and fun," and he walked over to a closed door and opened it for me, saying, "There is this."

I stepped over and looked through the door. It led to stairs leading down to the basement and at the end of the stairs was another door through which the cats came and went to their litter boxes. It smelled unpleasant and was altogether enough to discourage me from wanting to adopt a kitten.

"*Ohhh . . . right, of course. I forgot about the litter boxes,*" I said, *stepping back from the open doorway.*

"*Are you ready to go?*" asked Alex.

Alex opened the front door for me and ran ahead, down the steps. He turned and lifted me down, off of the porch, and onto the ground next to the SUV. I liked this sensation and wanted to go back up the steps to be lifted down again, but I didn't. We jumped into the SUV and Alex started the engine and sped off, taking us off-road again, moving fast over the terrain, until we pulled out of the woods and back onto the highway.

⊖━━━✗

I awoke as my alarm was just getting ready to sound. *What a weird dream,* I thought to myself. *What was that all about?* Since crossing the lake into St. Tammany Parish, I'd been having vivid dreams, but this one seemed to be trying to convey a message of some sort. I told Alex about the dream on our way to our last day of meetings at the Stennis Space Center. He laughed and said that having had cats off and on his whole life, it was good that I was warned.

That evening we went to the French Quarter so that Alex could see and experience it. It was pretty much as I remembered. Unless you're a local or have a local showing you around, it's easy to fall into the tourist-quality experiences. We had a mediocre dinner, stopped in a few bars for drinks that were mostly sugary mix and little else, and generally overpaid for everything. Alex didn't seem impressed, but now he could say he'd been there and had seen it. The most memorable event of the evening occurred on our way back to the car as we were leaving. I was wearing one of my new pairs of sandals. Avoiding stepping in liquid of any kind had been a high priority for me all evening. I'd been keeping a vigilant eye and pointing out places not to step as we walked around. When we crossed Bourbon Street on our way back to where the car was parked, there was a significantly large puddle of... something in our path. Alex leaped over it and onto the sidewalk. When I stepped forward to leap over it, my foot hit a patch of ice cubes. A bartender had dumped a bucket of ice in the street. I slipped and my entire foot slid into the depths of the puddle of unknown liquid! Alex caught me, preventing me from falling into the puddle, but my foot was soaked to the ankle. Alex doubled over with laughter. After my fussing all evening about not stepping in anything, karma got me in the end! We both laughed on and off the whole way back, but I was so grossed out that I made Alex stop where I could use a clean bathroom to wash my foot off. There was no way I could ride in the car for the better part of an hour with who knew what on my foot!

The next morning we headed to the airport. I sipped my coffee and looked out of the SUV window. The sun was rising on Lake Pontchartrain and the vast expanse of water was sparkling like thousands of perfectly cut diamonds. If I looked closely, I might see the Lady of the Lake nodding in my direction—her acknowledgement of our visit. It had been a magical week, there was no doubt in my mind that Northshore had its own kind of magic and Alex and I had been caught up in it, glowing with it. Some of the locals recognized it when they encountered us—I saw it in their faces throughout the week. From the moment we crossed the lake into St. Tammany Parish, we were enchanted. I wanted to come back, and I wondered if it would be the same if I did.

Chapter 19

Anticipation and curiosity shook me out of my state of sleepiness early Saturday morning and had me speeding down Route 7 toward Winchester. I couldn't wait to see what a week away from the house would mean. Last week was huge in the life of Merryhearth and I hated that I missed seeing the daily progress and checking on things. If everything had gone well, the house would be rid of the poorly constructed and falling down mid-twentieth-century outbuildings, the old kitchen and bathrooms, and the failing plaster throughout the gallery.

As I pulled into the driveway I noticed immediately that the 1960s-era barn that had been leaning forward at about a ten-degree angle was gone. In its place were two flat zones, one sitting below, the other above, with a gentle bank of soil joining them. My mind went immediately to the landscaping possibilities—no grading required! Next, I noticed that at the end of the driveway the same era two-story garage, which had been leaning about ten degrees to the right, was gone. Now there was an unobstructed view of the pretty little brick smokehouse, original to the property.

"What a difference!" I said out loud.

I made my way up the front steps, sidestepping the holes in the portico floor—*Note to self, have Josh temporarily cover the holes with plywood sheets*—and unlocked the front door. I noticed a difference in the hall as soon as I stepped into the house, the hall was much brighter. I followed the light into the drawing room. From where I was standing, I had a commanding view through the drawing room into the depths of the library. I gasped in amazement!

"Oh, how beautiful!" I said to no one at all.

When Josh and his crew pulled the old lean-to addition off of the back of the house, the big, six-over-six double sash library windows were exposed to the outside. Sunlight now streamed into the room, making it bright, and airy, and inviting. Before, the library looked into the dark, dingy lean-to interior. Now the view from the library was across the vast expanse of the back lawn, all the way to the woods with their understory of honeysuckle, blackberry bushes, and wildflowers, and their ceiling of a myriad of mature trees—maple, elm, and oak. The woods were one of the most pleasing features of the property and probably one of the least appreciated by former owners. They created an impenetrable curtain of tree branches and leaves that made for a natural and beautiful privacy barrier across the back of the acreage. This change to the library was a delightful and unexpected surprise!

"Merryhearth, how long has it been since your library windows enjoyed the warmth of the sunlight?"

She didn't answer me, but I could feel the positive energy of this epic improvement and I knew the library would be one of the rooms where I spent many hours surrounded by my books, looking out onto the peaceful panorama around me.

I walked through the library and into the far end of the hall on my way to the kitchen. Josh had not gutted the kitchen. I assumed the crew ran out of time or maybe out of room in the construction dumpsters. The same was true of the two old bathrooms. The tub, sink, and toilet of the 1940s-era bathroom was untouched, including the disgusting, dysfunctional toilet stained black by who knew what. The 1980s-era bathroom was also still in place. This one was pretty gross as well, but it functioned.

As I made my way to the gallery, I quickly realized I'd forgotten to open the doors and allow the air to start flowing through the house. It was getting hotter with each step upward, and more humid. When I reached the gallery, I estimated the temperature to be close to one hundred degrees and water droplets were sliding down the walls where the humid, hot air was coming in contact with the cooler plastered walls. *Welcome to the last week of July in Virginia*, I thought to myself.

Upon entering the gallery I encountered another surprise. The failing plaster had been removed and in its place was what I could only describe as a beautiful work of art. Thousands of hand cut and carefully pieced together strips of heart pine formed what looked like the hull of a giant sailing ship. The pine lath strips were still intact across the ceiling and looked like they had been preserved in a time capsule created the day they were cut. They had been fashioned into the shape of an inverted bowl across the span of the underside of the hip roof. When finished, the hand-applied plaster, clinging to the lath, would have created the effect of a subtle dome. I wondered why Josh had left it in place and I hoped there was a way to save it, but knowing the roof's support beam was broken, I couldn't see how the lath could be left intact, nor could I imagine that replastering the gallery was anything I could afford to do.

My cell rang, and I looked at the incoming caller on the screen, "Hi Josh! Your timing is perfect! I'm at the house now looking at the work from last week."

"I'm in the driveway. Want to come out? I'll fill you in on what we did. It's cooler out here."

As I stepped into the shade of the big maple tree next to the driveway, I felt the immediate drop in temperature.

"Wow, it really is much cooler out here," I remarked. "Central air-conditioning is a must for this house. Did you know it's raining on the gallery level?"

"Yeah, it gets pretty hot up there."

"So how did it go last week? The outbuildings being gone is a huge improvement! And I was so pleasantly surprised by the difference made to the library with that lean-to removed."

"We made good progress, but the guys didn't get to the bathrooms or kitchen, ran out of time, and I'll need to order more dumpsters. Would you believe they're out of dumpsters through the end of August?"

"I guess this is a busy construction time. Tell me about the lath on the gallery ceiling. Did you leave it up for a reason?"

"No, it has to all come down."

"That's kind of a shame, it's absolutely beautiful. I can't even imagine the kind of craftsmanship that went into measuring, and cutting, and piecing it all together. It's a work of art."

"Huh, yeah . . . I guess so."

"So is the plan still to examine the broken beam from inside and repair it without removing the metal roof?"

"Yeah, once we rip all that lath out," *I felt myself wince*, "we can get to the beam and replace or repair it. Then we can put spray-foam insulation up against the roof and frame it out for drywall. You won't have any heat loss through the roof anymore."

I wondered how much heat was actually lost through an inch and a half of horsehair and fine-ground clay plaster, lath strips, and metal roofing. I knew not much if any was lost through twelve-inch-thick, solid-brick, walls. I was so tired of hearing how the old ways were inefficient, and the new ways were better. I doubted new construction materials could have withstood the kind of damage and neglect that Merryhearth had been subjected to and been as resilient as the old materials had proven to be. How many new construction homes could have withstood what Merryhearth had for decades?

"So what will the guys do now that you don't have access to dumpsters?"

"We'll go ahead and pull the lath down, and I'll take it in my dump truck to the landfill. Then we'll fix the broken beam and frame it all out and get the drywall up. The drywall can be finished later when the drywall guys can come in."

"Sounds like a good way to keep moving forward. Has the bank paid you yet for finishing the phase-one work?"

"No, they're giving me the runaround when I stop in or call to see what's going on. I can't seem to get a straight answer out of any of them."

"That's ridiculous. I'll call them on Monday. You've done the work and I've approved it for full payment. I'll find out what's going on and let you know what I learn."

"Thanks. I appreciate that."

On my way back to Leesburg I thought about the bank giving Josh a hard time and wondered what on earth was going on. They were the bank—not a private checking account. Why would they be delaying in making the payments? Was there something Josh wasn't telling me? Did he owe them money and was there some private deal between them? I couldn't imagine what it was, but my powers of perception were telling me that something wasn't right.

⊖——⚞

Jill was the first one logged into our daily team sync-up video on Monday morning. As I was logging into the video call, I could see her reading emails on her computer screen. She looked anxious, and I wondered if something had happened at work on Friday while Alex and I were making our way home from New Orleans. I didn't have any emails from her or Rory to indicate there was a problem, but sometimes Fridays were not a day when problems got dealt with. I was thinking about this when Alex's face appeared in the Brady Bunch box on my computer screen.

In as cheerful a voice as I could muster, I said, "Good morning, team! Happy Monday!"

Alex groaned, "Is it Monday already?"

"Sounds like you had an eventful weekend."

"Something like that," he grumbled while reaching for his coffee.

Jill chimed in with only a slightly more energetic tone, "Good morning, you guys. How were your flights home on Friday?"

"Fortunately uneventful for me," I said.

"Same for me, easy flight back," added Alex.

"Jill, did anything develop in the office on Friday?" I asked.

"You have this crazy sixth sense! As a matter of fact, yes."

"Uh-oh, let me guess—before we could get to Rory to warn him and plan our defensive strategy, Delores Umbridge showed up in her pink business suit and heels and started trouble?"

"Pretty much—I don't have all the details but when I called Rory to set up the meeting with him for this week, like we discussed, he said, 'Is this about Deborah Callahan?' and I almost choked!"

"Did he tell you why or what was going on with her?"

"He just said she was looking for a lot of information and asked him a bunch of questions about the project."

"Okay, that's not too bad. There's still time to plan for how we'll thwart her attack if one is coming."

"I would have sent you an email or called you, but Rory said not to ruin your weekend and that it could wait until Monday."

I wasn't sure that waiting until Monday was the best course of action, but Rory's thoughtfulness was commendable. As soon as our video call was over, I pulled up Rory's shared calendar and scheduled an in-person meeting with him for the earliest opening, Tuesday morning, 8:00 a.m. I received his acceptance of my meeting invitation almost immediately.

⚊⚬⚊

My alarm went off at 4:00 a.m., and I was pulling into the parking lot at the commuter bus station by five thirty. From the vast number of people and cars, you'd have thought that five thirty in the morning was a normal time of day, rather than a time when we should all be sleeping. The workforce in the Washington, D.C., metro area were some of the most stressed-out people I had encountered. Most of these people started their workday as soon as the commuter bus pulled out of the lot. They'd be reading and responding to emails, working on their laptops, and making notations on documents they pulled out of their briefcases. The ride home would be slightly different. Many of them, due to sheer exhaustion, would be sound asleep within minutes of the bus making its last stop—mouths open, heads bouncing into the aisle when the bus hit a pothole, or worse, slowly migrating like the Leaning Tower of Pisa toward the shoulder of the person next to them.

There was an unspoken brotherhood among the nearly one million of us who put in twelve-to-thirteen-hour days, came home to families who needed our undivided attention for several more hours, and then woke up long before dawn to start it all over again. Like most big cities, salaries were high, but so was the cost of living. Before you knew it, you were in a loop of living that necessitated you sleep less, eat faster, multitask constantly, and sacrifice your quality of life, and sometimes your health. I'd heard of people who escaped and never looked back because they were better in every respect for their decision to get out. I hoped that Rory's decision to allow my team to work full-time from home would be a way to escape this loop of living that resulted in diminishing returns.

I tapped on Rory's office door promptly at 8:00 a.m. I reminded myself to start with the touchy-feely comments and not just jump right into the topic I was there to discuss.

"Good morning, Rory!"

"Hi, Amanda, how was the trip in?"

"Long, I definitely don't miss that commute."

"Come in, sit down, would you like some coffee?"

"No, thank you. I had a good bit already this morning. So, how was your trip with your son to check out the campus at William and Mary?"

"Oh, thank you for asking! It was great! He's going to love it."

We chitchatted for ten minutes. I had to tap my foot on the floor to keep my face calm. I only had thirty minutes with him, and I needed to cover a lot of territory. Finally, I had my break—*Now whatever you do, don't call Deborah Delores.*

"Tell me about Deborah's visit with you last week," I said.

"She wants all the documentation for the project, the cost analysis, project management plan, change management plan, risk analysis and mitigation strategy, everything and anything you've got."

"We have tons of documentation, including everything you just mentioned. We also have several comprehensive briefings that we've given to different audiences, customized for executives, agency stakeholders, and anyone who will be a

177

part of the new business processes."

"Did you ever brief Deborah on the project?"

"As the director's special advisor, she was invited to the briefing we did with the director."

"Oh, yes, I remember that now. She didn't come and when you circled back with her to set up a makeup briefing, she said to just forward the PowerPoint and that would be enough for her."

"Exactly. I really think we need to brief her. Just giving her all the documentation will open the door for her to interpret it the way she wants and put her own spin on it."

"Amanda, don't you think you're being a little harsh? I see her interest as a very positive sign."

Uh-oh, I thought. *As the saying goes, Houston, we have a problem.*

"I hope you are right. Unfortunately, past experience with her has established a pattern. More than once she has voiced complete confidence in our projects, then, once they are fully underway, she takes a deeper interest. That interest leads to her being a negative force and turning key supporters against the project."

"Why do you think she does this?"

"Honestly, I think it's how she survives in a very political work environment, and it's effective for her. With laser precision she picks out a piece of data or information and builds a reasonable argument for why its flawed or a problem. The director hears her argument, always alone, without the project leaders being present. He's grateful to have someone on his side who found this 'terrible thing' and saved his . . . umm . . . saved him from embarrassment."

"Is she going to find something?"

"She always finds something. However, most of the time we are able to either explain it or fix it."

"Okay, well then, let's give her what she's asking for, and

I'll ask her to come to me first if she thinks something is amiss with the project."

I wasn't in a position to debate the approach he was suggesting. I suspected Deborah was in full *derail the project* mode and the last thing she would do was confer with Rory first. That would totally defeat her purpose of making herself invaluable, again, to the director.

I nodded and added, "I think it will be best if the documentation comes from you. That will give you the opportunity to further establish your rapport with her. And, Rory, this is a transformative project for the agency. Our managers, our employees, and our HR department desperately need these modernizations, so please know I'll do whatever is needed to keep this project on track."

"Thank you, Amanda. I can't imagine that Deborah doesn't also see the value of this project for the agency. I just need to do a little more hand-holding than I have. It's really my fault probably for not making more of a point to reach out to her. I'll do that now. She'll be fine and the project will be fine."

On the way back to Leesburg that afternoon I crafted a long email to Jill and Alex, letting them know how the day had gone and that all the project documentation was being handed off to Delores Umbridge. I hit the Send button and leaned back in the bus seat. It was deathly quiet on the bus and, as I looked around, I noted that most of the exhausted commuters were asleep, including the man sitting next to me, who was precariously close to my shoulder in his comatose state. Danielle, who also took the commuter bus from Leesburg, liked to tell total strangers that she slept with a different man nearly every day. I guess that was true of everyone on the bus. With any luck, my days of commuting would be few and far between. Being able to work virtually from home would be critical after I moved to Winchester. And with that I texted Josh: "Hi, Josh. I called the bank today. They said the check's in the mail." I didn't get a reply, but hopefully that was one potential catastrophe avoided.

Part Three

Exploring

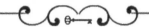

"Seldom, very seldom, does complete truth belong to any human disclosure; seldom can it happen that something is not a little disguised or a little mistaken."

– Jane Austen, *Emma*

Chapter 20

I wanted everything during the Italy trip to be perfect, so I spent the first couple of weeks of August getting ready. I bought clothes, went to the gym every day, and scheduled a session at the day spa for an expensive, top-of-the-line spray tan, something I'd never done before. I packed and repacked my suitcase. I mentally went through the outfits for each day and each evening. We'd be gone for eleven days and ten nights—including travel days. Since we'd be sharing a bathroom, I bought a set of matching pink-and-black toiletry bags so that I could keep my assortment of beauty products tucked neatly out of sight. I thought of every detail, including buying all new pajamas—really cute ones—a different set for each night, which included pajama shorts. I didn't want a T-shirt nighty getting twisted up around my waist under the covers. The day before we left, I had a mani-pedi and touched up a few gray strands in my hair that were making my curls look more like dyed platinum than the natural blond that they were.

Everything was set. I had planned and planned for the trip and had attended to every detail of our accommodations and sightseeing. The flight would be long, but we had a gorgeous historic Aventine Hill villa awaiting us when we arrived in Rome. It would be three and a half glorious days, eating wonderful Italian cuisine, touring a two-thousand-year-old city built by Roman emperors, exploring the wonders of Vatican City, and experiencing some of the most epochal architecture, sculptures, and paintings created by humankind. Then we would be off to Tuscany where we would be relaxing at a restored, historic, Chianti Region farm estate, learning about wine and food, cooking and tasting the delicacies of Tuscany, and touring historic hill towns full of ancient cathedrals, superb handmade artisan treasures, farmers markets, and wineries—lots of wineries!

No sooner would we be finishing our stay in Tuscany than it would be time to enjoy Venice, after a stop in the iconic city of Florence. In Venice, we would be staying in a historic palazzo with a spacious room that overlooked the canal from a set of French doors opening onto a private balcony. We would enjoy more gourmet dishes, this time from the sea, walk the narrow alleys and visit the shops, stumble across quaint churches opening onto unexpected tiny neighborhood squares, and spend a day shopping the island of Murano for the perfect chandelier for Merryhearth's dining room.

I would be doing all of this with Alex—gorgeous, fun to be with, incredibly considerate, smart, *and did I mention gorgeous*, Alex. We loved all the same things—sightseeing, historic architecture, unique shopping venues, tasting and learning about wine, and amazing food. Doing all of this in Italy was ramping up the fun factor exponentially! Alex seemed excited too. He texted me often about the upcoming trip, and we executed our planned absence from work very carefully. Everyone, including Jill and Rory, thought that Alex had decided to take the same days off as me because it would be a quiet time in the office. The last two weeks of August were a typical time for the federal workforce to go on vacation and enjoy the last part of summer before the kids had to be back in school. No one suspected that Alex and I were actually going to be vacationing together—in Italy no less! Danielle knew the details, of course, and was still not overly enthusiastic about the plan. Alex and I talked about being careful once we were back at work to not give away that we had been together. I would talk about Italy, and he would just be vague about what he did during his time off. I warned Alex against posting any photos to his social media that could be seen by people at work. He said that wasn't a problem as he kept work and his social life very separate. Nonetheless, we decided it was best that he not include me in any photos that he posted to social media while in Italy. We had thought of everything.

At last, the day arrived for us to start our vacation. We met at the international terminal at Dulles. Alex was on time for once, and we boarded the plane together. He took pictures of us with his phone, sitting in our seats, side by side, as the plane doors were being closed and secured for liftoff. I waved and smiled at the camera. Our vacation had begun!

As I settled into my window seat with Alex stretched out in his aisle seat next to me, I thought about how everything had fallen into place, more perfectly—more beautifully, than I could have imagined when I was trying to piece together what was left of my life after the explosion. I had not only discovered Merryhearth Manor, but had finagled the money to buy it, and the know-how and contractor crew to rehabilitate it. At work, I was able to have my cake and eat it too, with the arrangement that Rory had approved to work from home while the big project I was leading was being implemented. That meant at least a year of avoiding the life-debilitating commute, and hopefully it would evolve into a permanent work arrangement once the project was successfully launched and my value to the agency cemented—and the most unexpected twist of all was the friendship that had developed between Alex and me. A friendship that quite literally had brought me back to life. Because of Alex, I wanted to *be* fun again and to have fun. I wanted to feel young, and happy, and playful. I wanted to look pretty, and be sexy, and be noticed. Alex was so enjoyable to be with and so handsome, and I was better with him than I could remember being in a very, very long time. For that, he would always hold a special place in my heart. I maneuvered myself in my seat to take up a little more of the shared armrest between us, and this resulted in our shoulders touching, ever so lightly. I felt a tiny flutter of butterflies in my stomach. This was going to be the best vacation ever.

After the flight attendant finished the safety announcements, the pilot came on, "Ladies and gentlemen, this is your captain speaking. Welcome aboard this nonstop flight from Washington, D.C., to Frankfurt. The weather ahead is good, and we're expecting a smooth flight and on-time landing. Sit back and enjoy the ride."

The hum of the jet's engines was loud inside the cabin and Alex leaned toward me to talk. "The day we are in Florence, I need to do some shopping."

"How much time will we have in Florence?" I asked. That day of our trip was a bit of a mystery to me because Alex had made all the transportation arrangements, and we were basically going to Florence to turn in our rental car and catch the train to Venice.

"Depending on when we get there, probably no more than two or three hours."

"Oh, so probably not time to see much?"

"No. And I want to find the jewelry store where I bought my silver chain when I visited Florence a few years back."

"Oh. Did you want to buy yourself another one?"

"No. I want to get a gold bracelet for Dion."

I'd only heard Dion's name mentioned in passing, and didn't think he'd been on Alex's radar screen for very long.

"How long have you known Dion?"

"I met him about a month ago, but we just started going out very recently."

"And you want to give him an expensive gold bracelet from Italy?" I felt Alex stiffen at my question.

"Bracelets are my thing. I like to give them as gifts when I really like someone."

"Okay, sure. I like jewelry stores and if this one has good deals on Italian gold, maybe I'll treat myself while you are picking out something for Dión, or is it Díon?" The name kind of stuck on the tip of my tongue as I was trying to sound natural.

"De'On, he spells it capital D—lower case e—apostrophe—capital O—and lower-case n," said Alex.

"Oh, is he French?"

"No," said Alex.

I thought the bracelet seemed a bit excessive, especially after knowing someone for just about a month, but I had no insights to the courting rituals of the gay world. Maybe this was a perfectly average and expected event after about a month? And, there was his statement, "When I really like someone . . ." Was this the start of Alex's next *serious* relationship? I knew Alex was a bit of a player from things I had picked up on, especially when I went to happy hour with him a few times in D.C. Once he had taken me to his favorite gay bar. I was a little confused about why he chose to take me to the gay bar, but I was fine with it. After sipping our drinks, he had asked me what I thought, and if it was what I expected. I said that it didn't seem different than any other bar. He had replied, "I can change that if you like." At the time, I responded with, "What, with the snap of your fingers, the party will be on?" and he had smiled and said, "Yes, pretty much."

There had been other glimpses of Alex's D.C. reputation, but they weren't of any consequence when he and I were together, so I didn't give it much thought. Now I wondered what role De'On was playing in his life, and I wondered if it would alter the dynamic between the two of us. I felt uneasy.

As the pilot had promised, the flight was uneventful and smooth flying. We made our connection in Frankfurt, but not before making the mistake of ordering food at the airport. We were both starved, and we found a place to eat nearly as soon as we disembarked from the plane. After looking at the selections on the menu, mostly sausages of a multitude of varieties, we settled on German meatloaf and potato salad. I like meatloaf and I like German-style potato salad, so this seemed like a good option. We were both surprised when our plates were handed to us. I can only describe what appeared to be two bread-shaped and -sized, thick slices of . . . hot dog. Imagine a hot dog—same color, same consistency, same smell, the size and shape of a big slice of meatloaf—that's what this was. We each managed a few bites and then focused on our potato salad.

"Thank goodness where we're going, finding good food won't be an issue," said Alex.

I laughed. "No, if anything we'll have more options than we can deal with."

The last leg of the flight was over before we knew it and we touched down in Rome at 10:00 a.m., the day after we'd left Washington, D.C. Alex snapped a photo of us "post flight" before I could stop him. We were looking a bit ragged and even though I didn't want to admit it, the before and after flight photos were cute. I smiled as I thought to myself, *This is it— we're in Rome!*

Just after we collected our luggage, we spotted a white-haired gentleman wearing a black jacket with the hotel's in-signia on it. He was holding up a sign with the hotel's name and logo. We introduced ourselves and soon were settling into the back seat of a modest black sedan.

"Wow, that could not have gone more smoothly," I said to Alex.

"No, that was much easier than trying to navigate our way to the hotel on our own, and cheaper since it was included in the cost of the room."

Alex and I were quiet the remainder of the drive to the hotel. I couldn't believe I was in Rome. I absorbed everything I could see from the window of the sedan. I wanted to have a true sense for this place that I was visiting for the first time and which played such a major role in history and the evolu-tion of art, literature, and all the things that I found so fasci-nating. I soaked in the landscape, buildings, people, even the ugly graffiti—of which there was a surprising abundance, much of it sadly marring the façades of buildings that looked to be nineteenth-century historic beauties.

We pulled into the circular drive of the Aventine Hill villa, now converted to a four-star, boutique hotel, and I was thrilled to see that it looked as lovely in person as it had in the online photos. It was small, by hotel standards, and the recep-tion desk was immediately inside the front door. I looked around and although it had changed significantly during its metamorphosis from a home to a hotel, I could still make out the floor plan and layout from its private villa lifetime.

Another white-haired gentleman stood behind the recep-tion desk. He was dressed formally in a suit and tie and crisp, white shirt. His dark gray suit jacket bore the emblem of the hotel in an embroidered patch sewn onto his lapel.

"Yes, madam, how may I help you?" he stated in English, laced with exactly the Italian accent I had imagined, although not the warmth.

"Buongiorno. I'm Amanda Grayson, here for check-in." *I thought he must know this as his driver just dropped us at the door after retrieving us from the airport.*

"Buongiorno. Sì, we have you in our luxury, king-size bedroom, overlooking the garden, is that correct?"

At this point he looked at Alex, back at me, and then at Alex again with what appeared to be a look of absolute disdain. I might have thought I was imagining it if I hadn't picked up on Alex's reaction to his look. I watched as Alex took a step backward, straightened his posture, casually placed his right arm on the reception desk, and got a smirky half smile on his face.

"Yes, that's correct," I said.

"How will you be paying?" he asked.

"With the credit card I used to reserve the room."

"May I see the credit card, per favore?"

"Certainly," I handed over the credit card.

"I will need to see your passports as well."

I wasn't expecting this, but I guessed it was *normale.* "Here you are," I said, as I slid my passport to him. Alex slid his over as well without saying a single word. He placed our passports side by side on the desk. He looked at the names and photos, then lifted one eyebrow and flared his nostrils.

"Very well, madam. Here is the key to your room and your documents. Our breakfast is served in the garden each morning from 7:30 a.m. to 9:30 a.m. The elevator is down the hall and to the right. Enjoy your stay with us."

"Thank you," was all I could muster, and Alex said nothing at all as we headed down the hall, pulling our rollie suitcases behind us, stacked with our carry-on bags and Alex's backpack.

We found the room and the key opened the door effortlessly. We stepped into a small hall with two rooms, one to the right and one to the left—a spacious bedroom and a large luxury bathroom.

"This is nice, really nice," said Alex as he walked to the window to look out and turn down the temperature on the window air conditioner.

"Yes, no decoraphobia attacks here. It almost makes up for the chilly reception we just received downstairs."

"The hotel manager could use a lesson in welcoming his guests," said Alex.

"Was he the *manager*? I haven't felt that awkward and uncomfortable in I can't say how long."

"He seemed a bit judgy, and yes, his lapel pin stated 'Directorre Del'Albergo'," said Alex.

I continued, "I think he disapproved of me because we're an unmarried couple sharing a room. I felt like he thought I was, I don't know, some kind of *harlot*, or something. I can't believe in this day and age I'm saying that, but he clearly had some issue with us."

Alex said nothing in reply and began to unpack his luggage. His silence sent me into a spiral of worrisome thoughts . . . *Did Alex think the disapproval was because of our age difference? . . . Was Alex embarrassed to have the hotel manager think we were a couple? . . . Was Alex embarrassed because I paid for the room, leaving the manager to wonder what our relationship was?* Something was off balance, and the manager had made our first personal impression of Rome unpleasant. I didn't want our trip to start that way. I was accustomed to being welcomed by the Lady of the Lake and embraced by the snow-tipped mountains of the Rockies. I expected Rome to be even better, but instead I felt like a fish out of water and, for the first time ever, I worried that Alex was second-guessing being with me. Unlike work trips, this trip event made us a "couple" . . . of sorts. We weren't a couple that was sleeping together—well, actually we were sleeping together—but we weren't *sleeping* together. We were—however you looked at it—traveling as a couple, a man and a woman, just the two of us, sharing a hotel room, and meals, and everything—and it wasn't because of work, or any requirement—we were on vacation, by choice, just the two of us ... together.

Chapter 21

The thought of our first dinner in Italy was enough to overcome the jet lag that was starting to catch up with me. "Let's find a place to have an early dinner. I'd like to expunge the memory of my hotdog-loaf."

"Good idea. I'm starved."

"Where should we go?" I asked.

"There's what looks like a local neighborhood place within walking distance of here, and the menu has some nice options," said Alex, looking at his cell phone.

"Sounds perfect. I want to change clothes and freshen up, and then let's head out."

In the spacious bathroom with lots of mirrors, I donned one of my new cute outfits and sandals. I was feeling very chic in my polka-dot shorts and matching tie-up, sleeveless blouse. Alex changed into shorts and a T-shirt, and we headed out the front door. The judgy manager nodded as we passed the reception desk. I smiled awkwardly but said nothing. Once we were off the hill, the streets were much busier with a lot of traffic and quite a few stores and restaurants. We walked about five blocks, and it didn't take long to realize that Italy, in

August, was incredibly hot and humid. I was feeling sticky, and my face was beading with sweat. Heat and humidity are not my friends. My natural curls turn to frizz and my hair takes on the look of stringy cotton candy. To make matters worse, the hotter I get, the redder my face gets—not that cute blush of pink, I'm talking seriously blotchy red.

We found the restaurant, and it didn't take long for the waiter to recommend we try a sample platter to share of local meats, cheeses, bread, and fresh tomatoes and cucumbers, followed by their homemade pasta—we chose different sauces for the pasta. With this we ordered a bottle of wine, also recommended by the waiter.

"I like the selection of meats and cheeses. They all taste great, but they're a bit salty, even the cheeses," I commented to Alex.

"I think it's the way they make and cure everything."

When our dishes of pasta arrived, we sampled each other's, and neither of us could decide which one we liked better. The wine was especially nice, a rosé of Italian origin, of course. Things were feeling more normal now between us, more the way I imagined it would be. The waiter eventually brought the check to Alex. I loved how we weren't rushed, and the waiter and other restaurant staff were friendly and welcoming—thank goodness.

After paying, we left to walk around and check out the nearby shops. Alex also scoped out the buses and bus stops we would need in the morning to take us into the various sightseeing neighborhoods. One of the little shops we entered had an eclectic mix of artisan treasures including beautiful serving bowls and platters—hand-painted with lemons—leather purses and wallets, ceramic flower baskets, handmade garden pots, and jewelry. Alex decided to look for something to take home for his niece. While he was shopping, I wandered over to the jewelry counter. Something had caught my eye and I wanted a closer look.

"May I see the thimble please," I asked the salesclerk, who looked like she could be the shop owner.

"Here you go. It's ten-carat gold and can have a little ring added so that you can attach it to a charm bracelet or a necklace."

It was a tiny, dainty gold thimble, with what looked like intricate carving that didn't appear to be machine stamped. The quality was quite impressive.

"What does it say inside? I can't quite make it out."

"Oh, it has '*Roma*,' and the year inscribed on the inside edge."

"I really like it. May I ask what it costs?"

"Of course! Let me check . . . it's fifty-two euro."

I had an idea—a plan for the thimble—and the price was within my shopping budget, so I asked if they had little gift bags.

"I can give you a little red-velvet pull-string pouch to put it in, *senza alcun costo*."

"Oh, that would be perfect! Thank you! And I don't want my friend to see it, so let me pay you for it now."

Alex bought a couple of things to take home to his family and friends, and I slipped my purchase into my purse without him noticing it. My plan was to present the thimble to Alex as a memento of our trip and how much his friendship had come to mean to me. Like when Wendy presented Peter Pan with a thimble, telling him it was a kiss, I would give Alex this little gold "kiss." In so many ways, it was the perfect symbol of our unique friendship that had taken a more meaningful course with his pronouncement in Orlando that he was a "really good kisser." I would wait until our last day in Italy and then tell him that I wanted to give him a kiss, while handing over the little, red-velvet pouch.

Back at the hotel, we walked around the first floor to see

the decor and find the garden where breakfast would be set up. I kept a vigil eye out for the manager, feeling very much like a naughty teenager, but fortunately we didn't see him, or anyone else for that matter. We were both by now very tired and jet-lagged, not to mention soaked through with perspiration from the walk up the steep hill to the hotel. In our room, the air conditioner was running hard to keep the temperature cool, and Alex offered me first dibs on a shower while he caught up on his email and social media. He'd been taking a lot of pictures, including of our hotel room and our plates of food and wine at the restaurant. I asked him to send me the pictures of the trip after we got home. I figured with him taking so many pictures, that was one thing I didn't need to be focused on.

It didn't take long to realize the window air conditioner's cool air couldn't penetrate the closed door of the steamy bathroom. This was going to be a problem as I was as sticky after my shower as I had been when I started, and there was no way I could blow-dry my hair and apply makeup in the morning in this bathroom oven.

"The bathroom is all yours," I announced to Alex after I emerged in my new pink-pajama-short-set with my wet hair forming ringlets and my face scrubbed clean of all makeup. I was pretty sure he had never seen me in this state of "simplicity," and true to form, he politely made a point of not mentioning it or looking too hard in my direction.

"I have to warn you, it's very hot and steamy in there. The air conditioner doesn't cool the bathroom."

"Oh, great," he murmured and shut the door behind him.

Alex was in the bathroom for a really long time. I unpacked and organized my clothes, shoes, and toiletries for the duration of our stay, checked and answered emails—mostly from work—pulled back and folded down the coverlet on the bed, and placed the pillows that were in decorative pillow shams and the toss pillows on the chair in the corner. I was keenly aware that most hotels don't wash bedspreads/coverlets or the pillow shams, much less toss pillows, between guests. If you don't want to be in contact with the last guest's *essence*, keep your contact to the sheets and pillowcases, which are washed daily. Fortunately, the sheets were nice quality and the bed linens were immaculately clean, based on my expert inspection.

I was reading a tour guide of Rome by the light of the nightside table on my side of the bed, propped up on two king-size pillows, when Alex finally came out of the bathroom. I was exhausted from having not slept on the plane during the flight over, but I didn't want to be sound asleep when he came out of the bathroom.

"Feel better after getting a nice shower?" I asked.

"Much better! But you're right, there's no AC in there. It gets really hot."

"Maybe tomorrow morning we can take turns using the room to get ready. I can stay in the garden with my coffee while you get ready, and then we can switch?"

"That's a good idea. That way we can leave the bathroom door open," said Alex, with relief in his tone.

He slid into the bed wearing a pair of gym shorts and a T-shirt and turned out the light on his side.

"You can read as long as you like, the light won't bother me. Once my head hits the pillow, I'll be out," said Alex, followed by a considerable yawn.

"No, I'm exhausted from not sleeping in close to forty-eight hours. Lights out for me."

I turned off my lamp and settled into my side of the big king-size bed. I've always slept with a body pillow, so I pulled my spare king-size pillow out from behind my back and placed it in the middle of the bed between us. I was afraid that without the pillow, I might in my sleep mistake Alex for the body pillow! I had thought about what I would do if Alex mistook me for a body pillow—that would be okay I thought, however, I wasn't about to be the one to make a first advance. *Would he make the first advance?* In actuality, I couldn't picture more than spooning with Alex. That was as far as my desire was taking me. I knew what Danielle would say to this, "Yep, that's how it starts!" and maybe she would be right, but I wasn't feeling it, probably because I was so tired.

As my eyes adjusted to the minimal light in the dark room, and I adjusted myself on my side, body pillow pulled in—facing Alex—I didn't have to ponder the issue for long, or wonder what Alex was thinking as he lay on his back next to me. The loud hum of the air conditioner was suddenly interrupted by a thunderous, earsplitting sound. It made me jump, and in my startled state I lifted my head off the pillow, but before I had time to question the source of the noise, it repeated. Holy cow! The sound was loud enough to rattle the windows and be heard outside the room. It was Alex! He was snoring! Never had I heard anything like it—so loud, and so jagged, that it seemed unreal. I sat up in the bed and looked at him through the dark. He was completely passed out—dead to the world—and generating noises that seemed less like those of a human being and more like those of a cross between a humpback whale surfacing to exhale through its blowhole and a lion attacking a wildebeest in the Serengeti!

How was it possible that this beautiful man—and he was drop-dead gorgeous, even in his sleep—could be making these hideous noises? The sounds were excruciatingly loud, random in their pattern, of varying intensity, and continuous. I didn't know what to do. I didn't want to wake him, and besides, if he snored, waking him was only a temporary form of relief. I pulled my body pillow up and put it over my head to deafen the reverberations—no good. I looked around the room for ideas on how to minimize the sound. I could put my body pillow over *his* face—not a good idea. I could double the pillows over my head—*ewwww*—that meant using one of the pillow-sham pillows—*can't do it.* Maybe if I thought of the snoring as "white noise" I could fool myself into accepting it. I tried . . . I listened for patterns . . . I focused on pitch . . . I meditated with the noise . . . *NOT effing happening!* Then I remembered, somewhere inside a pocket, inside a cosmetic bag, inside a toiletry bag, I had a pair of foam earplugs. I kept them for travel, in case my hotel room ended up near an elevator or on the same floor with teenagers. I'd have to turn on the light to find them. I got out of bed, switched on my light, and began rummaging through my toiletry bags. The snoring continued uninterrupted, one minute it was the humpback whale creating a twelve-foot waterspout, and the next minute it was the lion going for the wildebeest. "Where are my earplugs!" I shouted frantically.

Ahh, I found them—two little bright orange foam earplugs! I squeezed first one and slipped it into my right ear, and then the other and slipped it into my left ear. As the gentle foam slowly expanded, the first noise to disappear was the high-pitched ring of the light bulb next to the bed, the next noise to disappear was the hum of the window unit air conditioner, and—wait for it—wait for it—*WHAT!* The snoric boom was still there! How could it be? The earplugs made only the slightest difference in the intensity of the noises Alex was making. I got back into bed with the earplugs in, I sandwiched my head between my pillow and my body pillow, and I made the ultimate sacrifice, I laid the icky pillow-sham pillow on top of that. I held the layers of pillows down with my arm, creating a small opening to breathe. It didn't make a bit of difference, none of it made any difference—the snoring continued, and I lay there wide awake.

The last time I looked at my cell, it was 5:00 a.m. I'd been checking the time just about once every hour or so, so I knew

I hadn't slept. Should I just get up now, I wondered. I tried one more time to fall asleep. When I next opened my eyes, Alex was sitting in the side chair in the room, dressed to go down for breakfast, reading the tour guidebook. Finally, I must have dozed off. What time was it? I looked at my cell, it was 7:00 a.m.

"Good morning!" said Alex. "I'm so glad you were able to sleep and didn't wake up too early like I did."

"Uh huh. What time did you wake up?"

"I woke up about 5:15 a.m. I must still be on D.C. time, but you seem to have adjusted quickly."

"It took me quite a while to fall asleep," I responded.

"It was probably all of those pillows you had stacked up around you. Maybe tonight, try scaling back, so you don't get overheated."

"I need coffee. Is it time for breakfast?"

"Almost, we can head down as soon as you're dressed."

"Okay. Coffee will be wonderful."

I put on a pair of jean shorts and a T-shirt, and hastily brushed my teeth. My hair was sticking out in all directions from going to bed with it wet and from tossing and turning all night. I tried to tame it a bit, but until I had some coffee, I couldn't function. I knew I looked a mess, but it couldn't be helped. Alex on the other hand was full of energy, looked rested and renewed, and had been up for a couple of hours getting ready for the day ahead of us. As we walked toward the garden, the breakfast spread was laid out in a room adjoining the outdoor tables. Attending the breakfast were three white-haired gentlemen in dark pants and shirts with the hotel logo. It wasn't my imagination that we got peculiar looks from them, and I wasn't in a great mood after two hours of sleep in three days.

"What do they do, clone these men? Aren't there any women that work here?" I said to Alex. Alex looked a bit surprised at my comment.

"The food looks great," commented Alex.

"Where's the coffee? I don't see the coffeepot."

"I'm not sure, I don't see one either," said Alex.

"I'm going to kill someone if there's no coffee," I said, not joking.

At this, one of the cloned, white-haired attendants invited us to sit at a table of our choice and asked if we'd like tea or coffee.

"Yes, coffee with a lot of cream . . . please," I managed to say in a somewhat civil tone.

"I'll have the same . . . black," said Alex.

The attendant motioned us toward the tables and added, "When you are ready, you may help yourselves to our breakfast selection."

Alex almost immediately helped himself to the food. I waited until I'd finished my first cup of coffee and had requested a second.

As I looked over the offerings, I was a bit surprised to find the same meats and cheeses and bread that had been in our dinner sample platter. In addition, there were sliced tomatoes with mozzarella, quartered tomatoes with cucumber slices, and diced tomatoes with hard-boiled egg slices and what looked like dill or cilantro. *That's a lot of tomatoes*, I thought to myself—I wasn't opposed to a charcuterie board and cheese and bread for breakfast, but I'd just eaten that the night before. Missing were cooked eggs, cooked bacon or ham, fresh fruit—albeit there was some canned fruit and a large assortment of jams and preserves, and any kind of bread other than baguette bread. *Okay Amanda*, I said to myself, *don't be an obnoxious American. You're in Rome, and the breakfast foods are different here. When in Rome, do as the Romans!* And with that I chose an assortment of salty meats, and salty cheese, some baguette bread, and a few tomatoes, *not my favorite vegetable.*

Alex seemed very pleased with the food selection and offered to let me take my shower first while he stayed in the garden.

"You'll probably need more time than I need," he said, "So why don't you go up first?"

What did that mean? If he was going to take as long in the bathroom as he did the night before, I doubted I would need more time than he needed, but I was glad to head up to the room. I needed to shake off the exhaustion and try to hit my reset button so that I was in the right frame of mind for the exploring we'd be doing. After all, I was in Rome!

Chapter 22

We had no problem using the local bus system to take us to Central Rome where we planned to spend our first full day seeing the historic sites. The people on the bus were much like people everywhere, women on their way to office jobs, kids on their way to school, and retirees who looked like they were headed to the market to do some shopping. They looked at us, so obviously American tourists. I smiled, nodded, and said *bonjourno* in response. I was determined to see as much of Rome as I could in our time here. We'd be walking everywhere we went, and I was dressed in comfortable walking shoes and one of my new outfits. We started at the Piazza Navona, arriving at about 10:00 a.m. Already the temperatures were in the nineties and the humidity, intensified by the sunlight, made it feel even hotter.

We entered the Piazza Navona and immediately the Baroque Roman architecture struck me with awe. It was magnificent, and I loved how the buildings formed an enclosed, rectangular oasis that featured the three fountains: Fontana dei Quattro Fiumi, Fontana del Moro, and the Fontana di Nettuno—as well as a glorious church, and a colorful cast of street artists, quaint cafés, and shops. This made for a great start to the day. Alex took a lot of pictures, especially of the sculptures and fountains, and I was glad I'd have these memories of our trip. Our wanderings, carefully navigated by Alex using his cell phone map, led us from one incredible site to another. I was fascinated by how one minute we were cutting through a narrow street between buildings and the next minute we opened onto a square with a beautiful Bernini sculpture, or magnificent cathedral, or—as was the case when we left the Piazza Navona, the Pantheon! Just like that, one minute we were enjoying seventeenth-century splendor and the next minute we were entering an ancient Roman building from the first century.

"I can't believe we just popped out from that narrow street and WOW, there's the Pantheon!" I said to Alex while looking at the surreal site in front of me.

"Yes, this part of the city is like that. It's a surprise around any corner."

We entered the Pantheon and marveled at its still in-use interior and architecture.

"It's much cooler in here than I expected. This heat is unbelievable. I'm already soaked through, and we've been at this for less than an hour," I commented.

"We need to stay in the shade as we walk. And we need water. Your face is pretty red. Are you okay?" asked Alex.

I could tell that my face was red, and my hair was damp. I was overheated, and it was only going to get worse as the day progressed. I'd never experienced anything like the heat and humidity in Rome, in August.

"I need to drink a lot of water and all the sodium we've had the past couple of days is not helping."

We found a little convenience store not far from the Pantheon and bought water. I quickly downed one bottle and opened a second one to drink more slowly. We continued our trek, walking through beautiful streets and stopping to look at statues and buildings, reading plaques—thankfully written in English as well as Italian. It was then that I realized drinking all that water meant I needed to find a restroom, and pretty quickly.

"Alex, does the map indicate where the nearest public restroom is located? I haven't seen any in passing as we've been walking."

"Let me see. No, I don't see anything marked on the map and I don't remember passing any."

"Will the cafés have bathrooms?"

"They should. I'm ready for a little break. Let's find a place to sit for a minute and cool off. You look really overheated."

Alex navigated the way to Campo de' Fiori, a nearby Renaissance- and Baroque-era piazza. We found a table under an umbrella, not far from the statue of the philosopher Giordano Bruno, burned at the stake for committing heresy on the spot where his statue now stands. It seems he angered the wrong people when he insisted the earth rotated around the sun. I was beginning to wonder if *Italy* was the sun. I couldn't believe how hot it was, and in case I had any doubts I was now completely convinced my anatomy was not designed for heat. Alex didn't seem to be nearly as overheated as I was.

As soon as the waitress took our order, gelato and ice water, I headed in the direction of the café's bathroom. It wasn't easy to find, but I eventually wove my way to the back of the restaurant and found the only bathroom in sight, door standing open. I looked around to make sure it was the right bathroom and convinced there weren't any other bathrooms, I stepped in and closed the door.

"What *is* this?" I said out loud to myself.

There was a single toilet bowl, completely devoid of a seat. That is to say, if you removed the toilet seat and had just the toilet bowl—that's what I was looking at. At first, I thought

I had entered the wrong bathroom. *Was I in the men's room? Is this the Italian version of a urinal?* No, I'd checked carefully, and this was the only bathroom. *Is it a bidet—can't be, there's no plumbing for that, and besides where is the toilet if this is the bidet?* I wondered what to do exactly. *Does one hover over the bowl?* I didn't want to sit on the rim—YUCK! As I was contemplating the least of the unpleasantries ahead of me, I heard a knock on the door and someone saying something impatiently in Italian.

"One minute please," I said in reply.

I chose the hover method. This was made much more difficult by the fact that my clothes were stuck to me with sweat and had to be peeled off like shrink-wrap. At one point in the process I lost balance and nearly fell in the ominous bowl but caught myself in time. I wondered if all the bathrooms would be like this one. *It was going to be a long day!*

We left Campo de' Fiori slightly refreshed and headed for Largo di Torre Argentina. Like with the Pantheon, one minute we were crossing a busy street with cars zooming through a congested intersection, and the next minute we stood on the sidewalk above the square looking down at the ruins of four temples and the Theatre and Curia of Pompey. It felt surreal. I was standing a few hundred feet from the very spot where Julius Caesar was assassinated by a group of senators on the Ides of March—March 15, 44 BC, during a meeting of the Senate at the Theatre of Pompey!

"This is unbelievable," I said to Alex.

For a moment the heat and humidity disappeared, and I was transported back in time, an invisible voyeur to the murder unfolding in front of me.

"It really is amazing," said Alex.

As I was comparing the ruins to a map of the site I noticed several cats meandering through the ruins. As I looked more closely, I saw that there were quite a few cats—more than the usual number of stray cats one would expect to see in a city square, much less a place of ancient ruins.

"Alex, did you notice all the cats?"

"Yes, I think I read this is a cat sanctuary. Let me see if I can find it again on my cell."

"How strange," I commented.

"Here it is, I found it. According to Wikipedia, 'The Torre Argentina Cat Sanctuary is located in Temple D of the Largo di Torre Argentina. The cat shelter was founded in 1993 and offers sterilization and adoption programs that house an estimated 350 cats. The shelter operates as a no-kill shelter under Law no. 281, enacted by the Italian Parliament in 1991. These laws introduced: (i) the cats' rights to live free and safe, (ii) institutionalization of cat caretakers. The shelter remains active, despite archaeologists' protests to dismantle the shelter in favor of protecting the excavation . . .' Not what you would expect," said Alex.

"Huh, 350 cats . . . inhabiting the site of the ancient Roman Senate. There's something strangely poetic about that, in a kind of cosmic reincarnation way."

"I know, right?" said Alex. "Pity the cat who was Julius Caesar."

"Or for that matter the cat who was Marcus Brutus, if feline Julius Caesar gets to him first. Rome is so full of the *unexpected*," I replied.

And with that statement, a street vendor wearing a colorful caftan approached me for at least the fifth time that day to sell me an African, hand-carved, collapsing wooden bowl, to which I politely replied, "No, thank you. I'm all set when it comes to hand-carved, collapsing wooden bowls."

It was suddenly very hot again, and I gulped the last of my bottle of water.

From the Largo di Torre Argentina we headed to the Capitoline Museums. It was now the hottest part of the day, and we hoped being indoors would allow us to cool off a bit. With two buildings holding treasures on multiple floors, we were assured of getting out of the sun and humidity for a couple of hours while we explored amazing collections. From the Capitoline Hill we looked out over the ancient Roman Forum down to the Colosseum. It was an amazing view. Once inside the museum, the first thing I noticed was that it wasn't cool. The air was quite heavy and warm. Oscillating fans were moving the warm air around, but it was like being in a breezy steam bath. I realized this was not going to be the respite from the heat that I had hoped for—no chance of my pink face and heat blotches disappearing anytime soon. We made our way through the museum rooms, with Alex taking pictures of everything—sculptures, paintings, ceiling frescoes, and ornate glass chandeliers. As I paused, waiting for Alex to get just the right angle on yet another fabulously muscle-toned, perfectly proportioned, realistically endowed Roman, I said, "Have you noticed how few female statues there are?"

"No. Aren't there any female statues?" asked Alex.

"I haven't seen any yet, despite seeing dozens of male statues."

"I guess you're right. I didn't pick up on that."

We wandered through several more connecting rooms, each featuring a center-stage sculpture of a naked Roman (*man* being the key descriptor in *Roman*). Alex took pictures of all of them, I don't think he missed a single one. And then . . . finally, we walked into another room, a lovely small rotunda room, and in the center stood a magnificent statue of Venus. She was over six feet tall and was perched on a three-foot-or-so-tall, round pedestal. She was lovely and looked so feminine, and modest, and vulnerable in her nakedness. This was the first full female statue we'd seen. There was little else in the rotunda room to distract from her presence. I looked at her with awe and thought she was perfection itself. I turned to

Alex to make sure he was taking a picture of her. *Wait ... where was Alex!*

"Alex?" I called softly, but got no reply. "Alex, are you here?" I called softly again, looking around the rotunda room.

Alex had moved on to the next room. I found him getting just the right angle for a photo of the ornate ceiling and glass chandelier. "Did you get a picture of the statue of Venus?"

"Oh ... no. I didn't really notice it. Do you want a picture? ... I'll go back and take a picture."

Didn't notice it? How could you miss it! I thought to myself. *Hell, he probably ran through that room, with his eyes averted, since it contained a naked woman!*

We eventually reached the room containing the famous bronze she-wolf dating to the fifth century BC. I found a chair in the corner in front of an oscillating fan and sat down. I was so hot I could have melted on the spot. Alex was thrilled to have found the she-wolf and the infant Romulus and Remus figures.

"Take all the time you need to get the pictures you want," I said, hoping I could buy as much time in front of the fan as possible. Alex didn't look like he had broken a sweat—and I was dying from heat exhaustion. The longer I sat in front of the fan, the less I cared about seeing another precious artifact, and the more I just wanted to sit there with the air blowing straight onto my face until I felt cool again.

"I got some great pictures. I think we've now seen most of the famous sculptures and paintings. Want to head to Trevi Fountain and find a café?" asked Alex.

"Okay," was all I could find the energy to say, as I managed to stand up and move away from the fan. I also realized that my two hours of sleep in three days was catching up with me. I worried that at some point I might just pass out, like those people who suffer from narcolepsy and suddenly fall asleep at any time, during any type of activity. That could be me—

209

maybe in the middle of a museum, or at the feet of a naked Roman while Alex took the one hundred and tenth picture, or perhaps in one of the fountains in the center of one of the endless piazzas. Just so it wasn't in a bathroom with a seatless toilet bowl—that would be bad!

I prodded myself onward with the promise of a fountain-side café table and something cool to drink. It seemed like visiting a fountain, especially one as large as the Trevi Fountain would be a cooling, refreshing respite from the heat, which I badly needed. I had reached the state of complete wet rag. My hair hung in damp, cotton-candy clumps, any makeup I'd been wearing melted off hours ago, and my cute "first day in Rome" outfit was soaked through and sticking to me like it was glued to my body. Perhaps a quiet table, near the fountain's water spray, and something cold and refreshing to drink would revive me. Anything that included cooling off and being able to go to the bathroom sounded great! As we reached the Piazza di Trevi, I wondered where the fountain was.

"I don't see the fountain. Where's the fountain?" I demanded.

"It's right in front of us," replied Alex.

All I could see were hundreds, maybe thousands, of people swarming together—practically crawling on top of one another, in front of the Palazzo Poli. "I hear the water. Is it behind all of those people? What are they doing?"

"Yes, unfortunately we've arrived at a very busy time. I don't think we'll be able to get near the fountain. If you look above the people, you can see the statue of Oceanus, standing under the arch."

"Why are so many people here, at *this* fountain?"

"It's a really famous fountain, and I think they're trying to elbow their way to the edge to toss a coin."

"Toss a coin? Why?"

"Legend has it that if you throw a coin over your shoulder into the water, you'll return to Italy someday."

"If this crowd is any indication, they must scoop dump-truck loads of money out of that fountain!"

"I'll hold my phone up and see if I can get some photos over their heads."

And this is how I saw the Trevi Fountain, from Alex's cell phone, not from a quaint café table, sipping something cool, while feeling the occasional refreshing spray of water.

On to the Spanish Steps. We were able to find seating at a café in the Piazza di Spagna. The area was beautiful with elegant ocher-colored buildings, Bernini's fountain—the Fontana della Barcaccia—and the celebrated Spanish Steps rising up to the Trinità dei Monti. It was very crowded here also, but the crowds were more dispersed, and they didn't interfere with the overall feel of a refined, eighteenth-century atmosphere. I found the café's restroom, and fortunately I also found my first toilet seat of the day. I was so happy to see it. *Be grateful for small mercies*, I thought to myself. I could never have imagined I'd be so delighted to see a toilet seat. We were able to cool off a little bit and get some light fare to hold us over until dinner.

"We've seen so much today, and it's all been amazing," I said to Alex as we made our way back to the hotel.

"It's been a full day. What do you want to do this evening?"

"Do you think we could get takeout and bring it back to the hotel? We could probably have the garden to ourselves."

"Good idea, and we could get a bottle of wine, that rosé we had last night would be nice."

"That sounds good. I can't wait to take a shower and put on fresh, dry clothes. Then I just want to relax. I don't think I have the energy to do anything else."

Back at the hotel, Alex volunteered to get dinner while I

took a shower and tried to rejuvenate myself. He texted me from the garden: I'm back with pizza and wine. Come down when you're ready.

Me: I'll be right there.

As I settled into the same table where we sat at breakfast, Alex lifted the lid of the pizza box. "I ordered the 'traditional Italian,' so I hope it's good." We peered into the box and both exclaimed, simultaneously, "Oh." Swimming on the top of the pizza, threatening to infiltrate the cheese and what was beneath it, was a raw egg with the yellow yolk intact. I suppressed an involuntary gag. Alex looked like he might be doing the same. Very quickly he grabbed two of the paper plates from the bag, scooped up the raw egg, and put it in the bag.

"I didn't expect to see *that*," he exclaimed.

"I wonder what else is on the pizza," I said.

We fought our way through slimy artichokes, rubbery pepper chunks, and sour tomato lumps, topping a wet-noodle-consistency crust with no flavor. I wondered where the world-famous Italian cuisine was. So far we hadn't really encountered it. Fortunately the wine was great, and Alex regretted not getting the food from the restaurant where he bought the wine—the one where we had eaten the day before.

"I just thought it would be good to try something different. While I was there buying the wine, I should have just ordered some food."

"In all honesty, more charcuterie and pasta doesn't sound appetizing. I think your idea of the pizza was a good one. It's just, well, not good pizza."

We finished the wine and headed to the room. Alex said he had some things to catch up on and suggested I get some sleep. He said he'd take a shower and work on his computer downstairs for a while. I was out the minute my head hit the pillow. I slept for about three hours before the snoric boom woke me. After that I mostly stared through the dark at the ceiling until it was time to get up.

☲━━━✗

After another day (and another sleepless night) in Rome, we had seen quite a bit, including all that the Vatican had to offer, the Castel Sant'Angelo, the ancient ruins of the Roman Forum, the Colosseum, the Circus Maximus, the Atrium Vestae (house of the Vestal Virgins), the Domus Augustana (residence for the emperors of Rome), and more beautiful piazzas, shops, and cafés. It was time to catch our train and head north to Tuscany. To be specific, a restored Tuscan farmhouse in the Chianti Region. Rome was otherworldly, and it was also the hottest place on earth in August, or so I thought upon checking out of the hotel and heading for the train station. The same judgy Directorre Del'Albergo who checked us into the hotel, checked us out the morning of our departure. He was no friendlier and seemed as disdainful as ever. At some point during our stay I stopped caring and I hoped whatever had bothered Alex when we checked in was no longer an issue.

We never did manage to find outstanding food in Rome, and I really hoped I wouldn't see any more charcuterie, boiled eggs, dry baguettes, or tomatoes for breakfast. I was ready to move on and I was looking forward to our time in Tuscany where I hoped some of the magic between us would return, and we'd be like we were on our work trips together. Rome had been amazing, but it was also disappointing on a personal level. *Tuscany would be better*, I thought to myself.

Chapter 23

The train ride from Rome to Orvieto was comfortable and uncrowded. We stretched out in seats facing one another and marveled at the scenery unfolding in front of us. We passed delightful fields of thousands of neatly planted sunflowers, and the vast expanse of green, open space was balm to my tired eyes and overstimulated brain. I leaned back into my seat and found myself thinking about Merryhearth. I missed being there to see the daily progress and chat with Josh and the guys. I wondered if Josh was getting regular payments now from the bank, and since it was the hottest time of the year, I hoped Victor, Ricardo, Carlos, and Felix were still taking their midday lunch break and enjoying their ranchera folk tunes under the shade of the big black elm tree.

Alex looked at his cell frequently to see if new messages popped up. I watched him smile to himself and start texting a reply to many of them. "A message from De'On?" I would ask, and he would grin and say yes. I knew he was sending De'On regular selfies from the iconic Rome locations we visited. There was definitely something different in Alex's demeanor; I felt his focus was directed away from me, and his priority was clearly his budding relationship with De'On. I was beginning to wish I was back in Winchester, not rumbling through the Tuscan countryside. *Amanda, stop it! Don't let sleep deprivation and heat ruin your Italy vacation and poison your perception of things.* I straightened my posture and sat up a little taller in my seat.

Upon arriving in Orvieto, Alex picked up our rental car and we loaded the luggage. It was as god-awful hot here as it had been in Rome—certainly no better, which I optimistically had hoped for. We locked the parked rental and caught the cable car to the hilltop where the historic town of Orvieto overlooks the Umbrian countryside. After checking out the spectacular cathedral and breathtaking sight line of the surrounding hills—we had lunch in a café with views of the main square and topped off our visit with a wine tasting.

"And this is why we included Tuscany," I said to Alex as we clinked our wineglasses together, toasting our arrival.

"This wine is outstanding!" replied Alex, taking a photo of the bottle and our pale gold glasses.

"Are you ready for a totally different Italy experience?" I asked him.

"Yeah, I'm ready to slow down the pace and relax a bit. Tell me about the farmhouse we're staying at."

"It's classified as an agriturismo, that's kind of like a combination working farm and bed-and-breakfast. From the website it looks pretty, the furnishings are simple, the breakfasts are farm-to-table from either the farm itself or nearby farms, and it's surrounded by miles and miles of grapevines and olive trees. The one I picked looked very nice in the photos and has private bathrooms in each room, but no swimming pool. I thought about one with a pool, but I didn't think we'd want to waste time sitting around a pool when we could be out tasting wine!"

"Refill?" asked Alex.

"Please."

"You mentioned before that it's historic. How far back does it date? What's its story?"

"Yeah, that's one of the reasons I picked this one. There are like hundreds of them, but this one is owned and operated by a woman who restored it from rubble. It dates to the eighteenth century. It sounds like a fascinating story, and I figured she and I have to be kindred spirits. I really want to talk with her, hear her story, and share experiences of trying to do the impossible with a big old house and property. I can see us sharing war stories from opposite sides of the Atlantic over a glass a wine. Women who, on their own, have taken on this kind of crazy project, have to have a lot in common."

"I'm glad you found it. I'd like to hear her story also."

"And . . . this one had another fun element . . . a cooking lesson is included for guests staying more than one night."

"Oh, that sounds great! I'd love to learn to make a traditional Tuscan meal."

We took the cable car back to the foot of the hill and picked up the rental car. No roomy SUV with deep leather seats here—not an option. Alex rented a tiny red car, almost too small to fit our luggage, and with a standard transmission. Cramped as it was, the saving grace was it had air-conditioning that worked really well.

"You're okay with driving a standard, in unknown territory, that looks to be very hilly?" I asked.

"They asked me if I had a preference, and I said I actually prefer a standard. They're fun to drive, especially on roads like this. My first car was a Volkswagen Beetle with a standard transmission. I loved that car!"

"Thank goodness you're doing all the driving. I can just enjoy the scenery."

And I did enjoy the scenery. The vistas were as pretty as the Shenandoah Valley, in a different way. The softly rolling green hills were decorated with orderly fields of olive trees and grapevines, creating a structured, yet natural, beauty like nothing I had ever seen. There was a soothing visual rhythm to the undulating landscape with its rows and rows of mature plantings that looked more like sheet music ledger lines filled with musical notes than agriculture. The mostly stone houses looked like they were drawn by hand, using a color palette chosen to complement their natural surroundings. As Alex shifted gears and navigated the narrow two-way roadways, I enjoyed being a living element of a landscape masterpiece.

We found our agriturismo easily and parked the car under a sunshade. We walked up a narrow flight of about 15 natural sandstone steps, hugging a gentle cliffside. When we reached the landing, a very pretty scene greeted us. A gravel walkway wound its way across a plateau, through flowerbeds and stone patios, toward the north end of the farmhouse. The farmhouse, made of brown cut stones, punctuated with red-clay bricks in a patchwork pattern, faced west. The front entrance was accessed by crossing a broad stone terrace, comfortably outfitted with umbrella tables, chaise lounge chairs, and glorious ceramic pots overflowing with colorful flowers and vines.

The terrace was elevated above a vast expanse of beautifully manicured grape vines that gently sloped downward, away from the house, and rose again on the far side of the hill, opposite the house. As we stood in front of the heavy wooden door, adorned with black-metal-strap hinges and ancient iron lock, taking in the picturesque surroundings, a woman who looked to be about sixty, with a stylish blunt-cut of silver hair, leaned her head out of an upper story window and instructed us to enter and come upstairs. After stopping to pet the two dogs on the patio, who had appeared from somewhere to greet us, we headed up. I glanced around as we ascended the stone steps to the second story. Its interior was incredibly authentic, and the country-quaint furniture and decor were perfect for the setting.

The woman who had called to us from the window met us in the narrow hall to the right of the stairs and ushered us into the big kitchen.

"Hurry, close the door tight. The air conditioner is on," she said with a substantial Italian accent, ushering us forward into the kitchen. She offered seats at the same long, wood plank, farmhouse table I'd seen in the website photos.

Glad to have arrived, I enthusiastically addressed her, "Hi, I'm Amanda Grayson. We've emailed back and forth a few times. You must be Nina?"

I noticed that Alex again—like when we arrived in Rome—stayed back and didn't say anything. His demeanor made me feel awkward. *What was going on with him*, I wondered.

"You're here for three nights, sì?" said the woman.

I guess we were going to get the business done before the introductions and the niceties. "Yes, three nights, and you may use the same credit as the one used to hold the reservation."

"And you want the cooking lesson?"

I looked at Alex, "We do, right?"

"When is the cooking lesson? We'll be out sightseeing during the days," said Alex.

"No, no, of course. The cooking lesson is at night after all the other guests have checked in. I have eight checking in between today and tomorrow."

Alex looked at me and nodded, and I said, "Yes, we want the lesson."

"That will be sixty euro each," she said matter-of-factly.

Whoa, I was taken aback. I had understood the cost to be included in the already very pricey rate for the room. Did I have that wrong? And, if it was extra, it fell into the category of *food and entertainment*, which Alex was covering. At this point

I really didn't want the cooking lesson anymore, but if I had said *never mind* it would have looked like we were being cheapskates.

"I prefer cash if you have it," she said, looking at Alex expectantly.

Alex pulled out his wallet and counted out one hundred and twenty euro and laid the cash on the table. He did not look pleased.

"Thank you," she said. "You want a glass of wine? Sit down, I'll get us some wine."

We sat down, saying nothing, I was still stunned. She returned with a quaint-looking round bottle, half wrapped in a straw basket (a fiasco), of what she described as a "locally produced Chianti," and poured the wine into two small juice-sized glasses. After filling the little juice glasses, she sat a plate of dry biscuits on the table.

"Thank you. You are Nina?" I asked.

"Sì, sì," she replied.

"And you restored this lovely old farmhouse yourself?" I thought maybe now that we were at her table, drinking wine, breaking bread, and had gotten through the business end of things, we could chat.

"No, no, I had workmen do that," she said dismissively.

"Did you have a difficult time finding workmen . . . who knew how to work with the old materials and historic construction?"

"Psst. They are many here. Everyone knows the old style."

"Oh. You're lucky. I'm restoring a historic home in the U.S. and I've had a lot of difficulty finding and hiring historic construction experts."

"What are you going to be doing while you are here?" asked Nina, looking mostly at Alex.

Alex responded with, "How old is the farmhouse?" *I smiled to myself.*

"Very old, eleventh century," replied Nina.

Alex looked a little confused. "I didn't realize it was that old."

"Sì, it is very old. Are you going to wineries while you are here?"

"Yes," I said. "Do you recommend any in particular?"

At this point, Nina produced a map of the region that she had procured especially for her guests. It documented two distinct routes with particular wineries marked. As we sipped our authentic, locally made Chianti, she explained the two routes—one for each day of our stay. She pointed out several wineries that were owned and managed by very good friends of hers, who always took good care of her guests when they mentioned her name. Alex asked a few questions about the wines produced in the area. Nina didn't seem to be an expert on that subject.

"These maps are helpful," I said.

"Sì, sì, I make these for the Americans. I don't know what we would do without the Americans. All the tourists we get now are Americans. The Americans are the only ones with enough money to come here now."

Alex looked at me and asked, "Are you ready to bring the suitcases in?"

"Yes. I'm ready."

"Okay, I will show you your room," said Nina.

We followed her out of the second floor that was her living quarters, down the stairs, and through a door into a small room to the right of the stairs. From this room, a sitting room of sorts, were two doors.

"That is your room," said Nina, pointing to a door to the left. "Another couple is in that room, and they are checking out today. The new people checking in today and tomorrow are in the building behind the house. You will have this area to yourselves."

I made a mental note that having the sitting room could come in handy. It was very dark in the sitting room, despite the intense sunlight outside, and it only had one small window toward the top of the wall at the low ceiling.

As Nina unlocked the substantial wooden door to our room and manipulated the antique iron hardware, she said, "You will want to keep your room's shutters and door closed during the day."

We stepped into the room, and I was pleased that it looked the same as the photos on the website, although a bit smaller. Like the sitting room, it was dark, but had more windows—one near the ceiling over the bed and the other in the middle of the wall opposite the door. The room was simple, cozy, and clean. It had a terra-cotta tile floor, and beautiful exposed wooden beams across the ceiling that seemed a little higher than the ceiling in the sitting room. The simple furniture included an antique armoire, a small credenza with tiny refrigerator, an antique iron double bed covered in a quaint quilt, and two nightstands with lamps on either side of the bed. A small door to the left of the armoire led to the bathroom, which also had a small shuttered window. I thought the room looked sweet and in keeping with a historic Tuscan farmhouse.

Before either of us could comment, Nina stated, "Okay, you must keep the shutters closed during the day to keep the heat out and open them at night to let the cool air in. If you do this, you will be very comfortable. Do not open them during the day, just at night."

I stepped closer to examine the windows. There were no windows ... there were NO windows ... just openings without glass.

"If you need anything, go outside and call up to me at my kitchen window. That's the only way I can hear you over the air conditioner," and with that, she scurried from the room, through the sitting room, up the stairs, and was gone.

When I turned around, Alex was examining the windows. He opened the shutters to reveal that both of our bedroom windows were topped on the outside by arbors covered with thick vines, and one looked out onto the patio while the other viewed the gravel walkway. The bathroom window opened at eye level to anyone outside on the main walkway leading to the house from the car parking zone.

"So . . . they don't have insects in Tuscany?" asked Alex.

"This is really strange. We're supposed to sleep at night with no glass windows, just the shutters open to the outside—which, by the way, is the big patio and main walkway to the house."

"There is so much wrong about this setup, like privacy, bugs, safety . . ." said Alex.

"Oh, I've got another one for you," I said. After my many black snake encounters at Merryhearth, I had snakes on my mind, and I was well aware that snakes could go right up the side of a vine or trellis and enter a house.

"What's that?" said Alex with trepidation.

"That arbor out there, over the window, is exactly the kind of place a snake would love to hang out—and at night when it gets cool, slipping through the open window to be in the warm room beyond would be just the thing."

"Maybe they don't have snakes *or* bugs in Tuscany," said Alex.

We unloaded the luggage and settled into our quaint, little farmhouse room. I couldn't wait to take a shower and cool off. It was unbelievably hot. The bathroom was tiny, and I kept my pretty pink-and-black toiletry bags as much out of the way as I could. Alex gave me first rights to the shower and I accepted with gratitude. After closing the door to the bathroom, I checked the window—shutters were closed, but I could hear other guests arriving and their footsteps crunching on the gravel walkway right outside. I pulled back the curtain to turn on the water and was very surprised by what I saw. It was half of a shower, truly *half-a-shower*. Having so much construction design experience in my recent past, I was able to accurately determine the shower's dimensions to be twenty-four inches deep by forty-two inches wide. *Good thing I'm petite*, I thought to myself. I adjusted the water temperature to a cool, tepid setting and stepped over the threshold and into the half-a-shower.

"What the heck!" I said out loud and jumped out of the shower and back onto the bath mat. The white tile shower floor was spikey. I reached down and touched it with my hand. It wasn't my imagination—the surface of the shower's tile floor was made up of blunt spikes! I'd never experienced anything like that. I desperately needed a cool shower, but not in a torture chamber! Once I determined that the spikes could not puncture the bottoms of my feet, I got back into the half-a-shower. I gingerly stepped around as I washed my hair and continuously flung the shower curtain away from my skin as it kept touching me in the small space allotted for showering. Each step was painful as the spikes found new flesh and my feet had to adjust. If the point of this shower tile was to prevent people from taking long showers—it worked! I was relieved to be done and to step onto the soft cotton bath mat, away from the half-a-shower torture chamber.

Once the horror of the shower itself wore off, the next awful realization was that I was now trying to dry off in what amounted to a steam room. The bathroom was full of condensation, the mirror was fogged over, and, as I dried my skin with the towel, it was damp again—immediately. I needed to get some air into the tiny room. I couldn't open the door to the bedroom, Alex could be out there. I looked at the window. *Should I do it? Could I open it just a crack to get some fresh air flowing?* I wrapped myself in the towel and climbed onto the ledge under the window so I could reach the shutters. Kneeling on the ledge I reached forward to open the shutter a crack and right there, not four feet away, were people walking straight toward me. I ducked, hiding my torso under the window, and quickly closed the shutter, hoping they hadn't noticed me. I got dressed, pulling my clothes on over my sticky, wet, skin. Forget the hair, that wasn't happening. I stepped out into the bedroom. Alex was there organizing his suitcase.

"Your turn. Enjoy your shower. Let me know if it leaves you with any lasting impressions."

"Uh-oh," he replied, and shut the bathroom door behind him.

We had a light dinner that night in a small restaurant nearby. It wasn't anything to write home about, and more enjoyable was sitting in the lounge chairs on the big stone terrace in front of the house. We were on a hill and the terrace looked out over vineyards that were so close, they appeared to be a part of the agriturismo. As the sun set and the sky grew dark, we could see the stars begin to appear. They were spectacularly bright in the perfectly clear night sky and looked closer than at home. They reminded me of how much I enjoyed star and moon gazing from Merryhearth, which was far enough from the city to avoid light interference. No one else was around, although we knew others had checked in after us. We sipped a light red local wine that we picked up at a store near the restaurant where we had dinner. I felt like maybe I might be able to get the first decent night's sleep since leaving home, when Alex yelled, "Ouch!" and slapped his arm.

"What is it?" I said, but my question was answered when I heard the familiar sound of a mosquito buzzing near my ear. Then it was my turn.

"Oh crap! There are mosquitos everywhere."

"They seem to be really attracted to us, they're . . . like, attacking!" said Alex as he slapped his neck.

They *were* attacking! Small, fast, abundant numbers of them were all around us, in our faces, buzzing by our ears, and going in for the kill on every exposed area of skin. Considering how hot it was, that was a lot of exposed skin. I felt one hit my cheek and decided: Enough!

"Ready to call it a night?" asked Alex.

"Yeah, I'm exhausted."

"Me too. It's been a long day."

Alex had the key to our room and as he unlocked the door, and we stepped in, the dense, hot humid air hit us.

"Oh, goodness, it's really hot in here," I said.

"This room's on the west side, all that afternoon sun heated it up like a pizza oven in here."

"But we kept the shutters shut like she said."

"HA!" exclaimed Alex.

"We need to let the cool air in," I said.

"You mean along with the killer, piranha mosquitoes?" said Alex.

"Maybe if we keep the lights off, they won't come in."

"And the snakes?"

"At this point, I'll risk the snakes."

"Okaaaay," said Alex.

When we were ready to get into bed, we turned the lights off, and I took the window opening on my side and Alex got the window opening above the bed. We unfolded the shutters in the dark and lay down. We were side by side, in the now much smaller double bed, not touching of course—that had become the norm—facing the ceiling.

"I don't feel a rush of cool air, do you?" I said to Alex in the dark.

"There's no cool air coming in here. I don't know what she was talking about," replied Alex.

"Maybe it takes a little while. It's so creepy knowing the windows are just wide open to anything that's outside, includ-

225

ing people coming and going. Seriously, anything could come through these windows—we're not even on the second floor, we're at ground level. Why don't they have screens here? I don't understand why they don't have screens in the windows. And honestly, if I'd known there was no air-conditioning, I would never have picked this place."

And then it happened, the sound I had come to dread . . . the horrific snoric boom! It was so loud, and he not only produced the noise—he slept soundly through it. I had never seen anyone fall asleep like he did. Contact with the pillow resulted in sleep within less than a minute. I lay there, hoping for some cool air; it wasn't happening. The room was so hot! I threw all the covers off and kicked them to the bottom of the bed. This resulted in Alex having no covers either, but I didn't care one bit. As I lay facing the ceiling, surrounded by the reverberating waves of snores, hoping, praying for a breath of fresh air . . . I felt it. Not the cool air I so desperately needed— but a mosquito . . . biting my thigh. I slapped at it and in the process I heard one buzzing by my ear. Oh no! They were coming into the room, they were infiltrating the room, they were going to be as bad as they'd been outside on the patio. I realized that I would soon be covered in mosquito bites, on top of my red, blotchy, overheated face, under my stringy cotton-candy hair. *NOOO!*

I jumped out of bed and closed the shutters tight on the window next to me. Then to reach the window above the bed, I had to stand on the bed. Alex was in the way. I didn't care. The mosquitoes were coming in, and I had to get the shutters closed! I stood with one foot on either side of his head while he snored on. *Oh please . . . don't let him wake up now!*, I thought. No chance of that—the snoring continued without so much as a pause. *Whew . . . I got the shutters closed. Now what?* I went into the bathroom and ran cold water over a washcloth and dabbed my face and arms and lay down to try to get some rest.

It was so hot. I went back to the bathroom again to refresh the cool water on the washcloth. The bed was springy and every time I got up Alex bounced around. I didn't care anymore. Walking back to the bed with the cool washcloth on my face, I realized the terra-cotta tiles on the floor felt cool. I reached down and touched them with my hand—they were cool to the touch. Maybe if I lay down on the floor and pressed my face against the tiles, and my arms and legs, I could cool off. I stood there motionless for a few moments, actually contemplating this, ME . . . the person who doesn't want the bedspread or pillow-sham pillows to touch me. "You're losing your flipping mind!" I said out loud. In response, Alex let out with a particularly snorty, multiple-syllable snore. I gave up. I lay down on the bed, with the washcloth on my forehead, and stared at the ceiling. Occasionally I swatted at a mosquito that tried to bite me—and I waited for morning to come.

Chapter 24

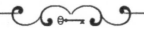

Alex was already seated at a table in the shade with his breakfast and coffee when I stepped out onto the patio dressed in my "first full day in Tuscany" outfit.

"Oh, this is lovely, and it's thankfully cool here in the shade. What's for breakfast?"

"Umm, the traditional options," replied Alex.

I stepped into the little kitchen, off the terrace, and saw an artfully laid out selection of . . . exactly the same items we'd had in Rome—fatty cold cut meats, salty cheese, dry baguettes, hard-boiled eggs, tomatoes, and cucumbers. To be fair, there were also slices of fresh watermelon and a small bowl of fresh berries and yogurt, and what looked like a homemade coffee cake. *That was nice*, I thought to myself. I heard Alex say, "The coffee's excellent and I already poured you a glass of orange juice."

We started our first day driving the Chianti Road, or Highway 222, as it's called. We'd decided not to strictly follow Nina's map, and to venture out on our own. Our first stop was Barone Ricasoli, known as the oldest winery in Italy. This stop was the first of many that day that were as delightful as I imagined they would be. The wineries were outstanding, the small villages and towns were postcard-perfect, and the only less than amazing experiences were with food. We really had not had a single meal that was outstanding. Alex navigated the roadways like a pro in our little red car with the standard transmission and incredible air-conditioning. After lunch, I found myself unable to keep my eyes open in the passenger seat. The hum of the engine and the cool air blowing on my face was a combination my sleep-deprived body couldn't resist. I had on dark sunglasses, and I hoped that Alex wasn't noticing that I was sleeping through much of the iconic scenery as he drove us through the countryside.

When we arrived back at the agriturismo, Alex suggested we ask Nina about dinner options. So far, we weren't doing well finding places to eat on our own, and we figured if there was anywhere in Tuscany to have a truly outstanding and authentic meal, it had to be found by word of mouth. Feeling a little foolish, we stood on the patio and called up to her at the window as she had instructed.

Sticking her head out of the upstairs kitchen window, she yelled, "Sì, sì, come up."

We were surprised to find the other guests sitting around the kitchen table drinking the locally produced Chianti out of the little juice glasses. It was a pleasant scene and Nina seemed to be in a much more jovial mood. Introductions were made around the table as glasses were filled for Alex and me. We met a couple in their midthirties from New Jersey (Matt and Sarah), a couple from Sacramento, California, in their midfifties (Diane and Don) and their daughter and her best friend, who appeared to be in their midtwenties (Kara and Jackie). It was the first time that explaining the relationship between Alex and me had come up during the trip, and so . . . we just didn't explain it. We left it at names and where we were from—Washington, D.C. All eight of us were in Tuscany after having been in other parts of Italy. Matt and Sarah had been touring all day, like Alex and me. The California group had just arrived.

Even though we hadn't been in Italy for that long, there is something comforting about being with other Americans (or people of your clan—whatever it may be). We immediately fell into easy banter about our travels, what we still wanted to see, and our impressions of everything. You would have thought we were longtime friends, not total strangers meeting for the first time. Matt and Sarah had done the wine route that Alex and I planned to do the next day, so we exchanged a lot of information on that subject. We all wanted to know if Nina had suggestions for a place to have dinner.

"I have this friend who is starting his own restaurant," said Nina. "He is amazing! His food is all fresh, made to order, excellent quality. You will not have food like he makes anywhere in Italy."

We agreed that this was what we'd hoped for, and none of us had really found it yet. We asked Nina if his restaurant was open yet.

"Let me call him now," she said excitedly.

We could hear her on the phone speaking with her friend in Italian and nodding her head vigorously.

"He says he can take all of you tonight if you are okay with a fixed menu. It will be four courses with wine."

We agreed this sounded great, and the reservation was made. We chatted for a while longer and then headed to our rooms to shower and change. Alex and I arranged to take turns staying out of the bedroom so that we could leave the bathroom door open while each of us showered. Dress was casual, and I put on another of my new outfits, black shorts with a white linen blouse tucked in, and black sandals with a low wedge heel and leather ruffle at a diagonal across the top of my foot. Despite being sleep-deprived and fighting the effects of the extreme humidity, I looked cute and felt happy to be in Tuscany at last. We met the others on the gravel walkway, and Diane and Don offered to drive us in the van they had rented.

It was almost dark when we arrived at the restaurant, a modest establishment with a little bar and a few tables. The chef and owner, Nina's friend Aldo, greeted us warmly and took us around to the back where a large wooden picnic table with attached benches was set up for us on a stone patio lit by a multitude of candles. The table was beautifully set with white linen napkins, silver flatware, pitchers of ice water, wineglasses, and baskets of big, soft loaves of homemade bread. It was absolutely enchanting and Aldo was gracious and welcoming. We introduced ourselves (that awkward moment again with Alex and me) and sat down at the picnic table. I was at one end with Alex, Kara, and her friend Jackie to my left. Across from me was Don, with Diane, Sarah, and Matt to his right.

"This looks like a scene right out of a movie," said Alex as we settled into our bench seats at the table.

"It really does. I love that we're sitting outside, under the stars. And all of these candles as the only source of light is absolutely magical."

Aldo proceeded to explain what we would be eating in each course and how he was preparing the food from scratch, with fresh local ingredients. A teenage girl in blue jeans and a white blouse, and a young man in jeans and a T-shirt, brought out three bottles of wine for the table along with the antipasti—verdure grigliate, a selection of grilled vegetables, including eggplant, peppers, and zucchini.

It soon became apparent that we would be taking a long time to enjoy and consume this dinner. The antipasti was outstanding, and so was the wine. Much to my surprise, the three bottles were empty before the next course arrived—albeit that was about forty minutes after the antipasti had been laid on

231

the table. I don't think any of us really noticed the time, we were talking and having a pretty good time. When the first course arrived, it was amazing. Aldo came with the two helpers, and three more bottles of a different wine were placed on the table, along with individual servings of black truffle pasta for each of us. Aldo showed us the actual truffle and explained how he made the dish, as we marveled at the presentation and the taste.

I was full after the pasta, but we had two more courses coming. Everyone was talking, and I noticed the wine bottles were going down again, pretty quickly, and they were all congregated in front of Alex, Kara, and Jackie. By this point in the dinner, Alex had completely turned away from me at the table and he and Kara and Jackie were having their own, rather lively, three-person party.

"I wonder how these two wines would taste if mixed together," said Alex.

"Only one way to find out," said Kara.

"Don't leave me out," said Jackie, holding up her glass for a refill.

"Don't worry, we won't leave *you* out," replied Alex.

"Yeah, it's more fun with three," said Kara.

Giggles ensued and Alex added, "I can attest to that."

Apart from the three of them, the congenial company, candlelight, starlit sky, and the fabulous food and wine were what I imagined Tuscany would be. Then, out came the main course, Tuscan grilled bone-in pork loin chops. And the table was presented with three more, yet different, bottles of wine. The previous three, some of which still had a little wine in them, were left on the table.

I noticed at this point that most of us had slowed way down on the wine, and other than a small taste of the new selection, didn't refill our glasses—but Alex, Kara, and Jackie were making up for the rest of us. The pork loins were to die for—probably the best I had ever had. We were now into a meal that had taken us over two hours to consume, and had included nine bottles of wine, and there was another course coming.

I noticed Alex was lifting bottles of wine, searching for the ones that still had contents, then filling his glass and Kara's and Jackie's glasses. I had no idea how many glasses of wine he'd consumed, but by the look of things, it was quite a lot. He and the two women were flirting and laughing, and Alex kept leaning in and whispering in Kara's ear, and putting his arm around her shoulders. I watched Diane and Don looking uncomfortable and embarrassed, Matt and Sarah kept looking at me with sympathy and tried to ignore the three of them, and I was mortified—absolutely dying a little bit as each minute went by. Suddenly, dinner couldn't be over soon enough. As Alex continued to openly flirt with the women, and they flirted back, everyone else at the table ceased to exist, especially me. I couldn't even get his attention as he was straddling the bench with his back to me and his front to them. I was embarrassed, humiliated, and angry all at the same time.

Dessert arrived—without additional wine. I don't re-member what it was. When the check came, I motioned to Don to work out our portion with Alex. I saw Alex produce cash from his wallet, and I hoped he was sober enough to do the math and count it properly. As it turned out, the cost was incredibly reasonable, about forty-five euro each, and I couldn't imagine how Aldo made much profit. I hoped we hadn't dissuaded him from pursuing his restaurant dream.

We were piling back into Don and Diane's van to head back when Alex, Kara, and Jackie announced they were going to walk back.

"Do you know the way back?" I asked Alex.

"Yes, we're only about a mile straight down the road from

the farmhouse," he replied with confidence.

"It's pitch-black out here and ten o'clock at night. Do you think it's safe?" I asked.

"We'll be fine. Do you want to walk with us?"

"No. Give me the key so that I can get into the room."

Diane, putting her arm around my shoulder, said, "Come on, Amanda. Maybe they'll get eaten by Apennine wolves on the way back."

I knew Kara and Jackie had their own separate suite, and I wondered if the three of them were going there to continue their partying.

I stepped alone through the farmhouse door into the dark hall at the foot of the steps. Nina's light was still on upstairs, and I could hear her air conditioner running hard. When I unlocked the door to our room, I was hit immediately by the stifling heat. I washed my face and put on my pajamas with the shorts. I couldn't believe what had just unfolded right before my eyes, in the presence of everyone at the table. I was crushed, and by Alex, of all people. *Amanda, you should have seen this coming. What did you expect? You're ten years his senior, not a twentysomething that takes life as one big party, whether it's kickball or a four-course dinner with wine. And of course, his infatuation with you was going to be replaced by his infatuation with the next enigma that crossed his path. At some point, this crazy illusion of ridiculous smitten-ness that you've been harboring was going to blow up!* Was I never to be free of explosions in my life?

I got out my laptop and started looking for flights home from the nearest airport, which was Florence. There were a lot of flights from Florence to Washington, D.C., with seats available the next day. I wanted to go home. I just wanted to be home. I packed my suitcase and put all but what I would need for the morning in my luggage. I was ready, and tomorrow couldn't come soon enough. I doubted I would see Alex until tomorrow, and I didn't care. Maybe I could *finally* get some sleep, except I was so mad, and so upset, and so hot, that I doubted I could sleep.

Just then I heard feet on the gravel walkway outside and Alex at the window, "Hey, will you unlock the front door? I can't get in."

Nina must have locked it, thinking we were all back. I contemplated not opening the door, I really did.

"Hi! It was a nice walk back. All the stars were out. Do you want to sit on the patio for a little while?"

I just glared at him. If looks could have killed, he'd have been a puddle of wax on the floor.

"I want to go home! I want to go home tomorrow! I found a flight out of Florence and you need to take me to the airport in the morning. My stuff is packed. I'm leaving!"

"What? Why? What's wrong?"

"You have humiliated me!"

"Wait, please ... just one minute ... I ... I have to go to the bathroom."

I sat down on the foot of the bed and took a gulp of water from a bottle I retrieved from the little refrigerator. Alex came out of the bathroom wearing his boxers and no shirt.

"What's wrong, why do you want to go home?" he said, sitting on the bed next to me.

There were a million things wrong, so I decided to go for the most obvious. "You flirted and came on to those women tonight." He didn't deny it. "You made a fool out of me. You completely humiliated me in front of those people!" My voice was rising with each statement and I wondered if we could be overheard, but I didn't care. "You and I know we are not a couple, but everyone else thinks we are. Do you realize how it makes me look to have my 'boyfriend' act like that? Everyone

the bed on his knees and positioned himself like he wanted to wrestle with me—wearing nothing but his boxers. He playfully pushed me from the side and with the expression of a little kid on the play mat said, "Come on!"

I had no idea what he was talking about. Then he pushed me again from the other side and said, "Come on! Do something." I had no idea what he was doing. He was bouncing on his knees and shimmying back and forth like we were wrestling.

"What are you doing?" I asked him.

"Come on!" he said again and then *bit* my arm right above the elbow.

"OUCH!" I yelled. "What are you *DOING*?"

At this point, to my total shock and surprise, Alex outright tackled me. I wasn't expecting it, not to mention I weighed a fraction of what he weighed, and so we went flying, head over heels across the bed, crashed into the nightstand, and landed on the floor.

I was a bit dazed and as I picked myself up off the floor, I could see that luckily Alex had broken my fall. No apparent injuries, the bite site was still stinging, but I was in one piece.

"Oh, my god, I'm so sorry. Are you alright?" asked Alex, now appearing to have snapped out of wrestle mode.

"Yes, I hope we didn't break anything. Are you okay?"

"I didn't mean to hurt you. Did I bite you too hard?"

"Too hard for what? What were you doing?"

"I wanted to make you happy again. I thought that's what you wanted."

"To wrestle and roughhouse with you? Why would you think that?"

"I'm so sorry."

"You know what, let's just straighten up the room and try to get some sleep. It's better to make decisions in the light of day."

"Okay, but I don't want you to go home," said Alex, looking very sad.

"What *did* you tell Kara and Jackie about us?"

"Nothing."

"Do they know you're gay?"

"I think so."

"How do they know? Did you tell them?"

"I talked about De'On."

"So they definitely know you are gay?"

"Yes."

"Well, that's a saving grace."

"Why?"

"Because they will tell their parents and I don't look like such a fool. It changes the story. Now, I'm a straight woman traveling with a gay guy who is my *friend* and who drinks too much."

"Oh."

"The whole dynamic is different. Thank god they know you're gay. Let's get some sleep and reevaluate in the morning."

Alex slept soundly. I couldn't sleep at all, and this time it wasn't just the snoric booming, it was intense homesickness.

Chapter 25

I was wide awake as dawn crept through the closed shutters
of the stone oven that was our bedroom. It was 5:30 a.m., and
at least it was daylight, so I could get up. I needed desperately
to clear my head. I was sleep-deprived, overheated, puffy from
salty foods, not to mention a little stiff from being tackled and
bitten. I hadn't been able to work out like I'd been doing at
home, and I needed a physical outlet and some space to clear
my mind. While Alex slept on, I dressed in my running shorts
and shoes, unlocked the front door, and stepped out into the
cool air on the stone patio that overlooked the expansive vineyard.

At this time of the morning it was even more serene and
beautiful. A gray mist hung low between the vines and everything was wrapped in an ominous silence, not a sound to be
heard. Being in and near nature had always been soothing for
me, especially in troubled times. I followed the gravel walkway around to the little dirt road that circled the vineyard
from above. I stretched and then started a slow, easy jog down
the little road. I could hear startled wildlife, probably squir-
rels, maybe deer—I didn't know—in the woods that bordered

one side of the road. I hadn't asked anyone if this road was public, and I hoped I wasn't trespassing or doing something that could get me into trouble. I'd left my purse, cell phone, everything back in the room and so if I had a mishap, I'd be out of luck.

As I jogged along, I started to feel uneasy. This was clearly not a very frequently traveled road, and it was getting more grown over the farther I went. I didn't know where I was, other than at an agriturismo near Siena. At home, it would not be a good idea to jog down a remote, little-used road, if you didn't know your surroundings. Why wouldn't the same rule apply here? I stopped to get my bearings and decide what to do. It was then that I spotted the farmhouse from where I was standing on the dirt road. It was at the same height as I was, but on the other side of the vineyard. I could cut down through the vineyard and come up on the other side and be at the patio. I headed down the hill enthusiastically, between the vines that were taller than I was, and felt good that I was moving pretty fast with downward momentum.

I reached the very bottom where the vines started to climb back uphill toward the farmhouse. It was then that I saw the brush in front of me rustling. I slowed out of instinct, and that's when I heard a thunderous noise come from the brush—a cross between a bull elephant roar and a grizzly bear growl. "What in the hell?" I said as I stopped dead in my tracks. Then I saw it. "Oh my god!" Out from the brush popped a very large ... *very large* ... wild boar. We made eye contact and I let out with a high-pitched scream that echoed through the still morning air, only to be outdone by another elephant-bear roar on the part of the boar—this one louder than the first. I didn't wait to see what would happen next. I spun on the spot where I was standing and started running as fast as I could back up the hill from where I came. I looked back once and saw the boar running too, but not after me, thank goodness, he was running in the opposite direction. I ran all the way back to the road and stopped to catch my breath. I walked back to the farmhouse at a fast clip. "Holy shit!" I said out loud as I reached the patio. I looked down into the vineyard but didn't see the boar, he was probably catching his breath somewhere else and thinking "Holy shit!" to himself.

I opened the bedroom door. Alex was exactly as I'd left him—he hadn't moved, and he was still snoring. Considering I could have been eaten by a boar, never to be seen or heard of again, Alex was luckier than he knew that I made it back in one piece. I could envision Lester Holt, the host of *Dateline* narrating the murder investigation, "Amanda Grayson disappeared one misty morning in the beautiful Tuscan countryside. She vanished into thin air, without so much as a trace of what became of her. Her purse, cell phone, and all of her belongings were untouched in the overly hot bedroom of her agriturismo. Her travel companion, arrested for her murder, claims to have been sleeping soundly and unaware that she disappeared. Other guests staying in the agriturismo heard them the night before her disappearance having a heated argument, and then the sound of loud thuds coming from the room. The local police found the furniture knocked about, but no overt signs of forensic evidence . . ."

I took a shower, put on a clean T-shirt and shorts, and lay down on the bed. Then a miraculous thing happened; I slept. It was 10:00 a.m. when I woke up. Alex was just waking too. We didn't say much to each other, except he asked me if I still wanted him to drive me to the airport.

"No, I've somehow survived the trip to this point, it has to be so that I can find a chandelier in Venice, for Merryhearth."

"I'm glad. And I'm sorry."

"We missed breakfast here. Do you want to head out and find someplace to eat?"

241

"That sounds great."

"Remind me later to tell you about my adventure this morning."

"Oh? Okay."

"It's a good one."

"I can't wait to hear it!"

❦━━╴

We spent the day doing the second route of wineries and historic hill towns. We both bought wine to have shipped home. I bought an artisan-made silver, orange, and blue bracelet from a jewelry shop in Montalcino. The little town was full of cute shops and quaint cafés, and we decided to sit for a while and just enjoy the sights and the people coming and going. We chatted about things going on in our personal lives—me with Merryhearth, and Alex with De'On. He showed me a picture of him and De'On together at a party. They were a nice-looking couple, and De'On reminded me of one of my favorite actors, Anthony Anderson. There seemed to be a new understanding between Alex and me, a more serious—grounded in reality—understanding between us. For me, the illusion was broken, and the surreal attraction replaced with a solid understanding of who Alex was—his strengths and his weaknesses. It wasn't that I now disliked Alex, far from it. But for me, he was no longer the hero of the song he had sung out loud as we cruised through the Rocky Mountains in Denver.

As we were getting ready to leave, an adorable kitten slipped under my chair and wound her tail around my ankle.

"Oh, how sweet, isn't she darling?" I said to Alex.

"I wonder where she came from?" he said.

"What interesting markings," I commented. "She's gray all over with a white face and neck and a perfectly orange tipped tail!"

She seemed familiar to me, like I'd seen her before. I

242

reached down to pet her and she purred. I picked her up and snuggled her in the crook of my neck, and she purred more. She was irresistible, and I'd have kept her if I could, but I had to set her down and say goodbye. A few minutes later, as we were walking back to the car, I remembered . . . *It was the very same orange-tipped-tail kitten from my dream.*

As we pulled into the farmhouse, I suddenly remembered, "OH, GOD! We have that cooking lesson tonight. With all those people."

"Do you want to skip it?"

"No, we—you, paid a fortune for it. And besides, it will look bad if we don't show up."

"Are you okay with that?" he asked.

"Yes, by now they have figured out we are not a couple, and they've chalked up the bizarre behavior to *some of you* having had too much to drink. It happens. *Normale!*"

When the time was near, we headed toward the stairs leading up to the kitchen for our cooking lesson. Alex saw an open door in the hallway next to the stairs, and said, "Let's explore. We never got a tour of the house. It's much larger than the areas we've seen and since it dates to the eleventh century, the architecture has to be unique."

"I don't think it's that old, but yes, let's check out the room."

We stepped into the opening of the doorway and found a deep, walk-in storage room.

"Huh," said Alex.

"Oh, my," I said.

"So much for locally produced, authentic Chianti wine."

"Yeah, so authentic it comes in traditional Italian fiascos."

In front of us were shelves loaded with box after box of cheap grocery store wine. It wasn't even Chianti; it was a *red blend*. With the boxes of wine were a dozen or so empty fiascos, ready to be quickly filled from one of the boxes of wine.

243

"You know," I said, "It's not that the wine is in boxes. Upon occasion, I've had some halfway decent boxed wine. It's that she lied."

"Yeah. There's really nothing more to say—she lied."

When we stepped into Nina's kitchen, promptly at 6:00 p.m., the others were already there. All of them, especially Kara and Jackie, went out of their way to welcome me into the fold of the group. The awkwardness I dreaded evaporated with the genuine rapport we shared as a group of newly formed friends. No sooner were we all together, than Nina stated we'd be starting our cooking lesson in the garden, picking the vegetables for our dinner. Out we headed, with big baskets over our arms, to a very comprehensive kitchen garden behind the house. Nina showed us where and what to cut—all the produce in our dinner was coming from the garden. I wished I'd had a large-brimmed straw hat like the one Nina donned.

Despite being late afternoon, the sun was hot, and the garden was humid like a hothouse. The gardening took longer than expected, and it was close to seven o'clock when we got started in the kitchen. Alex took over sink duty, washing vegetables, cutting boards, knives, and utensils, so they could be reused. Diane and I were cutting vegetables, Don was separating the chicken thighs and legs, Sarah, Kara, and Jackie worked with Nina to make the dough for the noodles, Matt kind of rotated around. Despite the air-conditioning, the kitchen was getting hotter by the minute.

We soon discovered that Matt would be the one to say what we were all thinking, "Can I get that fan from the hallway and set it up in here?" he asked.

"Sì, sì, get the fan," replied Nina.

Everyone took turns standing in front of the blowing air. We were all overheated and Diane pointed at her feet, "You know in all this heat and with all this salty food I'm so puffy I can hardly get my shoes on. This has to be the hottest place on earth."

"I know what you mean," I said, agreeing with her and looking at my own puffy feet.

Kara spoke up, "And the bedrooms are so hot at night. I can't sleep."

"Oh my god, it's horrible," said Jackie. "Last night I gave up and laid down on the tile floor. I actually put my face on the floor! Can you believe that? That's how hot I was."

I laughed. "I can totally believe it."

Diane, in a very sweet tone of voice, spoke up, "Nina, have you considered getting fans for the bedrooms?"

"I have fans for the bedrooms!" replied Nina matter-of-factly.

"Well, where the hell are they?" asked Matt. My thoughts exactly—*If she has fans, where the bleeeeep are they?*

"You want a fan for your room?" replied Nina.

At this point, completely unrehearsed, everyone in the kitchen looked up from what they were doing, and replied in unison, "YES!!"

"Okay, I get you the fans. You take them back after dinner to your rooms."

Diane spoke up again, "Maybe you could add to the information sheet in our rooms that fans are available upon request."

"Yeah," said Matt, "How would we know you had fans?"

Nina looked at Matt like he was about five years old. "You Americans. The problem with you Americans is that you never ask for what you want. I see this all the time. You leave here and give me a bad review, but you never asked for what you want. I need good reviews, so you want something . . . ask."

"Okay," said Matt, as we all looked on, except for his wife, Sarah, who had a little smile on her face and was very focused on the pasta maker machine. "I want something besides hard-boiled eggs for breakfast."

"What do you want?" asked Nina.

"A cooked egg," said Matt.

"Fine, no problem. You can have a cooked egg. Just ask the cook in the kitchen to make you one in the morning. You see, facile!"

It was now close to eight o'clock, and we were just beginning to cook the chicken thighs and legs in a sauté pan on the stove and feed the dough through the noodle cutting machine. I said to Diane, who I could tell was someone who entertained and cooked a lot, "At this rate we might be eating by ten o'clock."

"Not if she doesn't stop criticizing how everyone's doing their job. You'd think I never cut a carrot in my life."

Nina had called Diane out, rather embarrassingly, for not cutting the vegetables the way she had instructed us to do. Being a good little camper, mine were cut according to specifications and I didn't get yelled at—but my turn for total humiliation was coming.

Matt spoke up again, "I'm starved, can we unwrap the bread?"

We were all starved and didn't wait for Nina's answer. There were two loaves of bread on the table, and we wasted no time in unwrapping them and passing the baskets. Nina at this point brought out two fiascos of the "locally produced Chianti," and like so many ravenous vultures we gnawed on our bread, washing it down with the cardboard box wine.

"Don't eat too much bread, you won't have room for dinner," said Nina.

Diane asked her husband, who was overseeing the chicken simmering in the sauté pan, how it was coming.

"Nina," called Don, "how much longer do you think for this chicken?"

"Oh, the chicken is ready, but we have to let the pasta dry

before we can cook it."

Matt spoke for us again, "Let the pasta dry! Geez, how long does that take? It's nine o'clock now."

Nina didn't really answer. She was piling up all the dirty dishes and utensils at the sink and asked us to set the table as she brought out stacks of pretty hand-painted farmhouse plates. Diane and I decided to finally sit down, our duties being done. Alex had been very subdued, staying over in the corner at the sink and out of the line of fire. As I dabbed my hot, damp face with the soft cotton napkin, I was thinking that at least we all looked equally hot and miserable. But little did I know that miserable was to get a lot worse for me.

Nina walked over to Alex, and perhaps thinking she had ignored him, said, "You are a good boy—washing all these dishes." Alex said nothing, his back to us, and just kept scrubbing.

Looking over at me where I was sitting at the table, Nina said, "You have a very good son." The whole room was suddenly very quiet, and I saw everyone looking at me. I must have had a very strange expression on my face. I made no reply and just looked at her.

Then she made it worse, "He is your son, no?"

The only sound in the room was the fan blowing and the chicken simmering. Everyone, including Alex, was now holding their breath. No one was moving, they were frozen in place.

So many thoughts went through my head in that instant, the first being *Ewwww!* What—did she think I was sleeping in a double bed with my grown son! Then I thought, *Do I actually look that bad—old enough to be his mother?* Next came, *Is she fucking crazy?* There was just no way in hell I was going to explain *anything* to this woman, so . . . I simply said, "No."

She couldn't leave it alone. She kept going, "No? He's not your son?"

This time I didn't have to answer her. To my relief, everyone answered for me. In a loud, resounding, definitive response, they all said in unison, "NO!"

"Oh," she said. "Okay, it is time to cook the pasta now."

Diane leaned toward me, "Don't pay her any attention, no sane person would ever mistake you for Alex's mother!"

We finally served the chicken, salad, and pasta at 10:00 p.m. It was good, not amazing, but good—and homemade from fresh ingredients. I couldn't see that it was worth sixty euro a piece in ingredients, but we had the *benefit* of Nina's cooking instruction, so there was that.

We said our goodbyes that night on the starlit stone terrace before heading in different directions to our rooms, each of us carrying our big, white floor fans. We had bonded, and it gave me a whole new appreciation for "you Americans." I was ready to be done with Tuscany and glad we were headed out in the morning.

Chapter 26

We arrived in Florence at about ten o'clock in the morning to drop off the little red rental car that had been our only sanctuary from the miserable heat. The drive from the agriturismo was shorter than I had expected, and I was looking forward to seeing what I could in the short time we'd be in Florence.

When we stepped out of the rental car covered garage onto the sidewalk—dragging our multitude of stacked rollie suitcases behind us—the heat hit me in the face like an inferno. It was by far hotter here than anywhere we had been. Also complicating matters were the masses of people. The sidewalks were as crowded and busy as a stadium exit zone after a big sports event. It was nearly impossible to navigate the streets, with our luggage in tow, getting hotter by the second.

"Can we leave our luggage in a locker at the train station?" I asked Alex.

"No, and we have to be careful that it doesn't get stolen if we aren't watching it."

"Maybe we could get a hotel to keep it for us?" I asked.

"Maybe. Let's try that."

We found the nearest high-end hotel and immediately upon entering into the reception area a porter asked if he could take our luggage. At this point, I was hot and frustrated from navigating nearly ten blocks through the heat and crowds. I spoke up enthusiastically, "Yes, thank you! But we aren't checking in until this afternoon. Do you have storage for our luggage until we check in?" I fibbed.

"Of course. Let me get you a ticket. Your luggage will be very safe here until you are ready for it."

Alex tipped him, and we sat down in the hotel café and sipped iced coffee.

"I'm headed to a jewelry shop on the Ponte Vecchio. I'll show you some things on the way over," said Alex as we finished our coffees and got up to leave.

"Okay." I guessed this was the best I could hope for during our quick run through Florence.

It was unbelievably hot, and Alex was in a hurry, so most of what he pointed out was a blur to me. When we arrived at the jewelry shop on the Ponte Vecchio, I missed my cue that he wanted to shop alone. It didn't take me long, however, to figure it out. He and the salesclerk were all energy—dashing here and there, pulling out bracelets, comparing quality and cost, measuring the length since De'On's wrists were apparently large. I got the impression that I was very much in the way, so I slipped out the door and wandered around the other shops. Most were too expensive or too cheesy to buy anything, and again the crowds were unbelievable. I wondered if perhaps Alex wanted me out of the shop because while he was there, he was going to buy a little memento of the trip for me. A way to say thank you for all the work I put into the planning, and researching, and finding the hotels to make it the best trip possible. That would be nice, maybe a little Italian teapot charm—he knew I collected those, and I'd seen a case with charms in it near the front of the store.

After a couple of hours, Alex texted me that we needed to head for the train station. We picked up our luggage at the hotel and fought our way through the hot, overcrowded streets, dragging the suitcases behind us until we reached the train station. This was my Florence experience, and with one last look from my train car window, I saw Florence fade into obscurity.

The train from Florence to Venice was more crowded than our train from Rome to Orvieto had been. I didn't have a window seat, so it was hard to see the landscape we traveled through. Once the train had picked up speed and the passengers sitting around us were settled in, Alex asked, "Do you want to see the bracelet I bought?"

"Sure," I said as enthusiastically as I could.

"It's twenty-karat white gold. I had them add links to the chain while I waited so that it will fit De'On's wrist."

"It's nice, did you get a good deal?"

"Four-hundred euro."

"Whoa—that's a lot of money!"

"You think? I thought it was very reasonable," replied Alex with a broad smile, obviously very pleased with his purchase.

I thought to myself, *I hope he's worth it.*

⚷━━⚹

We disembarked the train in Venice and from the Santa Lucia Railway Station we caught the vaporetto, or water bus. Our hotel was in the Dorsoduro District, one of six sestieri in Venice. This meant we arrived to the opposite side of the island from where our hotel was located. I had chosen a four-star hotel in Dorsoduro because it promised to be one of the nicest locations in Venice. The long water-bus ride, for nearly the full length of the Grand Canal, was a delightful tour in

251

and of itself. The Grand Canal, curving in a reverse S through the heart of the city, is also Venice's main street, and it was very busy with traffic—boat traffic. We saw everything from water taxis, to water buses like ours, to gondolas, and even barges carrying produce and food goods. I was fascinated by the hustle and bustle of it all.

I knew from having studied my tour book to find a spot outside on the front bow of the vaporetto. I was glad I did because the unofficial tour started straightaway with a spectacular view of Santa Maria di Nazareth, an impressive seventeenth century Baroque church with a façade of columns and a multitude of statues—mostly saints. My tour book had me watching out next for a series of magnificent palazzi, or palaces, representing every style of architecture, from the twelfth century to the early eighteenth century. I left Alex watching my luggage as I dashed back and forth from one side of the open boat deck to the other to see the palazzi in the order the tour book said they would appear. I loved it—it was otherworldly, and the fresh air mixed with occasional water spray kept me cool.

After passing the Fish Market and the Ca' da Mosto, the oldest palazzo in Venice—dating from the thirteenth century—we came to the Rialto Bridge. I didn't need my tour book to recognize it. I also knew we must be about halfway to where we needed to get off of the water-bus at the Accademia C stop. I had selected a hotel that faced onto a quiet, alluring, side canal, near the Peggy Guggenheim museum. We stepped off of the vaporetto with our luggage and found the hotel easily. Fortunately, we didn't have to drag our suitcases all over the island to get to our destination.

Upon entering the hotel lobby, we were immediately greeted very hospitably by an older gentleman in a suit bearing the hotel's logo. He was incredibly gracious and seemed to understand immediately what we needed.

"Your spacious canal-side room is ready for you. We turned down the air conditioner so that it would be cool when you arrived. There are complimentary bottles of water in the room's wet bar refrigerator, and you may stop by the front desk anytime when you need replacements. Our American-style complimentary breakfast is served in the café until 10:00 a.m. and we are here to help with any arrangements for dinner, sightseeing tours, and transportation. Welcome to our lovely hotel and to Venice."

No judgy looks, no snide comments, no abrupt demeanor. *Very nice*, I thought to myself. Also nice, was that Alex didn't act weird when we checked in. It seemed he was over his ridiculous, mistaken impression that he was seen as a male prostitute, and I was his client. Our luggage had been whisked away while we were checking in and was already in the room when Alex scanned the key card and unlocked the door. When we opened the beautiful solid wood door with polished brass trim, a surprising blast of cold air hit us. The room was heavenly. Everything smelled new, and it was beautifully and tastefully decorated in a clean, modern—yet plush—style. The room was enormous, with two sets of French doors that opened onto Juliet balconies overlooking the quiet side canal. The bathroom was as big as the whole bedroom at the farmhouse and was separated completely from the bedroom by a full dressing room with its own chaise longue. The shower was huge with multiple shower heads. *No rushing us out of the shower here*, I thought to myself. The bed was enormous and when I opened the large wardrobe, I was delighted to see half a dozen pillows in clean, crisp, white pillowcases.

"Thank goodness! I think we lucked out with this one!"

"It's really nice," said Alex as he opened one of the sets of French doors overlooking the canal and took a selfie.

We unpacked, drank our bottles of water, and showered.

When I came out of the dressing room in one of the new out-fits I hadn't worn yet, Alex had prepared a little apéritif for us to share before dinner. The French doors were open, and he had set up the room's little table and chairs in front of them. There was a bottle of wine and some fruit, cheese, and crackers laid out.

"Oh, wow, how delicious this looks. Where did you get the wineglasses and the knife?"

"Our friend at the front desk was very accommodating," replied Alex.

"This is certainly a nice way to start the last leg of our Italy tour!"

"Cheers! Here's to our time in Venice and finding the perfect chandelier for Merryhearth!" said Alex as he held up a wineglass.

"Cheers!"

On our way out of the hotel that evening to get dinner, the man who had checked us in asked if we would be interested in a tour of one of the glassmaking factories in Murano.

"We offer transportation to a Murano glass factory, followed by a tour and glassblowing demonstration, completely complimentary—if you are interested?"

"As a matter of fact, we were looking to go to Murano to-morrow," said Alex.

"Very good. Does nine thirty a.m. work for you to have the boat pick you up?"

I nodded my head and Alex asked where we needed to be to meet the boat.

"The boat will be right here, in front of the hotel entrance, waiting for you."

"Thank you!" I said. This was working out very well.

For dinner that night, we found a restaurant with outdoor tables that faced onto the Venetian Lagoon. We watched the multitude of boats navigating the water and the moon rising over the lagoon to reflect its silver glow in the wavy seawater. I was able to sleep some that night. The sheer delight of being in a cold room, with exquisite quality linens that were cool and crisp to the touch, and a huge bed to stretch out in, made it possible to doze off.

⚬⟶

At 9:30 a.m. prompt, we entered the hotel lobby. A different person, this time an attractive woman, greeted us and motioned that our boat to Murano was ready when we were.

"How nice, she knew we are the ones taking the tour," I said.

"Yes, everything is done very well here," replied Alex.

"Including the boat! Look, it's beautiful!" I said, pointing through the glass doors of the hotel.

Waiting for us at the tiny loading platform was a gorgeous, vintage, solid wood Chris Craft boat. It was beautifully restored and maintained. I estimated it to be about twenty feet long, and it had soft white leather seats and a white canvas convertible top, that together made a stunning contrast against the gleaming wood. I practically felt like royalty as the driver took my hand and helped me step in. We took a leisurely drive from the south side of the island north to Murano. The driver made a point of calling out landmarks as we passed them and delivered us directly to the dock at one of the glass factories, where our tour began immediately.

For a free excursion, it could not have been done better—no crass sales pitch wrapped in an artisan demonstration here. We were treated like VIP guests at the factory. A very small number of us were taken to the glassblowing floor and provided a very thorough and informative demonstration of the process and skill involved in making the beautiful Murano glass chandeliers and other glass artwork. I met one of the master glassblowers, and we were able to ask him questions

255

about the process and his work. After the demonstration, we were assigned a salesperson, Mr. Lorenzo Fostano, who gave us a tour of the showroom. Lorenzo showed us around the enormous, multi-floor building and continued my education. He was very patient as I asked a million questions, and he wasn't at all pushy. I wasn't ready to pick a chandelier from the first factory I'd ever seen, but I got a good start on understanding what I liked, and didn't like, for Merryhearth.

Alex was an absolute trooper that day on the island of Murano. I dragged him through every single glass chandelier shop—every one of them! In each I asked questions, was shown unique examples of the beautiful chandeliers, and in several cases was taken to back rooms—only opened for serious buyers, where hundreds of glittering beauties sprang to life above my head when the light switch was flipped. He never lost interest and stuck by me the whole day.

We eventually took a break and stopped for lunch, sitting at a table along the waterfront. Toward the end of our meal two middle-aged American ladies, tourists like ourselves, asked if they could sit at our table as there weren't any seats available elsewhere. We motioned them in and made introductions. It wasn't long before we were chatting with Madge and Lisa from Ohio about our mutual impressions of Italy and our experiences. At some point, the topic of how the two of them came to take a trip to Italy came up. And, then it was my turn, but unlike our first introductions in Tuscany, I jumped right in, "Same for us. We became friends through work. When we realized we both wanted to visit Italy, we decided, why not? Good friends make great travel companions."

"Exactly!" said Madge.

"The best trips I've taken were with a good friend," said Lisa.

"I have to agree," I said.

Madge asked for how long we had known one another,

and Alex picked up the conversation from there, talking about our connection and the many places we'd visited while on work trips.

As I listened to their conversation from my corner of the table and watched as Alex carried on a lively discussion with our new acquaintances, I came to a realization. I was no longer smitten with Alex—my smittenness phase for Alex was over. I wasn't sure if it was the night at Aldo's restaurant and what came after, or Alex's newfound fixation with De'On, maybe it was spending so much time with Alex that I got to know who he was behind the public face, or all of those things combined. But whatever it was, I was sure of one thing—the new reality was better. It felt so much better to know and to say aloud, *What we have is friendship*, plain and simple. I was released from the guessing game, the pseudo roles that we'd both played since the Orlando trip, and the stress of a continuously "on the edge of something more—but never crossing the line" trajectory with Alex. It had been exhausting, and it wasn't real, and it wasn't fun—not anymore, anyway.

"No more," I said softly to myself.

"What was that?" asked Alex, looking inquisitively in my direction.

"Oh, nothing, just that I can't eat anymore. I'm stuffed." Everyone laughed and shortly thereafter we said our good-byes to Madge and Lisa and continued shopping.

☛

It was near the end of the day when we sat down for a few minutes to assess the best option for purchasing the chandelier for Merryhearth.

"You know, I think the first factory is the best option. After learning all that we did today, the first factory will make a custom chandelier to my specifications. I've seen elements of different chandeliers that I liked throughout the day, but none of them were all in one chandelier. I need a custom chandelier made in order to get all the features I want and omit the features I don't want."

"Let's head in that direction," said Alex. "Lorenzo will be very glad to see you. He liked you!"

We entered the building where we had started our day some six hours earlier. We asked for Lorenzo, and before we knew it, I was explaining to him in great detail what I wanted. We sat at a large table and Lorenzo began to sketch the chandelier I described. He offered us glasses of champagne, and we were served from the most exquisite handblown champagne flutes I had ever seen. Once the sketch was complete, we dashed (with our champagne flutes) between floors where Lorenzo pointed out different chandelier features that fit the design he had sketched. As I said, "Yes that base," and "No, not those arms, these arms over here," and "Just one set of swirls, not two," and "clear glass with *that* shade of pink edging," he took furious notes next to his sketch. As soon as the details were documented, and I was completely pleased with the design, he made a call to the factory floor. I could hear him speaking rapidly in Italian with someone on the end of the phone, "Io voglio Fabio per questo ordinazione. Sì, sì Fabio, Fabio."

"Good news for you, madam. Fabio Ongaro is going to make your chandelier. He is a master glassblower here at the factory and his work is exceptional. You met him this morning, on the glassblowing floor during the demonstration."

"Oh, he is the man who was answering my questions. That's awesome! I will think of him when I look at the chandelier."

"It will be beautiful ... just like you. You have designed a beautiful chandelier," said Lorenzo, smiling.

We completed the details of the sale and Lorenzo told me to expect the chandelier to be shipped to my home in about six weeks. He explained how it would be packed and provided general instructions for assembling it, but said detailed instructions would be included.

Feeling incredibly satisfied, as only a full day of hard-core shopping can achieve, we caught a water taxi back to our hotel. That night, over dinner, I pictured my pink Murano glass chandelier, handmade to order by the master glassblower Fabio Ongaro, hanging in the dining room at Merryhearth Manor.

Chapter 27

Our second full day in Venice was really the start of seeing the main island up close. After a delicious breakfast at the hotel we began our exploring, on foot like in Rome but with a little less heat and humidity. I was pleasantly lost as we wandered through the large cobblestone alleyways and the smaller, narrow calli lined with tall brick and stucco houses in a state of enchanting decay. The calli were so narrow that I could run my hand along the old walls as we walked and imagine the generations of Venetian families whose rich lives made each of these buildings a warm and inviting home over the course of centuries, *centuries*. Alex had a good sense of direction, and we would usually pop out onto a fondamenta that bordered one of the canals, and then we could head toward a bridge that would take us back into the interior to be lost again. Unlike Rome, we took a much less measured approach to our sightseeing. The destination here was Venice itself— the architecture, the alleys, the squares, the canals, and so we let our wanderings dictate where we ended.

We would find ourselves meandering into campielli, small squares, when we least expected them. Stepping into the campielli was like entering a time capsule. Regardless of the number of tourists out and about, these minuscule squares were mostly deserted, and we often found ourselves the only people in sight. They customarily contained an ancient well in the center, and a number of buildings with doors and windows flung open onto the square. Small songbirds called to one another across the balconies of these small squares, the bigger birds and gulls finding them too confined. Gauzy white curtains fluttered, laundry was hung out to dry across balconies, and frequently the aroma of baking bread all added to the sensation of having time traveled to a pleasant summer day in the past.

The larger squares, or campi, were frequently bordered by a beautiful, ancient church, and encircled by benches and huge clay pots filled with flowers cascading down their sides and resting on the cobblestones. Sometimes a statue or fountain was also featured in the campi. Typically, encompassing one corner of the square was a little café with tables set up in a shady spot under a tree or with colorful umbrellas. We took frequent advantage of these cafés to get a cool drink and use the bathroom. Like Rome, bathrooms were few and far between. Through our random approach to enjoying Venice, we also stumbled across significant landmarks—including Saint Mark's Square and the Doge's Palace. I was awestruck by Saint Mark's Basilica with its ornate Italo-Byzantine architecture, intricate vast mosaics, and stolen treasures that were a fascinating glimpse of the Crusaders and their daunting effect on civilization. After a late lunch in a restaurant near the Piazzo San Marco, we headed toward the Rialto Bridge. Alex said his sister had commissioned him to find an Italian gold ankle bracelet.

"Do you have a specific shop in mind?" I asked.

"No, not really, but it would be nice to say it came from a shop on or near the Rialto Bridge."

261

Everywhere we went were little specialty shops selling leather goods, exquisite stationery and pens, unique pottery, and many other artisan-made treasures. We spent the rest of the afternoon shopping for souvenirs for family and friends while we continued our meandering sightseeing. At the edge of the Rialto Bridge, we found a small jewelry shop across from a bakery. It was the bakery that first caught my attention. *Oooo*, I thought, *here are the scrumptious looking Italian baked goods I hoped to find on our adventures across Italy.* They were labeled with delightful sounding names: marantega cake, bussolà burenelli cookies, fugassa cake, zaleti cookies, fritoe cakes, and fried crème—to name a few! I would much rather have bought pastries than jewelry, but when I looked up from the bakery window display, Alex had already entered the jewelry shop, so I went in to see what they had. I looked at several bracelets, small ones that were reasonably priced, and Alex looked at options for his sister.

"They have a lot of silver charms. Did you see them?" asked Alex, pointing at a shelf on the far side of the store.

"Oh, they do have a large selection of charms," I replied as I began scanning them.

"Did you see this one? It's an Italian teapot."

I looked at a little silver charm he was holding up. It was actually a coffeepot, but I decided not to correct him. "No, I didn't see that one. It's cute."

"Would you like it?" he asked me.

His question took me by surprise and I thought to myself, *Aw, that's very sweet.* It was an appropriate gesture on our last day in Italy, and it showed he appreciated all that I had done to make this the best trip possible. It also helped to heal the still smarting wounds he'd inflicted—intentional or not—and it boded well for the future of the friendship that at present was on shaky ground.

As we finalized our selections and the salesclerk was

adding up our totals, the little coffeepot charm, at fifteen euro, was being added to my receipt by mistake.

"Oh, that's for his tally," I said.

The clerk seemed confused and sought confirmation from Alex with an inquisitive look.

"Oh, did you want me to get it?" asked Alex.

What! I was shocked. His question could not have hit me any harder if it had been a punch to the stomach.

He responded before I could answer, "It's fine—no problem. Add it to my stuff." Then he slid it across the counter to me to put in my bag.

Stunned by what had just transpired, I simply said, "Thanks."

☦━━★

On our last night in Italy, we decided to find a really good restaurant, if we could. The food in Venice had been okay, but not amazing to this point. On our way back from shopping, I stopped at our hotel reception desk and asked about options for restaurants while Alex went to the room to shower and dress. The same gentleman who checked us in was on duty.

"Your last night in Venice," he said with a warm smile.

"Actually, the last night in Italy. We've been to Rome, Tuscany, and here," I said.

"And was it all that you expected and more?"

I hesitated before I responded, "It was different in many ways than I expected." I was surprised to hear a hint of sadness in my tone.

"Ahh, sometimes we are *sent* the unexpected. I've come to learn in all my years in this lifetime, that those experiences are the ones that help us grow . . . they are gifts," he said very philosophically.

"Hmm, I think you may be right," I said. "There is always a silver lining if we look carefully enough."

"I can tell . . . you are very astuta and a beautiful person. The gift of your unexpected Italy experience will reveal itself in time."

"Thank you," I said with a smile.

"And now, let's find you the perfect place for an ottima cena on your last night in Italy."

He made several phone calls and was speaking in Italian, but I could tell he was asking about daily specials and reservations. He wrote the name and address of one of the restaurants on a hotel card and handed it to me.

"This is where you should have dinner tonight. I know the manager personally, and he is going to make sure you have a wonderful meal. I've made the reservation for you, and just let him know when you arrive that Giovvani sent you."

"Thank you so much!" I said, wanting to give him a hug but thinking better of it.

That night, I dressed in my last new outfit with matching sandals, and the little silver bracelet I bought in Montalcino, and we walked along the canal outside of our hotel to the restaurant. It was nearby, so I wasn't hot and sticky by the time we arrived. When I mentioned to the hostess that Giovvani had sent us, the manager came to the front of the restaurant personally to greet us. We were taken to our table and introduced to no fewer than three servers who would be attending us. The staff, the food, and the warm ambiance of the restaurant were amazing. We enjoyed a delicious four-course dinner and shared a bottle of wine recommended by our waiter.

It was a good way to spend our last night in Italy. I was so ready to be home, to be back on terra firma (literally and figuratively), and to focus on Merryhearth. I needed the grounding that I only felt when I was walking through her rooms, touching the smooth plaster walls, and imagining my life in that wonderful house. But before leaving Italy, I had one thing to take care of. Sitting at the bottom of my purse was a pretty little red-velvet pouch, with a kiss inside—a tiny, dainty gold thimble with intricate carving.

We walked back to the hotel and entered the lobby. I was sorry to see that Giovanni's shift had ended, and his replacement was at the front desk. She greeted us enthusiastically and asked about dinner.

"Go ahead up to the room if you like," I said to Alex. "I'm going to get a couple of bottles of water and will be up shortly."

"Okay. I'm going to double-check our flight information for tomorrow and then go to bed."

"Sounds good. I'll be quiet coming in, in case you're already asleep."

Of course, I knew that it wouldn't matter if I was quiet or not because nothing would wake him once his head hit the pillow.

When Alex was out of sight, I stepped back outside and took a leisurely walk along the canal. The night air was refreshing, and the people watching was superb, with happy tourists meandering alongside the water enjoying themselves. I walked toward the Calle di Mezzo bridge—the moon was bright in the starlit sky and I could see its brilliant light reflecting off the clear water. Standing on the bridge, I looked out toward the Grand Canal. Gondolas were navigating to and fro from both sides of the little bridge. It was a perfect scene and I couldn't help but smile at the beauty of it all. I reached into my purse and felt for the soft velvet. I opened the little pouch and took out its treasure. I ran my finger over the edge, feeling the inscription, and then held the kiss in the palm of my hand. Another gondola glided almost silently under me. I waited for a lull in activity and for the canal surface to become smooth again, like glass. I slipped the thimble back into the red-velvet pouch and pulled the drawstrings.

It was different now between Alex and me. The magical

allure that was born from blueberry margaritas, enriched by the mystical aura of the Northshore, and matured through shared, beautiful time together, was over as suddenly and un-expectedly as it had started. "Friends don't kiss," I said softly to myself, and I tossed the little bundle into the canal. I heard a faint splash and, leaning over the side of the handrail, I watched it slowly sashay back and forth, like a red-velvet feather, downward to the bottom, where it came to rest pret-tily on the sandy floor of the canal. Then I walked back to the hotel and enthusiastically packed for the trip back to Virginia. I very much looked forward to being home in a few hours.

Part Four

Loving

The Props assist the House
Until the House is built
And then the Props withdraw
And adequate, erect,
The House support itself
And cease to recollect
The Auger and the Carpenter-
Just such a retrospect
Hath the perfected Life-
A past of Plank and Nail
And slowness-then the Scaffolds drop
Affirming it a Soul.

— Emily Dickinson
The Props Assist The House

Chapter 28

I pulled into the driveway at Merryhearth and was surprised to see things looking mysteriously closed up and quiet. I had come straight from the airport, and it was early enough on a Saturday that the crew should have been on-site working, but they weren't. I unlocked the front door and stepping in I saw immediately that the construction debris was picked up and there wasn't a tool in sight. The house was hot and stuffy as I walked the rooms on each floor, looking to see what had been done while I was in Italy for almost two weeks. The only change was on the gallery level—the intricate lath was gone, and the nearly two-hundred-year-old original roof beams were exposed. I saw that they had new engineered beams sistered along their sides to reinforce them. The broken beam was securely supported, and it clearly had not required removing the standing-seam metal roof. *Thank goodness for that,* I thought, but what on earth was going on? Why had all the work stopped, and Josh and the crew packed up and left? I pulled up Josh's number on my cell and called him—he answered right away.

"Hi, Amanda. How was Italy?" he asked.

"Hi, Josh. It was okay. How was your week? How are things going at Merryhearth?"

"Have you been out there yet?" he asked.

"Yeah, I'm here now, and it looks like there may be a problem or something?"

"You could say that. Have you been home yet and did you check your mail?"

"No, I came straight out from the airport. Why?"

"You should have a letter from the bank."

"Oh, what's in the letter?" I asked trepidatiously.

"Amanda, the bank has shut down. It's gone . . . closed. They lacked the liquidity to meet their obligations. In other words, the bank that was lending you the money, and paying me to do the work, has failed."

"The bank went bankrupt?"

"More or less . . . yeah, the bank is bankrupt," said Josh.

"What does this mean for Merryhearth?" I asked.

"I'm not the one to be advising you, but I spoke with Gil, you know, the bank president, and he said existing loans would be transferred to a new bank for the amount owed, not the amount that was promised to the customers," explained Josh.

"So, in other words, no more money for the rehabilitation work?" I asked.

"Right—and it gets worse. Because the bank is insolvent, they haven't paid me for any of the materials or work we did during the last month. They told me it was up to me to seek payment from you directly."

"Oh no! This is a nightmare!"

"Look, I know you're tapped out and that's why I had to pull the crew and get them started on another job. I can't lose them. I have to be able to pay them, so we've moved off your house for now."

"Oh, of course. No, I totally understand. I need time to figure this out and find out what my options are."

"Yeah, they've left you in a real bind," said Josh.

"I will pay you what I owe you. I just have to figure out what to do now for money. I'll figure something out."

"I know you will. I've got the guys on a good-paying job now, so that actually buys you some time to figure things out. Just stay in touch and keep me posted on the progress."

"I will. Thanks for the info, and for being so nice about this mess."

"Hey, it's not your fault. It'll get worked out. These things always do. Hang in there."

"Thanks, Josh. Talk to you soon. Bye."

I spent the drive back to my apartment in Leesburg going over the situation. The construction loan through the bank was all the money I had for the work on Merryhearth, and it wasn't even enough to do everything—just the basics to get the house to *livable* condition and allow me to move in. I had very little cash, just a few thousand left over from the loan I took out against my retirement 401K fund for the down payment on the mortgage and the English basement work. I had good credit, thank goodness, and my salary was decent—but the rent on my Leesburg apartment was eating up a big chunk of that each month. I was going to have to get another bank to lend me the money for the rehabilitation work. I was also going to have to come up with the money I owed Josh. *How much was that*, I wondered. Other than the Italy hotel charges, my credit cards were at zero balance, and I'd already budgeted for paying for the Italy expenses from my next paycheck. I contemplated the feasibility of using my credit cards to purchase needed construction materials.

I called Danielle from the car, "Hey, it's me. Are you in the middle of anything?"

"No, just doing laundry. That's my exciting Saturday afternoon. Oh! Are you back from Italy?" she asked.

"Yeah, got in just a couple of hours ago."

"Ooh, I can't wait to hear all about it! Want to meet for dinner?"

"I can't afford dinner. Let's meet at my place in Leesburg. I'll make a pot of coffee if you bring the vanilla creamer."

"Hmm, sounds like you have a lot to tell me about Italy. I can't wait to hear it—but don't leave me in suspense . . . is Alex still gay?"

"This isn't about Italy. I've got much, much bigger issues to deal with, and I need your brain to help me think through it."

"Uh-oh . . . okay, I'm on the way with coffee creamer. I'll pick up some Chinese too, you're probably starved," she offered.

"Great, thanks! Oh . . . and Alex is still definitely gay, and very happily so. I'll fill you in on Italy much later. *This* needs full focus first!"

"Got it! See you soon."

Danielle arrived bearing crispy spring rolls, Szechuan beef, General Tso's chicken, steamed rice, and vanilla coffee creamer. As I opened the containers and slid in the serving spoons, she reached into the cabinet for the plates.

"Never mind that—I'll get the plates. Here . . . read this letter from the bank," I said while taking the plates from her and placing them on the table.

I watched her read through the letter twice before she looked up, "Holy crap! The bank is bankrupt?"

"Yep, the Merryhearth rehabilitation loan has evaporated into thin air, and with it went Josh and his crew. I'm dead in the water with a house that I can't live in—and a big old fat mortgage that I have to keep paying, regardless!"

"Oh, my! Okay—food first, then we'll brainstorm!"

After picking at my food and giving Danielle some of the easier to explain highlights of the Italy trip, I was ready to get down to business. We cleared the table and I made us a pot of strong coffee.

"So basically you are back at square one," said Danielle.

"Except now I don't have the option of *not buying* the house," I said.

"That was never really an option. You and that house were meant to be together," she said, laughing.

"Here's the thing, I need to prove the house has equity or 'potential equity' so that a bank will loan me money to do the work it needs. Banks aren't big on 'potential equity.' They want no risk, and that means proving equity now—not at some point in the future," I explained.

"Hmm," said Danielle, and I could see her wheels turning. "So you need to demonstrate the house is worth more than what you owe on it so that they will grant you—like an equity line of credit?"

"Yes, exactly. The more the house is worth, the greater the loan, or equity line of credit can be," I explained.

"What exactly is the state of the house now?" she asked.

"The basement looks great, but that's about it. The old, nasty looking kitchen is still there, with dead bees stuck in every nook and cranny. The two old bathrooms are still in place. The ceiling has been torn down on the gallery level. The storm windows are in a state of half missing, with vines and dead bugs caught in them. The porticoes are lethal with rotted boards more numerous than solid boards. The entire house is caked in brick dust, dirt, and grime from years of sitting abandoned. The grounds are a mess—but at least the old outbuildings are gone. Should I go on?"

"No, I get it. It looks pretty bad and that's what the lender will see when they send their representatives out to appraise the value of the house," said Danielle astutely.

"Yes, unfortunately. Hell, for all I know, they might say it isn't worth what I owe on it, much less, more than that."

"Now you're just being pessimistic. Anybody with half a brain can see that house is going to be amazing when it's done. The key is getting them to be able to see beyond its present state and imagine its future state."

"Exactly!" I said.

"How do you feel about hard labor and getting dirty?" asked Danielle.

"If you're suggesting I take on the construction work . . . not good," I replied.

"No, that's not what I was thinking. You know how real estate agents stage houses when they are trying to sell them?" she explained.

"Ohhh . . . I see where you're going with this. Clean the house up, make it look as good as possible, and help the appraiser . . ."

"See into the future!" said Danielle, finishing my sentence.

"You've got a point. In the state that it's in now, it's hard to see the value and potential. The banks are risk averse unless they get a decent appraisal. So, we make sure the appraisal is as high as possible by staging the house."

"Exactly!" said Danielle.

"See . . . this is why I needed your brain power!" I said, slapping my hand on the table.

"So, pick me up at eight a.m. tomorrow morning? I'll bring my cleaning supplies, and you bring yours. We'll make a day of it," said Danielle cheerfully.

"Danielle, I'm exhausted. I haven't slept in two weeks. I don't know if I have the energy, but okay . . . let's do it. It has to be done!"

"Great. I'm going to head out then, and you should go to bed and get some sleep. I'll see you in the morning!"

After Danielle left I straightened up the apartment and unpacked my suitcases. After a long, refreshing shower, I slipped into my own bed for the first time in what felt like an eternity. It was wonderful to be home, and I slept soundly for twelve hours. When my alarm went off at 7:00 a.m. I felt rested and ready to face anything and everything to save Merryhearth. *Thank goodness for Danielle*, I thought to myself as I headed out to pick her up—with every cleaning accoutrement I owned and two big floor fans.

It was the end of August, the hottest time of the year in the Shenandoah Valley. When we arrived at Merryhearth the outdoor temperature was already eighty-four degrees and going up. I opened all the windows that we could open, and all the doors. I set up the floor fans and got the air circulating as quickly as possible to prevent the heat from settling in. We decided to start on the lowest level and work our way up.

"The English basement looks amazing," said Danielle.

"Oh, that's right, you haven't seen it since they finished the work down here."

As Danielle studied the big summer-kitchen cooking fireplace, brick floor, and beautifully restored exposed brick walls in the future wine cellar, she said, "We need to make sure all four rooms down here are counted as living space by the appraiser. Amanda, do you know what an Old-World wine cellar like this, with a fireplace no less, does for an appraisal?"

"Hopefully a lot," I said.

We swept the floor and dusted the ceiling rafters in the English basement then migrated to the first floor which was in much, much worse shape. We worked side by side from high to low in each room. Everything was covered in grime, brick and mortar dust, cobwebs, and dead bugs. Using long handled dust mops and wet mops we cleaned ceilings and walls— knocking off as much loose paint as we could from spots where it was peeling, washed miles worth of wood trimwork, and cleaned the hardwood floors.

"This is unbelievable," said Danielle, "these rooms are

unrecognizable. What a transformation!"

"Did you notice that under this cheap white paint, everything is Philadelphia green?" I asked.

"Yeah, I've noticed that. The ceilings, the walls, the wood trim—everything is that same shade of green. I don't get it," said Danielle.

"The good news is that it looks like there have only ever been two coats of paint, the original green and this crappy-quality white. I'm thinking there must have been wallpaper everywhere. The walls are in such incredibly good condition that they must have been covered continuously over the years—then someone took down the wallpaper and painted over the green with this white paint. It was probably the developer who subdivided the land and thought he was going to make a big profit off the house by doing some quick cosmetic updates."

We took a break to run into town, cool off, and get a bite to eat. Downtown Winchester was crowded with weekend day-trippers who had come out from the suburbs and D.C. to explore the historic towns and wineries up and down the valley. We looked a mess, comparatively speaking, but we didn't care—we were on a mission and once we finished our lunch, we were back at it.

"Wow, are you ready to tackle the kitchen?" I asked Danielle after we walked through the now-clean sections of the house to the last room that needed our attention on the first floor.

"It's really bad, and it's torn up too. The ceiling is missing a section where they took the bees out, honey stains are streaked down the wall, chunks of plaster are all over the counters and floors," noted Danielle.

"Yeah, and there are still dead bees everywhere."

"No time like the present. Let's get started!" said Danielle.

It took both of us the remainder of the day to make just a

dent in getting the kitchen cleaned up. The things that were destroyed or broken we worked around. When it started to get late, we decided we had done all we could.

"Let's pack up and head home. I'm exhausted, and you must be too," I said, as Danielle wiped sweat from her face with her dirty T-shirt.

"Yeah, I'm dead on my feet," she conceded, "but we've barely made a difference in getting this house ready for appraisers. I knew the house was big, but you get a whole new appreciation for big when you're cleaning it!"

"If you're willing, we'll have to pick up where we left off next weekend."

"I'm willing, but I'm not sure if we can get it done in just one weekend."

"I hate to say this, but next weekend is a three day-er. We have the Labor Day holiday."

"Oh, right . . . I forgot . . . that extra day should do it. You are going to owe me big-time!"

"Name your price, anything!" I said.

"I'll think about it, but for now let's head home."

As we walked around to close windows and doors and unplug the fans, I couldn't help but notice how the house seemed to be appreciative of the hard work we expended on her behalf. I had to find a way to borrow enough money to keep the rehabilitation work going, I just had to.

Chapter 29

When my alarm sounded at 5:00 a.m. the next morning, I was pretty sure someone had hit me over the head with a heavy object. I staggered out of bed and every muscle in my body ached. The bottoms of my feet hurt, and my fingers were so cramped it even hurt to turn the coffeepot on. I had a video call with Rory at 8:00 a.m., his request, and that meant I didn't have time to check in with Jill or Alex before talking with Rory. I had planned to spend all day Sunday leisurely reading my email and getting caught up on work issues, but the unexpected marathon cleaning session at Merryhearth ended that plan. The next best thing to do was get up extra early and get caught up so that I was ready for the call with Rory.

Okay, hair in a neat ponytail, business attire blouse over shorts and flip-flops, hot mug of coffee in hand—I sat down to go through my emails. Scan the list first for emails from the boss, then from the execs above his grade level, *or should it be the other way around,* then emails from my regional project leaders across the country, then everyone else. *Wait, what's this . . . is this from . . . oh no! . . . here's one from Deborah Callahan—brace yourself, Amanda.*

Hi, Amanda,

I know you won't be seeing this probably until you are back from your vacation, but please check in with your boss as soon as possible.

Like I wouldn't do that anyway?

We have found a serious issue with the big project you are leading, HR Program Reengineering. There are a number of irregularities. The director of the agency is very concerned about the situation. You are to put everything on hold until further notice. Your boss has been briefed and he and the director have met. I'm sure he will fill you in on the details.

Thank you and welcome back after your vacation!
Deborah

DAMN IT! I knew this was going to happen! I continued down the list and read an email from Rory that basically said the same thing, but he added in his message that he was sure it would all work out. Sometimes his optimism was just damn annoying. I also had emails from several of the regional project leaders, including Jan and Sheryl from Denver, asking what the heck was going on back in Washington, as they'd heard from Rory to put all project work on hold. *What a mess!*

When Rory appeared on my laptop screen promptly at 8:00 a.m., he was all smiles and small talk. I wanted to scream, but I knew I had to get through the friendly chitchat and ease gently into the disaster.

"Oh, thanks for asking, my vacation was wonderful, and Italy was great," I gushed.

"How was the food? I bet you didn't have a single meal

that wasn't amazing?" he asked.

"Oh, it was amazing," I said—after all, he didn't want reality, he wanted the myth.

"I'm so glad you had a great time and that you are rested and full of energy for the upcoming week!" he said with the enthusiasm of my summer camp counselor from Lake Tikiwaka the year I was twelve.

"Oh, absolutely, never felt better!" *Now that was an outright lie.*

"I'm sure you've seen the emails about the project being put on hold, and I have some more details to share with you," he said as he moved into the business end of things.

"I'm all ears and, Rory, I hope you weren't caught between a rock and hard place with the director. The timing for Deborah's interest couldn't have been worse, with me out of the country for almost two weeks."

Of course, I knew "the timing" was intentional on Deborah's part, but I thought I should apologize, nonetheless.

"Oh, don't feel bad, that's just Murphy's Law, but I do have a follow-up meeting with the director this afternoon, and he'll be looking for answers from me."

"Okay, fill me in, and we'll figure out how to address all the issues to put him at ease and give you a little breathing room."

"Oh, I'm fine. Don't worry about me. None of this is about me. I'll be fine. My job is secure. Although, over the weekend, I was having chest pains. But I'm sure it was just gas. I'm fine," said Rory, unconvincingly.

"So Deborah mentioned 'irregularities' in her email to me and said that was the reason for the project work stoppage. Do you know what she is talking about?"

"Yes, she reviewed the tons of project documentation and couldn't find anything that addressed, in detail, how the finance processes and systems were being updated to accommodate the new HR processes and automation. When she questioned the finance office folks, they said it hadn't been worked out yet and was a focus point for later in the project. That sent her into a state of frenzy, and she wrote up a detailed risk analysis, bullet after bullet, of all the possible things that could go wrong. Then she briefed the director, in private, on her risk analysis. First on the list was employees not getting their bimonthly pay!"

"Hmm . . . she's right in one respect," I said, "and that's the fact that there isn't a lot of documentation about the changes to the finance processes and systems. That's because there is no need for changes to the finance processes and automated systems. The finance folks will keep doing exactly what they are doing now, they'll just get their data—the same data—through a new interface. Nothing on their end is changing."

"But what if the interface doesn't work? That's her point—people wouldn't get paid, benefits would be messed up, all hell would break loose. Oh, I'm sorry, Amanda, I didn't mean to curse," said Rory with real fear in his voice.

"That would never happen because we have testing built into the project schedule. We won't cut off the old interface until the new one is 100 percent. In other words, for as long as it takes—and that's usually only two pay periods—the new and old processes are run simultaneously and verified for accuracy for every employee, down to the most minute detail. That's standard protocol for a project like this," I explained.

"I don't think this explanation will be enough to convince Deborah and the director that things are fine as they are. We need to demonstrate to them that we are going to do something extraordinary to ensure nothing goes wrong," said Rory. "You see, it's as much now about Deborah having . . ."

I interrupted him in midsentence *(bad habit of mine)*, "About Deborah having been right and catching a horrible risk that could have wreaked untold havoc on the whole agency and every single employee, because no one else thought of this but her."

"Well . . . yes. So what can we do, Amanda?" asked Rory in a voice that sounded so desperate that I wanted to give him a hug and say, "Don't have a heart attack."

"Okay. I've got an idea. We will of course, that is, *you* will of course concede that Deborah is right to be concerned. And while we have testing of this very risk built into the project schedule, it's not enough—all things considered. To avoid the agency losing the money and investment in the project up to date, and to ensure we continue modernizing the HR processes and automated systems that are desperately needed across the country, we hire an expert onto the project team."

"An expert? What kind of expert? And what happens to the expert after the project is done?" asked Rory.

"That's the beauty of the plan. You see, we need someone who is a data scientist and systems integration expert anyway. Nearly every strategic project that the team has undertaken and will pursue in the future has an element of data management," I said with a smile.

"Oh . . . I get it. This new hire is to be responsive to the risk Deborah has identified and address her concerns. And, we get a new position and expertise that we need anyway!"

"Yes. I—you—will need to sell them on the long-term benefits after this project ends, but that shouldn't be difficult since they are always demanding data, and analysis, and reports," I added.

"I like this plan! So do you know of someone who could fill this requirement for your team?"

"I have the perfect person in mind. Her name is Ella Woodman, and she's doing this exact same work for another federal agency."

"Do you think she'd be willing to come to work here? And what about the other agency, won't they mind?"

"I think I can convince her to come over to our team as long as she can work from home—that will be the key selling point. And as far as the other agency, they won't be happy, but that's how the federal government operates. We pass the best talent around and create awful gaps in the process."

"I think this will work. I'll prepare my briefing with the director, scheduled for this afternoon, very carefully. I'll agree that the risk is significant, and it will take a significant solution. Then I'll propose adding an expert to the team and even let them know that we've already identified someone," said Rory, thinking aloud as much as stating his plan to me.

"One more thing, Rory," I said, "don't say 'we' when you are briefing them. Delores doesn't like me. It will be better if she thinks you alone came up with this idea. She will even like the fact that you have decided that I can't handle it on my own. That assumption on her part will make this idea even more appealing. She'll think this action puts me in my place."

"Oh no, Amanda. I don't think she feels that way about you. I'm sure she likes you! She's just a worrisome person who always looks for the worst-case scenario," replied Rory. "But okay, I won't mention you were part of this idea . . . just in case . . . but I don't think it's necessary . . . but I'll sell it as my idea alone."

"Great. Let me know how the meeting goes. My fingers are crossed, and I'm sure you can convince them," I said, as we ended the video call.

At this point I had had about all the crazy I could take and decided to walk to the coffee shop around the corner to clear my head. As I was walking, I went over all the current catastrophes: I needed to do some immediate research on finding banks that did construction loans to keep Merryhearth going, I needed to have a backup plan for work in case the HR Program Reengineering project was canceled and Rory couldn't sell the director on the "hiring an expert" idea, I needed to give the project regional leaders an update and do damage control with the key players across the country—and I needed to put my boss hat on and fill Jill and Alex in on what was going on without freaking them out. *OH, Alex . . . this would be the first time since Italy that I was shifting roles and would be "the boss" again. How weird would that be,* I wondered, as I subconsciously rubbed the place on my arm that sported a slight bruise in the shape of a bite mark.

"Hi, Amanda! Your usual? Large-vanilla-latte-low-foam?" asked Jess from across the coffee shop counter.

"Sounds great, thanks, Jess."

"Haven't seen you in here in a while."

"Yeah, I just got back from vacation."

"Really? I was going to ask if you'd been under the weather."

"Do I look that bad?"

"Well, wherever you went on vacation . . . I think I'd go someplace different next time, if I were you."

"Gee, thanks, Jess!"

"Anytime! Here's your latte. Have a good one and try to de-stress. Maybe you need a vacation!"

"You too!" I said smiling, as I stepped out onto the sidewalk and headed back to my apartment. *Time for the daily sync-up call with Jill and Alex . . . uhg.*

As the Brady Bunch boxes on my laptop screen filled with Jill's and Alex's faces, I couldn't help noticing how fantastic Alex looked. He was rested, chipper, focused—and Jill was absolutely glowing.

"Good morning, guys, how was your weekend?" I said.

"Mine was great! Hung out with friends and got great results from a recent purchase I made," said Alex.

Jill jumped in, "What a weird thing to say, what did you do, score big on a stock futures investment?"

"Yeah, you could say that," said Alex, looking like the cat

that swallowed the canary.

"I'm glad your investment in time and money paid off. That's good news," I said.

"Listen to you two, all cryptic like, it sounds like we're in a scene from *The Matrix*."

"I love those movies!" said Alex.

"I hate them, but Tom loves them," replied Jill.

"Okay. Switching gears . . . here's the latest on the project," I said.

I briefed them on the Deborah-made crisis, the director's position on the project, and the proposed solution that Rory was going to tee up that afternoon.

"What if the director doesn't go for it?" asked Alex.

"Then we end the project and move on to the next one, the director has spoken," I said.

"But," said Jill, "if the director agrees, we get a new member to our team—a really talented member."

"Yes. Keep your fingers crossed," I said.

"Well . . . the timing for getting a new team member could be excellent!" said Jill.

"I'll bite," said Alex. "Why is that?"

Oh, unfortunate use of phraseology. I rubbed my arm.

"Becaaaause . . . I will need to be out on maternity leave for a while!" squealed Jill.

"Oh, my goodness, Jill, that's fantastic news!" I said.

"Wow, congratulations to you and Tom!" said Alex.

"When is the baby due?" asked Alex and I simultaneously.

"*She* is due in five months! On January thirtieth!"

"Oh, Jill, I'm so happy for you and Tom! This is great news. See, eliminating all of that commuting stress and being able to work from home made a big difference!"

"It really did. Thank you so much, Amanda, for having our backs and making that happen."

It was moments like these when I realized wearing the boss hat had real benefits. In a world where everything we achieved was a struggle, and where we all worked so hard for our happiness—I could make a real difference in people's lives. It was within my power to improve the quality of life for my team, Jill and Alex, and by extension many others including Tom and De'On. I thought to myself, *I've got to fight for this project because it's the right thing to do and because so many people need me to make sure it doesn't get derailed!*

Chapter 30

The week dragged very slowly, with little good news on either front—Merryhearth rehabilitation funding or the director's decision on the project. I had spoken with half a dozen bank lending departments, and they all told me the same thing—construction loans were for relatively small amounts of money, and nowhere near what I was looking for. They recommended I refinance the mortgage and take cash out if the house had enough equity. Danielle and I would have to get the house looking as good as we possibly could before it was appraised—everything was riding on a high appraisal.

I went ahead and filled out some preliminary refinance paperwork with one of the banks and set up an appointment to have the house appraised. I hated going through this again. I'd just finished this whole process a few months ago, and now I was back at the start line. I had scheduled to meet the appraiser at Merryhearth the following Wednesday, so Danielle and I had our work cut out for us. There were two more entire floors to clean, windows to wash, and porches to patch so that the appraiser wouldn't fall through them. Then there was the grass and general lawn cleanup to deal with. I had a plan for that and called Christopher, Josh's teenage son, who cut grass for extra money.

"Hi, Christopher. This is Amanda Grayson. Your dad has been working on my house."

"Hi, Miss Grayson. My dad said you'd be calling."

"Please, just call me Amanda. I was hoping we could meet at the house tomorrow morning, about nine a.m.?"

"Sure, do you want me to bring all my lawn equipment?"

"That would be great. See you in the morning."

Next, I sent a quick email to Rory to see if he had any news on the director's decision for the continuation of the project. So much was riding on the project's moving forward, not the least of which was continuing our virtual team arrangement.

"Good morning, Rory, and happy Friday. Any word yet from the director on the project?"

I received his email reply almost immediately.

"Good morning and happy Friday to you too. Unfortunately, no word. Looks like we'll be going into next week with things still on hold."

"Okay. Thanks for the update and have a good weekend."

The only saving grace with having the project on hold was that I could focus on dealing with the Merryhearth catastrophe. I decided to drive out to Winchester and get in a few hours of cleaning at Merryhearth, on my own. It would put Danielle and I that much further ahead when we got started the next morning.

I glanced in the full-length mirror in the hall on my way out the door. I had to admit that, despite being stressed out, I looked good in my cutoff jean shorts, tie-dyed T-shirt, and running shoes. My hours at the gym, getting fit for skiing in December—*Note to self, invite De'On along on the ski trip*—meant I'd lost twenty pounds, was strong and shapely in all the right places, and looked young and healthy. I'd let my hair grow and now had blond, wavy curls that fell across my shoulders. My new clothes and a plethora of cute new shoes meant I was more stylish than I had been in years, and certainly since the eighteen months following the explosion. Feeling good, I opened the sunroof in my car and turned up the radio. A few hours connecting with Merryhearth would be great.

When I arrived at the house, I was surprised to see the grass neatly mowed in impressive stripes and someone, who I assumed to be Christopher, trimming around the trees with his gas-powered weeder. He looked surprised when I pulled into the driveway with my sunroof open and my radio blasting. I could see as he came closer that he didn't resemble Josh at all. This kid was tall, about six feet tall, muscular, had chin-length, light brown wavy hair, and a fair complexion. I surmised he looked like his mother. With more self-presence and confidence than I would have expected from someone so young, he held out his hand and introduced himself.

"Hi, I'm Chris."

"Hi, I'm Amanda. Nice to meet you."

"That was Dirty Honey you were listening to, wasn't it?"

"Yes! Are you a fan?"

"Yeah, and I'm surprised you're a fan."

"You mean because I'm so old?"

"No, I mean because you're classy, and you drive a sick car!"

"Oh," I said, laughing. *That took me by surprise.* "Well, when I'm alone, and can't shock people, I love to listen to rock. A lot of the newer bands are every bit as good as the old rock and roll legends."

"My dad said you were really uptight, but you're cool," said Chris with a broad grin on his face.

Did I seem uptight to Josh? I guessed I was particular about things, but that was because the house required a particular approach to everything. Chris was very friendly and talkative,

289

and I soon learned that he could be a wealth of information with just the right prompting.

"How's your dad doing? Is his new construction job going well?"

"Yeah, he says he should be able to make up the money he lost on your house when the bank went belly-up."

"That's good to know!" I had to laugh, this kid was awesome, and I liked him immediately.

"How come you aren't in school today? I didn't expect to meet you until tomorrow."

"School starts next week, after Labor Day, and I graduated last year."

"Oh, I see. Any plans for this year?"

"I've been accepted to trade school. I'm starting in January. I'm going to be certified to repair diesel engines and other equipment."

"That's great! I hear trade schools are really expensive. Are you saving for tuition?"

"Yep, been doing lawn work all summer, and I'll keep that going as long as I can before heading to Tennessee for school."

"Do you do more than mow and trim?"

"Yeah, I'll do anything."

"How much do you charge?"

"My rate is $35 an hour. Sometimes I have a friend help me, but it's still $35 an hour."

"Chris, you may have just become my new best friend. How do you feel about walking the property with me and scoping out the work that needs to be done to get this place looking respectable?"

"Sounds good to me!"

We walked the property and established a multi-month plan for dealing with decades of unbelievable madness. The first to go were the sections of barbed wire fencing that separated the property into illogical zones, next were piles of lumber scraps, concrete blocks, and other debris, that were littered all over the property. Any bushes that existed were marked for either removal or a good trimming. Zones of the acreage that had not been mowed over the summer were identified for bush-hogging. The woods would be cleaned up so that there was a clear understory, and mulch would be used to start to establish beds for future plantings. Nothing was out of the question for Chris. As long as I was willing to pay for the materials, renting the equipment when needed, and his hourly rate—he was willing to do it! As it turned out, that fall before starting school, he worked so hard that I felt guilty. I worried he'd burn himself out, but he never slowed down. He was always happy to see me and eager to show me the progress he'd made when I came out to the house. He single-handedly turned a mess of four acres into what became the foundation for a beautifully landscaped estate lawn.

After walking the property with Chris, it was really too late to get started on cleaning, so I headed back to Leesburg and texted Danielle to see if she wanted to grab dinner.

Danielle: Sorry, can't do dinner. Doug and I are on a date.
Me: Have fun. Pick you up at 8:00 a.m.?
Danielle: How about 8:30?
Me: [Smiley-face-emoji.] Okay, 8:30.

The next morning, Danielle started on the bedroom level and I focused on window washing and getting the ugly old aluminum storm windows to either close tight or open all the way—but not be half open and half shut. This was complicated by the number of vines that had grown through them and infiltrated the inside of the house. As I was working on a particularly stubborn window, my concentration was shattered by the sound of Danielle's excited voice.

"Amandaaaa! You better have a look at this!" Danielle was

calling from the bedroom over the kitchen—the one with its own back stair.

"What is it?" I said breathlessly after running up the stairs.

"Someone has shoved something up the chimney, and it's really gross-looking."

"Maybe it's treasure?"

"More like a dead body."

"Oh . . . well, let me take a look," I said, sounding more confident than I felt.

I got down on my knees, crawled into the fireplace, and stuck my head under the opening of the chimney, avoiding spiderwebs as much as I could. I could see what appeared to be a plastic bag, partially filled with slimy, brownish water, and there was something else in the plastic, but I couldn't tell what it was.

"What in the heck? People have done the weirdest things here!"

"What do you think it is?" asked Danielle.

"I don't know, but you're right, it's really gross-looking."

"What if they were trying to hide something?"

"Whatever it is, it has to come out. It can't stay here," I said with conviction.

"Why would someone shove something up the chimney?"

"Only one way to find out."

I wasn't about to stick my arm up the chimney to grab it, not even with my rubber gloves, so I looked around for something that I could use to get hold of it.

"Here," said Danielle, handing me a claw-end hammer.

"Perfect. Thank you."

"I'll watch from over here," said Danielle from the doorway to the adjoining room. "You know, just in case I need to make a run for it."

"Gee, thanks. Where does that leave me?"

"Running behind *me*!"

"Well, you better be fast!"

With that, I hooked the end of the plastic bag with the hammer and pulled gently. At first, it didn't move, and I was afraid of tearing the plastic bag and having the slimy water hit me in the face, but I persevered. The mass started to break loose and slowly shift downward.

"Can you see what it is?" asked Danielle from the safety of the doorway.

"Not really."

A little more of the mass shifted downward, and I felt it break loose. I jumped back quickly. With a thud, and a kind of sick *splat* noise, it hit the hearth. Danielle shrieked and ran into the next room, and I took her place in the doorway.

"Is it moving?" asked Danielle from the next room.

"No, but I can't tell what it is," I said, drawing near again. "It looks like it drowned in slimy water, inside a plastic bag shoved up the chimney."

"Oh, crap! Was it murdered?"

"I don't know, but I'm going to find out."

I was kneeling down to examine the watermelon-sized mass when Danielle suggested calling someone. "Like who?" I said.

"I don't know! Is Chris outside?"

"I'm not calling a teenage boy into the house to deal with the 'big scary thing in the fireplace' for goodness' sake."

"No, you're right—but he looks like he could handle it—but no, no, that wouldn't look good."

I poked at the object in the slushy bag, and it was soft. I was beginning to lose my nerve.

"Can you roll it over?" said Danielle, "Maybe there's a clue on its other side."

"Okay, I'll try."

I was concentrating intently on the mass and hooked it on the side with the hammer, getting ready to pull it toward me to roll it over and see what it had to reveal on the opposite side, when Danielle tapped me on the shoulder.

"Eeeeeeeek!" I screamed.

"EEEEEEEK!" screamed Danielle, louder. "What is it?"

"I don't know!!"

"But you screamed!"

"Because you scared the hell out of me, sneaking up on me like that!"

"Oh, phew! I thought you saw something."

Then startling us both, as we hovered over the drowned mass, came a deep voice, "Is everything alright in there?"

"We screamed again, in unison, "Aaaaahhhhh!"

"What's wrong?" asked Chris, entering the room. "I heard you two screaming from outside. Oh . . . what is that?"

"We don't know, it was shoved up into the chimney."

"Let's get it out of the bag," said Chris.

"Yeah, but let me find some rags to soak up the water before we cut open the bag."

I found a canvas drop cloth down in the kitchen that the workmen had left behind and brought it upstairs. We gingerly rolled the mass onto the drop cloth and with the three of us hovering over the object, I cut into the plastic bag with the hammer's claw.

Smelly, brown liquid poured out onto the drop cloth.

"Oh, that's rank!" said Chris, covering his nose with his forearm.

The mass started to come into view as the liquid drained away.

"What in the heck is it?" asked Danielle.

"I think it's . . . yes, it's a pillow with blue-and-white-striped ticking," I replied.

"Why would someone drown a pillow and shove it up the

294

chimney?" asked Danielle.

"I think I can answer that one," said Chris as we looked at him inquisitively. "My granny stuffs pillows up the chimneys in her old house to stop cold drafts."

"Ohhh . . . that makes sense," I said. "Someone probably wanted to keep the pillow clean, so they put it in a plastic bag before stuffing it up the chimney."

"Yeah," said Chris. "And rainwater probably built up over time and got inside the plastic bag, and the pillow absorbed it."

"Good grief, this whole episode took years off my life!" said Danielle.

Chris at this point was laughing, and I found myself starting to laugh too. Danielle joined us, and the three of us stood over the murdered pillow, laughing so hard we had to wipe the tears away with our sweaty T-shirts.

"The next time you need something, call me, okay?" said Chris, wiping tears from his face.

Still laughing, I promised I would.

We finished all the cleaning over the span of the holiday weekend, and Danielle said she'd never felt so tired in her life. I had to agree, the work was hard and dirty, but the house looked amazing and so did the yard, thanks to Chris. Josh stopped by on Labor Day to drop off the sheets of plywood he cut to place over the holes on the porches, and I let him know I had an appraiser coming on Wednesday at 9:00 a.m. The house was as ready as it could be, and looked as good as it could look, without actually being fully restored. There were still walls with peeling paint, broken windowpanes, exposed beams across the gallery level, the old defunct kitchen and bathrooms, and a million other things, but on the surface, it looked pretty good, and hopefully . . . good enough for an appraiser to see its future value.

Chapter 31

Kelly Dillar was walking around the side of the house from the backyard when I pulled into the driveway at 8:45 a.m. on Wednesday morning. I sensed her early arrival and unescorted exploring were very much intentional.

"Good morning. I'm Amanda Grayson. I'm guessing you are Kelly Dillar?"

"Hi. Good morning. Yes, I'm Kelly."

"I see you didn't have any problem finding the house."

"Oh, no, I was pretty sure I knew exactly which house it was when I saw the address. I'm very familiar with this area and have been doing appraisals for the bank for a long time."

"So then you already have a notion of the value of the house?"

"Yes, I do."

Just great, I thought, she was biased before even seeing the inside or hearing my plans for the rehabilitation work.

"Well," I said, "before you make up your mind entirely, would you like to see the inside and hear my plans for rehabilitating the house? That will give you an idea of its future value."

"Actually, I have to judge the house on its value today, as it is in its current state. The appraisal can't be based on your visions for the house."

"Oh. I guess I misunderstood then. When I spoke with the bank lending department, I told them the idea was to refinance with cash out so that I could restore the house. But what you are telling me is that you can't value it based on its 'finished' state, only on its current state?"

"Exactly. People have big ideas all the time for what they want to do, and then they fail to follow through. The bank can't be left holding the bag because someone decides to by a new car or a sport utility recreational vehicle instead of doing the work on the house."

Clearly, she didn't understand the commitment I had already undertaken to rehabilitate Merryhearth. I was taken aback by her statement.

I tried to explain, "But I've already started the work and …"

She cut me off, "I can see from looking around that you aren't living in the house, right?"

"No, it's not ready to …"

"So that's added risk. This isn't your primary home. We see it all the time. People get these ideas that they want a vacation home or something and then find it isn't practical and … well, you get my meaning."

I was totally floored. This was a disaster and was no solution at all. It would be better to have no appraisal than a low appraisal that could be used against me. I had to think quickly.

"Kelly, I'm so sorry. I've brought you out here on false pretenses, I guess. I was under the impression that you were looking at the house today in terms of its future value after the rehabilitation work was done."

"Right," said Kelly. "I don't consider any of that in the appraisal."

"Well, then, I think I'll save you the time to look through

the house—and I'll save myself the expensive appraisal fee."

I needed to get her out and fast, before she could tell me it was too late, and she'd be working up an appraisal.

"I'll move my car now so that you can back out of the driveway."

"Oh, I hope I haven't offended you? I can still do the appraisal, maybe what I come up with will be enough."

"No, no, you haven't offended me. Nice to have met you. Have a great day!"

I jumped in my car and backed out of the driveway as quickly as I could, letting her move her car and leave before there could be any more discussion.

After she was out of sight, I unlocked the house and went in. I turned on the fans and popped open one of the lawn chairs. Sitting in the shiny, clean, future drawing room, I rested my chin on my hands. What was I going to do? I couldn't *unbuy* the house, nor could I do any work on it. I was stuck with no way to move forward and no way to go back—and I owed Josh a lot of money for work that had already been done. I felt tears start to well up in my eyes, and then they began to cascade down my cheeks and drip off my face. The situation was hopeless. I'd bought a house I couldn't live in and maybe would never have the money to work on. My dreams were evaporating into thin air. And the chandelier, my pretty, pink Murano chandelier, handmade by Fabio Ongaro specifically for me, might never hang in the dining room. More tears came flooding onto my cheeks and dripped off.

"Merryhearth . . . what's to be done?" I said aloud. "You're going to have to help me solve this."

I walked around the house and examined the work we'd completed over the weekend. The house looked better than I had ever seen it, and certainly cleaner. All the brick dust was gone, the cobwebs had disappeared, there was a noticeable lack of dead flies and bees on the windowsills. Speaking of windows, they no longer had vines creeping through, and I had used clear packing tape to cover missing pieces of glass and to secure broken windowpanes. But all that hard work had been for nothing, the appraiser didn't even see the house. Her mind was made up, and not in a good way.

I heard my cell phone ringing from a distance and tracked down my purse. When I finally pulled the phone out, I saw I'd missed a call from Bob Norseman. I hadn't seen or spoken to him since closing on the house back in May. I pressed his number and he answered on the first ring.

"Hi, Bob! How are you doing?"

"Hi, Amanda! I'm doin' well. How 'bout you?"

"I've been better, actually. I just had a rather unpleasant experience with a home appraiser out here at the house."

"Ahh, let me guess, you're shoppin' 'round for a new mortgage?"

"How'd you know?"

"Word travels fast in the real estate business. When I heard the bank crashed, I figured it might've left you in a bad spot."

"You've got that right. Bob, I'm in a real bind!"

I filled Bob in on the particulars, including owing Josh money and being out of options. I managed not to cry, but a few times my voice got shaky. I finished by saying I didn't know if I was going to be able to keep Merryhearth. He listened intently without interrupting my flood of gloom and doom, and then he did what Bob had always done: he made something that could be just awful sound like no big deal.

"Oh, it's not as bad as all that, you've got options. First off, you just forget what ol' Kelly Dillar told you. I know her and she's a real piece of work in the appraisal world. You did right to run her skinny ass off. Now, answer me this . . ."

Bob proceeded to ask me a number of questions about the condition of the house. I had no idea where he was going, but I dutifully answered.

"So," he said, "you've got a dry basement, a solid roof over your head, one bathroom that works—toilet, shower, sink, and running hot and cold water in the kitchen, but no functioning air-conditioning or heat, and minimal electric with an old fuse box?"

"Yes, that about sums it up."

"Well, heck, girl, you've got it better than half the residents in our neighborin' state of West Virginia!"

"What do you mean?"

"I mean, you're gonna move into that house!"

"Move into it? As it is?"

"Look . . . how much are you spendin' on rent, utilities, furniture storage fees, and gas to run the wheels off that little car of yours as you go back and forth between Leesburg and Winchester nearly every day?"

"Actually, several thousand dollars a month, now that you mention it."

"Exactly! That's money that you can put toward Merry-hearth. And, if you're livin' in the house, you're gonna get better interest rates to refinance it."

"There's no heat, or stove, or refrigerator."

"Look, you won't need heat for a couple a months, and by then you'll have some financin' lined up."

"Umm, do you think this will increase my odds of getting a loan?"

"Well, I've got another ace up my sleeve on that front."

"Oh, do tell please," I said, feeling a little more optimistic.

"There's a special government-backed loan that only a few approved banks offer. It's specifically for the rehabilitation of older homes. It's called a 203(k) Rehabilitation Loan. A friend of mine recently switched jobs to a bank that offers 'em. We were talkin' 'bout it last weekend when Marie and I got together with her for dinner."

"I've never heard of it."

"Well, I'm in the business of sellin' historic homes and I never heard of it either, but from what she told me—it's ideal for your situation."

"So I have to be living in the house to qualify?"

"No, I don't think so, but it just makes sense to start puttin' the good money you make to better use than rent and furniture storage. Think how far that money'll go."

"You're right. And as long as I'm able to work from home, why not be living in Winchester? I'll have to buy a refrigerator and a microwave. I guess I can get by without a stove."

"Sure you can, and you can buy a couple of those portable, room air conditioners if the electric in the house will support 'em."

"Bob, you've given me a lot to think about. And you've given me renewed hope just when I was scraping the bottom of the hope well."

"Glad I could be of some help. And I'll send you my friend's contact information as soon as we hang up."

"I'll call her the minute I get the info!"

"Well, hang in there and let me know how it goes."

"I will. Thank you, Bob!"

And with one phone call, my world had gone from completely desperate to completely optimistic!

I looked up through the stairs that climbed three levels of the house and said into the sunbeams lighting the space, "Interesting timing on that phone call. Thank you, Merryhearth." It might have been my imagination, but in reply I thought I saw a twinkle of light, midway up the encircled stair space.

Back in the lawn chair in the drawing room, I called the number Bob sent me for his friend Jessica McCarthy. It was still early, and I hoped she'd be available to talk. The phone rang several times and went to voice mail. I left her a detailed message and decided to head back to my apartment where I could access my laptop and start to look logically at Bob's suggestion of moving into Merryhearth in its current state.

Throughout the drive back to Leesburg, I went over the numbers again and again in my head. Bob was right. If I could live at the house, I'd be saving a substantial amount of money that could be put toward rehabilitation expenses. The more I thought about it, the more I realized it was a no-brainer, I needed to move to Merryhearth. The only real obstacle—other than a few little things like no air-conditioning and heating system, no real kitchen, a gross bathroom, marginally adequate electricity, and tape holding some of the windows together—was work. If the project at work was canceled, and I had to go back into the city every day, moving to Merryhearth would make my life next to impossible. Of course, I knew that was a possibility when I bought the house, however, making the *forty-mile* trek between Leesburg and Winchester nearly every day gave me a new understanding of how miserable a *ninety-mile* trek between Winchester and D.C. would be. I decided to call Rory.

"Hi, Rory, it's Amanda."

"Hi, Amanda. Sounds like you're driving. Did the appraiser like the house?"

"Long story short, no . . . but I have another possibility in the works that may actually be a much better way to go."

"Oh, that's terrific! See, things always work out."

"Speaking of working out, it's been over a week now. Any word from the director on the status of the project?"

"Unfortunately no, and I'm getting worried that the longer it takes, the more likely it is that he doesn't realize the urgency."

"I was afraid of that. Do you think there is anything we can do to nudge him a bit?"

"No. I wouldn't want to do that. No, that could backfire on me, umm us. No, better to give him his space. Yes, we'll let him take the time he needs."

"Okay. Just keep me posted if you hear something."

"I will. You'll be my first phone call."

"Thanks."

I had another idea. I knew the Denver regional office was furious over the project being stalled, and I also knew the Denver regional director was outspoken, just like Jan and Sheryl—it was something in the water out there, they were all gutsy and fearless. When I got back to the apartment, I dialed Jan's number.

"Hi, Jan, it's Amanda."

"Hey, girl, have you gotten those folks in D.C. under control yet?"

"No, and I may need some help from the Denver Broncos."

"HA—that's good! What can we do for you?"

"How about a little gentle nudging from your regional director to the director? Without mentioning me, of course."

"I've been chomping at the bit—Bronco humor, get it—to turn Jean loose."

Jean was Margaret Jean Murrey, and she was one of the agency's longest tenured employees and was smart as a whip. She had single-handedly gotten the agency through some of its toughest times and managed to climb her way through the executive core to become the regional director of the agency's largest and most complex region. I had a lot of respect for her and the team she had built. If anyone could shake things loose, she could.

"Thanks, Jan. I owe you!"

"You certainly do. Next time you're out here with that hunk of a team member, Alex, we're going out for shots."

"Good grief, Jan, you'll get me fired!"

"We might all get fired, but we'll have fun in the process!"

"Really, thank you for this!"

"You got it, girl. I'll let you know after Jean makes her call."

No sooner did I hang up with Jan than my cell rang.

"Hi, Amanda? This is Jessica McCarthy calling you back."

"Thank you, Ms. McCarthy, for calling back so quickly."

"Call me Jessica. I understand you're a friend of Bob's?"

"Yes, and he mentioned you had information about a loan program for people who are restoring historic properties?"

"Yes, I actually just started a new job at a bank approved to manage the government-backed 203(k) rehab loans. They've appointed me the department lead for the program. I figured Bob might know some folks who needed this kind of loan, and here you are!"

"Congratulations on your new position! Where do we start?"

Jessica provided me the details on the 203(k) rehab loan program and set up a link for me to fill out the necessary paperwork and sign all the forms electronically. It didn't take me long because I'd just recently gone through the whole loan application process—a couple of times. By the end of the day, I had the loan paperwork accepted for review by Jessica's department and another appraisal scheduled to determine the value of the house. This time it *would* be based on the post-rehabilitation work, as specified in the contract I had established with Josh. The day had been a whirlwind of ups and downs, but fortunately ended on a positive note. I had regrouped and things were looking good again for the rehabilitation work. Now I needed things at work to turn around.

Chapter 32

Bob Norseman called me the next afternoon with more information on the 203(k) rehab loan. He'd had an after-hours conversation with Jessica and wanted me to know what she had conveyed.

"I'm glad you and Jessica connected," said Bob, "She's good people and I think you'll like workin' with her. I just wish I'd known about this 203(k) loan before you worked that deal with the bank."

"Don't beat yourself up, Bob. At the time, the deal with the bank was a good deal. And it led me to Josh Edden who, by the way, has been terrific to work with."

"Yeah, I guess everythin' happens for a reason, and you're gonna end up better in the long run, I think, having this 203(k) type of loan."

"We'll see. I hope so."

"Which leads me to what Jessica told me. She said she couldn't say this to you directly, bank rules and all that, but she definitely wanted you to know a few things."

"That's really nice of her."

"She said that if you can have the house staged with

furniture, rugs, curtains, a few potted plants, that sort of thing, your appraisal will come in higher. She said to tell you to make sure the bathrooms and the kitchen look like they work, even if they don't, and to get a refrigerator, even a cheap temporary one."

"But I thought this appraisal was based on the future state, not the current state of the house."

"It is, but she said the appraisers are picked at random from lists that aren't specific to just 203(k) loans. That bein' the case, no matter how many times they're reminded to overlook busted plumbing, missing appliances, and basically trashed houses, they can't totally overcome their trainin' and ignore what they see if the house isn't pristine."

"Oh, that's a shame."

"She said her loan department ends up arguin' with 'em and tryin' to figure out more accurate estimates of the future value by studyin' the construction contracts and similar properties that have undergone rehabilitation, basically doin' their jobs for 'em."

"So, in other words, I should move into the house sooner versus later, and before the appraiser comes out."

"Exactly right."

"Alright then. I have my work cut out for me."

"Have fun!" said Bob before hanging up the phone.

I felt like my life was taking on a life of its own. Events were dictating the course I took before I had time to comprehend the facts and weigh the pros and cons. Forget a logical approach—there was no time for *logical*! I started calling moving companies to see if any could accommodate a large move like mine within the month. After hitting a brick wall with the first four companies, I got a break with company number five.

"Yes, ma'am! We had a cancellation and can fit in a move to Winchester this Saturday. Will that work for you?"

I was stunned that they could accommodate my move to

Merryhearth in just two days. The previous week, my only goal had been to get the house cleaned up. Now I was looking at moving everything I owned from storage and the Leesburg apartment. I hadn't had time to mentally prepare. A million thoughts ran through my head, *Was I ready? Until yesterday, I was about a year away from moving. Would I have to move again when Josh started up the construction work?* So many unknowns, but this man was waiting for an answer, and I knew I had to give him one.

"Yes, that will work for me!" I said with more confidence than I felt.

After hanging up with the moving company, I called Jessica. She answered on the first ring.

"Hi, Jessica, it's Amanda Grayson."

"Hi, Amanda."

"I wanted to ask if you have any idea when the appraisal on the house will take place?"

"We're still going through your paperwork, which looks great, by the way, very thorough. I can't tell you how often we have to call our customers because they left something blank on the forms."

"I also wanted to know if you work with an appraiser by the name of Kelly Dillar, and, if you do, I'd like to unrequest her."

"Humph. Yes, I know Kelly Dillar. We called her Kelly Killer at my last bank because she killed about half the loan applications we got with her lowball appraisals."

"Interesting."

"But you didn't hear that from me."

"No, of course not."

"I've been told that she's now working almost exclusively with one bank, and so if her name does come up next on the list, she usually declines."

"If her name comes up on the list for Merryhearth's

appraisal, we need to find a way to have someone else do it."

"Say no more, I understand completely. As we've been talking, I just got an email from my loan processor who says your application has completed the review process and is good to go. So that means we can go ahead and schedule your appraisal. You'll need to be present so that you can go over the construction plans with the appraiser."

"Oh, that's exciting! How about the end of next week, maybe Friday?"

"You'll be ready that soon? Have you spoken with Bob recently?" she asked cryptically.

"Yes, and, as it turns out, I'm actually moving into the house this weekend!"

"Oh, wow! Then, yes, let's set up the appraisal for Friday, that gives you close to a week to settle in."

The appraisal was scheduled, and I just had to make sure that the move went smoothly, and I could get the house put together in the week that followed. *Oh, and I needed to order a refrigerator!*

As I was making a list of all the things I needed to do to be ready to relocate to Merryhearth in two days—including giving my rental landlord thirty-day notice that I'd be leaving—my cell pinged with an incoming text.

It was Alex: How are you doing? Haven't heard from you in a while.

He meant on a personal note, because we had talked every day at work.

I texted back: Crazy busy!

Alex: With Merryhearth?

Me: Yes, would you believe I'm moving in on Saturday!

Alex: What! How did that come about?

Me: It's a long story.

Alex: I'd love to hear it!

Me: Soon, we'll catch up soon.

I was glad he reached out. I was so busy though that I didn't have time to play. I had a million things to do—call utility companies, schedule the refrigerator delivery, and figure out the placement of furniture across Merryhearth's four floors and twenty-three rooms.

⊖——⚡

Saturday morning the moving van arrived at my apartment in Leesburg and in a matter of minutes I was caught up in a buzz of activity. There were half a dozen guys coming and going, asking me a million questions, and moving so quickly that I felt like I mostly just needed to stay out of their way. Once the movers had loaded my apartment belongings, we headed to the storage facility to get the mother lode. I had taken very little with me to the apartment. Most of my half of the cruise ship was in storage. After the explosion, Richard showed very little interest in the vast collection of furniture, rugs, and all the other stuff that outfitted the house. I assumed his girlfriend had her own furniture, and it was her taste, not mine, so he liked it better. He found the cruise ship furniture more of an albatross around his neck than a useful asset. That said, he didn't offer to let me have it, he and his attorney insisted on an even split of everything, right down to the outdoor patio umbrellas and pillow cushions. However, the list was left to me to create, so I selected for myself the items that I knew were easier to fit into any-sized rooms and were the style, colors, and fabric patterns I'd want for my next home.

The whirlwind of activity continued when we reached Merryhearth. I directed the movers to each room as they pulled sofas, chairs, tables, lamps, rugs, you name it, off the truck. I had gone out to Merryhearth the evening before and taped the names of each room onto the doors. The movers looked amused as I said things like, "The writing desk goes in the morning room, and the antique library table goes in the

309

library." I didn't have time as they were unloading to really appreciate how the rooms were coming together, that would come later. It took a long time to unload everything and disperse it across the house. The guys were hot, and the weather was typical for mid-September—hot, with a little bit of hot, followed by humid, and interspersed with hot. By the time they left it was close to six o'clock. I needed to unpack the bathroom box for the one bathroom that functioned so that I could take a shower, and I needed to have my bed made with my clean linens so that I could sleep. Once that was done, I'd grab something to eat and collapse.

That night, when I slipped between the cool percale sheets on my bed—fan blowing gently on my face—in my bedroom at Merryhearth, filled with all my pretty things, I felt unbelievably content. What a day!

When my eyelids fluttered open Sunday morning, the first view in sight from the softness of my down pillow was a vast expanse of green, dotted with grazing black cows, that filled the gap between the two ridges on the east and west sides of the rolling pasture. It was surreal, and I pinched myself to make sure I wasn't dreaming it. Waking up at Merryhearth, I would discover, was a never-ending delight.

That morning, as I wandered with my mug of coffee from window to window, I marveled at the beauty each had to offer. To the south was the soft rolling green pasture and cows that I had woken up with. To the east were the ancient apple groves, with their craggy trees loaded with round, red apples that shone brightly in the morning sun. To the west was the high ridge that sheltered the farms and groves, layered in rich foliage from the mature trees that covered it. And to the north was my own expanse of lawn, encircled by the wood line with its understory of wildflowers and blackberry bushes bending with the weight of their ripe fruit. *I could never get enough of this*, I thought to myself. I held up my thumb to block the visibility of one house out in the distance. This created a view from the house that hadn't changed in nearly two hundred years. I was standing on the same gently worn, heart pine floorboards, looking through the same handblown, wavy glass panes, at the same picturesque vistas, landmarks, and geography as the first lady of Merryhearth, on the first day that she woke up in her newly built home and looked out the window, holding *her* mug of coffee.

I consumed every minute of the day putting the house together, unpacking boxes, and making the rooms beautiful—as much as I could, considering their current state. I had not called Danielle to help me. I hadn't even had a chance to tell her I was moving—it all happened so fast. I knew she was on a camping weekend with Doug, their relationship had moved to a deeper level and Danielle seemed incredibly happy. But that wasn't the only reason, I wanted this time to myself—to connect with Merryhearth and to reconnect with the things from my former life—my life before the explosion. I spent Sunday making Merryhearth my own and putting the past in the past, by bringing the remnants of that life into the future. It was like I was home at last. I *was* really home, my home, that no one could explode, and that I would relish forever. It would just keep getting better and better over the years.

Chapter 33

I set up my laptop on the library table, surrounded by my books lining the floor-to-ceiling shelves, facing out onto the back lawn through the big six-over-six antique window sashes. Jill, Alex, and I continued to develop the project materials as though things were still on track, but unfortunately, we were in limbo on the future of the project. Our work could be for nothing, but we didn't want to risk the project being behind schedule if the director gave us the green light to start up again. I spent the evenings until nearly midnight unpacking boxes and setting up each room. As the rooms came together, the house looked even more beautiful than I had imagined. I still had peeling paint, a dysfunctional kitchen, no ceiling on the gallery level, holes under plywood on every porch, and a million other issues—but with the house furnished and lived in, it took on a whole new look and feel.

I was also learning the house's quirky issues and the things I would have to deal with—some sooner versus later. One of the most unsettling was what was becoming a pet black snake. I never figured out if it was the same snake or multiple snakes, but Dora the Explorer, as I came to call her, was everywhere. She especially loved sunning her five-foot-long self on the porches around the house. If I opened the door to shoo her away, she'd look up inquisitively and start to slowly come toward me, as though she thought I had invited her into the house. I researched how to get rid of snakes, and everything I found said the best solution was to eliminate their food source, mainly mice. Midway through the week, while in a video conference with Jill and Alex, I looked up and there was Dora, slithering across the library floor!

"Oh no!" I yelled.

"What is it?" asked Jill and Alex in unison.

"That damn snake is in the library with me. I swear it's being friendly."

"What?" asked Jill.

"What are you talking about?" asked Alex.

"How in the hell am I going to get it out of here?"

"How did it get in?" queried Alex.

"I don't have any idea."

"Try shooing it with a broom," suggested Jill.

I ran for the nearest broom, standing in a corner of the kitchen, and when I got back to the library it was still there, looking around, calm as could be. "Damn it! Why did it have to come into the house?"

"It's probably been in the house for years," offered Alex.

"Ew, I just got the chills," said Jill.

"Turn your laptop around, so we can see it," said Alex. "Damn, that thing's big!"

"Amanda, I'd be out of that house so fast!" said Jill.

"I have to deal with it. I'd like to just bolt, but that won't solve the problem."

"Shoo it toward the door," said Alex.

I approached the snake, and with the broom held way out in front of me, I started sweeping in the direction of the library door and the back door of the house. Dora, looking very surprised at my lack of hospitality, began wriggling furiously and maneuvered herself toward the library shelves, in the opposite direction of the door. From my laptop, I heard Jill scream and Alex exclaim, "Oh, man!"

"You guys aren't helping!" I said.

"Try again, it needs to go toward the door," said Alex.

I swooshed the broom again at Dora, and this time she did something I never expected—she circled behind me and went straight up the library chimney. The last thing I saw was the end of her black snake tail disappearing out of sight, up the chimney.

"Oh no! I didn't know snakes could do that," said Jill.

"Yeah, I didn't know that either," said Alex.

"That makes three of us," I said. "And the worst part is, this chimney is blocked off, so she can't get out. Unless . . . oh no."

"Unless what?" asked Jill and Alex in unison again.

"Unless she decides to come out in my bedroom. This chimney connects to the fireplace in my bedroom."

"That's it, I'd bolt," said Jill.

"Oh, wow, what are you going to do?" asked Alex.

"I'm going to leave the library and hope she comes down and goes back out the way she came in. What else can I do?"

I ended the video conference with Jill and Alex and called the pest service company that I had used for the cruise ship. They explained that snakes were a matter for the Department of Wildlife Resources and not to waste my time because they didn't come to people's houses to remove anything smaller than a bear. They told me what I had already learned from researching the internet, the only way to be rid of snakes was to remove their food source. Since the house had sat vacant for five years, it likely became a habitat for all kinds of rodents and that brought in the black snakes. They told me to be glad I had black snakes because that meant that I likely didn't have other kinds of snakes. *Oh, goody,* I thought. I signed up on the spot, over the phone, for their vigorous routine to rid the house of mice, but they said it would take a while for the snakes to leave for destinations where the smorgasbord was more plentiful. I never saw Dora leave the house, but she also didn't appear in my bedroom, so I assumed at some point she did leave. I hoped her exploring inside the house scared her enough to stay outside until she moved on.

By Friday morning, the day of the appraisal, the house was looking as good as it could look under the circumstances. I had taken Jessica's advice and staged the kitchen and the completely off-line bathroom to look functional; it had hand soap, towels, toothbrushes—it looked like it was in use. I prayed the appraiser didn't try running the water or lifting the lid on the toilet, if he did, he'd see black slime. The kitchen wasn't quite as scary if you ignored chunks of plaster that were missing from the walls, a huge gaping hole in the ceiling where the beehive had been removed, and the general state of ugliness of everything that was in the room, especially the circa-1985 seamless, linoleum floor. Fortunately, the temporary refrigerator had arrived just in time on Thursday afternoon.

At 9:00 a.m. prompt, a tall, thin man in his midthirties knocked on the door. He introduced himself as Adam Parker, the appraiser. He was friendly in a professional sort of way and spent a little over two hours looking over the house and grounds and having me provide a very detailed explanation of the planned rehabilitation work. In addition to the contract I had with Josh, I explained that I intended to do more, if funding was available based on the appraisal. I could tell Adam liked the house and was fascinated with the items in the contract and my explanation of how sensitive the work was.

"Where did you learn the craft of historic house restoration?" asked Adam.

"I've learned from research, no formal training."

"To hear you talk, I'd have thought you were schooled on the subject."

"Thank you! I do feel like I know a tremendous amount of information, and I love learning about historic construction and rehabilitation."

"I'll be working on the appraisal throughout the weekend. It's going to be hard to find comps, considering how completely unique this house is, so I'll dig deep. Some appraisers just look at comps with similar square footage and building façade materials, but I don't think that fairly represents a house like this one."

"I appreciate your understanding of the house and how it differs from modern-day homes."

"Yes, it really does. They simply don't make houses like this anymore. And this one is so original . . . right down to the glass panes in the window sashes. You have such a rare gem with this house!"

"Oh, thank you. I can't tell you how many times I've heard 'You better get rid of those old leaky windows and put in new energy efficient windows.' I want to strangle those people."

"Ha, I can imagine. I'll send the appraisal directly to the bank, hopefully on Monday or Tuesday."

"Thank you! Have a good weekend."

"You too."

That seemed to go really well, I thought to myself. What a difference from my encounter with Kelly Killer. I was seeing that people fell into two categories when it came to old houses. They either loved them, having an actual physical reaction of excitement and wonder—or they thought they had no value at all and should be totally modernized, if not torn down entirely and replaced by new construction. No one really fell in the middle of these two camps.

As the appraiser pulled out of the driveway, I heard my cell ringing from the table in the library. Picking it up, I saw it was Rory. I braced myself for bad news, as I answered.

"Hi, Rory, what's up?"

"Hi, Amanda. I decided to call you instead of sending an email. I just came from upstairs in the director's suite. By the way, how's your day going?"

Oh, for goodness' sake, just get to the point!

"It's going well, thank you. What did the director have to say about the project?"

"Good news ... we have the green light to start it up again! It took him a while to decide because he was consulting with some other federal agencies who recently completed HR modernization projects like ours. Turns out they told him the 'big scary risk' isn't much of a risk as long as we are doing thorough testing before completely cutting the interface over to the new process and system."

"Oh, wow—that's great news!" I practically jumped up and down as I responded. "And what about the new position? Is he approving it?"

"Well, kind of bad news and good news there. He is not approving the new position. But the reason is that he has complete confidence in the project work you are leading across the agency to make this happen."

"Oh, wow again. I didn't know he had any real understanding of my role or even who I am in the big scheme of things."

"Turns out he definitely knows who you are and thinks very highly of you. He said he was inundated with calls from the regional directors, who had gotten an earful from their regional project leaders. They all sang your praises, and the regional directors told him in so many words that this project was being managed better than any big project the agency has undertaken in recent times. They also told him, in so many words, that they were tired of Deborah's meddling and making a mess of things. I guess they've also been on the receiving end of her involvement in their stuff."

"This is better than I could have hoped!" I said, almost in shock.

"Yeah, the Denver region was really vocal and is calling for Deborah's head on a platter. But you didn't hear that from me."

"No, of course not."

"The director has asked me to work with the HR department on some options for moving Deborah out of her current position and into a role where she can't do anymore harm. I think he felt like she made a fool of him with this project derailing."

"I think she's eligible to retire. Maybe she would prefer a way to leave with her dignity intact. It would be kinder than the humiliating move to the proverbial broom closet," I suggested. That was how federal agencies generally dealt with problem executives, they made up a fake job with no responsibility or staff, gave them a fake title, and just got them out of the way without actually firing or demoting them. Often an email would go out to the workforce having it sound like so-and-so got a big new job—but everyone would know it was a broom closet move.

"Good idea. I'll look into that. So full speed ahead now and, Amanda, . . . the agency values you, the whole agency!"

"Thank you. I am SOOO relieved. This is great news. I'll keep you posted as we fire up the engines again."

"See, Amanda, I told you everything would work out just fine. You really worry too much."

I called an impromptu video chat with Jill and Alex to fill them in. They were thrilled with the news, and we spent the rest of the afternoon working out our next steps to get the project back up and running. One crisis was averted. *Now*, I thought, *If the appraisal would just come in high enough, I could breathe again.*

Chapter 34

Monday, midmorning, Jessica's number popped up on my cell. This was the do-or-die moment I'd been waiting for.

"Good morning, Jessica."

"Hi, Amanda. Did you have a nice weekend?"

"Very nice, how about you?"

"Great weekend. We took the kids to a splash park. They loved it. I've never been to a splash park before, but it was really a lot of fun, and there were so many families there. The kids played and played, and then slept the rest of the afternoon. It was great."

Oh, pleeease, enough with the small talk . . . is it a good or bad appraisal—my whole future is riding on this!

"That sounds like fun and a nice way for the adults to have a little break also."

"Exactly!"

"So did you hear from the appraiser? He seemed very open to the value of historic homes."

"Yes, he sent over his appraisal this morning, that's amazing turnaround by the way, I need to give him a good review, anyway, I just finished looking it over."

"Good news or bad news?"

"Pretty good news. He appraised the house for quite a bit more than you owe on it. We should be able to get you $160,000 for the rehabilitation work."

The number sank in—it was much less than my original $215,000 loan—which was much less than the $300,000 I needed to have all the work done. Whoa, I was ending up with half of what I really needed. It was a sobering moment.

"Amanda, are you there? Did we lose the connection?"

"No, no, I'm here. I was just letting the number sink in."

"Oh. Are you disappointed?"

"I'm very grateful for the amount, it's just far from what I was hoping for."

"It's actually one of the better loan amounts that I've seen."

"Then I'm pleased."

"It's okay. I understand. There is another benefit with this loan. We add the cost of temporary housing to the loan amount, based on an estimate of the time needed to finish the work."

"Oh, how much will that be?"

"In your case, it's $18,000. You don't have to accept it, but it's available."

"Oh, that's good. How does it work? I mean, does the money go directly to the temporary housing source or is it paid to me?"

"It's paid to you directly, up front. No one requires proof of how much of the money is used for temporary housing. You pay it back the same way as the rest of the loan, through your mortgage payments."

"Oh, okay."

"So the next step is to set up your meeting with the rehabilitation counselor and inspector."

"The rehabilitation counselor and inspector?"

"Yes, because these loans are federally secured and backed, the homeowners are required to work closely with a rehabilitation counselor who also functions as an inspector, reviewing the work that's been done and signing off before the bank releases payment to the contractors."

"Oh, I had no idea."

"Will that be a problem?"

"No, not at all," I said as I imagined how thrilled Josh would be to know every aspect of his work had to be signed off on by the bank's inspector before he got paid—and now the total of what he would be paid was less. I hoped he wouldn't lose patience with me.

"Perfect, your counselor will be Gavin Hasting. I haven't met him yet, but all the loan processors here think he's terrific."

"What is his background?"

"I'm not really sure. You should ask him when you meet him. I know there is a vigorous vetting process, so I'm guessing he has a pretty impressive résumé."

"Great, I'll wait for his call."

"I'm so glad this worked out for you, Amanda. We'll plan to close on the 203(k) refinance on Wednesday, if that works for you?"

"Yes, that works."

"Okay, see you Wednesday," said Jessica as we ended the call.

My life was back on track, and now I needed to call Josh. He answered on the third ring and as he wasn't one for small talk and the niceties, thank goodness, we jumped right into the heart of the discussion.

"I'll have $178,000 from the bank, if I include the temporary housing allowance."

There was silence on the other end of the line, and then

in his best Eeyore voice, Josh replied matter-of-factly, "That's a good bit less than what's needed for everything on the list."

"I know, I've been thinking about that and I have an idea."

"What's your idea?"

"I'll definitely be prioritizing carefully what we do and how and when it gets done. Also, I need you to put as many of the expenses as possible on my credit card, it has a ceiling of 25K and right now I have a zero balance. That will save the cash for things that can't be done on credit."

"Yeah, I can do that. But what do you mean you have $178,000 if you include the temporary housing allowance?"

"Hmm, good question. Josh, I moved into the house last weekend . . . and I'm going to live at the house through the construction phase."

"You moved into the house? How? Why? And you want to live there during construction . . . oh, I don't advise that. You have no idea how rough it's going to get as we tear out the bathrooms and kitchen, the old plumbing . . ."

"Josh, I don't have any choice. I need every last dollar that I can scrape together for the work. You know better than I do that this amount falls short to cover everything that I need to do."

"Yeah, I guess you have a point there. But to live at the house while the work in ongoing, that will be a nightmare."

"The way I see it, there are three rooms that don't need to be touched for the major stuff—the dining room, the morning room, and my bedroom. We'll seal them off as much as we can, and I'll live in those three rooms while chaos reigns around me. I don't have any choice."

"But you said you've moved in. What about all your stuff?"

"I'll have a few of those portable storage pods delivered to the house, and we'll put the stuff in those during the construction phase."

"Okay. We'll have to time things so that you have one

bathroom or another at any given time. What will you do for a kitchen?"

"Microwave and refrigerator, set up in the dining room."

Next, I filled Josh in on the 203(k) loan counselor and inspector. He took the news better than I thought, saying that it wouldn't be any different than dealing with the county inspectors. I kind of thought it might be, but I decided to leave him with that understanding. *Cross that bridge when you get to it*, I thought to myself. By the end of the call I was relieved that Josh didn't waiver on continuing the work, and he said he would get started again next week. That meant I'd have the month of October before I needed heat in the house. It could work out if everything went smoothly.

⚷⟶

The work week went well, and I found I was able to work from Merryhearth with ease. Jill, Alex, and I were full steam ahead, pulling in the regional project leaders to get things moving again on the project. We decided that due to lost time, nearly a month, we'd cancel our next in-person planning session and meet via conference call as needed. I told Jill and Alex about the new loan program and let them know I was going to be staying in the house during the construction phase. They were both more than worried that it would be a disaster, but I repeated my new favorite phrase, "I don't have any choice." Everyone understood when they looked at it that way. After I hung up from our conference call, my cell pinged with a text from Alex: Don't forget to notify the Murano factory that there is a new address for shipping the chandelier.

Me: OMG. I totally forgot. Thanks!

Alex: My Italy wine arrived yesterday. Has your shipment come in yet?

Me: Yes. I retrieved it from Leesburg yesterday.

Alex: I was thinking when Merryhearth is ready, I'll bring

some of the Italy wine out and hang the chandelier with you. We'll make a day of it.

Me: I would love that. Hey, been meaning to ask . . . how did De'On like the bracelet?

Alex: He really liked it. But he lost it while changing a flat tire the week I gave it to him.

Me: Totally lost it, it's gone-gone?

Alex: Yes, it was too big and slipped off his wrist.

Me: That's awful. All that money and time that went into getting it for him.

Alex: It was an accident. He feels really terrible about it.

Me: Accidents happen.

I wondered who might have found the extra-large, Italian, white-gold bracelet and if they had any idea that it was from a jewelry shop on the oldest bridge in Florence—or maybe it was lying along the road somewhere, embedded in gravel from cars running over it. I hoped it wasn't a bad omen for the relationship.

***

I had set up a time to meet Gavin Hasting on Saturday morning. He preferred a coffeehouse in Winchester for our first meeting. He said we would go over all the aspects of the program and his role in working with me through completion. I knew completion of the rehabilitation, true completion, would be a work in progress over many years— but I kept that knowledge to myself.

After my meeting with Mr. Hasting, I planned to spend the better part of the day at the library. The iconic Handley Library in Winchester contained the Stewart Bell Jr. Archives, a local history and genealogy center jointly operated by the Handley Regional Library and the Winchester-Frederick County Historical Society. The archive was known to be a treasure trove of holdings, including a variety of materials documenting the history of the Lower Shenandoah Valley from 1732 to the present, with an emphasis on the City of Winchester and Frederick County. I increasingly wanted to know more about the family who built Merryhearth, as well as the following three families who occupied the house. In essence, I planned to create the genealogy of the house. This would also help me to complete the necessary paperwork to have the house accepted for placement on the Virginia Landmarks Register, something I wanted to do once the primary work on the house was completed.

I easily found a parking spot on Cork Street next to the coffeehouse and entered a few minutes before ten o'clock. I looked around and didn't see any male customers, so I walked to the counter and ordered my favorite: large-vanilla-latte-low-foam. I sat down at a table close to the door and checked the time on my cell. I had a tome of documentation with me, as Mr. Hasting had requested, and I laid the pile on the table next to my coffee. I had an open view of the area outside the coffeehouse through the big picture window. From a distance, I noticed a man walking toward the coffeehouse. It had to be him because he was definitely headed toward the door. I had ample time to observe him from afar as he neared the building. He was a man in his late forties, blond curly hair, round horn-rimmed glasses, nicely built, and about five feet eleven. He was wearing well-worn jeans and an untucked, light blue chambray button-down shirt, with the sleeves loosely pushed up. He carried himself with an air of confidence and purpose, but not with an unfriendly, get-out-of-my-way demeanor. He reminded me of someone. My brain always connected people with their look-alikes . . . . Who was it? *That's it*, I thought, *he looks like the actor, Simon Baker.*

As he opened the door, a whoosh of warm air announced his arrival and as the warm breeze wafted toward me, I couldn't help to notice that he smelled like he had just stepped out of the shower, a pleasant blend of fresh bodywash and mint. I smiled as he stepped into the coffeehouse, and, seeing my pile of paperwork and expectant expression, he smiled back. He had a warm, genuine smile, and his blue eyes made contact with my green ones in that instant of curious acknowledgement that you have when you first meet someone.

"Hi, you must be Amanda Grayson?"

"Yes, and you must be Mr. Hasting?"

"Oh, please, no one calls me that, I'm Gavin."

I stood and shook hands with Gavin. He had a firm handshake, not too firm, and I thought he held my hand just a little longer than ordinary as we continued to make eye contact.

"I see you already have coffee. Do you mind if I grab some before we get started? I don't function without my morning brew. I've been known to set my whole day off course because I had to stop for coffee."

I smiled, "Of course. I totally understand."

I heard him greet the barista. Clearly, he knew him and must have been a frequent customer. "Will you be having your usual, Gavin?" asked the barista.

"Yep. Large-vanilla-latte-low-foam."

I noted his "usual" brew was also my favorite and shook my head, smiling.

He pulled out the chair opposite me and, taking his first sip of coffee, said, "Ahh, I'm restored."

"I understand," I said, feeling a little like a broken record. *Couldn't I come up with something better to say?*

"It's really nice to meet you, and I can't tell you how much I'm looking forward to learning about your historic home rehabilitation project. I live for the weekends when I can work with my 203(k) clients."

"You only do this on the weekends?"

"Yes, my real job is running my small architecture firm."

"Oh, you're an architect? Do you have a specialty?"

"I design houses mostly. I focus on residential properties, but sometimes I get pulled into commercial projects, which I really don't like."

"Do you have partners in your firm?"

"Yes, one other architect, my longtime friend Bruce Wainfare. We graduated from Virginia Tech together and started the firm in our late twenties. We had a lot of lean years, but I'm happy to say that, at forty-eight, the business affords me a comfortable life now. But I don't get to focus on my true passion as much as I'd like."

I noticed he wasn't wearing a wedding ring, and he didn't mention a wife or family.

"What's your true passion?" I asked.

"I love restoring historic houses. I like working with the natural materials that were used for historic homes, and I've studied the construction methods and how to rehabilitate without destroying or causing problems down the road. Once you learn about it, it's not rocket science, but I see so many contractors really mess things up."

"Yes, my house was slated for a terrible remuddle, before I bought it."

I didn't mention that I hired the very contractor that would have remuddled it. In fairness, Josh had come a long way from that point.

"I love that expression, remuddle, it sums it up perfectly. But enough about me, tell me about you and your wonderful house. When was it built, what's its architectural style, what original features remain? Forgive me, I tend to talk too much when historic houses are the subject."

I laughed. "Not a problem. I can't tell you how nice it is to have someone to share *my* passion with. And someone who speaks the language! That's a rare occurrence."

"Exactly, it's hard to find someone who isn't bored to tears when you start talking about historic houses with them.

That's why I do this work on the weekends. It pays almost nothing, but I get to share in people's journeys to bring beautiful old homes back to life . . . the right way."

"Do you have your own historic house?"

"I do. It's an early twentieth-century Craftsman bungalow, here on Cork Street—above Washington Street. It's small, but I love every square inch of it, and I wouldn't trade it for new construction if you made me."

"That's saying a lot, coming from an architect of new homes."

Gavin laughed. "You sound like Bruce, he says I'm a walking contradiction. But tell me about your house."

"For starters, my house has a name, Merryhearth Manor, but I call her Merryhearth for short."

"Oh, so she's a *she*. I like that. I can tell already that working with you for the next six to twelve months is going to be fun."

"Six to twelve months? I was hoping the house would be done by the end of April—that's a little over seven months from now."

"I'll help you achieve that finish date in every way that I can."

"How closely will we be working?"

"We'll be in touch throughout the week and will likely see each other in person every weekend. Will that be okay with you?"

I felt the old, familiar flutter of butterflies in the pit of my stomach—stronger than ever, and thought to myself, *hmm . . . Is the mitochondria the powerhouse of the cell? Is the pope Catholic? Do bears poop in the woods?* I responded with a bright smile and felt my cheeks blush, "Umm, yes. I think that will work very well for me."

He responded, "Good! I'm really looking forward to our time together. Now, let's break into that pile of paperwork you have there."

Epilogue

I slipped through the white picket-fence gate in the ancient stone wall that surrounded the cemetery at the Hopewell Quaker Meeting House. It was the last day in May, and the serenity of the cerulean blue sky was only outdone by the brilliance of the fluffy, white puffs of clouds. Birds chattering noisily fluttered from tree to tree over my head and bees hummed softly as they hovered, then disappeared into the wild dogwood blossoms.

I stepped through the soft turf, headed for the headstones that were tucked behind the one-hundred-and-twenty-eight-year-old American holly bush. The bush was neatly trimmed away from a series of headstones standing side by side. The holly was planted from a cutting of the same holly that grew at Merryhearth, the one that stood at the end of the veranda running the length of the east side of the house. Mary Rebecca had planted it when her darling son, Albert, was the first of the family to be buried at the Hopewell cemetery. He was in good company. Surrounding him were his mother's parents and grandparents. It must have broken her heart to lose her first-born at the age of twenty-three in a swimming accident.

She followed him just four years later at a young age herself, only fifty-one. Her daughters and husband, in loving tribute to her, penned the epitaph that I had read when I visited the cemetery the day I discovered the house.

Mary Rebecca Wife and Mother
She was the Sunshine of our House

This house—now my house—reminds me constantly of the happy people who called it home before I did. I sat my bouquet of yellow and purple pansies at the base of her headstone, as I do frequently now, and ran my hand across the top of all of their tombstones as I made my way back to the gate, closing it softly behind me.

⚬━⚓

As I pulled into the driveway at Merryhearth, I smiled. The house was done—well, mostly done. The construction mess was replaced by a well-manicured lawn and landscape plants that would mature over time into a beautiful balance of color and texture. The temporary storage pods were gone, and their contents returned to the interior of the house, which looked amazing. And best of all, Gavin's familiar dark blue SUV was in the driveway.

I hurried through the tea room door and into my new, dazzling kitchen with exposed brick walls, restored cooking fireplace, two-level center island with custom vent hood, and top-of-the-line appliances, some of which were hidden behind wooden panels that blended with the custom kitchen cabinets.

"Hey, you!" said Gavin, giving me a bear hug. "How was your visit with Merryhearth's first family?"

"I always love visiting them. It's such a peaceful setting and I feel grateful to them, in a strange sort of way."

"Maybe because *we* fell in love through them?" said Gavin with a smile and raised eyebrow.

"You know, you are right about that. I fell in love with you that first afternoon at the Handley Library as we spent hours and hours researching Merryhearth's genealogy. As we discovered one clue after the next and each of us was more excited than the other—I knew I loved you."

"I knew I loved you when I walked through the door of the coffeehouse, and you had that pile of paperwork in front of you and couldn't wait to dive into the details of the house and the work you wanted to do."

"And now the work is done, and it turned out amazing. Although it will never really be done," I said.

"Speaking of done, I brought your mail in, and I think you have something from Bob Norseman."

I picked up the stack of envelopes, flyers, and home improvement catalogs. I found the envelope from Bob and opened it. He and Marie had sent a card congratulating me on my one-year anniversary in my new home. It was exactly one year ago that I closed on the house after struggling with whether I should buy it. I shook my head that I should ever have doubted.

There was another envelope in the stack with a return address of Alex Jenkins, Washington, D.C. In January, Alex bought a historic townhouse in Northwest, D.C. It was in terrible shape and I occasionally provided him with advice on how to handle one catastrophe after another that kept surfacing.

I instinctively looked through the kitchen door to the dining room, where I could see my beautiful pink Murano glass chandelier twinkling. Alex had come to Merryhearth to help me hang it when the house was ready. We'd had a good day, drinking the Italian wine we had sent back and eating cheese on slivers of fruit like we had in Mandeville, on the Northshore. I would always harbor a soft spot for Alex.

I opened the envelope to find a wedding invitation.

Alexander Jenkins and De'On Jones
Request the Pleasure of Your Company at Their Wedding
Saturday, July 24, 2:30 p.m.
At the Residence of Their Good Friends
Mitch Fries and Ken Anderson
Middleburg, Virginia
Reception Following

I smiled. "How do you feel about going to a wedding with me?"

"I'd love to, when is it?"

"The end of July, at a historic house in Middleburg."

"All the better!" said Gavin. "Now, you said you had some drawings for me on your ideas for the garden terrace outside the tea room?"

"I do."

"Great, let's spread them out on the island. Oh, I made a fresh pot of coffee. I'll fix you a cup while you lay out the drawings."

Gavin handed me a cup of coffee with just the right amount of vanilla creamer, adjusted his glasses, and focused on the drawings. We'd been spending nearly equal amounts of time between his in-town bungalow and my country house, as he liked to call them. I loved watching him when he was working. When his mind was in full focus on an idea, I found him irresistibly sexy. I hoped the projects at Merryhearth would never end as long as Gavin was planning them with me.

"You realize what you have here, don't you?" asked Gavin.

"No, what do you mean?"

"Come outside with me."

We stepped out into the space where I planned to establish

the garden terrace.

Gavin pointed at the sky, "The moon rises here most nights and sets in the morning over there. It travels a path that arcs this space, like a rainbow. When the terrace is done, you'll be able to sit out here, with a nice glass of wine, and stargaze and watch the moon travel the night sky, like your own private planetarium."

"Oh, that sounds wonderful."

"You'll have a 'moon garden,' to go with all the other named rooms at Merryhearth," he said.

"I love that idea, and more so when I picture being in the moon garden with you. As a matter of fact," I said, touching my forefinger to my lower lip, "did you know that I'm considered a really good kisser?"

Acknowledgements

For so generously offering me the roadmap to publish my book and providing me with every imaginable service from book cover design to editing, a million thanks to my publisher. I could not have made it across the finish line without your guidance and support.

Thanks so much to my friends who put up with me while I talked about my ideas, read them excerpts of my rough drafts, and previewed chapters of the book. Without your input I was just stumbling in the dark.

And my forever appreciation to the many people in my life who inspired the characters in my book and motivated me to nourish the storyteller within. We are all storytellers and thanks to you, I was encouraged to let my storyteller flag fly.

Abigail Darby wrote her debut novel, *Merryhearth Manor & Me*, as a full-time writer after leaving her day job as a strategic planner for a number of different federal government agencies over the span of twenty years. She lives in the Virginia countryside outside of Washington, D.C., in a historic nineteenth-century house that she rehabilitated herself. In addition to writing fictional literature and talking her friends into buying and restoring old houses, Abigail loves hiking with her dog, visiting historic villages and towns, and going to wineries—and preferably all three of these at the same time.

Connect Online

DaegbrecanPublishing.com

 @Daegbrecan

 DægbrecanPublishing

 Dægbrecan Publishing

CPSIA information can be obtained
at www.ICGtesting.com
Printed in the USA
LVHW030708081122
732536LV00003B/188